TIES OF
POWER

TIES OF POWER

The Trade Pact Universe #2

JULIE E. CZERNEDA

DAW BOOKS, INC.

DONALD A. WOLLHEIM, FOUNDER

375 Hudson Street, New York, NY 10014

ELIZABETH R. WOLLHEIM
SHEILA E. GILBERT
PUBLISHERS

DAW TRADEMARK REGISTERED
U.S. PAT. OFF. AND FOREIGN COUNTRIES
—MARCA REGISTRADA.
HECHO EN U.S.A.

PRINTED IN THE U.S.A.

For Everett Norman Starink

Hi, Dad. I'm going to blame you for a lot of things, starting with my sense of honor, my self-worth, and my insatiable curiosity about the world. Then there's that tendency, surely hereditary, to save everything interesting.

I suspect it's also your fault that I never doubted myself or my dreams, since I knew you would be proud no matter what. Thank you for all your support, love, and encouragement, as well as the way you still wiggle your ears like a true elf.

Love, your Julibeth.

ACKNOWLEDGMENTS

Book three! I've noticed one difference already—I need to thank more people each time, which is a truly wonderful problem. For those who aren't listed here, please understand the lack is space and not my most sincere gratitude.

If my first effort at a sequel reads well, I give full credit to these hardy souls. Any mistakes or omissions are mine. Thank you, Sheila Gilbert, for unerringly spotting the flaws. Thank you, Merilyn Vyse, for volunteering to read the manuscript even after you learned this meant hundreds of scribbled sheets of paper. And a very special thanks to my alpha reader, Roxanne BB Hubbard, who somehow caught just about everything possible, including all those interesting words spell check leaves behind!

I'd also like to thank my fans and readers for all those "made my day" moments this past year. It means a great deal to me to find out my stories and characters have given you pleasure.

My thanks to the great folks at DAW Books, including Sean, Debra, and Amy. I'd like to thank Luis Royo for making each cover even better than the last. And thank you, Ellen Asher, for your kind words and the beautiful hardcovers from the SFBC.

I'd also like to express my warm appreciation to these individuals for their tremendous support and interest: Roberte Fournier, Mark Lefebvre, Stephen Christian, Patti Vickers, Ann (Pat) Methe, Mark Askwith, Don Wright, John Rose, Raymond Alexander, Nicky Blum, Dave Switzer, James Schellenberg, John Kahane, Peter Halasz, and Mici Gold.

Thanks, Jennifer and Scott, for allowing me to bend the family schedule around writing and signings. You are the best.

And thanks to my fly guy. Roger, this is far too much fun for one person—which is why I'm so happy to share it all with you!

PRELUDE

MEMORIES and socks.

Barac sud Sarc, Third Level Adept and former First Scout of the Clan, shook his head as he added the holocube image of his murdered brother Kurr to the clothes already in the travel case. Memories, indeed.

I wondered when you would go, the words formed in his mind, the touch soft and familiar.

"First Chosen," Barac acknowledged out loud, continuing to pack. "Come in—" He triggered the locking mechanism on the door with a thought.

His mother entered, her movements gracious despite the pain he could sense rippling the unseen M'hir between them. The M'hir. Barac swallowed, suddenly unsure how long it would be before he could touch another of his kind this way. Clan philosophers debated if the M'hir had existed before Clan thought, some believing it to have been an emptiness waiting to be filled with Clan power, others arguing it was a construct of Clan minds and not truly a place at all. Like most, Barac merely accepted that every Clan mind existed in part there, in that nothingness through which Clan thoughts and form could pass at will. It was the medium making them one, regardless of strength or ability. Or dispute.

Barac studied his mother's face, feeling as though he had to memorize every detail: the delicately pale skin and fine bone structure he saw in every mirror, the dark eyes and generous mouth edged by laughter lines.

Not at this moment, however. "Where will you go?" she asked calmly enough, aloud. It was her right to question his intentions—

not as his mother, Clan family structure was almost nonexistent—but as Enora, First Chosen of the House of sud Sarc.

Barac tossed an old coat on the lopsided pile of discards covering his bed and some of the floor. "Must be time to move on," he commented instead of answering directly. "Look at all this junk!"

"You could stay."

He hesitated in the midst of closing the final bag, then made his decision. He turned to face her. "If you knew what I do, First Chosen, you'd send me yourself."

Enora frowned, taking a step closer to her son. Her elegant hand waved in a complex gesture, as if drawing threads from the air. "What are you talking about, Barac? Why would I—?"

Barac shook his head. *It's time you saw the Clan Council as I do,* he sent. He opened his thoughts to hers, using his greater strength to forge the gentlest of links with her ordered mind, then drew her into his memories, letting Enora relive with him events of which she'd only been told. And, as the Clan knew well, words were the easiest way to lie.

It didn't take long. Barac withdrew, soberly watching his mother as she groped one-handed for a chair's back, oriented herself, then sank down into it slowly. "Sira—" she whispered, shying from the intimacy of mind touch as she sought to control her emotional response. "A lawbreaker. She did all this, herself?"

Barac waited, knowing what his mother struggled to reconcile. Enora had been a Chooser herself, once, as all Clan females were.

Choosers possessed the Power-of-Choice, an uncontrollable force within themselves that instinctively tested the strength of unChosen males within the M'hir. Win or draw, and the Joining formed, a permanent connection between a pair through that other space, regardless of distance, severed only by death. The Chosen female Commenced, her body altering to its reproductive state.

Losing males were rejected. A Chooser could be patient, since their bodies, untouched by physiological aging, would wait as long as necessary for the moment of Choice.

But with each generation, the Power-of-Choice had become stronger, more dangerous. The Clan Council, hungry to increase the abilities of the Clan, hastened the process by preselecting the strongest male candidates for Choice. After all, to the Clan, power was everything: status, currency, and life.

It took only two generations for Choosers to be born who were powerful enough to kill weaker males during the Test. Fewer and fewer Joinings were successful. The inevitable result? The birth of Sira di Sarc, a Chooser so powerful, so potent, that no male could survive her testing.

Barac's memory of Sira carried the taste of longing, the overwhelming desire any unChosen felt for such power, and a self-preserving dose of fear. Yet he knew the person as well as the legend: outwardly fragile and ordinary, an easily-overlooked shadow with wide-set gray eyes and solemn expression; inwardly, self-willed and brilliant, brimming with power awaiting release.

Sira had willingly gone into seclusion to protect the unChosen. She had used the years of her isolation to study the population dynamics of her species. She was given access to the old records, from the time when the M'hiray—the 730 individuals possessing the mutation allowing them to use the M'hir—had been forced to leave the Clan Homeworld during the Stratification of their species. It didn't take her long to discover that not only were the M'hiray in trouble, her own existence, a female who could not find a mate of her kind, meant that extinction was close at hand. She proposed alternatives, the most promising being to test the Power-of-Choice against the mind of another telepathic species, such as a Human. The subject might die, but perhaps the Chooser would Commence and become reproductive without risking more Clan lives.

The Clan Council accepted her conclusions about the danger to the M'hiray. The Council didn't accept Sira's proposal, utterly rejecting any possibility of a Choice involving a Human. Such a violation of Clan ways was unthinkable. Instead, they decided on a different solution. They would erase the mind of the most powerful and desirable Chooser, Sira herself, in an attempt to destroy the Power-of-Choice and bring her precious genetic makeup back into the Clan pool.

Sira was warned. She selected a Human for her experiment, a telepath named Jason Morgan. To protect any unChosen she might encounter, she underwent stasis, the procedure that temporarily blocked a Chooser's powers. To make it possible to undergo Choice with a Human and a stranger, her memories were ruthlessly suppressed, ridding her of all identity, substituting compulsions that would send her directly to the Human and the moment of Choice.

"She broke the Law," Barac agreed. "But so did the Council."

Enora shook her head. "I know. What they tried to do was wrong. But Sira— I saw for myself how she cared for this Human, even after her memories were restored. She learned to control the Power-of-Choice in order to save him. How could she—"

"Justify herself to Morgan?" the Clansman smiled. "All I can say is, Morgan is a remarkable being. He risked his life to save her, and risked losing her to bring back her past."

"Such caring is rare among the Joined," Enora said almost wistfully. "I can see she would value it." Her voice firmed. "Nothing you've shown me explains why you are so intent on leaving."

"Efforts were made to keep Sira from Morgan. One of them resulted in Kurr's murder."

"Yihtor di Caraat killed your brother," Enora said, her face growing pale but still composed. "Yihtor's mind was erased for his infamy and his House name removed from the M'hiray. It is over, Barac."

"Yihtor was merely the weapon, First Chosen. Kurr was someone's messenger—an expendable messenger."

His mother's eyes narrowed. Barac felt the troubling in the M'hir between them as she fought to keep her thoughts private. He knew better than to reach for them. "Whose messenger? Who is responsible for Kurr's death?"

Barac shook his head sharply. "I don't know. But Sira does. She wouldn't tell me, not in front of the Council."

"So you would seek her out now." Enora paused. "I agree you should go. But even if you can find her, Barac, she may not want to see you."

Barac closed his eyes briefly. Then he picked up both travel bags and said without facing Enora: "She'll see me. We have something in common now."

He began to concentrate, preparing the mental image that would guide his passage through the M'hir, sidestepping space and leaving his troubles behind on this planet that was no longer his home.

We have both been driven into exile, he sent into her thoughts, surrounding the bare words with the taste of his despair and a glimmer of what might have been hope. *Good-bye.*

Barac *pushed . . .*

And disappeared. The air in the room shifted slightly to fill the space where he had been.

Enora, First Chosen, walked slowly over to the pile of unwanted clothes. She picked up a shirt, faded gold threads taking fire from the light as she folded it in her hands. "Imagine saving this," the Clanswoman murmured.

She brought the shirt up to her cheek. The fabric trapped a tear. "One son murdered," she whispered to the tiny damp spot. "And now, the other son gone. Who is doing this to us?"

"So. Here to see the Witch?" a silky voice breathed into Barac's ear. Maintaining an expression he hoped wasn't too forbidding, Barac turned to look at the being standing next to him along the bar's edge, only to frown in distasteful recognition. *A Drapsk.*

Worse still, there now seemed to be a full ship's complement of the creatures arranging themselves in seats vacated as if prearranged. The Spacer's Haven—at least this end of the long, dim room making up the public area of the popular gambling den—became almost totally Drapsk within minutes.

Barac sighed. This was the right world. No credit to his Talent: Morgan's ship, the *Silver Fox,* stood age-dark yet sturdy among the ranks of other traders in Pocular's shipcity, name and rating for cargo posted with the rest. The Haven might even be the right place, although it had been almost a standard year since he'd heard Sira declare a desire to learn how to gamble. Who was to say how long that had lasted? At least it was a place to ask discreet questions. He did know a chorus of Drapsk was hardly the right company if he wanted to find his cousin without arousing attention.

On the other hand, the Haven was warm and dry, his cautious searching thus far had lasted three long and unsuccessful days among backward, unhelpful beings, and Barac found himself simply too tired and comfortable to care.

Resigned to the moment and his new companion, the Clansman took another sip of inferior brandy, shuddered, and asked
the obvious question. "What witch, Captain?" Polite to avoid
under-ranking a Drapsk; all individual Drapsk appeared identical, with no recognizable features or expressions on their flat,
eyeless faces. Polite and also wise. The huge Drapsk trading
ships were crewed by tribes, every member closely related in
some fashion they'd never shared with aliens. Drapsk thus had a
regrettable tendency to respond as a unit to any real or imagined
insult against their own; a trait which granted them respectful
treatment even in a cesspool like the Haven.

"Oh, a true Ram'ad Witch, Hom," the Drapsk persisted, taking a seat on the stool next to Barac without so much as an
acknowledgment toward its former occupant (a Human who had
quickly decided to blend into the surrounding crowd). Six fleshy
tentacles—bright red and distractingly mobile—surrounded its
tiny bud of a mouth. A pair of truly spectacular antennae plumed
in purples and pinks rose from the alien's brow. They dipped
toward Barac, then fluttered as if confused. "Since you seemed a
watcher rather than a games' player or backer, I assumed you
were another fan. Am I in error?"

Barac ordered a drink for his new and uncomfortably observant source of information, finding it easier to talk over the
Drapsk's shoulder rather than look directly into its tentacled
globe of a face. "A fan of magic, Hom Captain? Not particularly. But I enjoy new experiences." The Drapsk's weakness for
the occult was well-known. Barac remembered several jokes—
all concerned with the gullibility of a Drapsk and the size of its
purse. Then he glanced at the silent group of Drapsk around
him—quiet, well-armed, and intent—and decided this joke was
not necessarily complete. Perhaps he would wait and see this
"witch" for himself.

Two hours later, Barac tossed yet another handful of currency gems on the bar and decided enough was enough. The
Drapsk had proved able to consume seemingly endless amounts
of its chosen beverage; more to the point, there was still no sign
of its "witch." High time he tried his luck elsewhere. "Well,
Maka," he announced, eyes flicking to the container firmly
affixed to the creature's mouth by the cluster of tentacles. "I
can't stay all night waiting on your witch, pleasant as your com-

pany has been." Frustrating company as well, for anyone else Barac might have questioned about Sira or Morgan had given the Drapsk—and their chosen companion—wide berth indeed.

Antennae fluttered in acknowledgment; the container didn't budge. Barac stood and bowed his farewell, praying that the creatures didn't take it on themselves to follow him out of this bar and into the next in line along the street. But he had only started to raise his hood, the water streaming from the clothing of latecomers a warning of conditions outside, when the lights flickered and dimmed. The myriad sounds of the place—voices high, low, and mechanical, music competing in volume, the click of playing pieces—stopped, except for the rolling of one die as it hit the confining wall of a table and bounced back into the center.

"Behold, my impatient friend," said the Drapsk with too-loud satisfaction in that hush. "The Ram'ad Witch. The owner—nay, the Queen—of this place."

Barac stood as spellbound as the rest as a form ever so slowly materialized out of the haze-filled air to become solid, living, seated on the black throne. But in the silence, his quick gasp turned nearby heads his way with unwelcome attention. Barac subsided, though his eyes remained fixed on the graceful figure dressed in flowing white.

A delicate hand gestured, and the lights returned, the noise becoming deafening once more as the various patrons accepted with the ease of familiarity the dramatic appearance of their mistress. Barac was unable to look safely away before wide-set, *knowing,* gray eyes pierced the yellow smoke and confusion to meet and hold his.

The Drapsk, mistaking the direction of the witch's gaze perhaps, chittered excitedly among themselves. Barac ignored them, breaking free of the thrall that had held him, but answering the summons of those eyes nonetheless—moving slowly, inexorably toward the platform.

A path cleared for him as others became aware of what was occurring. There were comments whispered in his ear as he passed—suggestions that would have made him turn on the speaker had this place not given such words unspeakable conviction. So when at last Barac stood at the steps leading up to the occupant of the black throne, he refused to look into her face any longer, lowering his gaze to the heavy barbaric jewelry barely covering the whiteness of her breasts, to the gleam of gem-encrusted bands around each wrist and ankle.

Of all the possible fates he had imagined for his dear cousin, of all the places he would have sought for her—that gentle, tormented Sira might descend into the darkness of a fringe-system hellhole where all things were for sale, if they weren't stolen first—that possibility had never even entered his mind.

Chapter 1

"PREPARE us something warm, Kupla. Some sombay with that spice of Meragg's," I ordered briskly, making my own sound and movement cover the statuelike immobility of my most unexpected guest. My personal servant scurried away without a backward glance. For myself, I couldn't take my eyes from Barac's lowered head, his thick black hair immaculate as always despite the weather outside this night.

Outwardly, nothing of my cousin had changed. If he thought a cheaply-cut coat and a slouch could hide the natural arrogance of the Clan, he was sadly mistaken. *His elegant charm,* I thought to myself, *stands out more in contrast.* I was surprised a thief hadn't tried his pockets yet. Or maybe one had, and soon learned not to trust appearances. By Clan standards, Barac sud Sarc might be weak, but he had other defenses.

But why was he here? Why now? What did it mean? Questions I hesitated to ask in such a public place tumbled through my thoughts.

Any joy in seeing him was held hard in check by the suspicions racing through my mind—suspicions of Council interference in my plans, suspicions of the old struggles beginning anew.

The drinks arrived, carried with skill through the crowd and deposited on a small black pedestal within reach of my hand. "A seat for my guest, Kupla," I was able to say. "Then you may leave us." Barac's eyes flashed up to mine at this—ablaze with some emotion—yet he moved stiffly to climb the dais and sit on the offered stool. The corner of my mind I permitted to have such concerns registered amusement at his obvious distress, admiring the way he accepted the steaming cup and deliberately turned his attention to the milling crowd. I sipped my own; I couldn't taste it.

"Welcome, Cousin," I said quietly. "At least, I'd like to think so. Why are you here?"

Barac refused to meet my eyes. "Why are you, Sira?" he asked in an oddly anguished whisper. "What are you doing here? Do you know what they call you? What they say about you?"

I laughed; I couldn't help it nor did I try. The bulbous-eyed croupier at the nearest table lost his concentration to stare at me and so also lost half the credits stacked before him to a quick-fingered neighbor. "Excuse me, Cousin," I apologized, just as glad for a chance to absorb the shock of Barac's arrival. "Business."

Ignoring Barac for the moment, I sought through the thickness of bodies for the one I wanted. *There.* A conveniently vulnerable mind. Quickly, I pinned the stealthily moving culprit in place, sending a quick mental summons to my nearest guardsman. Ripples of awareness spread from the spot where the wild-eyed Human stood immobilized by my will. Beings moved away on either side, leaving her exposed and encircled.

I stood with deliberate slowness. My guardsman pounded up, stun whip loose and ready in his hand. The regular patrons of the Haven looked expectant, while the croupier's thick-featured face oozed satisfaction—one of the less pleasant aspects of hiring Foweans being their tendency to secrete a glistening green mucus when cheerful. I wasn't the only one to swallow uncomfortably as the croupier hastily wiped his facial glands on a sleeve. From the glazed look of his garment, the House had been winning steadily tonight. No wonder his table was almost empty.

"Win from me if you can, Human," I said into the attentive quiet. "But no one steals from me." I released the control of her body back to her mind and watched her stagger only briefly. Coolly, the thief reached into one voluminous sleeve and removed more metal disks than I'd seen her steal.

"Only in the Haven have I met my match," the woman said in a low pleasant voice, inclining her head to me just so, holding on to her pride. Doubtless a professional criminal; this world had many such. "One cannot steal from those protected by magic," she continued ruefully.

I hid a smile. "But anyone can steal from a fool," I countered. At this, the crowd rumbled approval, and the croupier's triangular mouth gaped open anxiously. With a dramatic, and quite unnecessary, gesture, I performed my most popular feat of "magic." The figure of the croupier vanished with a sigh of displaced air.

"Keep your winnings," I continued, sitting, quite as if nothing untoward had happened. The Drapsk at the other end of the hall hummed in delighted unison. The would-be thief clutched her booty and melted into the crowd. Things returned to normal.

"Where did you send the Fowean?" Barac's voice was his own again, level, expressing polite interest and little else. *Much better,* I thought, but to myself.

"Just out in the rain," I pitched my voice for his ears alone. "Such tricks are good for business—and keep my dealers honest."

"And they amuse you. Is that what you've found here, Sira? Amusement?"

Maybe I'd been wrong about Barac regaining his composure. His eyes held some of the same uncomprehending wildness as had the pinned thief's.

"Barac sud Sarc," I said softly, adding the configuration of heart-kin to the bare words. "If you've come to see me, you don't seem very pleased about it."

Barac shuddered—his hand made a short violent gesture at the seething mass of noisy, gambling beings around us, many almost oblivious to their surroundings and certainly oblivious to us. "How can I be pleased to see you like this, to see you waste yourself with such filth, to be part of the port scum of this trivial waystation of a world? How can you even let yourself be seen in this place?" A pause as his eyes bored into mine. "What have you become, Sira?"

I tried not to smile. "Well, I doubt I've become what you've so unflatteringly decided, Cousin. Nor what you see. You forget, not all have your perception." Delicately, I reached into the M'hir between us, not touching his shields but offering a different vision to his eyes—a face whose features were smudged and hard to discern, the hint of an exotic gem on the forehead; a body coated in a mist that confused. An illusion easy enough to offer drink- and drug-hazed minds. A confusion of descriptions to confound any who saw more. No two who left the Spacer's Haven ever agreed on the appearance of her witch.

A flicker of astonishment crossed his face, leaving behind a raised eyebrow. "I won it, you see," I continued. "The previous owner, Sas'qaat, really wasn't as good at Stars and Comets as it thought. And you're right. I stay here because it amuses me. Until now, I've missed the shadowy edges of life, its variety and color."

"You've picked a hell of a way to start experiencing variety and color," Barac countered. A loud scuffle, ended by heavy thuds as guardsmen moved in, served to underscore his comment. Then with more characteristic dry humor: "Did you have to become a witch in order to hang out in a bar?"

"It was easier than telling the truth."

Barac's lips twitched as though I'd unwittingly scored some point. "The truth, Cousin? Which one?"

I considered him as I took another sip from my cup, politely refraining from exerting my presence in the M'hir against his, then said, "Why, our truth, Cousin. That as Clan, you and I can lay claim to a rare heritage of power, power used by our kind to live very well as parasites among the unsuspecting species of the Trade Pact. Let me see. Is it two hundred or three hundred Human worlds we grace with our presence? Or more?"

He couldn't help but glance around, checking if any being had overheard. I knew better. Once bets were placed, an earthquake wouldn't rouse the Haven's clientele to self-preservation, let alone curiosity. "I see. You sit *here*," he accused, eyes back to me, "and presume to judge the rest of us."

"I presume nothing," I replied firmly, raising one hand to stop his outburst. "And nothing is exactly what I want from the Clan. I've started a new life, Barac, one that allows me to use my Talent without claim to a heritage I renounced a year ago." Purposeful movement from the floor caught my eye, changing what I might have said next. "Actually, the Poculan version of a user of power, a Ram'ad Witch, has an interesting and useful status off this planet as well—as our friend Maka would testify." I nodded a regal acknowledgment to the approaching Drapsk. I'd been wrong about the earthquake. The parade of over thirty Drapsk was enough to dislodge even the Haven's gamblers, if only temporarily.

"Oh, Most Mystic One," the Drapsk halted a cautious distance away, antennae aquiver. "You have given us a tale to carry back to the Tribe tonight."

"Good business," I said offhandedly.

The creature began shifting from one foot to another and the other Drapsk followed suit in unison. Beyond them, I saw smiles carefully hidden. "Business is what my ship-kin and I would like to discuss with you, Mystic One."

"Captain Maka," I began. Indulging the alien night after night was becoming tiresome. "How many times must I give you my answer? I am not interested in accompanying you to your home system. As you've seen tonight, I'm needed here or my bumbling staff will bankrupt me."

If body posture were to reflect a stubborn set of mind, Maka the Drapsk should have been rigid by now. "We have searched two full cycles for a truly mystical personage such as yourself," the being protested. "Do not doom us to failure before our Tribe. Just a short voyage—amply rewarded and enjoyable."

The Drapsk sounded almost desperate—hardly a wise trading tactic. *Why?* "Not now," I compromised. "I have matters that require my personal attention." True enough, given who was sitting, rather puzzled, beside me. "Perhaps another time," I offered.

Foot-shifting ceased, replaced by mad feathery waves as the antennae of all the Drapsk fluttered. I sensed no mind-to-mind contact, but I was convinced the beings were communicating with one another. If it was some form of chemical signaling, I frankly doubted its effectiveness in the maelstrom of odors from the various bodies and innumerable smoke sticks surrounding us.

Maka came right up to the edge of the dais, lowering his voice conspiratorially. "Mystic One, you are kindness itself not to remove all hope. But time is short if the happiest of conjunctions is to occur this season for my ship-kin and me. Allow me to send my cargomaster to you with gifts—the merest indication of the treasures you would receive from the grateful Tribes of Drapskii."

I shook my head impatiently. I needed to talk to Barac, not these creatures. I had to find out which part of my past was intruding into the present. "Send your gifts," I agreed loftily.

"I'll provide you my final answer in return. Good evening, Captain."

Then, regretfully, for I truly enjoyed watching this cross-section of the cosmos each night, I put down my cup and brushed my fingers over Barac's sleeve. I *pushed* . . .

. . . and gained us the privacy of my rooftop garden. The storm had ended. The first pair of Pocular's smallish moons showed through openings in the clouds, casting doubled shadows and distorting silhouettes. It was the part of the lunar cycle when younger children were kept indoors after dark, old superstitions giving parents a practical defense against night-mares. I took a deep breath of fresh, clean night air and pre-pared to confront my own.

"Now, Barac," I said. "Why are you here?"

"Glad it's stopped raining," he commented instead of answering, as he paced around the rooftop.

"Don't go close to the edge," I warned, following him to the near side with its view of the shipcity's lights.

It was too dark to see his expression, but I detected a shade of patronage in his tone. "Really, Sira. I thought you had a good head for heights. And this is hardly the Cloisters, set on a mountaintop."

"No?" I said softly, taking my own advice and halting a good two paces away from the rail. "You could be wrong about that, Cousin."

Barac's fingertips touched the finely wrought metal. Almost instantly he cursed and yanked back his hand. "You've set pro-tections on this building." He sounded surprised.

"Of course. Do you think for an instant I believed the Coun-cil would allow me to leave in peace? I'd rather sleep at night, thank you." I felt Barac explore the unseen boundary with a tendril of power, knowing what he would find. The Haven was a fortress against our kind. No Clan could send thought or form into this place using the M'hir. And, I smiled to myself, if any tried a more physical approach, they would be in for a similar disappointment.

I switched on the lighting, adequate to let me see his face yet night-soft. Random beams played among the rain-soaked leaves and still-closed evening blossoms, sparkling like gems. I wasn't the gardener, but I loved the exuberant life here—in its way as novel to me as the hordes of beings beneath our feet. "You can test my protections, Cousin," I said dryly. "I assure you they are adequate against—" I hesitated, and he pounced cheerfully.

"The rest of us? Don't worry, Sira. I've no intentions of testing them again. I, a humble sud, remain glad you and I are on such good terms." His fine-boned face was open, freed of the guarded tension it had borne in the tavern, revealing lines of stress and—*was I wrong?*—what seemed to be the beginnings of hope. "But you asked me why I'm here. I've been chasing rumors of the *Silver Fox,*" Barac confessed willingly. "I was looking for you."

I sat and waved him to another of the lounge chairs. There were sufficient puddles to make me glad Meragg had insisted on rain-resistant furnishings for this retreat of mine. I raised one brow at the Clansman, refusing to be charmed. "I was never hidden—not to eyes like yours. You waited a long time to visit, Barac. Why now?"

Barac's smiling face settled into a mask, his voice dropping to the sharp edge of a whisper. "I did as you demanded, back then. You know that, Sira. I gave up my brother Kurr and the search for his true murderer—the name you knew but wouldn't give me." He paused, his voice gathering strength, yet oddly without bitterness. "But it wasn't enough for the Council, Sira—that I stopped my awkward questions. This past month I was to be offered Choice by the daughter of Xer sud Teerac," an impatient wave silenced my question. "A minor House. They live on Asdershal 3. But it was a good match; assured of success. Then, just before we were to meet, I was refused."

I winced. I'd known Barac remained unChosen from the moment I'd felt his presence in the Haven—those of the Clan who were incomplete carried their overwhelming need in the M'hir like a flag of warning. There would be pain as well as hurt pride in being refused. "It's not the end of things, Barac," I said awkwardly, remembering what had been said to me time and time again. Unhelpful, meaningless words, but all I could offer. "There will be other Choices—"

"Not for me!" Barac snapped, his power flaring so that I narrowed my perception as well as my eyes. "You don't understand, Sira. It was my third refusal. The last. The Council has

no intention of allowing me fulfillment—ever. I—" He bit back
what he might have said, then continued heavily, quietly.
"When I realized the game they played, I took the only honorable course left to me. I am now exile." When I didn't speak,
Barac smiled—a thin, hurt expression with none of his usual
confidence. "Got room for a warlock, Cousin Witch?"

"You are always welcome," I said quickly, gesturing respect
and commitment. "Curse them all for fools!" This last burst
from my lips before I could close them.

Slowly Barac nodded. "Especially one, Sira. No," he added
immediately, reading my sudden stillness correctly. "I can wait
until you are ready. I didn't come to open old wounds, just to
be with you for a while, to think things through." A mischievous grin took years from his face. "Do you know, I've even
missed your Human—the redoubtable Morgan. How is he?
Where is he?" He glanced around the garden as if expecting the
Human to appear at any moment.

I knew where Jason Morgan was—I always knew. Just the
sound of his name in my mind sent echoes along that subtle link
that bound me to the deepest part of his cool, crisp thoughts. I
stopped the reverberations before they troubled his peace.
"Morgan sleeps," I said, bringing a soft smile with me from that
tenuous contact. "You will see him before long, Barac," I promised, and said no more.

My kinsman would learn soon enough about the man who
had changed so much about our lives and been forever changed
himself.

INTERLUDE

"There." The compactly built, brown-haired Human input the last reading, then stretched from his huddle over the locator with satisfaction in his clear blue eyes, one hand brushing shreds of moss from his faded spacer coveralls. "We'll be able to find them next season without a problem. Should be as good a crop or better, don't you think, Premick?"

Premick, as befitted a hunter of his rank and dignity, did not quite laugh, but there was a suspicious twitching at the corners of his narrow mouth. "I am no expert on lumps in the ground," the Poculan answered in passable Comspeak as he rose to his full height, head and shoulders above the smaller Human. "Ask me about the nasar." Typical of the jungle-dwelling race of his species, Premick was spider-thin, the warty surface of his skin a light yellow, a color shared by the outer rim of his eyes. He was humanoid only from a distance, having triple-jointed arms and legs, each joint with its fleshy protrusions—a curious adult trait Poculans were unwilling to clarify for aliens. His legs didn't drop from his hips, as would a Human's. Instead, they began about a third of the way up the straight torso, originating sideways before bending toward the ground. It was a feature Poculans commonly used as a convenient horizontal ledge to support the weight of not-inconsiderable waist packs.

Jason Morgan, trader and Captain of the *Silver Fox,* patted his own well-stuffed carrysack. "As I've told you before, my friend, each of these tasty lumps will bring in the price of ten of your pelts—and at much less risk to our own hides."

This time Premick did laugh. "Maybe offworlders value them. I will settle for those ten pelts." The delicate fur of this planet's largest carnivore was both status and currency for his people, and the hunter was understandably bemused by the Human's search for the rare merle truffle. *To each his own,* Morgan said to himself. Having the *Fox* sitting planetside with empty holds ate far too many credits each day for comfort—the truffles rounding out his sack should ease that problem nicely, if the information on their market value provided by a certain restauranteur of his acquaintance was as reliable as ever.

Premick waited impatiently as Morgan collected his equipment, including the sketch pad and stylus the Poculan was convinced the Human slept with, and finally announced he was ready to leave the glade. With a snort of relief, Premick gathered up his own carryroll with one easy sweep of a long, bare arm, the other already cradling a snub-nosed rifle. Primitive though his people might seem in appearance and lifestyle, they did not scorn technology that gave them an edge against Pocular's many predators.

Morgan hurried to follow the rapidly-moving form of his guide along the narrow forest trail, his mind already calculating the number of truffles needed this season to cover docking fees.

"Ghsst!" Premick's irritated hiss moments later brought Morgan back to himself. The hunter must have found some sign of a worthwhile quarry ahead, and Morgan's steps were careless and noisy. Morgan accepted the rebuke, slipping into the lithe stalk that he had learned on another world, when his quarry had had reasoning brains and weapons more similar to his own.

Following Premick, often no more than a glimpse of yellow-brown deliberately allowed so that his companion would not be lost completely, Morgan once more let his mind wander. Not back to the *Fox,* and his own marginal credit; rather, he returned to his practice, to playing a game that had begun almost a year ago.

Premick, whose people had a trace of mental talent—his own sufficient to have led him to choose Morgan over other would-be trappers—acknowledged Morgan's preoccupation with a resigned shrug and a roll of his eyes. The Human knew when to free himself of the extra burden of concentration. And his now-silent, graceful movements were not bad at all for an offworlder.

The game. Morgan first dove deep within his mind, seeking the warm and golden place, the presence that was part of him yet had once been another's. *Ah.* It was akin to being shocked, that initial sensation of contact reestablished. Then came the recognition of power, of mental abilities stretched far beyond what he had ever known before. But it was power without complete control—which was, after all, the purpose of the game. The game imposed by the powerful daughter of di Sarc without consultation or appeal. She called it survival.

Morgan gave less of his conscious mind to his external surroundings, depending on Premick to warn him if he was needed to do more than follow quietly. At times, these stalks could lead them for hours down dark, mossy trails. More often than not, their quarry would elude them, though never because Premick lost the scent. So there was time to resume the game. A flash of power sent along a well-used pathway in that other place, the M'hir, would be enough. Morgan paused, ready—defenses in place, signal sent.

But the almost instantaneous reply was not the mind-wrenching test Morgan had expected. Instead, words formed softly around his thoughts: *Hello, Jason. I've been waiting for you.*

He hadn't heard her mind voice for weeks, yet the exquisite balance of Sira's mental strength was as familiar as his own. Past the faintest of barriers, all she ever truly held against him, emotions trickled through. Concern and, alarmingly, uncertainty.

His own answer was swift. The game, and indeed the living forest around him were forgotten. *What's wrong, Sira? Are you all right?*

Warmth, sudden and rare, as quickly gone. Morgan fought the temptation to respond in kind, keeping his mind voice light and comfortable; he had learned to respect, if not enjoy, the distance Sira kept between them. *We have company, Jason. An old friend has arrived. Come, please.*

Morgan stood still, then nodded, though she could not see the gesture. Sira would not call him out of the jungle for anything less than trouble, regardless of what she chose to reveal. He opened his eyes, surprised that he had closed them, to find Premick seated in a patient crouch, the flesh-crowned knobs of second knees at ear level, yellow-rimmed eyes steady and patient on his own.

"I've been called. I must leave," Morgan said simply.

The being nodded, then went on, his tone curious but tentative, as if unsure with a topic they always had avoided: "You serve a strange mistress, Morgan-friend, who summons you home in the midst of a good hunt."

Morgan's unusual blue eyes retained some of his power's glow. Premick might have imagined a flash of something in those eyes that made him shiver. Yet Morgan's voice was good-humored. "You complain about my witch, Hunter?" the Human said, shifting his load of truffles to his other shoulder. "And what about your sisters? Are they not why you enjoy my company and hunt the poor nasar?" Amid mutual laughter that hid both regret and apology, the pair turned back toward their camp of two seasons, disappearing into the trees as easily as their reprieved prey.

Chapter 2

THE harsh voice held no doubt and permitted none. "You will join with our Choice for you."

I was surrounded in darkness, so detached from my sense of self I was unsure if I stood or floated in that place. Despite my dread, I shouted: "I have made my Choice!"

A different voice, still faceless in the dark, soft and sad. "There is no Choice for you. There never was. There never will be. You are the most powerful Chooser to ever live. How could there be a candidate for you? Would you kill him? Kill him? Kill him?"

Did I begin to spin, or were the echoes making me dizzy? "I won't kill him. I won't—"

A new voice, with the crackle and snap of a campfire behind it. "It is the most unnatural self-control—what will you do when it breaks and he dies at your touch? What will you do when you've murdered him?"

Somehow I closed my eyes, seeking an inner, more tangible darkness, a point of reference to lead me out of the old, familiar nightmare. I felt my body under the sheets and knew I was awake.

More sleep would elude me. I accepted this as normal; my eyes snapped open to stare at the city-dimmed stars that showed through the ceiling ports. This was my weak time, when the tasks I had set myself seemed both futile and hopeless, my life as muted as those distant stars. It was part of what I had become since restoring my memory—this self-doubt that I acknowledged only in the dark and alone. Life had been clear to Sira di Sarc, who had plotted to risk the life of a Human to save her kind. It had been clear to Sira Morgan, the person I'd become when my memories and powers had been stripped away, leaving someone who learned to love.

Now? Now I was something lodged between those two, like a piece of meat stuck between teeth. And my life and loves were anything but clear to me.

Impatiently, I reached for the lights, only to have them come on before my hand touched the control. I blinked at the figure revealed half-curled in a lounge under a circle of brightness.

It's good to see you, my thought sped out, unchecked and honest.

Morgan stretched, a lazy, familiar movement, almost feline. His coveralls were jungle-stained and his blue eyes smudged with weariness. "You called me," he said aloud. "You knew I would come." And unspoken, without reproach: *I would have come before.*

"You are still at risk," I countered, aloud, and stood. Part of me felt the effect of my nakedness on Morgan, shared it as heat on my skin; part of me was fiercely glad of the strength in him when he brought this under control, too, even as I shivered in the abrupt shared chill. It gave me hope.

I slipped my arms into a robe and led the way into the galley. I didn't ask how long Morgan had been there, or what he thought of my sleeplessness. How he'd arrived unnoticed in my bedroom was simplest of all—the protections around this building were his.

We were partners once more; a transformation as easy in the end as shared sombay and toast. Our conversation was of small, immediate things. Although there was no good reason to delay telling Morgan that Barac was here—in the next room, in fact—I was loath to do so. It was the newer part of me which had grown sensitive and which I was continually torn between exorcising and sheltering. Once I recognized the weakness, I put my cup down firmly to announce, "Barac came to the Haven last night."

There was, of course, no reaction to be read on Morgan's regular features, a lack perhaps more meaningful than any surprise. His eyes glowed slightly. "How is he?"

I looked at him sharply, suspecting humor. "Aren't you more interested in why he's here, Jason? This is no casual reunion as your kind are prone to do. It is not the Clan way."

A definite chuckle. Morgan leaned back comfortably, contemplating his callused, broken-nailed hands. I noticed his body looked well-used: hardened, made leaner and more graceful by his time in the jungle. I knew his mind would show the same toughening. "Point taken, Clanswoman," he said after a moment. "But if you knew why Barac had come, you wouldn't have called me. So perhaps my question is important after all."

The Human continually impressed me with his insight. I knew better than to judge those insights as lesser in value because they were not always based on his Talent. That was the trap my kind had fallen into when they first encountered his species—so outwardly alike, so inwardly different. In my partnership with Morgan, our differences were our greatest strength. Rising, I collected our cups and tossed them into the kitchen's receiver. I could have left them for the servants in the morning; I didn't choose to share that much of him. "Barac says the Council has forced him into exile," I explained. "They have refused him Choice."

"Do you believe him?"

"Why shouldn't I?" I countered sharply. "He's my kin." Morgan just raised one brow. I sighed. It was my obligation to give Morgan only the truth. "Barac believes it, at any rate."

"So we don't really know why Barac's here," Morgan said, a small frown forming between his eyes. He tapped the table thoughtfully. "I don't like this, Sira. I don't like this at all."

"What do you suspect?" I lifted one hand and waved it in the air. "That he's been subverted by the Council to seek us out and infiltrate us as though we were one of those secret societies your species delights in?"

Morgan met my eyes, his own dark blue and somber. "And who has more secrets than any Human society ever known, my dear Clanswoman?"

"Fair enough," I acknowledged the truth of what he said. Only a very small, select group of Humans and other aliens knew of the Clan or of its settlements on Human worlds—information spread when Morgan and I had become an interspecies' experiment gone astray. The taste of it was still in my mouth: the bitter hurt of being used by my own kind. My own role in that experiment didn't improve the flavor.

"It's something happening now, something new," Morgan

pondered aloud. I listened, shaking myself from the black mood I knew perfectly well he'd sensed in me. As usual, I wasn't sure if I was annoyed or reassured by such empathy.

Morgan had continued, "On the other hand, Sira, we could be looking too hard for answers. Once in a while, things are as they seem." A humorless grin. "But let's be mildly careful. No need for Barac to know that you were concerned enough to call me. If he asks, let's say I came back on my own—my hunt having provided too little profit and too much discomfort. As Barac thinks walking on a sidewalk in the rain is suffering, he'll have no trouble believing that!" Decision made, Morgan stood, sweeping some crumbs into one hand and pushing in his stool.

"Was it?" I stopped my own movement to ask.

Morgan paused and looked at me, wiping the crumbs into the disposal. There was no missing the warmth in his eyes now. "When you are finished with this place, Sira, I have a world to show you—a world bursting with life that refreshingly cares nothing about the affairs of Clan or Human." A shrug. "As for profit, well, Premick will sell enough after our expenses to dowry one sister out of his hut at least. And I was able to trade for express passage here—and this." With a small flourish, Morgan opened the closure of his upper chest pocket and reached in to withdraw a ball of soft, white leather. "For you."

I made no move to take it from his hand, regarding Morgan and his gift with equal distrust. "Why?"

A smile that might have been wistful. "Now you ask the wrong question. Aren't you curious about what it is?"

I found I had to close my eyes briefly to regain control over emotions this Human persisted in arousing. Anger made my voice less than steady. "Is it your purpose to test me, Captain Morgan?"

He knew what I meant. He knew the chaos within me, the struggling dual reactions that only the discipline of years held in rational balance. Yet he continued to smile down at me, seemed to move closer. "A test, Fem di Sarc? Would I presume so against my own teacher? No." He reached out carefully, as if afraid I'd disappear, and pressed the ball into my unresisting hand. Words, borne over the barest hint of deep emotion, flooded into my mind. *Humor my humanity. This reminded me of you.*

I clenched my fingers into a fist around Morgan's gift, feeling a hard roundness within it. All I could do was to hold myself rigid, looking down at our hands still touching, using all of my will to stay apart, to refuse to acknowledge the currents of need charging the air.

My hair betrayed me, slipping over my shoulders, alive, twining up his arms, brushing softly against his cheeks. I followed its movements with my eyes, unwilling witness to the paling of Morgan's tanned face, the working of his throat, the triumphant darkening of his clear blue eyes. The straining between us was intolerable as our eyes maintained that contact.

I broke first—tearing away, turning to lean against the counter, breathing heavily in near sobs. "There is no other way. You know that. We must be apart, I your teacher only, or we are both doomed."

"Sira—" softly, a sound like warm air stirring my hair.

I shook my head, glad I wasn't facing him. "Unwise, Jason. You are very unwise."

There was no answer.

He was gone. I reached up to order my now-obedient hair and felt Morgan's gift still in my hand. Rage at my lack of control—and Morgan's easy accomplishing of it—made me start to fling the thing across the room.

I forced myself to stop. There was nothing to be gained by continuing to react on this emotional level. *So Human,* I thought, without the scorn of my heritage and training. In many ways, the time I'd thought myself Human had been the best, or at least the simplest, of my life. I put Morgan's gift on the counter and smoothed out the leather. I gasped at what lay within its wrapping.

It was a small gemstone, crudely shaped and polished by hand, yet arresting in the clarity of its deep blue color and fierce reflection of light. Its shape, like a pair of merged ovals, was very familiar. I created an illusion of this same stone on my forehead each time I appeared as a Ram'ad Witch in the Haven—for this must be a true witchstone such as given to initiates of magic among the tribes on this planet. Morgan must have had enough truffles to keep the *Fox* out of debt for months, yet he had bought this.

The gift, and its giving, held a message I could not misunderstand. Morgan wanted an end to the illusions—for me to return to an existence where I could be who and what I was. With a sudden deep calmness soothing my mind, I knew he was right. I might be his teacher in matters of power, yet Morgan was my teacher in matters of life. So be it.

INTERLUDE

"It does not matter who or what she is," insisted the voice, faceless as any gathered here in the darkness of nonreality, distinctive in its flavor of overwhelming power and purpose. "What matters is what Sira becomes."

"Fine words, Jarad di Sarc." The M'hir carried the taste of scorn far better than any expression, a scorn leavened by a hint of wariness. "You try to convince us the House of di Sarc would abandon its prize? That you view the future of our kind above your personal ambition?"

A rippling of force, as though something huge passed under the surface of an otherwise placid lake before diving deeper. Shields tightened without alarm. Meetings of the Clan Council were often laced with threat. It was expected that power would be tried, tested, and used—else why have it?

Jarad's mind voice was without emotion. "I view the future of my House as the future of our kind, Degal di Sawnda'at. Would any dispute this?" The M'hir was silent. "Are we agreed, then? The Council stands prepared to act?" A feeling of building pressure. "I warn you. If you continue to delay, we will face the ultimate perversion. Are you willing to taste Human in the M'hir?"

A different silence, as purpose and thought gathered into one. They were agreed.

It was time to end the exile of Sira di Sarc.

Chapter 3

"YOU want me to what?" From the look of him, Barac had slept better than I, but he was definitely not enjoying our breakfast conversation.

Neither was Meragg, my household attendant who, along with her favorite life-partner Kupla, were the only employees of the Spacer's Haven I allowed into my personal quarters. Meragg had stopped all pretense of serving fruit from the dish in her hands, eyes wide and swimming with black-flecked tears. I ignored her. "You need a place to stay," I reminded Barac. "Kupla and Meragg will help you learn the details. The Haven essentially runs itself, anyway."

Barac so far forgot himself as to contact me mind-to-mind. *I'll be the laughing stock of the Clan. Barac the bartender. Barac the innkeeper. Barac—*

"Barac the warlock," I added out loud, shutting my mind to his protest. "It's done, Cousin. The Haven is yours, to do with as you wish. I would suggest that you keep the personal staff that I have chosen—they're good people. Those working in the Haven itself range from reliable to predictable. Use your own judgment with them."

Barac shot a despairing look at Meragg, who had by this time buried her face in a towel and was wailing softly, the deep yellow of her skin flushing orange with distress. "This wasn't quite what I had in mind, Sira, when I came here."

I'd taken the dish from the poor creature and was helping myself to some strips of green pya fruit. Its juice was deliciously sticky, and I licked my fingers, growing happier by the moment. The tiny gem was a still-unfamiliar and exotic weight on my brow. "Adapt, Barac," I advised him cheerfully. "It will be an interesting challenge for you. And the place makes a tidy profit, after all."

Barac sighed dramatically, but I could see he was beginning to consider the possibilities. Meragg was peeking at him from over her towel—I could tell her agile mind was already at work judging the type of employer Barac would be. "Will you be back?" he asked, giving a shrug in surrender.

"And where are you going?" This from the apartment doorway. As Morgan walked out on the balcony to join us, Meragg discreetly slipped past him to disappear into the galley—I could guess what cheery gossip she was readying for Kupla's ears concerning the two now sharing my breakfast table. Poculans tended to multiple spouses.

Barac's smile of greeting was warm, as if he sensed an ally. "Morgan." He stood and held out a hand that Morgan was quick to take in a firm grasp. A Human custom—the Clan did not engage in idle physical contact. Barac would make a good host for the Haven.

Yes. I was making the right decision, and my newly gained peace of mind gave me the composure to greet Morgan calmly. His clear blue eyes flicked to the gem on my forehead, then came to rest steady and warm on my face. "Have you breakfasted, Jason?" I asked quickly, forestalling any conversation about that.

"I'll join you," Morgan accepted, dropping into a seat. He was carrying his sketch pad and slid it my way as he said cheerfully, "Nothing like civilized food. What's new on Camos, Barac?"

I eyed Morgan warily, pouring myself another drink and passing him the container. As I flipped open the sketch pad, I found it impossible to concentrate on Morgan's latest work, despite the lovely lines of the orchidlike flower he'd caught against the ragged surface of a cliff and the painstaking detail of a fern wet with dew. There was something odd in Morgan's bearing, a sliver of steel beneath the friendly voice. I knew him too well. Morgan had had time to clean the jungle from his body and change to new clothes. I decided he had also had time to develop some suspicion concerning Barac.

Barac didn't notice anything untoward with the question. He began to talk about neutral things: changes in Human politics that occurred after the Clan had agreed to remove its influence from the Camos Cluster, the cost of transport, the promotion received by an Enforcer Morgan and I knew well.

"So Bowman's Sector Chief. Good for her," Morgan replied to this last bit of news. "She'll surprise a few who thought they were untouchable."

The next logical topic was the Clan and my remaining family, a conversation I preferred to avoid. They both rose politely as I stood. Morgan sat back down, looking immovable.

"I'll stay and talk to Barac. We've a lot to catch up on." If there was a message in his eyes, I couldn't read it. Nor would mental contact be wise—Barac would at least sense it happening if not decipher it, and quite rightly feel offended. I nodded my farewells and left.

Let Barac be the one to tell Morgan that the papers I was working on were the transfer of ownership of the Haven and the closing of all my business dealings on this planet.

INTERLUDE

As a meeting place, it was perfect. Far from hidden, which would have aroused suspicion just by that fact, the four gathered in bright daylight—to all appearances enjoying a casual lunch just like the hundreds of others around them. Gaily colored umbrellas dotted the huge square like flowers in a garden. The babble of voices and movements was deafening close at hand. Rael di Sarc was pleased.

"All this, and you even arranged a decent meal. I am truly impressed, Ru."

The smaller Clanswoman, Ru di Mendolar, waved a self-disparaging hand, but her round cheeks flushed with pleasure. "Be more impressed when we have a better reason to share a table, Rael."

"True enough," Rael said. She spent a moment walking her long fingers—presently stenciled with the silhouettes of tiny flowers—over the moving lines of the menu in the table surface, tossing back the heavy black hair threatening to fall in front of her somber eyes. "But that time will come soon enough if we are successful."

"And how likely is that?" The speaker, a heavyset Clansman whose faint accent marked him as hailing from one of the Ruaran worlds, frowned at Rael. Larimar di Sawnda'at had never been known for his patience. "My sources indicate the Council is ready to move against the firstborn daughter of di Sarc."

"An old rumor turned into a new one," she retorted quickly, green eyes flashing. "It would make your sources more credible, Larimar, if they could tell us what the Council is planning. Why they have waited until now? What is this new threat? How are we to protect Sira, or warn her—"

"Hush, girl." The fourth member of the group was the only one present who dared use that quelling tone with the powerful Clanswoman. Rael flushed but settled back in her chair. "Better. Now Larimar's sources are good, and they have given us a place to start, but do not ask for miracles from them. If too many questions are asked, or too specific information is drawn from certain minds, the reprisals will be instantaneous. They could even reach back to us. We must never underestimate the strength or determination of the Council—or the threat they pose."

Rael nodded meekly. "Yes, Grandmother."

Ica di Teerac eyed her kinswoman suspiciously. "Don't use that tone with me, offspring of Sarc. Without my presence, you would not have had an acceptable excuse to gather this kin group in safety. And without my wisdom, you will fail."

Ru stirred restlessly, her dark red hair squirming as if equally resentful of the constraint of jeweled pin and net. "And what does that wisdom suggest, First Chosen? That we wait on the Council—cowering under your protection (for as long as that is respected)—and so let them act as they choose?"

"And what about Sira—" Rael began.

"I know impatience will not help anyone," Ica interrupted sternly, her blue eyes, washed pale with the years, focusing on each in turn. "But I agree the time has come to move as swiftly as possible. We must warn Sira, of course. Whatever the Council plans, it will not be an acceptable solution to the doom facing our kind. They are too blind, too set in maintaining all as it has been. It has become dangerous to so much as suggest change, as you all know."

There was a pause as the food and drinks ordered earlier arrived. After the servo was safely distant, Rael leaned forward, eyes intent. "I know where Sira has gone. It's time I went to her. I can convince her to come to you, Grandmother—"

Ica smiled thinly, a chain reaction compressing the fine wrinkles framing her lips. "Don't make the mistake of believing your father that Sira has been exiled by the Council. It was her decision to dwell apart. She is powerful, resourceful, and full of anger. That anger is a force to be reckoned with—both by us and by her. You, especially, must remember this, Rael."

"I don't understand."

The old Clanswoman's eyes glittered. "Sira is no longer

Clan, not wholly. Since imprinting upon the Human—" Ica deliberately avoided the more potent term, Choice, "—she has become unpredictable at best, clouded by emotion, tainted with unusual ideas. I agree you must go to her," this with a gesture that silenced Rael's protest before it was uttered. "But she is no longer the sister you admired. She is no longer the helpless 'Human' you aided on Acranam. She has become someone else—someone who has learned to wait, to prepare, and, I suspect, to hate. I would rather know what Sira di Sarc plans than what the Council of the Clan has arranged. It may matter more in the end."

Larimar pushed his dish away and leaned back in his chair. "I've heard a great deal about Sira di Sarc—who hasn't? But nothing that suggests that she would be capable of resisting the will of the Council."

"She resisted the will of your former leader, Yihtor di Caraat, easily enough!" Rael snapped. Larimar's jaw clenched.

"Acranam is not being called to account here," Ru interjected quickly. "We are gathered in an effort to save our species. Old disputes have no relevance."

Although Ru was an unfamiliar peacemaker, being one who usually ruffled, rather than smoothed, feathers, Rael made the gesture of appeasement. "Sira and I have always been heart-kin."

Ica sighed softly, as if for once she wished to acknowledge her great age. "Just as long as you realize, Rael, that our cause must be held as greater than any emotional ties. It may be that Sira will judge us—and you—as much her enemy as the Council."

The others were silent, eyes carefully averted. Rael gained no help from them. She met the implacable face of her grandmother with pleading in her eyes, their luminous green grown dark. "It will not come to that. Sira will understand and help us willingly. You'll see."

"I hope so, Rael. But willingly or not, Sira di Sarc must help the Clan. We can permit her no other choice."

Chapter 4

"PLEASE reconsider, Mystic One," the cargomaster's plumed antennae were drooping below his shoulders, giving the Drapsk a comically tragic look. "These gifts were ill-chosen—give me time to make a new selection—"

I sighed, quite sorry I'd let the Drapsk in the door. But it had seemed only polite. "Your gifts are magnificent," I said, and not for the first time. "Perfect. I can't accept them because I'm not coming with you. It is my decision to make, Cargomaster, and I have made it."

The Drapsk stood mutely, double-elbowed arms wrapped around a collection of packages continually threatening to topple. I hadn't exaggerated in my compliments. The gifts were magnificent: gems, intricate sculptures, rare perfumes, and tapes of antique Human literature. I'd been taken by surprise, both by their quality and by the unexpected aptness of their selection. Then again, perhaps I shouldn't have been; the Drapsk were master traders, always careful to scout ahead and know their customers. "This is your final decision, then, Mystic One?" the creature, who could have passed for Maka or any other of his crewmates, asked despondently.

"It is, Cargomaster. And—as I've told you repeatedly—even if I wanted to attend this Festival on your homeworld, it would be impossible for me to leave immediately on your ship. I've made other plans which can't be delayed further." A satisfied flicker of thought that was not my own. I resisted the impulse to throw something at Morgan, who was stretched out on a nearby bench, eyes closed, basking in the afternoon sun. "Your gifts were perfectly selected. Your timing is not."

"As you say, Mystic One." A bow that ended in an abrupt scramble after a package. I caught it and set it on top.

"Do you wish me to 'send' you back?" I offered politely.

Both antennae jerked upright in alarm. "No. No, thank you, Mystic One. My transport waits below."

"Then accept my thanks to you and your kin for this offer. Perhaps some other time." But this politeness was wasted breath. I watched Kupla intercept the rapidly fleeing Drapsk at the doorway to my apartments, catching several packages as most finally slipped through the being's hold.

It was just as well the door closed quickly—it would not have been the best of manners to laugh in its hearing.

Still chuckling, I threw a cushion at Morgan with a delightful mix of impatience and expectation. "When do we leave, oh mighty jungle guide?" How good it felt to be on the move again, to be shaking off the dust of this shabby city. I should have made this decision weeks ago. *I'll have to thank Barac,* I thought to Morgan.

One blue eye opened. "We can go whenever you're ready, chit. And our guest."

Chit? If he meant to evoke memories of that simpler time, when I was Hindmost crew on the *Silver Fox* and technically deserved the nickname used for the youngest and least, it didn't fool me for an instant. I grew still, alert to a return of that edge to his voice, to the feel of his mind, despite his casual tone. "You want Barac to come with us?" It was impossible to keep disappointment from my voice.

Morgan opened his other eye and raised his head onto his arms, the better to look at me. "I don't like leaving him unwatched behind us."

I walked over to a raised planter, staring down at the clustered flowers without seeing them. "What is it you sense that I do not?" I paused, feeling Morgan stand and come to my side. We looked out over the rooftops together for a moment; the distant mountain ranges were hidden in cloud. We'd had our share of rain, I thought, digging my fingers into the damp soil. It was loose and freshly turned. So Morgan had found time for his garden; the plants had that indefinable air of being loved again.

"I'm not sure what I sense," he confessed quietly. "It would be easier if I were. But I've learned to trust my instincts—my Talent at tasting trouble," he corrected. Morgan's precognition had saved his life many times before I'd arrived to give him a name and source for it. It was a Talent I lacked.

I dusted my hands and looked up at him with a frown. "There is one way to test Barac," I heard myself say, as if the calm voice came from someone else. "I could scan him." The part of me that remembered when I was pure Clan cringed at the thought of breaking the law; the newer, less familiar part of me was distressed at the thought of my cousin's probable reaction. I shoved both responses from my consciousness.

There was a grim set to Morgan's mouth and a troubled look in his eyes as they studied me. "We already know the most likely reason he's come. And you know my feelings about it."

"To find the one responsible for Kurr's murder," I said in a low voice. Yes, I knew Morgan's opinion. I caught at his hand, clenching it in my own. "Jason, swear to me. You won't tell Barac. He can't go against Jarad di Sarc."

"He can't go forever without knowing." Morgan's hand turned, his fingers lacing between mine. "When were you planning to tell him it was your father behind it all? Your father who arranged for Yihtor's kingdom on Acranam. Your father, Sira, who sent both you and Kurr into Yihtor's reach. Barac deserves the truth."

"A dangerous truth." I shook my head, feeling my hair rising in agitation. "If Barac is to live, he mustn't know any of this. Jarad—his allies on the Council—they'd destroy him in an instant. Your knowledge is more than enough for me to worry about. Promise me, Jason."

Morgan had a way of smiling strangely at times, a smile I couldn't interpret despite my experience with his expressions. He did it now, the slightest upturn of his mouth coupled with a darkening of his blue eyes until I could have drowned in their depths. "My lady witch," he said ever so softly. "You have my promise. Always." His hand stole mine and brought it up to his lips.

A second hazardous moment in only one day, but at least this time I had full control of my emotions. I took back my hand, stepping away slowly, deliberately. "Barac's search for his brother's killer is not why you suddenly distrust his presence," I said more breathlessly than I'd planned.

Morgan wisely allowed the change in subject, shrugging as he came back to his seat. "How can we be sure this visit is Barac's own idea?"

"A scan would tell me."

He looked uneasy. "If Barac has been somehow controlled by the Council, sent here to do some mischief, I imagine that control will be too subtle to be easily found. That subtlety might even be part of the trap, to draw you beyond the safety of your own defenses, to expose you to their attack or control." And under the words, I felt Morgan's determination to perform the task himself, if need be.

I shook my head violently. "No," I responded to the unspoken. "You overestimate yourself. It will be your downfall yet, Jason."

"I don't overestimate my ability to sense trouble coming," Morgan insisted quietly, eyes narrowing. "Things are not as they seem."

A new voice. "They rarely are." It was a sign of the intensity of our conversation that Barac had been able to materialize behind us unnoticed. I thought, too late, it would have been a fine idea to add some internal protections to the Haven. But I hadn't planned on Clan guests.

My current one stood as though ready for a battle, arms loose, legs slightly bent. His face was white, except for angry red flashes over each high cheekbone. Morgan matched the Clansman's posture in an instant, sliding to his feet with a deadly grace I knew Barac would remember.

I gestured appeasement, soothing the emanations of my own power touching the M'hir between us, feeling Morgan withdraw into his customary cool detachment—invisible to all but mere sight. "You carry with you echoes of the past, Cousin," I told him bluntly. "Your simply standing here is like a hull breach alarm light-years from the nearest port. Why shouldn't we be concerned?" I paused for emphasis. "How can you know your desire to find me was entirely yours?"

Barac's eyes flickered to Morgan's unreadable face, then back to mine as if he were unsure which of us needed to be convinced. "Why should the Council go to such lengths to send me into exile when they could find you directly? My power is no threat to either of you. And this place is a fortress. Between

your wards and Morgan's traps, you could withstand a siege in
here."

"And you could be their gate, Barac," I reminded him. "You
know that."

"That's ridiculous!"

"Is it?" Morgan asked, his voice definitely knife-edged now.
Almost automatically, he stepped closer to me.

Barac threw up his hands. "Why don't you scan me, then,
Sira?" he said furiously. "That's what this is leading up to, isn't
it? Or aren't you capable of taking that last step away from your
own kind—of breaking the one law you've left intact? Well?"

Words would not solve this, I knew with a sudden sense of
calamity. I summoned my will, brutally suppressing both my
compassion and my anger. What remained was the icy, sharp
logic of my upbringing and a dark determination which was far
newer. Raising my eyes to meet Barac's immediately frightened ones, I entered his mind with all the speed and force I possessed—choosing the approach of an attack rather than the
delicacy which should have been my preference as heart-kin—
ripping past his shields as though they were cloth. Whether this
would save me from any traps I didn't know.

As if carried along by a wind, I felt Morgan's mind following mine; its powerful force remaining checked, quiescent,
on guard.

Mercifully, my cousin fainted. Morgan, sensing the moment,
was ready to ease Barac's limp form down gently. I remained
rigid, blind, my mind racing along forbidden corridors, exposing connections, motivations, ignoring all decency in this
rapelike exploration.

And all for nothing.

There was no touch that did not belong, no feel of anything
remotely foreign to Barac's own ordered and intricate thought
patterns. I'd trampled through his innocence and his hope for
better, exposed the haunted depths of his unChosen emptiness
and his grief, leaving violation and pain behind me.

I withdrew, swallowing bile, shivering not with cold, but
with the aftermath of my own self-disgust. What had I become,
that I could do the unspeakable without hesitation? How deeply
had I been maimed by hate that I would attack my own kin on a
suspicion?

Arms around me—a fiercely tight hold that spoke of trust, of faith, of things I doubted I deserved any longer. I opened my eyes, blinking tears away, and stared up at Morgan with my own barriers in shreds. "What have I done?" A whisper in a voice gone strange to my own ears.

Morgan's face bore a new, unfamiliar expression, one I recognized with an inward shock as pity. "What was necessary, for all of us," his tone remained level and soft. "You couldn't leave Barac wondering if he was being used by them—for all his bluster, you know he feared it was true as much as we did. And I wouldn't want to face him without knowing who was looking back at me through his eyes." I didn't need to touch Morgan's thoughts to share his memory of Gistries, the woman he'd killed at her own request to release her from the mental bondage imposed by Yihtor.

I pulled away, going to my knees beside Barac, sending now-gentle tendrils of thought seeking through his unconscious mind. "I—Barac is damaged," I said at last, my voice closer to normal. I looked up at Morgan. "I wasn't careful. He will be in pain when he awakes."

Morgan nodded in understanding, mimicking my position on the other side of Barac's still form. "Show me," he ordered.

Despite the circumstances, I felt the anticipation that always accompanied a chance to witness this difference between our powers. Among the many things we had discovered during the past year was that Morgan's mental strength was linked to an empathic sensitivity that made him a potentially gifted healer-of-minds. It was a rare Talent even among the Clan. In another universe, perhaps the Clan would have accepted his ability and trained him to its peak. As it was, Morgan relied on his instincts and what little I knew.

I felt his hands lightly upon my own as I once more sought Barac's unconscious mind. As I came to areas of pain, I entered them, absorbing the discomfort almost gratefully. Morgan's power slid around mine, soothing, sealing, restoring Barac's disordered thoughts.

When it was done, I could sense Barac's return to consciousness and withdrew rapidly. Before I had to face his condemnation, look into his reproachful eyes, I *pushed* and . . .

... threw myself down on the pile of fragrant branches, willing away emotion and regret until at last I could do so no longer. Then, I wept for what I had done.

Perhaps even more, I wept for what I had become.

INTERLUDE

"How do you feel?"

Barac rubbed one hand wearily over his eyes. "Better than I should," he confessed slowly. "Which of you—?"

"We are partners, Sira and I," Morgan reminded the Clansman.

"A Human concept," Barac noted with a scowl. "But it was Sira alone who scanned my mind. Sira—who now cares nothing for law, or kin."

"You offered." Mildly.

"Only as an act of faith!" Barac said bitterly. "Faith that was broken." He rose unsteadily, staggering once but ignoring Morgan's proffered hand, and looked around the rooftop garden. "Where is she?"

Morgan paused, looking inward through the golden haze that marked his own interface with the M'hir. *There.* "She's gone where she could avoid your judgment, if not her own." He felt a momentary unease at her leaving the defenses of the Haven; a concern made easier knowing she'd left Barac to him.

"Her own." Barac shuddered. "Ossirus. Let's hope such power answers to any judgment." There was something fractured in his eyes. Morgan saw it, but, unlike Sira, felt no impulse of remorse. As a Clan Scout, permitted by Council to interact with Humans and other species, Barac and others of his kind had routinely done worse to those others who suspected Clan abilities in the M'hir— or even its existence. To Morgan's way of thinking, there was a certain amount of justice served by Sira's actions and Barac's resulting headache. He only regretted the cost to her.

So Morgan tilted his head and regarded the ashen-faced Clansman with a small, grim smile. "So it was unpleasant. Be grateful she didn't find you under Council control." He left the obvious unspoken.

Barac seemed not to have heard, sunk in his own thoughts. He spoke slowly, as if to himself. "If Sira could do this to me, perhaps she would have been a fit mate for Yihtor the Renegade after all. And who could have saved us from the two of them?"

Morgan's light but swift openhanded blow caught Barac completely by surprise, shocking alertness back into dull eyes. The slender Clansman put one hand to his mouth, wiping blood from his split lip with a trembling finger. "Good," Morgan said, his mental barriers tightening as he felt Barac instinctively strengthening his own defenses. "You know me well enough, Barac sud Sarc," he went on, thinking back over the years when Barac and his brother Kurr had been frequent passengers on the *Fox,* years when Morgan had found information about the Clan a profitable item to trade, a seemingly ancient past before Sira gave him a new loyalty. "You know I'm not restricted to your methods—or by your laws. You'd be wise to remember that."

"I know you defend her," Barac said after a long pause during which he searched Morgan's implacable face. He made the gesture of appeasement, seeming soothed by the ritual whether or not he expected Morgan to appreciate its meaning. "I respect your rights as her Chosen," he added slowly, sitting down on a nearby bench. "Perhaps I should respect your judgment also. My own is not operating too well at the moment."

Something dark eased out of Morgan's face. "I still sense trouble coming."

Barac's eyes lost focus briefly. He winced then said ruefully. "I'm tasting nothing beyond this ache in my head."

Morgan considered the Clansman for a moment. "It was my suspicion Sira tested, not her own, Barac. If the trouble I sense isn't you, I'll apologize. If."

Barac shrugged gracefully, though his eyes were smoldering. "Be sure I shall be there for it when you're ready, Morgan," he promised tautly.

Chapter 5

"PUT it inside the door this time, please," I said wearily, poking my head around the woven grass inner wall of the hut. The Poculan who'd been about to put the village's latest offering of food safely distant—and thus out in the rain—started so violently that he almost dropped the basket and gourd.

"Yes, Lady Witch," he said courteously enough, considering the dilation of his pupils. The provisions were rapidly pushed into the entrance hall, their bearer obviously torn between a desire to escape my notice and a fear of offending. Irritated, I waved him to freedom, less than pleased to be beginning my adventure by accepting the homage—and unpleasant reputation—accorded to real Ram'ad Witches.

Still, the quarters were comfortable and I was given all the privacy I could desire. Morgan's memory of the place had promised at least that. I sat cross-legged on a thick, rust-red mat to examine the contents of the basket, careful to taste only those fruits I knew from the city markets.

It should have been good to be alone, to have time to think. I scowled at the fruit I was disassembling with unnecessary force. *Think?* I had too many thoughts rattling around in my mind already, the focus of most persistently straying from the steady purpose I had held foremost for so long. I blamed the quiet, the peaceful sleepiness of this remote forest village.

Then I shook my head, knowing better. This was Morgan's hut, his things. I had fallen asleep where he had slept for so many weeks, my cheek on a pillow his had warmed. I'd been so careful to avoid any physical association with the Human—to keep an insulating distance.

Coming here was a mistake.

I was so tired of battling myself. Such conflict was unproductive and damaging; better to make the best of my time in this new environment, learning from it, gaining every scrap of information I could—as I had in the Haven. *As I had from Barac's mind,* I recalled with a shudder.

"Lady Witch." I looked up in surprise at that soft summons from the door. An older hunter/warrior stood there, head respectfully bent. No fear here, I noted with relief. No fear, but I detected a strong sense of purpose.

At my "Yes?" the hunter stepped boldly into the hut, pulling the door cloth closed behind him. Unlike the race who preferred the city, familiar to me as patrons and staff of the Haven, this Poculan was tall and lean, his color closer to cream than the more vivid yellow-brown I'd seen previously. The pattern of soft, fleshy knobs covering each of his joints differed as well, although I couldn't quite name why I thought so. I did know better than to ask.

Intrigued, I motioned him to join me on the mat. "You are the Lady Sira," the hunter announced in quite reasonable Comspeak, dropping into a practiced crouch, second knees level with his head. Well enough. My own grasp of the local dialect owed a bit too much to the Haven's clientele to be reliable or always polite.

"Names have power, Hunter," I replied, warned to caution by the gleam in his eye.

A slow blink. "I am Premick, Lady Witch," the hunter said with a quicker courtesy. First naming was an important moment among these widely-scattered people. I'd been right not to ignore his slight insolence. "These past two seasons I have been a furseeker."

So. "You've been guiding Captain Morgan." I examined this Premick with increased interest.

"We have been brothers in the hunt," Premick corrected. "And thus I have in truth been your faithful gatherer as well." This last came out a shade too quickly, as if to forestall any denial.

I restrained a smile, aware now of what this enterprising hunter was after. By the standards of his culture, Premick was well within his rights to assume that my appearance without Morgan meant that the Human's place in my household was now available. There was valuable status to be claimed by one chosen to serve a Ram'ad Witch. I arched one brow before pointing out: "You are already burdened with three sisters, Hunter Premick."

Premick removed a leather pouch from his belt with one thin-fingered hand. He spilled its contents nonchalantly on the mat between us. I picked up one of a dozen large, green-streaked teeth. "Most impressive," I said honestly, quite willing to believe that considerable effort and skill had been required to remove the objects from their original owners.

Encouraged by this admiration, Premick drew his knife and held the carved handle out to me. "I can provide for you, Lady Witch," he said earnestly.

"And for your own flesh as well?" the question from the doorway was sharp, and in almost accent-free Comspeak. I kept my face smiling, although there was an unusually strong feeling of menace about the two figures shadowing the net of the door cloth.

"Enter if you have business with me, lurkers at doors," I suggested coolly. Premick had stood, knife still drawn. I wasn't sure if it was for my defense or his own.

The two hesitated only briefly before pushing through the door cloth to stand just inside its shelter. One was Withren, the village's headwoman, her collection of memory bones making a heavy, tinkling rattle as they swung around her legs. I dismissed her immediately as the source of the menace I felt—her concern was more for my reaction to being disturbed.

No, it was the other one. The rudimentary mental abilities I sensed in Premick and others of his kind were keener, more controlled in this old male, though scarcely a match for a child of the Clan. The sense of menace was his, based in a considerable anger directed solely at Premick.

"I am within custom, Laem'sha," that worthy was now protesting, looking very distraught as he felt the other's fury.

Laem'sha. I nodded respectfully, having heard of the village wise man from Morgan. "Welcome under my roof," I said politely, but firmly. "What is your business with me, Laem'sha, Withren?"

With that naming of names, the wise man seemed to recollect himself, damping the emanations of his own emotions with acceptable skill. "Greetings, Lady Witch," he said smoothly. "Forgive our intrusion, but we need to speak to this hunter—"

"Before I can accept him as my provider?" I finished for Laem'sha when he paused. "That seems more my affair than yours." It could be an error on my part to give in too easily; theirs was a society painfully conscious of status. On the other hand, I had no wish to become embroiled in local politics. I frowned slightly. "What is your concern here?"

Surprisingly, it was Withren who answered, her voice calm and placating, her Comspeak heavily accented but, again, better than my smattering of Poculan. "Our village has given four hunters to the service of your sisterhood, good Lady. It is a high ambition, and one which brings honor to us all." A delicate pause. "We wish only to remind Premick of his—obligations—elsewhere." The scowl on Laem'sha's face indicated he would have stated the village's preference in more forceful terms.

I could hardly fail to understand their predicament. Poor, sister-ridden Premick (who now sat looking quite deflated and stripped of his bravado) was in truth a dreamer to think the village would allow him to traipse off in my wake. And, although custom was on their side, who were the Ram'ad Witches to take the cream of the hunters from their families, leaving the burden of support on those less able? I was no such parasite, even though I posed as one.

I thought furiously for a moment, then reached out to touch the hilt of Premick's knife with my right hand—touched, but didn't take the blade to hold in completion of the ritual I'd seen through Morgan's eyes. "I am honored by your offer, noble Premick," I said solemnly. "But I am not free to accept your service."

The elders were obviously pleased, though they carefully avoided expressing that emotion in front of Premick. It was likely Premick wouldn't have noticed. His pupils dilated in shock. I sighed. "Jason Morgan stands at my door, Hunter Premick, even when I send him from me in the hunt," I searched for words to save his pride and to keep their support. "I am sworn to him as much as he is sworn to my service. It will always be so," I added very quietly, knowing it was true.

"Morgan is worthy," Premick said with commendable dignity. "I shall remain at your service, Lady Witch. And at my village's." This with a sideways glance at the two village leaders. I was amused to feel Laem'sha send a flow of comfort to soothe Premick's troubled thoughts.

Withren smiled openly, I presumed grateful I'd salvaged the situation without costing anyone status. "The sun will come out by afternoon, Lady Witch. Will you honor our village by attending our feast-night?" I raised a brow at Laem'sha, not overly sure of the wise man's opinion of Ram'ad Witches. But he smiled, and there seemed no trace of animosity left in his thoughts.

"Yes, Lady Witch," he echoed quickly. "You have chosen a fine time to visit us. The last hunt was a good one, and many of the fruits are at their best. It will be a night to remember."

Why not? I accepted their invitation at face value, suddenly weary of my hermitage between these walls. The three took their leave, to all appearances harmoniously.

I gathered up my dishes and left them at the door, pulling open the cloth as I did so. Withren was right: the rain was little more than a drizzle, and the clouds were breaking open in the distance. I drew in a deep breath, enjoying the smell of the rain-washed air.

A whisper of a step from the empty room behind made me whirl around.

Morgan took another soft step to come fully around the grass wall dividing the back storage area from the rest of the hut. He had changed back into his jungle-used garb. I hadn't heard an aircar arriving or leaving—or his entry through the rear door. I might have blamed the rain and my guests, but I knew perfectly well how silently Morgan could move if he chose.

Mentally, I slid into a cautious guard, unsure how I felt about him arriving so soon.

"Thank you for the use of this place, Captain," I said, my voice formal. *Give me distance,* I asked with my eyes.

He understood, taking hold of a long, hook-ended stick that had puzzled me. "Your comfort in it is my duty, Lady Witch," Morgan said easily, mimicking the village courtesies in Comspeak. He reached up with the stick, pushing it against what I now saw were a series of wooden strips covering a good third of the ceiling. As he worked the stick, the strips swiveled to admit the brightening afternoon sun, creating mote-filled beams of light. The interior of the hut took on an unexpected airiness. "Primitive, but well-adapted," Morgan said, leaning the control stick against one wall. "It pays to give close attention to all they do."

As Morgan went about the hut, intuitively ignoring me, pausing to examine a stack of orange-red blankets (gifts from the village upon my arrival), I relaxed. Things were as before. Reassured, I felt some tautness in the small of my spine let go. But as my inner guard opened ever so slightly, I sensed Morgan's own mind, thoughts rippling in clear, cool waves I had only to dip into to read.

So he had heard my conversation with Premick and the elders—and having heard my commitment to him, he'd become complacent. Without a word, I attacked.

This was no invasion, such as had devastated Barac. No, what I sent against Morgan's arrogantly exposed mind was pain, wave after wave of pain in hammer blows no less dangerous because they were unseen.

I watched him stagger to his knees, hands going to his head, his defenses struggling into place, then was jolted by the reflected force of my own power as Morgan belatedly added his inner strength to his shields. From then on, he moved only once, to stand up, legs spread apart as a brace. Our eyes met and held.

I raised a hand to signal enough, breathing more deeply myself from effort. Morgan's barriers were impeccably in place now. His face had gone white, sweat gleamed dully on his brow. There was an unfamiliar tightness to his mouth. All he said was: "I thought the testing over."

"How can it be?" I said sharply, echoes of strain coursing through my mind. "How can I consider you safe when you forget so easily? How dare you enter the power sphere of any Clan without your shields in place? You are not ready. Your power is barely under control."

"Barac said the same about you."

I felt the blood drain from my face, but held myself stiff and erect. "I did not expect him to understand." *I thought you would,* I added to myself.

Morgan deliberately relaxed his stance, though I noticed that his shields remained firmly in place. "And somehow I must?" he said, as though hearing what I'd left unspoken. Before I could answer that, he waved one hand in a gesture that had never been part of his Human upbringing. "That was uncalled for, Sira. I do understand." A small, mischievous grin. "And when my head feels better, I'm sure I'll appreciate this latest lesson."

Good enough. I rubbed my own head at that reminder. "Withren told me of a village feast." A peace offering. "I promise no more instruction for tonight."

Morgan's eyes were warm again. "And I promise to keep up my shields."

His tone was light, but I couldn't keep a sudden irrational fear from edging my own. "Be sure you do, Jason. The day will come when it won't be me testing their strength."

INTERLUDE

Hastho'tha, a being inclined to bemoan his fate as less than he deserved (an opinion shared by his three maternal and two paternal parents), was uncharacteristically silent as he walked among the tables of the Spacer's Haven. His fellow employees gave him wide berth, aware of his mood. Fortunately, there were few conscious patrons at this hour to take offense at his surly mien.

Hastho'tha focused a glowering eye at the black thronelike chair centered among the gaming tables at the other end of the tavern. His table wiper, an elderly, wit-wandering Queeb named Krat, shivered nervously, careful to avoid the heavy hands at the ends of the larger being's muscular arms. "Warlock!" Hastho'tha spat the word, but quietly. "Things were hard enough under Herself, without bearing this pretender. I tell you, Krat, there is no man-thing born that has the power of a Ram'ad Witch."

"Yes, Master Hastho'tha," Krat whimpered automatically, having listened to this particular complaint since waking. Its four flexible tentacles wrapped around cutlery as two more deftly smeared last night's grime into an even layer on the table. Then all six froze precariously in midmotion. "A lady, Master Hastho'tha," Krat said almost loudly.

Hastho'tha grunted his opinion of that likelihood, but then he stopped to stare at the richly cloaked female who had just entered. There was something about the tilt of the veiled head, an aura of power and wealth in the way she stood and waited.

The instincts of the head server took over quickly. With an ungentle nudge to Krat to continue working, Hastho'tha moved to guide the newcomer to an already cleaned table, eyes busily assessing the quality of her insystem clothing, so different from that seen on Pocular's streets. "What does your ladyship require?" he asked almost wistfully.

"The owner. To me," her voice was pleasant, but with an underlying firmness unused to delay. Hastho'tha bowed gracefully, a courtesy so unlike the burly Poculan that the watching Krat put a heavy smoketray down on top of its wiping tentacles and had to restrain a cry of pain.

Had Krat continued to watch Hastho'tha, it would have certainly understood the gleeful expression on the head server's face as that worthy headed toward the communications panel behind the bar. Nothing would have pleased Hastho'tha more than the idea of trouble coming to the new owner of the Haven, Barac sud Sarc.

"I showed her to the best table, Lord Warlock," Hastho'tha greeted his employer moments later, noting with barely disguised contempt that the being had used the lift from the apartment above instead of appearing in midair as had the true witch. "She said only that she wanted the owner of the Haven."

Barac took more notice of the squat, overweight Poculan, something he'd tried to avoid until now owing to the truly repulsive elongation of the protuberances over Hastho'tha's joints. Some of the pale, wiggling things were almost long enough to wave with the Poculan's gestures, and stood out against his mustard-toned skin. Barac didn't know if these were considered attractive or not—and didn't really want to find out. What he did know was that Hastho'tha must be one of the group of employees Sira had aptly labeled as predictable. A hard worker only when certain of the superiority of his employer. Hastho'tha would have been horrified to know how plain his emotions—including his hope that the lady in question meant trouble for Barac—were to the Clansman. "Take me to her," Barac ordered, voice deliberately bored.

Barac's assumed boredom vanished as they approached the table. "A bottle of the best Denebian wine, Hastho'tha," he ordered, his hands echoing an elaborate gesture the veiled woman was quick to offer him. Hastho'tha's surly scowl returned, and he managed to cuff Krat as he passed by on the errand, muttering about the unfairness of it all. Krat nodded mute agreement.

"Rael," Barac said softly, dropping into a seat beside her. Although her features were concealed behind a high-fashion veil, the Clanswoman had made no other attempt to hide herself. Barac half-closed his eyes as her power explored the edges of his own in delicate reacquaintance.

"Well met, Cousin," Rael nodded regally, though her voice was warm. "Though an unanticipated pleasure."

Barac, despite a conscious effort, could not keep the bitterness from his voice. "You expected to find your sister, of course. The mighty Sira."

Rael became still, a more than superficial motionlessness. When she spoke, her voice was sharp, driven, yet a whisper. "Why do you speak of her so, feel so? What has happened between you?"

"Not here," Barac cautioned, shaken by Rael's quick perception. Hastho'tha had come with the wine. Barac took it absently. "We are not to be disturbed," he said to the head server, eyes fixed on Rael. "Empty the tavern and send the staff home, including yourself."

Hastho'tha's brown-rimmed eyes blinked in astonishment. "Close the Haven, Master? It's never been closed—"

Barac turned swiftly, allowing his power to swell into a pain-filled emphasis that made the Poculan cower. "Close, lackwit. It may be permanently. Tell the staff to return only when I call on them."

"As you command, Lord Warlock," Hastho'tha stumbled back, black tears streaming from his eyes, a healthy new respect for his employer in his thoughts.

What has been happening, Barac? Rael sent mind-to-mind. Barac's quick wince told her much. She switched considerately to verbal communication. "You are damaged. How did it happen? Is Sira all right?"

"Sira!"

The name, spoken with all of Barac's resentment, told her enough. Rael raised her veil with two fingers, reaching with elaborate casualness for the wine. "You were wise to close this place, Barac," she ventured, voice as silken as the strangely mobile locks of blue-black hair revealed under her loose hood. "I think you and I have a lot to discuss tonight."

Chapter 6

"I COULD almost believe in magic, like the silly Drapsk."
Full of dreamy contentment and more than my share of deli-
cious white-fleshed fowl stuffed with grains and fruit, I leaned
back against Morgan's strong shoulder, wishing time could
stand still a while longer.

"Aie," he agreed quietly, arm opening to offer me a more
secure resting place. My hair quickly entwined itself around his
shoulders and neck, then lay quietly as if not to attract my
attention further. Perhaps I should have moved, altering a posi-
tioning that was clearly a caress, but why? My fears and indeed
the rest of the universe were far away tonight, driven into
shadows by the soft monotonous rhythms of the villagers'
songs.

And the dancers. They had come and gone throughout the evening on a stage defined by a circle of fragrant fires: sometimes
whirling, twisting, stamping their belled feet to drumbeats that
ached in my bones; other times slow, sinuous movements coun-
terpointed by piercing notes on a wind instrument. There seemed
no end to it, and yet I was amazed the dancers could maintain the
pace demanded by the hours already passed. "Withren says they
usually dance until dawn," Morgan added to my thought. True to
his word, his shields were in place, but our surface thoughts
mixed easily, unguarded in a peaceful truce.

"Will you join us, Lady?"

I eyed Withren lazily as she approached, leaving the current
group of performers. The headwoman looked wildly exotic
with her face, upper body, and multijointed legs coated in paint,
the colors glistening with sweat. I sensed her satisfaction. This
night was important to the village, a measure of the bounty

readied against lean months, a chance to draw together. *Why not?* I said to myself and Morgan with an inner smile, though the mere thought would have shocked me earlier in the day. I glanced at my empty goblet suspiciously, then shrugged.

Withren led me into the circle of light cast by the fires. Fortunately, the dance step of the moment was admirably suited to the rank amateur. The drums were lighthearted and steady; I was soon surrounded by what seemed to be all of the mature females of the village. The pattern of the dance was a stamping circle of eight that brought us closer then farther from a chanting outer ring of males. I laughed at Morgan as I passed him and, following the actions of my nearest neighbor, used my hips to give a fairly good imitation of her swiveling torso. There was an innocence here that could heal.

I don't know how long the dance lasted. At some point, the male villagers began to join, causing hilarious confusion as they crowded the already tightly packed females. I was bounced from one painted, stamping body only to rebound against another. There seemed to be a large and significant amount of elbow rubbing involved. Breathless, I began to seriously consider moving to the relative safety of the edge. Then I noticed the edges of the dance were spreading out past the fires as pairs of dancers whirled off into the darkness beyond.

A hot arm slid around my waist. I looked up in surprise.

Premick's painted face was puckered in a foolish grin that was certainly unusual on the dignified hunter. I could smell the local brew quite strongly on his breath. Fighting a temptation to giggle, I glanced around to see how the others handled this sort of thing. As far as I could tell, they were all happily being claimed. I tested his grip and found it to be like iron. "Premick," I began, as we moved, continuing to stamp up and down quite madly in unison, toward the nearest gap in the fires.

"Premick," a deeper voice echoed. Morgan stood, unmoving, in our path. Premick's drink-clouded mind took note of the barrier, and slowly he stopped dancing. I waited motionless in his hold, uncertain all at once of Morgan's intention. Surely the Human knew all this was in fun, that I was more amused than perturbed by this evidence of the villagers' acceptance of me and my part in their celebration.

But why did the music falter and stop? Why was I suddenly trembling as if in a cold breeze?

It was power. Morgan's inner power, combined with the portion I had given him of myself. Somehow, the humor was gone as I recognized that something else—rivalry, possession, claiming—was going on between the two males. It didn't matter that I was alien to both, not at this moment, with blood hot from the dance, and judgment smudged by drink. Morgan stood expressionless, hands loose at his sides, but Premick knew. The hunter released me, pushed me aside with one rough hand, the other fumbling for the knife that, thank custom, was left behind for the feast-night.

"Stop this," I said, aghast at the change in things, still shuddering with the impact of Morgan's emotions amplified by his mental strength. At least that was kept to the two of us, those now moving to surround us seeming to feel no more than anticipation. They were a basic people, I realized. The tense posture of the two males had its place in their feast-night, too.

Premick let out a low grunt and launched himself at Morgan. The Human moved with incredible quickness, but was brought to the ground with a thud as Premick's long arm caught one of Morgan's feet. Frantically, I looked around for Laem'sha, Withren, or anyone with authority. Surely they would help me stop this meaningless war between friends.

There. I was certain the lone figure to the right of the crowd was the wise man, though his costume made it impossible to be sure from a distance. I pushed through to his side with difficulty, the villagers having changed from peaceful dancers to hot-eyed encouragers of the battle.

Despite my urgency, I had to stop and stare at the apparition Laem'sha made in the fires' light. From the mid-torso origin of his legs to well above his head, he had been mummified within an immense basketlike contraption. It was filled with fruit and other foods, much of it pressed so firmly against the wicker the pulp was oozing through, attracting insects and somewhat larger visitors who peeked at me before rustling out of sight. I could only imagine what it felt like to be on the inside. Between the ripe food and garlands of flowers, competing aromas blasted my senses.

There was, as the living larder turned toward me, a hole at

face-height. In the shadow, I could make out a pair of eyes. I supposed he had to be able to see where he was dancing. "Laem'sha," I said, gathering myself. "You—" Then I leaped back, startled into a cry by a hideous creature lunging at me from its hiding place at shoulder-height. It was the size of my fist, but had jaws that opened much wider, revealing multiple rows of green teeth and two forked tongues. The protruding eyes were glazed over, as if the creature were blind. I wasn't sure which was more repulsive: its bloated, four-footed body, or the yammering screech with which it continued to threaten me.

Laem'sha, for I had been right in that identification, quickly produced a pulp-smeared hand to soothe his pet, if that monstrosity could ever be called such. Amazingly, the creature calmed at once. With its huge mouth closed, body slimmed, and its eyes more reasonably held in sockets, it looked better, but remained more nightmare than nature. "My truthsayer, Lady Witch," the wise man said by way of introduction, stroking the thing on a patch of brown fur between its eyes—the only part of it not coated in small, irregular spines. "You are troubled by this?" Laem'sha waved his fingers at the two figures now rolling perilously close to one of the fires, the crowd roaring its approval.

"It may be your custom, Laem'sha," I said dryly, recovering from the scare his creature had given me. "It's certainly not mine. Can we stop it, without offending your ways?"

Laem'sha's hand disappeared for an instant, then suddenly the entire top half of his costume split in the middle. He squirmed free of it—wiping a mass of crushed fruit from his head as his pet climbed determinedly back to his shoulder—and looked at me with a twinkle in his eyes. "Oh, it doesn't offend us, Lady—whether it goes on or ends. We of the jungle understand the needs of the flesh. But consider. Do you not feel flattered to have two such admirable suitors? Would it not be interesting to see who remains standing to claim his place as your provider?"

"I have no intention of allowing a brawl to determine who is to be my provider or anything else." I drew a breath, steadied my voice. "We have enjoyed your feast-night, Laem'sha. I fear too much so. Morgan may be more serious than Premick realizes."

Competing shouts greeted some move by a visibly battered Morgan to throw Premick against a hut wall, collapsing part of the structure. Laem'sha put his fragrant, sticky arm around my shoulders in a fatherly way and drew me in the opposite direction. Frustrated almost to the point of some violence of my own, I allowed him to do so, keeping a wary eye on the truthsayer beast as it adjusted to the movement by digging paired claws into Laem'sha's skin. "Yet Premick needs to lose some of his ambition, Lady Sira," the wise man said reasonably.

"Especially with regard to a certain Ram'ad Witch?" I suggested, grasping his meaning quickly enough, but unable to listen to the noise behind without wincing. "Isn't having Morgan defend his place physically rather demeaning to me?"

Laem'sha laughed, then looked down at me with a knowing smile. "I have been to the spaceport and its city, Lady Sira. I know of other worlds—and other powers."

Why, the old faker. "You know I'm not a witch," I said, pulling away to look at him searchingly. His large yellow-ringed eyes met mine without evasion. "Then why have you permitted Morgan and me to live in your village? Why haven't you exposed us? And how did you know?" Pride as well as curiosity prompted my last question; I had done my research thoroughly, I'd thought, before assuming the role. The fight became rather less important.

Laem'sha seemed quite entertained by my reaction, although he looked around carefully for eavesdroppers. "In part, because you paid your way, giving the village its fair share of Morgan's hunt. Of course, you did not fool Horhy here at all." The creature waggled its oversized head at the sound of its name.

I was puzzled. "Why permit our imposture, if you knew?"

"Magic, Lady Sira," was the soft answer. "We must have magic in our lives. And yet the true practitioners, our witches, are—shall I say—hard to live with at best? You provided a resident magician without causing any harm." I looked at Laem'sha with new respect. "And in return we gave you some peace, did we not?"

It was a reflex to check my mental shields; his perception must come from a deep knowledge of people. "You are a good and wise being, Laem'sha," I said, stopping to offer him my hands. A smash from the distance made me close my eyes briefly. "But don't you think Premick is convinced by now?"

What Laem'sha would have said I never learned. In that instant, as we stood isolated and partially hidden, there came the whine of a falling object before a dagger of light drove consciousness from my mind.

INTERLUDE

"You cannot enter."

Others who knew Jason Morgan would have been warned by the icy flash of his blue eyes. But then it was likely Withren had faced down enough hunters during her reign as virtual monarch of her tribe to be unimpressed by either rage or calm argument when they went against her wish.

Even so, Morgan was amazed to find himself still obeying the dictates of the village headwoman. He stared past Withren's narrow shoulder at the closed and guarded door of the hut, fists clenched, straining every mental faculty to reach Sira's mind, to assess her condition. Again, all he sensed was the peacefulness of deep sleep. But why hadn't she awakened by now, and why were Withren and her people so determined to keep him away from her?

He tried another tack. "Our ways are not yours, Withren. Lady Sira would want me to be with her, I assure you."

"You are male," the headwoman pronounced as if this explained everything, her face grim under its mask of cracking festival paint. She held her arms folded in front of her, a complex wrapping which Morgan didn't need to have translated to read as determination. Two other Poculans, female, stood silently to either side of her, folding their arms as well.

"What does—?" Morgan changed his mind, closing his lips over the question. He'd found the Poculans made very little distinction between their sexes in any role beyond the ownership of land and huts: usually held by their females, but not exclusively so. Even the provision of dowries—here a question of property ownership rather than bridal price, to allow younger members to become independent from family—was the responsibility of the oldest family member, male or female.

There was another way to ask. Morgan held out his hand. Withren touched her fingers to his palm without hesitation. Through the contact, Morgan sent a tendril of exploring thought, finding respect and concern for Sira—along with a surprisingly deep commitment to keep him from Sira while she was helpless. He withdrew before the sensitive Poculan detected his mind touch.

But he wasn't about to give in while Sira needed him. "I've respected your customs, Withren," he gritted out in as polite a voice as possible, fighting the tendency of his immediate surroundings to darken around the limits of his vision. It had been a long night. "But keeping me away from her now offends us both—and possibly endangers my lady. Let me see her. Please. She may need me."

Withren's eyes took on a hooded look. Through her fingers, still lingering on his palm, Morgan felt a startling rush of pity. "We know how to care for her—"

"What care does she need?" His alarmed voice cut across hers, and the women on either side of them reached for their knives at its tone. Morgan ignored them, twisting his hand from Withren's sudden grip as she tried to hold him back. "All I sense is sleep. What happened to her?" Enough was enough.

He tried to step past Withren, only to find his feet unable to take him any closer, pinned in place by some, some *thing* between himself and Sira.

"What?" he gasped, staggering back.

Withren looked suddenly tired. "You cannot enter past Laem'sha's magic," the headwoman pronounced heavily. "He left it in my care. Your lady will be awake soon from the sleep of healing. Please trust me, Morgan."

"I don't understand," Morgan felt, or rather tasted an ominous recurrence of the foreboding he'd experienced when Barac arrived. His eyes were dazed and pleading. "What happened? Laem'sha couldn't tell me much before he—died." Withren clicked her tongue in acknowledgment of echoing pain.

The attack had been sudden and deadly to those close to the once-gay circle of fire. Stun grenades, tossed from shielded aircars into the crowd of celebrants, had released a gas that meant harmless sleep to Human and Clan—asphyxiation to any Poculans caught directly in its cloud. Laem'sha had miraculously clung to life long enough to gasp what he had seen to Morgan. A vision of Sira floating up into the night sky.

Morgan shuddered at the memory. He suspected he'd gone more than a little mad then, sending searing questing thoughts into the night, ignoring any self-protection in his fear for her. *Sira would have his head for it,* he reflected ruefully. She had trained him to do better.

But he had found her at last, a pitifully crumpled figure tossed like so much refuse to lie unconscious in a clearing across the river from the village. The sight of her deathly still form alone in the moonlight burned behind his eyes when he dared close them. This was exactly the type of assault he'd feared and she hadn't; the type he'd fortified the Haven to withstand with every bit of his knowledge and skill. What good were sophisticated alarms and deadly traps when he'd let Sira leave their protection?

What good was he?

Warm, twiglike fingers wrapped around his. Withren's face was slightly frightened, a common expression among the villagers as they learned how much power lay within both him and his mistress, but she offered comfort anyway. "You haven't blamed us," Morgan said wonderingly, meeting her eyes. "The attack was aimed at us—at Sira. You lost eight of your own. I don't understand."

"You did not expect your enemies to follow you here, or you would not have come. And we are the Fak-ad-sa'it," she said with a note of tired pride. "We face life, accept it. There is no comfort in guilt or revenge."

Revenge. Morgan's eyes narrowed at the word, nostrils white as he took a shuddering breath. But he did not speak whatever was in his mind, saying instead, "I'm sending for help. My lady has kin in the city." He closed his eyes, forming an image within his mind of Barac, forcing himself to focus calmly. But his mental message to Barac was brief and forceful enough to wake the Clansman from a sound sleep: *Sira's been attacked. Come.* Beneath the words, Morgan drove the locate, his memory of this place, into Barac's thoughts. He'd need it to move through the M'hir to the village.

Morgan staggered, then caught himself, knowing he was near the limits of his strength and determined not to fail again.

"Ah," the satisfied whisper made him look up again. "The sisterhood draws together in trouble." Withren seemed beyond surprise as she beckoned to the slim figure forming out of the air beside them.

Morgan breathed a name in startled recognition.

"Rael . . . ?"

Faster than reflex, Morgan drew and aimed the weapon he'd tardily begun to carry, moving to put himself between the Clanswoman and the hut containing Sira. Suddenly, everything made a kind of terrible sense: Barac's arrival to drive Sira from safety and time the attack, and now Rael's to check on its result. The two members of the Clan Morgan halfway trusted, that trust a key to unlock their defenses. His mouth tightened as Rael became solid, her beautiful face turning ashen as she saw his welcome.

"What is the meaning of this, Human?" she demanded, her voice imperious. "Where is Sira?" Under the question, Morgan felt the lash of Rael's power as she sought her own answers, that power glancing from his shielding with a lack of success she acknowledged with a measuring stare and a raised brow. Rael took a step toward him, choosing to disregard the weapon aimed at her, her attention now on the hut. "What keeps me out?" she asked, head tilted as though she'd finally found the real puzzle.

Before Morgan could answer, the air was shattered by a scream. Forgetting Rael, he turned and ran toward the hut, finding the unseen barrier gone but landing right in the arms of the villagers Withren had placed as guards. He struggled frantically. Then, a second scream, unheard, burst through his mind. *Morgan!*

Chapter 7

I WOKE up screaming.

It was an understandable reaction, since the first sight to meet my eyes was the drooling grin of Horhy, Laem'sha's truthsayer. At my scream, the small creature let out one of its own, scrambling back from its perch on my chest to huddle in a ball on my stomach, quivering as though terrified.

I immediately lost my fear of it, reaching a curiously heavy hand to scratch its tiny patch of fur. When I touched it, I recoiled again. The thing had Talent!

I placed fingers on its warm fur again, curious. Strong impressions of fear, loss, loneliness; a lighter one of pleasure at my caress. Exhaustion and relief as well, as though it had been somehow exerting itself and had just now dared relax. This explained a great deal about Laem'sha's "truthsayer."

Thinking about the wise man was enough to drive the creature to a near madness of grief. I reached with my mind to calm it. The ease with which the small thing accepted my presence in its tiny thoughts suggested its master had used such techniques often. *Former master,* I reminded myself. What had happened to Laem'sha?

We had been attacked at night, but daylight shone through the roof vanes of the hut. Where was Morgan? He would never have left me alone, with only an alien beast for company, wrapped so, as I now discovered, that I couldn't rise from the sleeping platform if I tried. Instantly alarmed, I sent his name flying outward, *Morgan!*

Sira! Warmth, joy, burning out a black desperation I had never felt in Morgan's mind before.

What is going on? I replied, thoroughly alarmed by the violence of his emotions. What could have happened?

A sudden upwelling of sound: voices, a suspicious thumping, then footsteps. My welcoming smile for Morgan froze on my face at the sight of him.

Morgan's eyes were sunk in puffy, blackened flesh. One cheek was scraped open from ear to chin: a raw, oozing redness blending into his split and swollen lips. Knowing Morgan, I supposed Premick looked worse, though it was hard to imagine.

Morgan gave me no time to assess his wounds. He came to my side in long strides, dropping to his knees as though he'd lost the ability to stand, then buried his face in great handfuls of my hair. I was astounded to see his shoulders begin to shake. Words struggled out of him, none making coherent sense: ". . . gone . . . could have lost you . . . my fault . . . my fault . . ."

Jason, I reached mentally; at the same time my hands tried to hold him still. He had to be exhausted, irrational—how long since he'd slept?

It was horrible, feeling the depths of his torment and relief, knowing I was the cause.

But was it not also wonderful?

My mind cleared, leaving the simple truth. *Beloved and foolish Human,* I sent, and under the words gave him all I had always kept locked inside, a tide of love and need that surged over my other senses until I was blind and deaf. I felt him quiver and come to life under my arms.

A joy close to pain as the tide turned, was amplified, and came back to me. I felt tears pouring from my eyes. Emotions flowed back and forth between our minds until we couldn't bear any distance between us. I knew when Morgan pressed his wounded lips gently to my skin, the touch echoing my desire as well as his own. I knew when his eager hands released my body from its wrappings.

Then I knew sudden agony, reeling as a flash of dismay, horror, and rage roared from his mind to mine before Morgan slammed down every barrier, leaving me breathless and terribly alone.

"What's wrong?" I said, my eyes fighting to focus. I could see his face, dimly make out that Morgan was staring down at the lower part of my body. He seemed to hear me after a moment, and moved slowly, dragging the blanket up again. Then his eyes slid reluctantly to mine, anguished between their swollen lids.

I grew cold, summoning reserves of will to control my emotions. It would be easier to talk, to work out what had happened (or almost happened, an aching emptiness reminded me), if I were sitting up. I told my body to rise.

And I couldn't. The muscles of my abdomen would not respond. Attempting to twist, to roll to a sit resulted in a searing agony that left me gasping for breath. Morgan quickly seized my shoulders and eased me back into the pile of blankets. "Don't, Sira," he ordered hoarsely. Then in a rush: "You've been hurt. I didn't know. Withren wouldn't let me see you—she said you needed to sleep. I didn't know—" He seemed unable to go on.

"Jason," I began, my hands cupping his bruised face, bewildered by the chill feel of his skin, the depth of pain there. "What happened? I remember something falling—a blinding light. An attack?" He nodded within my hands but didn't speak. I sent a gentle summons, and a light weight landed on my legs. The truthsayer clung there, apparently willing to accept Morgan's presence. "This creature has Talent; it told me Laem'sha is dead. Others?" Another nod, slower. I searched his eyes, wishing he'd let me reach deeper. Then I thought I knew. "Do you want me to admit you were right about the Haven? I do. But it's not your fault. I was the one who left its protection, remember? You can't guard against my poor judgment—"

A violent negating gesture. "What, then?" I asked, drawing my hands away. "Surely not whatever wounds I have," I chided. "I'll heal."

Morgan's face was like a mask. I missed the feel of his thoughts as he chose to speak almost matter-of-factly, like some report. "Stun grenade. The gas killed eight villagers, including Laem'sha. The rest of us were unconscious. You were taken—" He stopped in mid-sentence. I realized with a chill of apprehension it was because he had to force himself to continue and I'd never known Morgan to hesitate, no matter how dire the news. "I found you hours later," he went on at last. "You'd been dropped near the river and left. After I brought you back, Withren and her women insisted on caring for you. I couldn't add to their grief by disobeying her."

The Human might have been carved from stone, his control was so devastatingly complete. The warmth we had shared, the happiness given and received was gone. We might never have touched thought-to-thought, flesh-to-flesh. I tried to smile at him, to awaken some softness in his eyes. "Obviously, I underestimated our opponents," I admitted, keeping my voice light. "A Clan failing, isn't it, to overlook technology? I promise I won't do so again. We must make plans to protect ourselves, to help the village." I left my mind open to him, but he continued to shut me out. "But you must tell me what's wrong, Jason."

Instead of smiling, he took my hands in a too firm grip. "You must promise me something first, Sira."

I blinked. "Of course—"

"By your love for me." Flatly, confident of his power and grimly willing to exploit it. I nodded, my turn to be unsure of my voice. "Promise me you'll stay here. That you won't go after them."

Stay where? Go after whom? Humor him, part of me said. Clearly, sleeping through the entire nastiness had been easier, and Morgan would have known the villagers who died. Add that to the fight with Premick and you had a massive strain on even Morgan's immense resources. Humor him? Another part of me screamed to silence him, to avoid hearing whatever Morgan felt required such a promise.

"I promise—by my love for you, Jason Morgan," I said finally, bowing to his need, hiding my grief that this moment and those words were stripped of the joy they deserved. "Tell me."

"There are two incisions on your body, Sira, sealed with medplas, just below your ribs," Morgan said with brutal directness. "From what I know of your physiology, that's where your—reproductive organs would be located." He stopped. For a moment, all I could hear was the pounding of blood in my head. "They're long cuts, Sira. Precise. They look deep as hell." Morgan's voice trailed away slowly, the pressure of his grip crushing my fingers; at the same instant I felt an inflow of his strength, an easing of pain.

"The Clan Council." I'd renounced their power over me,

their right to dictate my future, when I'd Chosen Morgan over my own kind. I hadn't been fool enough to believe they'd accept my Choice. But this? "Am I sterile?" I asked after what seemed like a century or so, my mouth so dry the words hurt.

"I don't know. I've tried to sense the damage. I can't—" This last with a familiar frustration. Morgan always refused to accept the limits of his healing gift. He went on, "That was never their aim before. Why now?"

I looked at him, feeling my cheeks burn. "Because they feared I would complete the Joining. That we would— If it were possible for us to—" I stopped, completely unable to bring words to the thwarted desire still senselessly pounding through my body.

"Simpler to kill me, don't you think?" Morgan countered without visible emotion. "I was lying there, completely at their mercy. No. I'm betting they took what they wanted. Wouldn't it suit the Council's goals to produce your offspring engineered to their requirements? Even better, to grow new Siras guaranteed to have your power?"

He was speaking nonsense. "It's forbidden!" I protested, cautiously flexing my body to isolate the pain, to confirm for myself its location. "Even if someone dared—the Clan does not have that kind of knowledge or technology."

His eyes bored into mine, their blue as hard and cold as aeons-old ice. "Knowledge is a commodity. A thing forbidden merely becomes—expensive."

What if it were true? I stared at Morgan's beaten and bruised face, trying to sort thoughts that raced in wild tangents. Then, slowly, piecemeal at first, I felt myself hardening, my thoughts coming together in a burning focus. It thrust aside all emotions save one: rage.

I looked into the face of my love and saw, Ossirus forgive me, only the weapon I had been unconsciously forging over the past year. A weapon ready for use.

"Recover what was stolen from me, Jason Morgan," I said through lips that were numb. "Seek them wherever they hide. As you love me—"

Our minds locked in one awesome moment of empathy; we were one being, dark and purposeful. Allowed inside his shields, I flooded his mind with my rage, shocked for an instant by the overwhelming response of his own.

As if aiming a beam of dreadful energy at my enemies, I *pushed* . . .

. . . and wrenched my thoughts out of Morgan's as he materialized in the control room of his ship, the *Silver Fox*. My eyes opened, blind to the sunlight streaming into the hut.

It was done.

As I lay there, hearing a chaos of voices and footsteps approaching, I realized my most familiar nightmare had just come true.

I was alone.

INTERLUDE

The crew? *Untrustworthy.*

Whether this conclusion was accurate or not, the lone figure sitting aloof from the frenzy on the bridge of the starship nodded his head at the thought, quite content to view all who were not his kind—and most who were—with distrust. It was usually justified, as Faitlen di Parth, Second Level Adept and Councillor of the Clan, knew.

The crew was also incompetent. What he had expected, considering the amount of local currency which had changed hands and other varied appendages, was an efficient, well-run ship. The task was simply to take care of the mundane detail of moving his group and their precious cargo quickly yet discreetly from this fringe-hole of a system. Faitlen rubbed his long, slender fingers against the fabric of his cloak, trying to rid them of their clammy moisture. It was unseemly to rely on aliens like this. He hadn't thought it potentially disastrous.

"Port Jellies are yammering about something, Captain," a voice shouted above the general din.

At this, a relative hush fell as the six Denebians turned as one to look at their passenger. "I thought you'd taken care of Pocular's Port Authority," growled the Captain, a large and florid-faced Human, his small, bloodshot eyes watering in one of the characteristic downs of ysa-smoke addiction. "We don't need trouble—"

Trouble? Faitlen sneered to himself. If he didn't need their revoltingly slow ship to keep his journey secret from those who Watched the M'hir, he'd show these pathetic Humans what trouble could be. Still, he didn't require further inconvenience.

"I remind you, Captain, you've been paid enough to compensate for any—difficulties." He considered the problem for a moment. "Continue on your posted course," he ordered. "I'll speak to—"

Anything the Clansman might have said was swallowed in the shrieking of the proximity klaxon. The crew scrambled to their seats, triggering holding fields with disquieting speed. Faitlen followed suit, fumbling once with the control, then feeling the reassuring grip pulling him deeper into the bench. He assumed those below were as prepared.

"Most likely some rec-sat or debris in an unmarked orbit," the navigator tossed over her shoulder. "These fringe worlds aren't known for their record keeping. Nothing to touch this ship—" She paused. "Mind you, Enforcers don't have to post a course."

Faitlen thought it entirely predictable this was the moment when the alarm screamed again in torment and all the lights went dark.

Streams of profanity located the crew. Just as the Clansman readied himself to leave the ship, deserting all aboard without hesitation, the lights returned and fields relaxed. The Captain's shouting into the com turned abruptly conciliatory. "Here's the confirmation of our course, Constable." A pause. "No. No problems with Port Authority." Another pause. "Tourists."

When the Captain leaned back, wiping the sweat from his forehead with one arm, Faitlen asked, "Well?"

The Denebian turned and glowered at his passenger. "Maybe you're not paying us enough to play bump and run with an Enforcer patrol. They were lurking out here, dark to scans, probably waiting to snag a poacher. That was close, hear me? They could have easily taken it into their heads to search us. I don't know what you've got below, and I'm not asking, right? But nothing about this deal says we take the fall if you're running Trade Pact contraband."

"Trust me, Captain," he said calmly. "They would not have thought to board this ship." Faitlen allowed his power to swell outward, sending a flare of pain against the Human's mind, observing the resulting parade of shock, fear, and loathing on the being's face with clinical interest. "And you have been paid enough."

Chapter 8

"SHOULD she be doing that?" Rael's question, pointedly addressed to Withren, was intended to provoke me. I ignored her, concentrating instead on the novel problem of walking without using the muscles of my abdomen. *Finally.* I leaned against the doorframe, back to my watchers, and was rewarded for my efforts with my first look at the outside world since last night.

There was no evidence of disaster in the peaceful scene greeting my eyes. Nothing remained of the happy preparations made for the village feast either. Villagers walked by, some carrying bundles, others with babies underfoot or riding on the Poculan version of a hip. Regardless of their age or business, voices were hushed, eyes glancing my way with a new furtiveness.

And why not? I asked myself grimly. It was my fault—the deaths, and more. My fingers dug into the thatch-wrapped wood as I strained again to reach Morgan. It hardly mattered if Rael witnessed this, too; she'd entered the hut behind Morgan, an intrusion neither of us had been in any condition to notice, and had seen what I would never have shared otherwise.

A bead of sweat stung my eye, and I began to shudder with the dual effort of fighting the pain lancing up from my abdomen and summoning the strength to concentrate in the M'hir. *Morgan!* I sent, driving forth his name with more desperation than power. Dimly, almost imagined, I sensed the golden glow he carried with him; between us was the impenetrable shielding I'd trained him to raise in battle.

Spent, I fought to hold myself upright, consoling myself that Morgan was safe, if not within my reach. Horhy nuzzled his/her/its? prickly snout against my ear, accurately sensing my mood. My hair was the creature's preferred roosting spot, a position which offended Rael's Clan sensibilities. I could feel her hovering behind me, the M'hir between us full of concern warring with frustration. There was something else there, too, but I was not inclined to search deeper.

But I was inclined to get help before falling flat on my face in front of the entire village, I decided, glancing back at my sister. "Rael?" She hastened to my side, wrapping her arm carefully around my shoulders to half-carry me to the seat Withren indicated.

"Time to eat, Lady Witch," the headwoman announced, her thin face more weary than grim. I touched her thoughts briefly, very lightly, encountering the core of firm loyalty to me, "her witch," underlying her thoughts. Here was one who felt she had failed me, rather than the other way around. My thanks for the meal Withren placed on the table before me were perhaps more deeply meant than she realized.

Before I could take a bite, however, Horhy jumped down to land with its two front feet accurately pinning the piece of meat on my plate. Glazed, slightly protruding eyes glared up at me warily but with determination. Rael winced and even I felt a little queasy as those tiny, sharp claws dug in and held, its body beginning to puff in threat. Withren, showing less than respect for a creature her people were convinced harbored the spirits of past tribal elders, snatched up the plate and dumped it, and its now-yammering rider, outside. "I'll bring you another, Lady," she promised as she went out the door.

Laughing was torture; I blinked tears from my eyes as I tried to resist the impulse. Rael reached one hand toward me, then left it poised in midair. "Please, Sira," she said again, her dark eyes anguished. "Let me do something."

Her power throbbed against what remained of mine, promising comfort and strength. Fully trained and powerful, Rael had the Talent to speed healing, an ability tied to an intimacy of mental touch I dared not allow—not while I remained so weak and vulnerable. "I'll be fine," I said, wishing futilely my voice sounded more convincing even to myself. "It's blood loss and shock."

"That's not all that's wrong." She hesitated, chewing on a

full lower lip for an instant. "If you won't leave here or let me help, at least let me call Barac—"

"Oh, he'd love to see me like this," I said without thinking, then flushed. She hadn't mentioned our cousin until now, but his absence and her presence told me most of what I needed to know. "Forgive me, Rael," I said, relenting before she had to reply. "That was—inappropriate."

"True," Rael agreed, suddenly absorbed in selecting a piece of fruit from a bowl on the low table. "Barac warned me you'd—changed."

"Come now," I chided, feeling every one of the years I had lived before this sister had been born, despite her reaching adulthood and Choice before me. "Surely Barac used a different word."

"Given the circumstances, I'm hardly worried about a sud's injured pride." Rael had asked me no questions about what had happened. She didn't need to, having, I was sure, plucked whatever Morgan and I hadn't revealed to her from Withren's thoughts. The minds of the Poculans were uncommonly accessible. Fodder for their witches and now for the Clan.

Her dark eyes rose to meet mine, uncertainty warring with something harder to decipher. A graceful gesture; a voice of quiet reason: "I understand what you did to Barac better than I do your remaining here, Sira. I understand it better than I do your Human abandoning you to these primitive—"

"Morgan," I protested firmly, if faintly, "would never abandon me. You know that, Rael. And these people, primitive or not, have shown me far more goodwill than any others of recent memory. Morgan trusts them, and so do I."

"Then where is he?"

"Where I sent him." For an instant, my eyes saw nothing but a whirling darkness, then I refocused on Rael's face with an effort. I studied her features: the strong cheekbones and delicate line of jaw so like our mother's and unlike mine; the look of an aristocrat, accustomed to power and control, despite the tendency of her lips to quiver and her eyes to darken, as now, when distressed. Her lustrous black hair, longer tamed than mine, still seethed restlessly over her shoulders. A passionate Clanswoman, sure of her place and our kind, and, I knew, someone who would agree completely with my loosing Morgan against my ene-mies—regardless of the risk to his life.

More than agree, I said to myself, guarding the thought behind my own shields. *Rael would see my actions as proof I was finally recovering my senses and returning to what I was born—a member of the Clan, the M'hiray.* For my sake, she had tolerated Morgan and reluctantly accepted that my feelings for him existed. Equally, for my sake, she'd be overjoyed to think I'd use him, treat him as Clan had treated Humans since our species first met. If he died in my service, freeing me from Human contamination, so much the better.

Oh, I knew how she'd react, how any of them would. I shifted carefully in my seat, trying unsuccessfully to find a more com-fortable spot among the blankets and my own thoughts. I knew exactly what it meant to be Clan, which was why I had chosen exile.

"Morgan will be back," I stated out loud, before Rael said something I wouldn't be able to forgive, no matter how true it might be.

Brief alarm in her eyes and thoughts, rippling the M'hir. In my weakness, I must have let some of my own emotions trickle through. Then she confused me, saying: "Soon, I trust."

Her shields were in place; keeping out my emotions or keeping in her own? "You surprise me, Sister."

"How so?" A too-innocent look from green eyes unused to secrecy. "You won't listen to reason. Maybe you'll listen to your Human and seek proper medical care. It's the least he can do after last night."

"You know what happened here, Rael," I leaned forward, clutching my middle, feeling my hair lashing my cheeks. "Morgan saved my life—"

"Really? After endangering it!" The M'hir was locked from us both, but her anger was plain. "You're right—I know what happened here. Do you?"

"I'm in no mood for riddles, Rael," I warned her.

"Who knew you were here?" she snapped. "Who was sup-posed to protect you? Oh, I know how Morgan engaged in a drunken brawl, leaving you defenseless—distracted! How con-venient! What was your Human paid for his service?"

All that saved Rael's life in that moment was my weakness. I had no mercy, no compassion left in me, only blinding fury, but the power I could slam against her shields was barely enough to widen her eyes with pain and fear.

It was enough to open the smallest of cracks, to let me reach her mind and surface thoughts. I hadn't intended such an invasion—I wasn't sure what I'd intended, beyond striking back—but suddenly I was there.

Almost instantly, Rael thrust me out. We stared at one another, both breathing in heavy gasps. I found it hard to focus until I blinked fiercely, feeling hot moisture trail down my cheeks. What I read then on her expressive face wasn't righteous indignation or anger—it was guilt.

"You aren't here to see me, to help me," I heard myself say incredulously. "You were sent to find out what lies between Morgan and me—to experiment on us—to learn how I controlled the Power-of-Choice. You came . . ." my voice failed me, then I knotted my hands into fists and found it again. "How dare you accuse Morgan! *You* came to steal what I wouldn't give the Clan!"

"No! Ossirus as my witness, Sira. No!"

"Yes, Rael. Yes and yes!" I stood, somehow, staggering back, desperate to put more distance between us. "You want Morgan here so that you can take us both to the Council. A nice, tidy package. Well, I'll never let you have him, do you hear me, Rael? Never!"

"Sira, wait!" Rael pleaded, standing and coming toward me. "Please listen. Read my thoughts. I'll open to you. You're wrong!"

There are moments when need transcends strength, when one reaches inward and finds what is necessary can be done after all, no matter the cost.

As Rael dropped her shields, driving her thoughts toward mine for whatever reason, I concentrated. She was quite capable of following where I went: her particular Talent, M'hir tasting, let her identify and track Clan power through that other space. But there were ways around it. With a whispered apology to Morgan as I broke at least part of my vow to him, I *pushed* . . . .

. . . and was adrift in utter darkness. Lines of brilliant power shimmered and crossed, enticing and beautiful. Most I'd created, spun during journeys on this world. Others traced well-worn routes between Morgan and me, as I'd sought out his presence in the M'hir to test and train his power. I held myself free of any of them, holding all I was together in the nothingness, holding until I began to fray at the edges and still I waited. My mind wandered, losing all fear, almost lost.

At the edge of my own existence, I saw—or imagined—a distant brilliance, a path once so wide and great its passing burned an echo in the M'hir itself. I lingered in this timeless place to wonder at it: had I stumbled across what remained from the exodus of the M'hiray, a legacy of that passage forged by the merged power of my kind? Or was there some other power out there—something unimaginable, something greater . . . ?

I caught myself thinning, dissolving, lured toward it.

Morgan . . .

His name became the only anchor left.

INTERLUDE

The Watcher stirred.

There were others holding vigil here, connected by the most tenuous of links, valued for their endurance and commitment.

Theirs was the most sacred task of any Clan: to taste the messages reflecting through the M'hir, to warn of any intrusion, to guard against contamination.

To watch.

This Watcher had tasted many things in the M'hir over the long years. Most had been the threads of energy left by Clan as they pushed themselves, their thoughts, or objects from one place to another, some the fierce brilliance traced by the temporary links between mother and offspring, the longer-lasting ones between Joined pairs, each fading into the network of pathways which those of lesser strength used as they journeyed. A few had been the danger they all sought, flickering touches tasting of metal and technology, everything feared and loathsome to the Clan. And speedily dealt with, whenever found.

This taste was familiar, yet not; recognized, yet momentarily disbelieved. The flavor of the daughter of di Sarc waned as though fading, dissolving in the M'hir—impossible in one so powerful.

The Watcher prepared her message. It was her duty to inform of loss in the M'hir, not to prevent it. The death of Sira di Sarc must be announced to the one on Council most affected: the head of her House, Jarad di Sarc. Sira's loss would mean changes to his plans; Clanlike, that he was Sira's father mattered not at all. What concerned Jarad, as it would any Clan, was power, its existence and potential. The loss of Sira meant the loss of her doubtless gifted progeny, should any Clansman at all be found her match.

Such things were not the concern of Watchers.

Wait.

At the limits of possibility, coalescence into form, survival.

The message was shunted to memory, unsent. The Watcher turned her attention elsewhere, vigilant and unsleeping.

Chapter 9

... I ALLOWED myself to materialize. Rael was no fool—even if she traced my path, she'd know she could never last so long in the M'hir. I almost hadn't, despite Morgan's memories of this place. Shaking my thoughts free of the journey, I staggered and reached one hand to hold on to the smooth pink wall. *Pink?*

"Greetings, Mystic One."

I peered down at the two identical Drapsk in front of me, their plumes fluttering, but otherwise not obviously surprised to see me. "I've decided to accept your invitation after all," I announced, finding it strangely difficult to catch my breath. "If you still want a Mystic One to bring home."

More fluttering, this time accompanied by a loud sucking noise as both Drapsk inhaled most of their mouth tentacles. "Wonderful, wonderful," they said together, having exhaled the tentacles. "We'll take you to our Captain."

"... med-tech? ..." I countered, unsure if I managed that aloud, knowing the cost of my journey through the M'hir as a warm wetness grew under the fingers still pressed to my belly and I began sinking to the floor.

You'll never find Morgan, Rael, was my last conscious thought. *Not while I live.*

I hadn't planned to stay on the Drapsk ship a moment longer than it took to regain the strength to leave, to follow Morgan, and elude Rael. While this was a schedule I didn't share with my new hosts, it was also, according to the Drapsk med, one I was unlikely to keep.

"How long do I have to stay in there?" I eyed the med unit with a sinking feeling. Surreptitiously, I tried stretching my abdomen and felt only a sensation of tightness. Of course, the Drapsk had dosed me thoroughly with pain medication after replacing the blood-soaked medplas. The being had been reassuringly confident about dealing with humanoid physiology—something I took on faith. "Are you sure I need this?"

The Drapsk, whose appearance differed from the Captain's only in the diagnostic scope dangling from a lower mouth tentacle, rocked back and forth with a pleased croon. "Quite sure, O Mystic One. As for how long, I must observe how well you respond. Perhaps only a few hours. Perhaps a day or two. Are you ready?"

I glanced around the room; if there were any answers or signs here, they were well-hidden. Except for the med unit and the scope the Drapsk held, I could be anywhere on the Drapsk ship, the *Makmora*. Her appearance might have been deliberately designed to fool the senses—humanoid senses, at least, I corrected to myself. Her pale pink interior lacked any marks or variation. Both corridors and rooms were softly lit, either for my benefit or because the Drapsk possessed vision despite their lack of obvious eyes.

There was little to see. Any equipment, including the ominous rectangle of the med unit and its cocoon, was lodged inside cupboards until needed, cupboards with doors that only showed when a Drapsk activated them. I thought of the med's infirmary as a room for my own reference, but it, like others I'd passed on the way here, was more as though the walls of the corridors cooperatively bulged at random to allow floor space for clusters of Drapsk activity.

Forget privacy. More than a dozen Drapsk had quietly passed by during the med's examination and treatment of me, on their way to tasks elsewhere. Each gave a dip of their feathery purple antennae my way, either polite acknowledgment or curiosity.

Mystic. I looked down at the Drapsk's blank globe of a face, unable to keep a frown from my own. "You must know from your scans of me that—"

"You are not a Ram'ad Witch?" The being's fleshy red tentacles blossomed out in a ring that could mean polite disagreement, personal affront, or an extreme of joy, its right hand ready to catch the scope as it came free in what looked like a reflex. I wished I'd paid more attention to Morgan's vistapes on the species, then realized I was likely wrong on all counts when the Drapsk tipped his plumes to softly stroke the back of my hand—a gesture I did know meant profound gratitude. "Drapsk know the true nature of things, Mystic One. The Ram'ad Witches are a lie accepted by their kind. You, as all on this ship know for truth, are a rare and magical being, forced to coat your power with that lie in order to survive."

A touch melodramatic, but closer to the reality of my life than I liked. I hesitated as the Drapsk indicated the cocoon with one small hand, not ready to relinquish consciousness just yet. "How do you sense this truth about me, Med?"

"Oh, the Scented Way holds the truth, Mystic One."

Huido Maarmatoo'kk, Morgan's huge Carasian friend and now mine, used a sense he called smell to detect a being's *grist,* a characteristic with a confusingly vague resemblance to what I would sense as Talent. I was reasonably certain what he meant had nothing in common with mammalian olfaction, but Huido could tell quite remarkable things about those with mental abilities. Not bad for a creature whose thoughts registered as a painful maelstrom to even a cautious touch. Perhaps these odd little Drapsk possessed a similar sense. *Great,* I said to myself with disgust, glaring at the oh-so-helpful med. *So much for secrets among this lot.* Caution would be in order until I knew more.

But first came a rare amount of trust. I looked at the cocoon and sighed, then let the Drapsk help me recline on its surface. His antennae drooped toward me with a slight quiver, as though the Drapsk relied on his own senses as much as the scope in his hand. Lying back left me short of breath, a symptom I couldn't very well dispute. The Drapsk med had been equally convincing. While he couldn't say exactly what had been done to me, not knowing how Clan physiology differed from humanoid standard, he confirmed someone had performed surgery on my reproductive organs. I must allow my body to heal or pay the price.

As the price was remaining vulnerable and of no use to Morgan, I had no choice. When the lid came down and servo-handling arms bestirred themselves with a most alarming number of needlelike points interested in my anatomy, I ordered myself to stop trembling. It would only be a safe, undisturbed rest. My mental shields did not need my conscious direction to keep me hidden from prying Clan. Warm gel began pooling along my bare skin.

"Will I dream?" I asked the med, perhaps a confusing question. I didn't know if Drapsk dreamed or, come to think of it, if they slept.

"If it's needed," came a soft, equally confusing answer.

I wished I could count on a dream to show me what I needed: where Morgan was and how I could bring him back to me before it was too late.

INTERLUDE

"Let me help your memory, Ancoma." It wasn't difficult to lift the smaller Poculan up and fling him against the cold, rain-splattered brick. In fact, Morgan decided it was the first thing he'd done in hours that satisfied the black rage boiling inside his mind.

Maybe he should do it again.

Ancoma, a shipcity slinker better known for his ability to access locked doors than for his courage, wiped a shaking hand across his face and cringed. His yellow-brown eyes were wide and dilated. A green line of blood-tinged drool slid down his chin, adding its fresh mark to the line of such stains on his ragged jerkin. "I can't remember what I didn't do!"

"Odd your good friend Sleva'tha saw you plain as could be. Now, all I want is a name." Almost idly, Morgan flexed his right hand. A tiny hilt dropped into the palm, as if by magic, its blade humming into life between his fingers. There was nothing idle in his grab to capture the Poculan's pendulous ear, a handle he used to pull the cowering being to his knees, then up against Morgan's own chest. "Who paid you to rent those aircars and leave them at the edge of the shipcity, Anco'?"

"Slev's crazy! I wasn't there, Morgan!"

The passing roar of a docking tug, a giant Drapsk freighter cradled in its immense arms, should drown out the screams quite nicely, Morgan decided. He waited serenely for the machine to come closer, staring into the terrified eyes of the Poculan, knife poised between the two orbs like a snake choosing a target.

Abruptly, sanity returned, pouring through Morgan's mind and body like a wash of icy water, drowning out the rage. The knife dropped from his numb fingers; the Poculan, released, crumbled into a quivering heap at his feet.

What was he doing?

Morgan shuddered. He retrieved the knife, turning off its blade, then snagged Ancoma as the being tried to slip away, and pulled him, almost gently, to his feet. "Sorry about that," he said brusquely. "Now, where were you last night? Just think about that, okay?" Morgan pressed a pair of four-sided coins into the being's clammy hand, keeping them in place with a firm grip.

The Poculan was understandably mistrustful, but it didn't matter. Morgan needed only a second to skim his surface thoughts. "Off you go," he said, disgusted both by the slimy feel of the being's mind and his own inexplicable loss of control. Ancoma didn't need further urging to scamper away, muttering darkly about insane Humans and mindcrawlers.

But, as Morgan listened to the pulse-driving din of the tug, creeping along the shipway, he had at least part of his and Sira's answer.

Ancoma didn't remember renting the aircars for the raiders, because he couldn't. Someone had erased his memory of last night.

The rage surged up again, welcome antidote to the exhaustion he kept barely at bay with drugs and determination. The only beings Morgan knew with that skill were the Clan.

And he knew where to find at least one.

Chapter 10

"MYSTIC One."

If I'd dreamed, the visions hadn't lingered. I squinted at the featureless face close to mine and wondered helplessly what else I'd lost in the time spent healing. Hours? Or had it been days? I sat up, too quickly, and gratefully clung to the Drapsk's small, round arm for support while the *Makmora* made its mind up to stop spinning around. "How—long?"

"Five hours, Mystic One. Please don't try to speak yet," a note of concern. "Drink this, please." A cup pressed into my hand brought up a memory, more dreamlike than any from my sleep, of another cup and another cocoon. I'd helped Morgan once, like this, as he recovered on the *Fox*.

Morgan!

I closed my eyes and sought that golden place, hunting frantically through the M'hir for the other half of myself, realizing two things at once: I'd only regained a limited portion of my strength, but even that was enough to tell me my search was futile.

There was no sign of him, no glow, no warmth. Morgan was gone.

He was properly cautious, I reassured myself. Of course, he would be. It was the Clan Council Morgan knew as the enemy. He'd camouflage his power as I'd taught him, avoid any exposure.

Even to me.

I sat, lost myself, too weak to chance travel through the M'hir, wondering where and how to start looking.

I couldn't believe what I'd done, what I'd *ordered* Morgan to do. I was supposed to protect him. By what leap of logic had

I turned that protection into a thrust right into the hands of his and my deadliest enemies?

It had to be done, argued thoughts that were pure Sira di Sarc, pure Clan. *Morgan might succeed. At the least, the Human could distract the thieves until I recovered enough to take the trail myself.*

If I could have bitten open my wrists at that moment and let my lifeblood pour out, I would have, if only I had a guarantee that part of me would die first.

The warmth against my fingers and a commonplace aroma roused me from my dark thoughts after a moment. I moved my tongue experimentally within my mouth, feeling as though I'd been chewing dust. I took a cautious sip from the cup in my hand, then a deeper swallow, glancing up in surprise. It was warm sombay, spiced exactly as I liked it. "Thank you," I began, then let my voice trail away. The med wasn't listening.

The Drapsk no longer hovered by my side, eager to help. Instead, when I wasn't paying attention, the small being had somehow curled itself into a compact white ball, almost round enough to roll along the floor if I were to nudge him with my closer foot. The gaudy antennae were tucked somewhere completely out of sight, or perhaps retracted.

I drained the cup, considering my companion. Morgan was the expert on other species, especially nonhumanoid ones. I hadn't seen this posture in his records for the Drapsk. Was it polite to disturb the being? Or was he in some distress?

I slid my feet over the side as I assessed my own condition. Still a bit dizzy, but that was fading with each breath. Sore, but compared to what I'd been through, I felt improved enough to assert some sort of control of events which, to all extents and purposes had, until now, been controlling me.

Speculatively, I gazed down at the ball of Drapsk. *Perhaps I could start here,* I decided, extending a very cautious tendril of power toward the seemingly unconscious being.

Nothing. I might have been alone.

There were species whose thoughts the Clan couldn't touch at all. *Not that many,* I recalled uneasily. It was simplicity itself for an Adept of reasonable ability to read the unshielded minds of other telepathic beings, although none but the Clan had thoughts able to mingle within the energy-laced blackness of the M'hir. I thought of Morgan's presence there wistfully. Only he, of his kind, made his own light within the M'hir.

It took more power and some practice to make sense of the thoughts and emotions within the minds of receptive nontelepaths. Morgan's Talent differed from Clan in that physical contact enhanced his ability. I'd learned his technique, and had begun to teach him mine—using the M'hir to convey his questing thoughts into other minds—but we'd had no time to finish his training before the attack had struck and changed everything.

No, I whispered soundlessly to myself, insisting on honesty. I'd been intent on turning Morgan's mind into a fortress, deliberately ignoring consequences as I honed his natural Talent into a defense, blending it at every level with the power I'd given him in the M'hir. I'd known, but conveniently ignored, that everything within the M'hir was two-edged. What worked to protect one mind could readily twist to destroy another. I'd convinced myself I was keeping Morgan safe from the kind of attack I expected, the revenge of the Clan Council for my refusal to risk Morgan to help them solve their problems. If— when—they came after me, I'd known he would need everything I could give him in order to survive.

In so doing, I'd forged him into a weapon against the Clan.

It hadn't only been the Council I wanted to save Morgan from—I wanted him safe from me. *And look how well I'd accomplished that.*

I had done one thing right. I had refused to Join with Morgan, no matter how strong the urgings of my heart. The Power-of-Choice, that M'hir-bound energy females of our kind used to test, and then Choose their life-partners, hadn't destroyed Morgan's mind as some of my kind had hoped. Instead, somehow, Morgan and I had controlled its dark force, tamed it. There had been no permanent link driven through the M'hir between us; my Power-of-Choice had flowed to him as a gift, enhancing his Talent a hundredfold. It didn't matter that it left behind an aching emptiness, a need deep in my mind that I controlled as tightly as I'd ever fought the demands of Choice.

Because if I died—something I had enemies willing to almost guarantee in the near future—and we were truly Joined, I would not die alone. Morgan's consciousness would be dragged into the M'hir, and he, too, would be lost. It was not a price I was prepared to pay for completion. He must survive, even if I did not. The Sira di Sarc part of me, all cold practicality, had long ago lost that argument. Making it even harder to believe what I'd done to Morgan on Pocular, and more urgent I do something about it.

The Drapsk didn't stir when I rested my hand on the warm, curiously firm curve that might have been his back. I opened my perception as Morgan had taught me. Again, nothing.

There was one last test. I straightened, closed my eyes, and extended my awareness into the M'hir, reaching outward until I was quite sure. There were no minds I could read within my currently limited range, a range I was confident encompassed most of the ship. It made an unsettling contradiction between what I knew to be reality and what my inner sense told me.

The Drapsk were here. They were also invisible.

I stepped carefully around the curled-up Drapsk. "I'm going to talk to the Captain," I whispered. The ball of Drapsk didn't move. "I'll tell someone about your—state—as soon as I can. And," this fervently, "thank you."

To the Captain, I told myself, choosing a direction at random in the corridor. The Drapsk appeared to be practical beings, despite this newly revealed tendency to remove themselves from action. I expected no problems in convincing the oh-so-helpful Captain Maka to provide me with transportation to the *Silver Fox,* docked, if my memory served me, a mere five rows east of the *Makmora*'s position within Pocular's shipcity. Morgan's search for the source of the attack surely hadn't taken him off-planet so soon.

I decided to hurry.

INTERLUDE

You lost her.

Rael thought this judgment rather harsh, considering the circumstances and Sira's relative power, but kept the opinion to herself. The result, as her grandmother rightly noted, was what mattered. *At least she survives,* Rael replied instead, straining slightly to keep the mindsend focused. There were few pathways etched in the M'hir between their physical locations, fewer still safe for their thoughts to slide along, an absence requiring a greater expenditure of power as they essentially built their own path with each thrust of communication. *When I find Morgan, I'll find Sira—*

Larimar will deal with the Human, Ica di Teerac responded, with no trace of effort Rael could detect. *He has some experience with them.*

I suggest, Grandmother, that Larimar wait until we know more of what Sira intends Morgan to do. Barac and I—

Ica's sending overrode Rael's, an interruption the Clanswoman experienced as an instant's pain and disorientation. *Do not confide in Barac sud Sarc under any circumstances. He is unChosen and now exile. The Council will be watching his every move through the M'hir.*

Barac is also no fool, Grandmother, Rael said, refusing to back down. It was somewhat easier to do given she was sitting cross-legged on the floor of Sira's hut in the village of the Fakad-sa'it, and the formidable First Chosen of the House of di Teerac was safely distant on the wealthy inner system planet Tinex 14. *I didn't confide in him—but we would be wise to consider adding him and his knowledge of events here to our group.*

Wise? Only if he gets a mind-shielding implant from the

*Trade Pact Enforcers. He's sud, Rael. Or have you forgotten
how weak his power truly is? He would be only a liability to
our cause.*

I thought the unChosen were our cause, Grandmother.

The M'hir subsided from Rael's consciousness as the link
was severed from the other end. She stretched the stiffness
from her back and shoulders. The conversation hadn't gone
well, but she hadn't expected it to, having no good news to
report. It looked as though the Clan Council had indeed anticipated their moves thus far, striking against the daughter of di
Sarc and stealing what they valued. Rael swallowed bile. If
only she'd been able to keep Sira with her and take her back to
Deneb.

Rael shivered, remembering the deadly cold of Morgan's
eyes when he'd defied her on Pocular, the unmistakable and
unexpected strength of his power. She'd never imagined a
Human could be a threat; now, she would never dismiss the
species as readily again. It gave a regrettable sense of vulnera-
bility to her life as the only Clan on the Human world of Deneb.

Her thoughts of Morgan were also laced with an odd sense
of envy, as if the raw passion she'd unwittingly seen explode in
him, echoing like thunder through the M'hir, was something
her kind lacked, and had never, until now, known to miss.

Larimar "deal with" Morgan? She'd take a bet on the probable
course of that encounter.

Not that they could afford to gamble. Despite Morgan's
abilities, their need was too great to allow him to resist them
any longer.

It was the survival of their species, the M'hiray itself, on
the line.

Chapter 11

WHILE my sense of urgency pricked at me like the needles of the med unit, the interior of the *Makmora* proved more challenging to navigate than I'd expected. I walked her maze of corridors, taking lifts here and there. In some sections, the pale pink ceiling dropped down as if supporting something too heavy for the floor above. I didn't have to duck to pass these areas, but found it impossible not to, my imagination quite willing to distrust unfamiliar technology.

The Drapsk freighter, I soon realized, was so huge the *Fox* herself could have been tractored into one of her main cargo bays, three of which I found in my journey. Worse, I couldn't begin to remember my way around the featureless place.

"I give up," I said at last, turning to look at my comet's tail of Drapsk. I'd passed several, each identical to the others, and each immediately putting down tools or packages in favor of a new, apparently engrossing pastime—following the Mystic One. Unlike the med, these were too shy to talk to me or answer questions; their shyness was an assumption I made to reassure myself as I listened to the soft pad-pad-pad of the disconcerting and increasing number of Drapsk feet behind me.

I'd tried telling them about the med's condition, which occasioned a synchronized series of low hoots but no alarm I could detect. I'd tried asking directions to the Captain, only to have the entire group flutter antennae at me each time. I was buffeted by the resulting breeze until I had to move to escape.

Now, weary and truly beginning to wonder if I shouldn't try to 'port to the *Fox* after all, in spite of my weakness and the chance of having Rael follow, I leaned against the nearest bulkhead. "Will one of you please, please, show me the way to your Captain?" I asked again, without much hope.

"But we have, O Mystic One," came the unexpected answer from several Drapsk, tentacles proudly ringing their mouths. "Oh, we have. There."

I swiveled my head around, very slowly. Not an arm's length from me was another in the interminable bulges in the corridor wall, this one almost as large as those leading into the cargo bays, and at the moment curtained by a fringe of purple-pink Drapsk plumes pointing in my direction.

When I turned to thank my entourage, I found myself looking at their retreating backs, as though the Drapsk had done their duty and were now returning in haste to their neglected tasks. I shrugged philosophically, quite sure if I were wiser, I might have just learned something important about the small beings.

One thing I already knew—too well—was their enthusiasm for my presence. "I appreciate all you and your crew have done for me, Captain Maka," I said sincerely, if with mounting exasperation; forced to cut abruptly into the Drapsk Captain's passionate and lengthy welcoming speech. "Allow me to offer some form of compensation—"

"Absolutely not, O Mystic One," Maka said with what appeared to be agitation, sucking in several of the red tentacles ringing his mouth.

"As you wish." Somewhere along the line, I'd lost most of my social graces, traded for being tired, sore, and short of breath. "I do have a request."

"Anything, O Mystic One. The *Makmora* is yours—" He spread his short, chubby arms as wide apart as they could go, presumably to indicate his ship's bridge. I looked around obediently, trying to get my bearings.

Having spent most of my life isolated both by choice and the dictates of the Clan Council, I'd only recently been exposed to the realities and economics of a spacer's life. That brief exposure had, through Morgan's insistence and my own curiosity, included a thorough apprenticeship in the operation of commercial shipping. So I found I recognized much of what I saw behind Captain Maka and around me on two sides.

We could be standing on the bridge of any large, long-haul

freighter, her operations crew of a dozen or so Drapsk intent on reasonably familiar control panels. There were, however, some distinctions which made it quite plain to me that this was not a ship designed for Humans or similar beings. The doorless corridors were only the first and most obvious.

The next distinction was invisible. As Maka began extolling the virtues of his ship to me, I was distracted by a tickle on my forehead. I reached up my hand and discovered the cause. I'd stepped into a breeze. Now that I thought about it, everywhere I'd been on the *Makmora* had been drafty. This was more than just powerful ventilators clearing the air. Intrigued, I raised my hand higher, discovering a variety of currents crossing over my head.

"Please refrain, O Mystic One."

I looked down at the Drapsk who had spoken. "Pardon?"

"You are influencing the com system. Please refrain, O Mystic One."

"That's all right, Makoisa," Captain Maka said quickly. "The filters can cope."

Com system? I surveyed the crew, paying more attention this time. All their antennae were erect, plumes widespread. Directly above each station, there seemed to be a separate air intake. I sniffed experimentally. If they were relying on odor for communication, it was nothing I could detect.

"Now, your request, O Mystic One?" Maka, trader-fashion, came right back to the point, his plumes restlessly twitching with what I hoped was eagerness to serve and not some preparation to argue.

"I'd like to visit one of your neighboring ships, Captain. It's a matter of some urgency—"

There was an unexpected pause. The Drapsk all turned to face their Captain. He shuffled his feet twice then said in a very determined tone, "I do not presume to know what your magical nature may inform you, Mystic One, but our scans indicate we are quite alone in this region. Should we check this again?"

I didn't like the sound of that, but found myself fighting a novel tendency to tip to the left before I could utter a word. If they hadn't turned down the lights, I decided, then this dimming of my vision was likely a prelude to a faint. I truly didn't want to land on one or more of my small hosts.

There hadn't been chairs, I told myself a moment later. I'd seen the bucketlike contraptions the Drapsk used at their stations, but I knew the chair I found myself sitting on had not been there when my surroundings started to fade. I peered at the circle of concerned Drapsk suspiciously. Either they were more magical than I'd ever claimed, or something was wrong with me.

"I don't feel quite myself," I decided.

Crimson tentacles writhed in nauseating harmony at this announcement. "Our Med, Makairi, assures me you will make a full recovery, O Mystic One. He believes you should not be moving around so soon after your magical exertion to reach the safety of our ship. We would have rushed to your aid had we known you were in danger." This last very sternly, as though he reluctantly found some fault in me. "You must take better care, Mystic One. A good thing you came to us at last. We will care for you."

All of this sounded reassuring on one hand, and a bit too final on the other. I focused on Maka, at least I thought the Drapsk speaking was the Captain. I'd have to tie ribbons on them to tell them apart. *Dear little Drapsk.* Where to fasten them was an interesting question. Some wore tool belts; most did not.

I noticed but oddly wasn't perturbed by this novel tendency of my mind to drift aimlessly from thought to thought. I remembered Morgan falling asleep abruptly after leaving the healing cocoon and hoped they'd understand if I followed suit and toppled off the stool. Did Drapsk sleep or did they curl up into little balls at night? Had I wondered this before?

"Back to the med unit, O Mystic One," a second Drapsk insisted, the mere concept encouraging me to close my eyes. Several of them took hold of my arms, very gently, tugging me to my feet. I struggled to stay alert. Here I was, being sent to bed by hopefully well-meaning aliens, while at any moment Morgan could be leaving me behind on Pocular, going who knew where—

I must have said it out loud.

"Oh, we are not on Pocular, O Mystic One," this with distinct, unmistakable amusement. "Why would we delay there when the Contest is about to begin?"

I found myself suddenly very wide awake, staring down at the chorus of Drapsk holding me upright as though they were about to bite. "Where are you taking me?" I demanded.

An agitated fluttering of antennae, then a single voice announced triumphantly: "Why, home, O Mystic One. We are taking you home to Drapskii."

"Please come back to the cocoon, O Mystic One." The med, Makairi, had arrived—my best guess, given the Drapsk circling around me carried a scope in one tentacle. I didn't bother asking what had happened to him earlier. I had enough to worry about.

"What I want is this ship to return to Pocular." Unfortunately, repeating this was having no effect whatsoever. Well, almost none.

They weren't happy. Even given species' differences, I could read that much. "But, Mystic One," Captain Maka approached closely, reaching out as if to touch me, but refraining. "We've informed the Makii of your Candidacy. You have a Place in the Ceremony, assured by guarantees from our Tribe, though this forced a delay. We travel at our best speed."

"We warehoused our cargo," said one Drapsk so quietly I barely heard.

Another, behind me, whispered: "Is the Mystic One deserting us?"

What had been deserted was Pocular, and my best chance to catch up to Morgan. I shook my head, then added: "No," aloud in case they couldn't detect the gesture—though in my experience the Drapsk managed very well without obvious eyes and experienced traders such as these probably read humanoids better than humanoids read them. "No," I repeated firmly. I thought it quite likely I owed these beings my life; I didn't owe them Morgan's. "I'm not deserting you. But I have something I must do on Pocular first. Surely there will be other Contests if I don't make this one. You have my promise."

A hush deadlier than the last one as those Drapsk previously occupied in operating equipment turned to add their antennae to the veritable forest aimed at me. "Mystic One," the tone of authority assuring me this was likely Captain Maka speaking— that and the now-familiar agitated hand waving. "Mystic One, I cannot emphasize too strongly how vital your appearing at this

Contest is for the Makii. If you do not, there may be other Contests, but there will be no Makii on the *Makmora* to have the
honor of supporting you as Candidate."

"I don't understand, Captain," I countered, although privately I was afraid I was beginning to see the trap I'd entered
without a thought. "This Contest of yours—you say it's about
magic? I have none. I can't be a contestant!"

This brought antennae up. "Have no doubt of your abilities,
Mystic One," Maka said, suddenly cheerful. "We believe in
you. All on this ship have witnessed your feats on Pocular."

"Parlor tricks. Fancy tech."

"True magic, such as you performed for me earlier today, O
Mystic One." This earnest statement from Med Makairi. I
looked askance at him. *What did he mean?* I wondered, ready
to doubt the stability of a being who curled up into a ball in the
middle of a medical examination. Or had he somehow detected
my effort to reach Morgan through the M'hir? I shrugged away
the uncomfortable notion.

"Then may I send a message on your com system?"

"Your presence on our Tribe's ship must be kept secret."
This from one of the unnamed Drapsk.

Captain Maka, I think, hastened to add: "The Heerii mustn't
find out about you, Mystic One. They mustn't!"

I closed my eyes tightly, then opened them. "Why, Captain?"
I asked with what I thought remarkable calmness.

"If other Tribes learn the Makii are bringing such a won-
drous Mystic One as yourself, they might resist any delay in
the Competition. If they succeeded, we would not make it to
Drapskii in time. It is a tactic the Heerii have used before."
Maka rubbed his little hands together, a parody of the Human
gesture I callously decided he used on purpose to convince me
of his stress. "And secrecy will be to your advantage in the
Competition, O Mystic One; much better to be a surprise to the
others. Please accept my assurance on this matter. And please
accept our total joy at your willingness to help us fulfill our
quest. Your kindness, your generosity, your—"

Maka had sucked in sufficient air before answering my question—which I noticed he hadn't actually done—to continue in
this vein for some time.

"Captain Maka," I said as sternly as I could, given my present state of imminent collapse. "My generosity does not extend to allowing you to being-nap me. Now, either get me a comlink, return me to Pocular, or—" I hesitated. "Take me to Ettler's Planet."

Ettler's Planet was Morgan's fallback plan. He'd insisted we set a rendezvous, insisted the day might come when we were separated and pursued—and would need a safe place to wait for one another. I'd gone along with him to end the uncomfortable discussion, quite sure nothing would make me leave his side. I didn't actually know where Ettler's Planet was from the *Makmora*'s current location, or from Pocular. It hadn't seemed important to know. *But now,* I said to myself, breathing in carefully light gasps, *it might be the best of several poor alternatives.*

Apparently, the Drapsk weren't about to agree with me. Five of the bridge crew curled up into little white balls, one rolling until it lodged against the base of a console. This solved one mystery: I saw how the plumes of their antennae flattened and the entire structure folded within the curve of their bodies.

The rest of the Drapsk stood absolutely still, antennae drooping until they hung like purple capes over nonexistent shoulders. There wasn't a word.

After a very long moment, a delicate breeze traveled across my forehead, teasing at my hair before it went on to ruffle the plumes of the nearest Drapsk. I assumed someone elsewhere on the *Makmora* was getting worried about the lack of hands on the ship's controls.

When even this didn't rouse my hosts, I decided it was time I worried as well.

INTERLUDE

Consorting with Humans was bad enough, Barac sniffed disdainfully. One could, in time, get used to them. But this, this conglomeration of aliens was infinitely worse. At least Humans and Clan shared a similar body plan. *Here?* There were more sizes, shapes, and colors of eyeballs watching him through the smoky haze than he'd imagined in his wildest nightmares. How had he let Sira talk him into running this place?

"The credit limit for the Auordian Ambassador, Lord Warlock?" Hastho'tha's oily voice intruded. A pause, then an impatient cough. "Lord?"

Barac's attention snapped back to his head server. "Double what she's asking," he said, ignoring the bewilderment on the Poculan's thick features. "After she gives you the access codes to her yacht for safekeeping." Had Barac cared in the slightest about the opinions of his staff, the sudden respect in the look he was given would have been gratifying.

Bah. It was nothing but observation. A Human could do as well. There was no need to touch M'hir and sample the thoughts of the old Auordian hag to know she was a compulsive gambler. Sufficient luck beads for twenty of her kind, jeweled to be sure, were braided in her mane of red hair. And she'd bragged enough about the yacht to him during the tedious ritual Hastho'tha had insisted he join, that of dining with the high rollers in the more luxurious private room.

Barac turned so he could hook one long leg over the arm of Sira's black throne. It was comfortable, despite its appearance of being carved from some stone. He appreciated the humor of the deception. The deception she'd used to smudge her own appearance in the minds of the Haven's clientele was something else again. Barac acknowledged without bitterness that such a use of power was well beyond his own Talent. He glanced around the sea of heads and other cranial arrangements bobbing through the seemingly permanent eye-level smoke in the Haven's main room. *They hadn't deserved her notice anyway,* he concluded, closing his own eyes briefly. They certainly didn't deserve his.

"Lord Warlock?"

"Go away."

A shiver of pressure in the M'hir startled Barac's eyes open and pulled him out of his slouch. Rael floated in front of him— image only, he knew in the next instant. He ignored the exclamations from those patrons sober enough to notice. Something was wrong. Rael was supposed to be with Sira and Morgan. He'd been glad enough to relay Morgan's warning to his more powerful cousin, not in the mood to jump to the Human's call—or to help Sira while his head still throbbed from her lawless violation of his most intimate thoughts.

Rael's eyes were the sharpest part of her image. They drilled into him now, their expression haunted. Barac felt some of his anger fade, replaced by something closer to fear. She chose not to speak out loud. *Is Sira—or the Human—with you?*

Puzzled, Barac shook his head. *Why?*

Sira was attacked, the words cut into his mind, the M'hir crystal-edged with anger. *She was—damaged. I thought she might go to you.*

Barac's first reaction was disbelief. *Who could harm* her?

The image shifted as Rael, wherever she really was, appeared to sit in midair, resulting in a flurry of activity in front of the dais as even more customers stopped gambling to watch the apparition, some dropping drinks in the process. *Sira is not invulnerable, no matter what a* sud *thinks,* her mind touch chastised him. *At least she lives. They used weapons, the cover of darkness—it was premeditated, formidable.*

If they used weapons, where was Morgan? Barac sent back, quite certain of the Human's own formidable ability with such technology. The Haven's defenses were convincing—the elevator alone was capable of turning unauthorized visitors to ash. He resisted a sudden feeling of guilt. It hardly mattered that he'd been the cause of Sira's leaving this stronghold; Morgan was her defender. And, Barac reminded himself, there was no doubt of Morgan's unfortunate and bizarre attachment to the firstborn daughter of the House of di Sarc.

You think so highly of her Human? Rael's dark eyes clouded, but she kept her emotions out of the M'hir between them. Most of them, anyway. Barac tightened his own defenses at the taste of her disgust. *His role in this is suspect, Barac. If he wasn't in collusion with the attackers, he certainly wasn't protecting Sira. Drunk and brawling with a primitive. At least he was able to pull himself together and find her. Sira*—a sudden distancing of their contact, as though Rael thought more to herself than to him—*Sira's belief in this alien is as stubborn as ever.*

But you don't know where Sira is now?

I don't know where either of them are—

Barac lifted his hand to interrupt his cousin.

I seem to have found Morgan, he sent, peering past both the illusion of Rael's form and the fascinated crowd to the disturbance spilling in through the main door of the Spacer's Haven.

Chapter 12

THEY'D won. So far.

I conceded the Drapsk their temporary victory as I shivered under the blankets they had thoughtfully piled on me: brand-new and very expensive issa-silk blankets stubbornly holding the chill from storage in the *Makmora*'s hold. Stubborn as the Drapsk themselves.

For such polite little beings, they were becoming an astoundingly large obstacle in my plans. Without the strength to 'port, I couldn't leave on my own. Worse, since my second several-hour bout in the cocoon, the *Makmora* had traveled who knew how far from any place I could locate through the M'hir.

This led to an unpleasant scenario, one I considered from several viewpoints as I eased my still-sore body under the covers and tried to rest. To use the M'hir to leave the ship, I needed a locate, a remembered destination. While travel through the M'hir sidestepped normal space, much like a tailor's needle could pass almost instantly through vast amounts of fabric, there was the problem of subjective time. I had the power to remain in the M'hir longer than most, if not all, of the Clan. That didn't mean my time was limitless. I'd already come too close to dissolving in the M'hir. Legend held that what was left became a ghost, a tastable consciousness to haunt any who traveled in that space. I didn't intend to be so flimsy a threat to my enemies.

Not knowing where I was meant not knowing the types of distances I'd need to travel through the M'hir. So I was trapped on the *Makmora* until I found out where we were and thus where I could go.

Or until we reached the Drapsk homeworld, where I might wind up discovering firsthand what their Ceremony was all about. Finally warm, and certainly drowsy, I admitted to some curiosity. The standoff on the bridge had only ended when I agreed my imminent danger of collapse was a more pressing issue than our destination. This capitulation didn't affect the rolled-up members of the crew; they were gently nudged to one side as though their comatose state might last a while— something that was apparently my fault.

Their obsession with me was no whim or trader's ploy. Even Maka had been close to what passed for hysteria in his species when I continued to resist their plans. Yet, as far as I could judge, they didn't seem to be any threat to me. A perplexing and frustrating complication, yes, but nothing worse.

What did they want from me? I nudged the thought away. I had other priorities than the affairs of the Makii Drapsk.

"All I want is for you to be pleased, I assure you, O Mystic One. This is the traditional garb for Contestants of the Makii Drapsk," this particular Drapsk, Makeest, sputtered anxiously, this largely due to the tendency of his tentacles to remain inside his mouth. I'd never seen a Drapsk try to speak around them before and, while interesting to observe, it did cause an inordinate amount of drooling. "Perhaps I failed to render the words properly? Is that what displeases you?"

"It's not the words, Makeest," I assured the anxious tailor. "I just don't see the need for you to prepare this—garment. I've told your Captain: I cannot participate in your Ceremony—" I wasn't sure whether to shout in frustration or burst out laughing. I did notice the combination of emotions was becoming very common around the Drapsk.

"What's wrong here?" said two voices at once, a note shy of harmony. "Have you offended the Mystic One, Makeest?"

"No, no," I assured the new arrivals: the Captain and his first officer Makoisa by the ribbonlike tags on their tool belts. I was becoming guilt ridden by the effort the Drapsk were willing to make to accommodate my every wish, whether I expressed one or not. The belts, complete with tags inscribed in glowing Comscript, had appeared on every Drapsk within an hour of my mistaking one of the deck crew for the med.

"There must be something that has offended you," Captain Maka insisted, antennae at the alert and his chubby four-fingered hands working the air as if in search of a foe. The three of them began rocking back and forth in perfect unison. I kept from smiling by an incredible act of will.

"This isn't exactly what I'm used to wearing," I temporized, feeling like a coward but quite sure I didn't want to start another unproductive round of Drapsk upset. In emphasis, I shoved my hands into the nicely convenient pockets of my spacer-blue coveralls. The color was right, but it seemed my fate to find castoffs from giants. I hadn't quizzed the Drapsk on where they'd found clothing for me in their spacious holds. Likely some poor Human was going to find his or her luggage had jumped ship in the wrong direction.

My kindness was for naught. All the tentacles were sucked into their adjoining mouths simultaneously. And stayed there.

Oh, dear, I thought, relenting. I picked up the dress, a filmy, almost translucent creation patterned along its considerable length in black over red, doing my best to avoid the mirrors cunningly set in the bodice as if to catch an admirer in the act. Not exactly what I would have imagined as a Drapsk item of apparel. Then again, I'd never actually seen any.

The one feature I did like was on the upper left shoulder. Makeest had lovingly reproduced my name in fine irragold thread. My true name, as the Drapsk would say. Sira Morgan.

"I suppose I could try it on," I said. Antennae perked up. "That doesn't mean I'm agreeing to anything." I tried to ignore how three sets of purple plumes dipped toward the deck.

The general air of bustling activity throughout the *Makmora* was evidence that the unusual gown wasn't the only preparation underway for my supposed appearance at the Drapsk ceremony, despite my continued objections. I closed the door to my cabin—one having been welded complete with frame and lock into the corridor wall after I'd shivered in a draft—and continued to wonder uneasily about my future with the seemingly harmless Drapsk.

They were not forthcoming about what I was to do or expect, repeatedly answering most questions with a maddening and unhelpful: "This knowledge could affect your performance, O Mystic One."

My performance in what? I sat down on my bed, bringing up

my knees and hugging them to my chest. My hair, strangely limp if well behaved since that night on Pocular, slid down over one eye as I thought.

That night. *I hadn't reacted at all well,* I decided with a shudder. I should have kept Morgan with me. He would have questioned the villagers, including Withren. He might have used the devices from the *Fox* to look for clues about the type of weapon used against us. I could have had him with me as I healed.

I hugged my knees even tighter. Given what was happening between us, I could also have easily lost all sense on the spot, wounds or no wounds. My body warmed with treacherous heat just at the memory. There was no doubt in my mind that our physical union could trigger Joining through the M'hir. All it would take would be my loss of control, something Morgan's touch apparently guaranteed.

Well, I didn't have to worry about that at the moment, I thought with disgust, since I had no idea where he was or into what peril I'd sent him.

Of course, I didn't know where I was, either. Or where I was going. The Drapsk homeworld, Drapskii as they referred to it when they didn't call it simply Home, was the fourth planet from their sun and the most beautiful world in the known universe. That was the extent of my hosts' volunteered information.

I gave the soft cylinder the Drapsk euphemistically called a pillow a sincere and forceful punch. One thing I did know. I wasn't about to be swayed from my own purpose, no matter how desperate, charming, or difficult my hosts became.

INTERLUDE

"What now? You're going to break my nose, too?" While Barac's voice sounded skeptical, he looked poised to disappear at an instant's notice.

Morgan winced, a movement sparking pain from several abused muscle groups. Premick likely felt the same. "That—was an accident."

"Your fist. Hastho'tha's admittedly ugly face. An accident?"

As the Human couldn't remember much from the moments immediately following his arrival at the Haven, he shrugged. *Let the Clansman make what he would of the gesture.* "I wasn't in a patient frame of mind," Morgan admitted, feeling hardly less impatient now. But he was after information, not another fight. Though the readiness of the bar's clientele to return shove for push had been remarkably easy to share.

His blue eyes glinted. "Has Rael told you what happened?"

"To Sira?" Barac asked. "No. No details anyway. You'd been fighting there, too?" the Clansman raised an elegant eyebrow. Morgan shrugged again. It would be several more days, unless he went comatose in the *Fox*'s med cocoon, before the marks of his battle with Premick faded. Add to that the fresh cut above his left eye, courtesy of the Haven's bartender. "Rael just said there'd been an attack and Sira was injured. How is she?"

Sira's name coursed through Morgan's veins like some hype-drug, rousing anger until he barely kept it from edging his voice. Odd how hard it was to picture her face or remember the color of her hair—only the feel of her rage came easily. "I don't know. She's recovering at the village. What did Rael say?"

"But—" the Clansman shut his lips over what he'd planned to say.

Morgan took a quick step forward, hands clenching. They were alone in Sira's—now Barac's—office; the Clansman had *pushed* them both there once it was plain the Haven would be the scene of an all-out war, at least until the combatants sobered up enough to realize they had no idea why they were fighting.

Morgan read what he needed to know in Barac's eyes. "Sira's left Pocular," he stated.

Barac nodded. "Rael believes so. She felt Sira enter the M'hir from the village but couldn't follow her." The Clansman appeared to hesitate. "Rael said it was an incredibly long 'port—one she didn't dare attempt."

Sira had sent him after her enemies. And now she was gone, breaking her promise to him before she could conceivably have healed enough to move safely on her own. He couldn't search for her without lowering his defenses against the Clan, including the slender being waiting for him to speak.

It was too late to pretend he'd known she'd leave. Barac, more experienced with Humans than most of his kind, had seen enough of his reaction. "Where did she go? Did she leave any word?" Morgan asked numbly.

Barac's eyes lowered, as if the Clansman saw something in the Human's face he couldn't bear to watch. "No." Silent for a moment, Barac walked over to a side panel, opening it to reveal a small bottle flanked by two glasses. It was Sira's favorite—a gift of Brillian Brandy from a mutual friend. "We could both use this," the Clansman said apologetically, pouring a generous amount of the rare liquor into each glass. "Here. And do you mind sitting before you fall down?" He squinted at Morgan. "How long since you've slept?"

Morgan ignored the question and accepted the drink; following Barac's example, he sank into one of the chairs Sira kept near her shelves. He stared up at them, wordlessly, only now noticing they were bare. She'd taken the time to pack her collection of bits and pieces, but he knew what should be there: shells and sand from her first walk on a beach, the first gambling chits she'd won at the Haven's tables—on her way to winning the business from the previous unlamented owner of the place—a series of vistapes on hold stowage that rightly should have stayed on the *Fox* but he hadn't the heart to insist, and other things. Nothing valuable, except as markers to a life expanded beyond all expectations, a life and individuality she'd earned.

A life he would give his own to protect. "It was the Clan," Morgan said slowly, taking a sip of brandy, feeling its soothing burn trickling into the depths of his throat.

"The Council?" Barac shot back.

Morgan shrugged, wincing as the movement jarred his bruised shoulder. "I don't have a name—yet. Or proof. But I don't doubt it. Unless you know of anyone else interested in harvesting the reproductive organs of your cousin?"

The blood drained out of Barac's face, leaving red blotches on each high cheekbone. His voice was a whisper. "What—what did you say?"

The Human reached out and lightly traced two straight lines against the issa-silk of Barac's evening jacket. "Unless you've something else there I don't know about," he said grimly. "They'd sealed the wounds with medplas—nice of them—then dumped her in the wilds where I don't think anyone else could have found her in time. So I'd say we're dealing with at least one individual who was squeamish about blood in the aircar, or compulsively tidy about their surgery."

"Baltir."

The last thing he'd expected was a name. Morgan felt the room spinning and focused hard on the Clansman's pale features. "Who?" he demanded hoarsely. "Who did you say?"

"It's a guess—but I'd bet on it. Sira didn't—no matter, I'll show him to you." Barac raised his hand as if to place it on Morgan's forehead, then hesitated. "If you wish."

"If you dare," the Human said softly, owing Barac the warning. He couldn't be sure of his own control anymore, or what might trigger the bottomless rage he carried.

He also knew—and Barac's sudden swallow as their eyes met and locked confirmed the Clansman's understanding—that he was after more than what Sira had asked. Recover what was stolen?

After he'd dealt with the thief.

* * *

Morgan watched the green flashing light on the com panel, debating whether to accept the link. It should be Pocular's Port Authority, giving him clearance to lift and the schedule for the docking tug to carry the *Fox* to the launch area, safely distant from the other ships on the ground and their valuable cargoes. His index finger hovered in the air above the control.

If it was Port Authority, Morgan knew accepting the connection and the notification sure to follow would mean he'd be irrevocably (unless he could find the credits for a very significant fine) committed to leaving this world.

"We were happy here," he mused out loud, comfortable with the habit of talking to his ship. Most of his adult life had been spent alone, like this, with the *Fox* herself as company. It was a preference both of his personality and for real protection from the unwanted thoughts of others. Until Sira's teachings, he'd been reluctant to test his ability to screen out the mental noise of those around him, to risk exposing his own telepathic skills. Now, that was the least of his concerns.

Morgan touched his fingertip to the top of the button, feeling its coolness in contrast to the burning rage buried inside him. He guessed what it was—at least some of it: Sira's parting gift. He doubted she'd meant to pass along so much of her anger; there was no question she'd honestly tried to protect him these past months. But he'd been aware of it, as he'd known most of her emotional turmoil. The link between them went both ways—he'd just made certain she wasn't aware of how deeply.

He regretted nothing, yet hesitated to push the button.

The rage was something that, identified, seemed controllable enough. He'd left Barac intact, Morgan recalled, despite temptation. But it colored his every thought of her, spilled darkness on the love she'd offered to him at last, pouring like poison over everything he felt in return until all that remained free of confusion was their common purpose.

"She wants me to recover what was stolen. To seek them wherever they hide," he reminded the ship. *Didn't you know that would have been enough, Sira?* he added as if she were still close in his thoughts, listening to what was more than speech. *Didn't you realize I would do it for my own sake—that what harms you, harms me? You didn't have to say: 'As you love me.'*

Morgan pressed the button, accepting his destiny, his other hand reaching for the yellow trip tape to insert at Port Authority's request. That it had nothing to do with his true destination was a detail the Human deemed Pocular's Port Jellies could talk to him about later.

If he ever came back.

Chapter 13

ONE advantage to having been a working spacer was that I knew the moment the *Makmora* dropped from translight and began docking maneuvers. The cessation of the almost soundless engine vibration, coupled with some abrupt shifts in gravity, left me in little doubt we were about to clamp on to something. *But what?*

This being a curiosity I couldn't satisfy from the warmth of my bed, I pulled on my coveralls as quickly as possible. Time to head to the bridge and ask some determined questions.

The door handle wouldn't budge.

Despite a sudden flare of anger, I had to smile. Did the Drapsk seriously think this could hold me in place? The locate of the bridge was easy to form; my Talent felt nearly normal again. I *pushed* . . .

. . . and felt as though I'd hit a wall. A prickly wall, at that. *This was not good.*

As if to underscore my growing apprehension, the ship connected with something else with a clang and thud. Their pilot lacked Morgan's finesse.

I calmed myself, using the discipline learned by Sira di Sarc over decades of honing her power to counter the newer and overly vivid imagination of Sira Morgan. I was constantly blending what I'd been with what I'd become; as constantly, I worried about recognizing the end result.

How were the Drapsk keeping me imprisoned? There was no opposition to the tendril of thought I cautiously allowed out past my shielding, no detectable change in what I could sense of the M'hir.

Not drugs, then, I decided with an immediate rush of relief.

There was at least one, of my personal experience, capable of temporarily blinding my kind to the M'hir, of trapping our thoughts within flesh. *So what else could it be?*

For no particular reason, I remembered Sector Chief Lydis Bowman, the Trade Pact Enforcer whose intervention had likely saved both Morgan and me from the plans of the Clan Council and my father, Jarad di Sarc. I could almost picture her round, stern face, wrinkled around the eyes and corners of the lips as though equally ready to grin or scowl on an instant's notice. She and her Constables had taken the risk of having experimental mind-deadening devices implanted directly at the base of their brains in order to protect themselves from possible Clan influence.

Now, as I looked around the very small space that was my prison, its walls soft pink and inclined to bulges more than corners, I found myself wondering for the first time if the Humans had invented that particular technology or purchased it—and if the latter, from whom.

I settled myself back on the bed. The Drapsk might be impervious to my other sense, but a seeking within the range of this ship might net me a mind I could touch.

Or more than one. *Whew!* The *Makmora* was no longer alone in space and no longer populated only by the Drapsk. I rubbed my forehead, blinking furiously, trying unsuccessfully to ease the painful impact of several hundred minds on mine. There was a cosmopolitan flavor to the confusion outside, making me quite certain that several different species were nearby, specifically on another ship limpeted to this one by prearrangement, not in attack.

Which was both good and bad—considering the clearest images I'd received suggested the *Makmora* was clamped lovingly to a very large, very well-populated pirate.

"The mechanism must have been stuck, O Mystic One," groveled the Drapsk who opened my door a short time later. His antennae were almost twisted about each other in what I charitably took to be sincere distress. "We should have provided you with a com system to use. I will see to it personally—"

Before the Drapsk could leave me on its worthy mission, a

move sure to mean letting go of the door currently held open in its right hand, I lunged forward and took hold of the handle myself. "Thank you," was all I bothered to say on my way out.

"O Mystic One. My apologies about your door," Captain Maka began. "It—"

"Must have stuck," I finished for him. "While I'll be grateful for the com system your crew mentioned, I'd really prefer not to have this occur again, Captain."

There was a concerted round of tentacle sucking at this, a general response from the bridge crew who continued to take a great deal of interest in my conversations with their Captain.

"Of course, O Mystic One," Maka said in that very reasonable voice of his, antennae slightly dipped my way as if seeking more information about my frame of mind.

This time I saw where the bridge seating came from as three stoollike objects budded up from the floor upon coaxing by a Drapsk crewman, offering perches overlooking the rest of the bridge to myself, Maka, and his first officer. I'd missed it before, being too busy trying not to faint. Fainting was not part of my expectations of this visit to the *Makmora*'s bridge. Answers definitely were.

I seated myself, placing my hands on my knees and then interlacing my fingers into as magical-looking an arrangement as I could comfortably maintain, having no reason to assume the Drapsk would miss such a detail. *Which one?* Ah, there was a shift change occurring at the com post. I focused on the Drapsk waiting to take his post, pointed my entwined fingers at him in what I hoped was a suitably magical gesture, and *pushed* . . .

The crewman vanished with satisfying promptness, providing the first piece of information I needed. It was something about my room, then, that inhibited my use of the M'hir. My Talent was potent enough here.

And every Drapsk on the bridge appeared to know it, too. Every plume was aimed in my direction, a focusing of attention I suddenly had absolutely no doubt was a reaction to my use of the M'hir, as I grew equally convinced the Drapsk were the source of the mind-deadening technologies used by the Enforcers. Yet the small beings had no presence in the M'hir, something I quickly tested again. *What were they? Did they know about the M'hir or was this some type of instinct?* Serious questions, I realized, unsure if I wanted the answers or the complications they implied. "Had Makoori displeased you, O Mystic One?" Maka asked in a faint voice, antennae vibrating furiously.

Since said Makoori immediately reappeared, almost falling out of the nearest lift as its doors opened, the question seemed moot, but I wasn't about to lose any momentum with the credulous Drapsk. "You've all displeased me, Captain Maka. I came on this ship in good faith—only to be imprisoned while you dock with strangers. I feel my good name endangered," I asserted, warming up to the tirade. "I feel my very existence endangered! How can I perform at the Ceremony on Drapskii in this state?"

They could have been slightly bizarre lawn ornaments for all the movement occurring through the next long moments. Perhaps the tips of various antennae fluttered. I relaxed, letting the Drapsk do whatever they needed to do in order to converse privately, hopefully having made my point.

"It was not our intention to alarm you, O Mystic One," Captain Maka spoke finally, one four-fingered hand warm on mine. It was the first voluntary touch I'd experienced from a Drapsk, the ministrations of the med aside, and I immediately tried Morgan's method to see if I could read the being's thoughts. *Nothing.*

"Then what was your intention, Captain?" I asked coolly. "And to what ship are you clamped?"

"The ss-ship is-s the *Nokraud,* Fem," hissed a new voice familiar enough to send an answering shiver down my spine. As I whirled to look at the intruder entering the *Makmora*'s bridge from the second lift, accompanied by a trio of Human-looking guards, I felt as though time had reversed itself—and not in my favor. "And the intentions-ss of your hossts-ss mussst have been to hide you from us-ss."

I knew that body plan, similar to mine in size and shape but built with a predator's abrupt agility. A pair of thin, tall crests rose from its snout to forehead, curling like a frame behind each forward-pointing eye. The crests were a mottled purple and yellow, the colors more like stains than natural pigmentation. The scaled snout, tilted down to better examine me as I remained seated, bore irregular knuckle-sized knobs along its length. Each of those eyes holding me pinned were bigger than my fist, with jet-black pupils slicing their gleaming yellow in half. The last individual of this species I'd encountered, Roraqk, murdered with less compunction than a cat, viewed primates as less-than-palatable entrées, and kidnapped me for a renegade Clansman. This being could have been Roraqk's twin, save for the smooth curl of a stump marking the loss of most of its left arm. In an attempt to kill Morgan, Roraqk had used his ship as a weapon, casually ripping open a space station and killing dozens of innocents as well as most of his own crew in the process.

I saw no reason to assume any differing tendencies in the individual before me.

Or, I observed with a sinking feeling, in the second one stalking out of the other lift, frills pulsing with color.

INTERLUDE

Let me come with you. Barac witnessed the intensity of his mindsend in the darkening of Rael's eyes as she turned to look at him. She easily held his urgency at bay.

"It is not necessary," his cousin answered coolly, choosing to speak. Perhaps, Barac thought bitterly to himself, she preferred to avoid mental touch with a sud, especially one unChosen and an exile. "Stay here. Tend your bar."

Barac spoke aloud as well, glad of Rael's attention at least, though smarting over her casual flick of fingers at their surroundings, the currently deserted gaming area of the Spacer's Haven. "This place?" he protested. "It's Sira's joke at my expense, nothing more. You can't think I planned to stay here."

Her gesture turned into the more gracious finger patterning of mollification and apology. "Forgive me, Cousin. I assumed this was what you sought when you left Camos."

"What I sought," Barac said slowly, holding her gaze with his, daring to send an underlying emphasis of power into the M'hir, "what I still seek, is justice."

"Ah, yes," Rael said, tilting her head thoughtfully. "Your hunt for those behind Kurr's murder. Were your answers here?"

"Sira knows. She didn't tell me." Barac paused for a moment, then added honestly: "She might have—if things had gone better."

Rael hesitated as well, raising his hopes. He'd caught up with her just as she'd been leaving for the shipcity, a choice of travel suited to secrecy from their own kind, despite the inconvenience. Her transport waited outside the Haven and her hood was already pulled up over her head: as much to confuse any observers, he supposed, as for protection from the evening's rain. Rael wasn't fond of uncontrolled weather. Actually, neither was he.

"If I come with you," Barac coaxed, "we might be able to catch up to Sira."

Rael smiled without warmth. "A chase we've run before, Cousin, without much success, if I remember. I'm going home, not hunting." Before he could speak, she added in a low voice, "If it helps your search for justice, Barac, I can tell you that Kurr's murderer, Yihtor di Caraat, has been dropped into the M'hir. He died three weeks ago, according to my source. They—the Council—tried to keep his body alive, to preserve his power in some way," her generous lips twisted as if around an unpleasant taste. "Fortunately, Faitlen's pet toad was unable to accomplish this feat, and Fem di Caraat dispatched her son's remains personally."

Barac put his hand on the back of the nearest chair, shutting down his awareness of the M'hir, slamming tight every barrier he possessed. Against Rael it might be enough. "Baltir again," he said, drawing on his Scout's training for that carefully neutral voice.

The Clanswoman's eyes narrowed. "Why have you closed to me?"

Barac felt her power at the edge of his own; not a pressure, an exploration. "The memory is—painful," he said. "We told you what happened that night in the Chamber. How the Council tried to force Sira into Choice with me, and when she refused to kill me by the attempt, they brought in that—creature. It promised to be able to impose some kind of physical bonding with Yihtor, something to—" he strangled on the words. From her expression, he didn't need to elaborate.

"Games," she spat. "They broke the Prime Laws and played with all our lives."

"You can see why I don't care to relive it."

"All this is true, Barac, but not the truth." Rael stepped closer, pushing back her hood so her eyes caught the light. Their expression was strange, as though she found something in him to fear, unlikely as that was. "You knew about Yihtor already," she concluded, surprise in her voice. "Was that why you made your decision to leave Camos? Knowing he was out of your reach?"

Barac shook his head, checking the strength of his mental walls. Dangerous, conversing with the more powerful. They frequently took offense at suds who tried for secrets. His purpose was greater than any accustomed caution. "I decided when I was refused Choice for the last time," he insisted. "That's when I knew there was no longer a place for me under the Council's rule."

Rael was definitely alarmed now. "You're trying to lie to me. Why?"

"How could I dare such a thing?" Barac taunted, glorying in being unafraid for the first time in his life of a superior power. *How far could he push her for reaction?* he wondered to himself.

Her voice hardened. "Hasn't being scanned once been enough pain for you, *sud*?"

Barac shrugged, allowing his defiance to leak past his shielding to trouble the M'hir touching them both. "Sira I can understand. What would be your excuse for lawbreaking, Rael di Sarc? Why do you care so much about why I came to Pocular? What secrets are *you* holding tight?"

The air whooshed past his ears to fill the space where the Clanswoman had stood an instant before, speechless, her delicate features drained of blood. He'd rarely seen so clear an expression of guilt and remorse in his life.

Rael should never gamble.

The trouble was, why? He'd stirred up something unexpected.

Barac realized he was still gripping the chair's back. He gave it a hard shove, sending it spinning into the nearest table, knocking the smoketrays and other glassware to the floor.

Maybe if he stirred enough pots, the truth he sought would finally rise to the surface.

Chapter 14

GRACKIK and Rek were their names, the former pirate being the one who'd lost an arm and the latter prone to flexing the corresponding taloned hand each time they stood in proximity as if it enjoyed making the comparison. Their voices and mannerisms were otherwise identical. For no particular reason—certainly their anatomy gave no obvious clues—I concluded they were both female.

And, despite the threat of their presence, I also concluded I was not currently on their menu. The Drapsk, it seemed, were good customers. *But of what?*

"You see, O Mystic One, it is merely business. You should not be alarmed." This assurance had been repeated rather frequently by my new companion, the comtech Makoori. The Drapsk was basking in the glory of having been part of my "magic" in front of his kin, and had attached himself to me ever since.

I kept my shields up, my expression pleasantly neutral, and refused to budge from the *Makmora*'s bridge or even my stool, hard as it was becoming. Roraqk's kind—called the Sakissishee to their snouts (the true name being so long and sibilant few others could manage it) and Scats when safely out of range—was a species even the unusually broad-minded Morgan refused to trade with, since Scats were firmly convinced all others existed as either food or disposable commodities. They would have constituted a serious threat to other species, had more than a handful ever left their cinder of a world. It also helped that they competed fiercely with each other at every opportunity, with cannibalism rumored to be quite acceptable on the winner's part.

Which made them lousy mercenaries, unreliable partners-in-crime, and excellent pirates. It was a wonder to me the Trade Pact didn't simply lock them on their world and wait for evolution to produce something more civilized. But that wasn't the way the quasi-government worked, as I knew full well. Species who signed into the Pact agreed to cooperate in trade, maintaining embassies at major ports, and providing starship facilities on their worlds. Although there was an interesting variation in the quality of those embassies and spaceports, overall the system worked just ponderously enough to keep the peace.

The Trade Pact had its teeth, the Enforcers, but their mandate was simply to protect the treaty. Piracy that affected major shipping routes, interspecies' slavery, price gouging on publicly-traded commodities were within their jurisdiction. Wars, bad manners, and internal species' politics were not.

Not that I could call on their protection anyway. The Clan were not signatories of the Trade Pact or any other agreement. Call on my own kind? There were less than a thousand of us, the strongest living one to a planet, most of those within the well-established and rich inner systems first settled by Humans in this quadrant. Status and rank within the Clan was determined instantly and without question by comparison of power. Any issues affecting us as a whole were ruled by the Clan Council, a group made up of the most powerful individuals from the eight main family lines. I could have been a member, had I wanted to continue to be Clan: keeping myself isolated, secret, and pure of other species' influence. Clan xenophobia would not serve them well in the future they faced, I thought with a familiar grimness. Not well at all.

But that wasn't my problem. My problem was prowling through the decks of the *Makmora,* likely drooling over what wasn't locked away, while busy doing whatever the Drapsk had arranged. Not surprisingly, they weren't telling me much about that, either.

"O Mystic One?"

"I'm here," I sighed, resting my elbow on my knee so I could support my chin in the palm of a hand. It was hard for me to think ill of the small beings, but I was getting plenty of practice. "And I remain quite sensibly alarmed by the actions of this ship, Makoori. You are aware that these beings you've allowed on board are not—how can I put this delicately—trustworthy?"

A thoughtful moment of tentacle sucking ensued, then the Drapsk nodded his blind head, antennae drifting back and forth with the movement. "The *Makmora* has explosive piercing grapples locked around the *Nokraud*'s hull," he said matter-of-factly, as if the knowledge of the Drapsk possessing and using banned tech weaponry would be reassuring.

It was. I grinned and felt at least one knot of worry letting go. "Forgive my lack of confidence in the Makii Tribe, Makoori."

From the deepening pinks of his antennae, I thought the Drapsk was pleased. "We pride ourselves in knowing our customers' preferences and habits, O Mystic One," he said smugly.

If the Drapsk wouldn't tell me, there was another means to find out for myself what the *Nokraud* was doing clamped to a Drapsk freighter. First, I had to find a suitable source of information and a moment's privacy. Scats weren't among the confirmed, or suspected, telepathic species, but I believed they were at least sensitive to the feel of an invading mind. Roraqk had been fanatically careful to avoid what he'd termed "mindcrawlers," though his precautions were, in the end, useless. Morgan had used his mental abilities to stop the pirate's heart, something he'd learned to do on his own. I hadn't asked where or why, grateful for the rescue if horrified by the method.

No, I wouldn't risk reading one of the Scats, not that I'd want to put my thoughts anywhere near theirs. But there were Human and other *Nokraud* crew moving throughout the *Makmora*'s corridors. I should be able to dip into one of their minds.

However, my newly appointed friend and guide, Makoori, wasn't making that effort easier. "Where exactly do you wish to go, Mystic One?" he asked, taking two steps for every one of mine. I suspected this was a tactful way of asking if I was lost. We'd been through this section of the ship twice, forced to move aside regularly as a steady stream of *Makmora* and *Nokraud* crew hurried by carrying packages or towing laden grav sleds. Which was the reason I kept returning here, although the reason for the hands-on cargo switch still escaped me.

"Exercise is very important to my mystical abilities," I lied straightfaced. *There.* A Human-looking pirate had paused in one of the doorless rooms just steps from us, putting down his crate to make some adjustment to a list affixed to the top. Before Makoori could so much as draw breath to try and stop me, I hurried forward and touched the *Nokraud* crewman on the shoulder.

"Excuse me. Haven't we met—" My voice stuck in my throat as the being turned to look down at me out of his trio of muddy green eyes. A Goth. I'd have better luck using a drill to read its thoughts than the M'hir. "My mistake."

The pirate grunted something incomprehensible and went back to its work. Makoori caught up to me. "Was there some difficulty, Mystic One?"

"No, Makoori. No difficulty at all." I surveyed the bustle in the corridor critically. All I could do was keep trying as long as the Drapsk was willing to follow me, puzzled by my behavior or not.

Success was somewhat more serendipitous than I'd expected. I was paying attention to something Makoori was trying to say; the oncoming pair of pirates were arguing about who had the heaviest load. Our collision was inevitable, convenient, and uncomfortable. I ended up on the bottom of a pile of limbs, cargo, and strange smells.

I wrapped my hand around the warm bare skin of some being's ankle, hoping for the best, and sent out a quick tight tendril of thought. Flashes of the argument appeared behind my closed eyelids. I sought deeper. *The cargo hold. The contents of the crates . . .*

"O Mystic One. Say you are intact! Get off her, you immense louts!"

I accepted Makoori's frantic help to dislodge me from beneath the cursing pirates, quite willing to regain both my lung capacity and fresher air to inhale. The contact hadn't done my abdomen any good. A flash of red-hot pain bent me over with a gasp.

The contact had been good enough to reveal what the dreaded pirates were doing here. They were delivering Tidikian fireworks—prohibited goods, since the Trade Pact took a dim view of cargo used as weapons by some species and as entertainment by others—but hardly a major crime. And in return, the Drapsk were offloading a variety of valuable spices and other luxury goods.

The pirate had been scornful of the Drapsk's passionate desire for the fireworks, but not of the profit involved.

"O Mystic One! I have summoned the med, but the com system is unreliable with so many filthy biologicals in the corridor. Can you walk? Mystic One?"

And why fireworks? All the Drapsk had told the *Nokraud* was that they were essential for an upcoming victory celebration.

As the Drapsk panicked even further, I tried not to laugh. It would have hurt.

INTERLUDE

Within the utter black of the M'hir, dread stirred and found a soundless voice: *It's too risky.*

The stronger mind of the two linked here deflected the fears of the weaker. *The only risk lies in failing to act. There are avenues to be tried—because they are dangerous or repugnant is of no consequence to our need. This is but one more. Are they ready?*

They are Chosen!

Clear amusement. *If they were not, they would hardly be of use.*

No doubt of acquiescence—the weaker knew his place—but a sliver of apprehension remained. *They will be missed. What then?*

You will ensure there is good and reasonable cause for their absence. A flood of determination: *They will thank us, some-day. You will see.*

And Sira?

Jarad di Sarc's confidence filled the M'hir until Faitlen could hardly breathe around it. *She will be grateful. Or no longer of concern.*

Chapter 15

I DIDN'T plan to go to Drapskii. I certainly didn't want to go to Drapskii. But when the Drapsk announced with glee the *Makmora*'s arrival in their Home system, it was a little too late to worry about my plans or desires.

And it was, I decided, *as reasonable a destination as any.* Much as I resisted the notion, the damage done to my body had been significant. If it hadn't been for the Drapsk med—I turned the unproductive thought away. The pain was gone, I could feel my strength returning by the hour, and two hair-thin lines were all that remained of the incisions on my abdomen. I was ready to take advantage of any opportunity to find another ship and set forth on my true quest. There was, I realized, just one flaw.

Any opportunity would depend on the intentions of the Drapsk.

Drapskii was an unusual planet in many respects, not only in the behavior of its inhabitants. At least the Drapsk had been overjoyed to supply me with geographical information—if little else.

There was no moon, and what free water existed spent most of its time in a series of deep cracks etched in parallel to its equator as if the world had been stretched from its poles by a playful god. With the exception of streaks of tawny desert nestled in the lee-side of mountain ranges, the land itself was completely carpeted with patches of agricultural land and sprawling Drapsk cities. I wasn't sure if this indicated a lack of interest in wilderness or a lack of wilderness to be interested in.

It was an old, civilized place—as set in its ways as its weather, having a climate strangely lacking in variation, though the Drapsk didn't bother with control technology as did many species. The only winds of consequence were mild, steady, and predictable, arising from the spinning of Drapskii herself; in turn, her almost circular and solitary orbit around the small white dwarf star of the Drapskii System provided little in the way of seasons. There were no great exposed bodies of water to store heat energy or release it to the atmosphere—a characteristic I thought responsible for the frequent caution on the tapes to bring in livestock twice daily: once during the nightly freeze-up and once during the searing heat of midday. The additional caution to roll up and perform *eopari* at those times was something I assumed would not apply to humanoid guests.

There were plenty of mountain ranges to break the flow of air into predictable local patterns. Not surprisingly in a species dependent on chemical communication, the Drapsk had identified hundreds of types of air movements and breezes due to microclimate effects, ranging from the slide of air down night-cooled mountain ranges to the scheduled bursts about the landing and launch fields of their shipcities. I skipped that part of the vistapes.

What I hunted for in vain was information on the Drapsk themselves. All I remembered from Morgan's tapes on the species was an impression of a civilization so private yet polite, so well-mannered and orderly, no one bothered to question anything they did—this and their obsession with magic. To me, alone in my cabin on the Drapsk ship, this lack of information seemed more alarming than anything I knew of the Scats.

Well, I said to myself when Makoori arrived to inform me we were about to land, *I was certainly in a position to add to the* Fox's *database.* Morgan would be pleased; he collected information the way others hoarded credits.

I didn't allow myself to think any more than that. The place in my thoughts where Morgan belonged was like some festering wound, a wound safer to avoid than examine too closely, especially here and now, when I had no way to heal it.

One of the first additions I was able to make concerned the seemingly identical appearance of the Drapsk. It was misleading. While I still couldn't distinguish any of my Drapsk, the Makii Tribe, from one another without their tags or some other clue, the three Drapsk who met us as we exited the *Makmora* the next morning were distinctly different: from each other as well as from the Makii themselves.

The Drapsk shipcity was, predictably, more civilized than Pocular's—a better match for those found on the rich, established worlds of the Humans' Inner Systems, such as my former home of Camos. An automated lift offered us easy passage from the ground-level port of the ship to an overhead series of moving walkways. I peered around me, unsure how the docking tugs would be able to move ships in and out through such a maze of seemingly permanent structures. Obviously they could, or we wouldn't be enjoying the luxury. I was reasonably sure the Drapsk considered my constant gazing around me as curiosity or as a compliment to their shipcity. I didn't bother informing them I was attempting to memorize potential escape routes.

The individuals who had been waiting outside the *Makmora*'s port didn't speak to me or to the two Drapsk with me: Captain Maka and my shipside companion, Makoori. Neither appeared to notice anything odd about this silence, so I presumed there was adequate communication going on—just not shared with the olfactorarily-deprived guest of honor.

I studied the new Drapsk. Of the three, one was considerably taller—almost my height—so the plumes of his antennae, yellowish-red as opposed to the familiar purple-pink of my hosts, occasionally tickled my ear. I had no idea if this was intentional or an accidental contact distressing the Drapsk as much as it startled me; all I could do was try not to swat the likely sensitive organ away in an ill-advised reflex.

The remaining Drapsk were similar in size and shape to the Makii, differing only in the plumes of their antennae. It might have been cosmetic, to mark some difference between Tribes, or a true physiological difference caused by age or sex. *If the Drapsk had different sexes,* I added to myself. Certainly one referred to all Drapsk as he—a convention they preferred. No matter why, one of the new Drapsk bore plumes of eye-piercing orange, while the other's were an equally intense shade of turquoise. The overall effect, as I looked down at my escort, was one of walking within a garden of animated feather dusters.

By the time the walkway carried us through the shipcity, I'd grown used to the feeling of gliding along without moving my feet, quite entranced by the sensation. The surface of the walkway was not truly solid, dimpling slightly underfoot. I'd never seen or heard of anything like this before—not that the Clan was overly fond of technology in the first place. My kind acquired from Humans any gadgetry they chose for comfort or convenience, scorning any understanding or overt interest, relying on Talent whenever possible. I had little sympathy for that attitude, having learned Morgan's love of his ship.

Unfortunately, my knowledge of technology was woefully limited, in spite of my newly gained interest in it. There wasn't much I could do in a year to counter the effect of a lifetime spent as Clan. Still, I was convinced this walkway was something even the Humans would find unusual. I noticed how connecting paths flowed into this one or branched away, a system more like a watershed of force than any mechanical device. I found myself comparing it to the blurring of reality that was the floor of the Clan Council chamber when suspended partially within the M'hir, and again regarded my tiny hosts with suspicion. *Not a good time to experiment,* I reminded myself, stopping the opening of my inner thoughts just in time as I recalled how the Drapsk crew seemed to react to my presence in the M'hir.

My outwardly-silent Drapsk escort and I flowed along until reaching the boundary of the shipcity. I'd expected a transfer from the walkways to some other type of transport—aircars perhaps, ubiquitous travel on other worlds. Not here. Perhaps they created too many errant breezes for my hosts. I watched the never-still antennae, more than a little frustrated at being unable to eavesdrop.

The type of walkway did change shortly after ours poured its way over the edge of the city itself, moving between windowless, curved structures I assumed were buildings. We intersected a larger area, more like a sand-colored pond than pavement, on which rested numerous bowl-like objects. One slid forward obediently to hold position in front of our small group. It was larger than the groundcars of my experience, smooth and soft as I was beginning to expect of Drapsk construction. There was no driver or visible controls. We simply climbed in and sat on the warm, yielding surface of its floor, the bowlcar moving off slowly at first, then with gathering speed in what must have been a predetermined direction.

To where? I couldn't see out of the bowlcar. There were no identifiable features to the structures I could see overhead, unless one counted a steady increase in their size. After a few moments of staring at the equally featureless faces of the four Drapsk, I struggled to kneel so I could see over the sides and watch where we were going. The ensuing unanimous tentacle-sucking brought me back down to a more dignified and boring position.

Well, stoic silence wasn't working. *Time,* I decided, *for a more direct approach.* "Surely now you can tell me where we're going, Captain Maka," I suggested, trying for a tone midway between irritation and expectation.

"Of course, O Mystic One," Maka said immediately, delicately spitting out his tentacles in what I took for relief. "Of course."

I waited three long breaths, before prompting gently: "So where are we going?"

"The Judgment Hall," said the tallest of the strange Drapsk, his Comspeak heavily accented but clear enough. There was none of the Makii's subservience to a "mystic one" in his voice or bearing. Out of the corner of one eye, I saw half of Makoori's tentacles slide back inside his mouth. *Oh, dear.*

"And why—" I paused involuntarily as the bowlcar accelerated upward at a growing angle, finding myself entangled in an armful of passive Drapsk. They were warm, smooth, and a little fuzzy to the touch—much like their furnishings. As the bowlcar settled back into something more horizontal, the Drapsk and I disengaged carefully. "As I was about to ask," I continued, trying hard not to laugh, "why am I going to your Judgment Hall?"

The tall Drapsk answered with a definite note of satisfaction: "To be tried on the charge of impersonating a being of true magic, of course."

Of course, I repeated to myself, laughter forgotten. "Captain Maka?" I asked, narrowing my eyes at the one I personally considered to be the guilty party.

He'd been sucking the odd tentacles, too, but mumbled around them clearly enough: "A formality before the Competition and Celebrations, O Mystic One. You will meet your Skeptic and be judged favorably, I assure you."

Not a word of agreement or disagreement from the others. I found I could clench my fingers into the spongy surface of the bowlcar's flooring with satisfying tightness. "And what happens if I'm judged unfavorably?"

"There's no doubt—"

"What happens, Maka?" I interrupted sternly.

The turquoise-plumed Drapsk said something in a soft, lilting language I didn't know and assumed was their own, before inhaling his own circle of fleshy red tentacles in what seemed final emphasis.

Maka's antennae drooped, as did Makoori's, but he answered me. "We—the Makii—lose the *Makmora,* O Mystic One, to another, more worthy Tribe." The antennae struggled valiantly upright again, and his small four-fingered hand touched my knee. "But we have no doubt of you, Sira Morgan. No doubt at all. You are the one we have waited for—"

"Silence," scolded the tall Drapsk. "The Skeptic will determine her worthiness for the Competition. It is not for us to say." His voice became less harsh-sounding, his globe of a face turning in my direction. "Do not be apprehensive, Fem Morgan. You will be our honored guest throughout the Festival, regardless of the Skeptic's findings. It is a privilege granted to few aliens."

"Thank you," was all I could find to say. I somehow didn't think *no thanks* was an option. But I glared at Maka and Makoori, hoping their experience trading with humanoids would be sufficient to let them read my expression. I hadn't asked to be responsible for 445 tiny Drapsk and their ship. Even if I accepted the role, I had absolutely no idea what the Drapsk's Skeptic would be judging.

All I could do was hope the Makii knew what I was doing here.

Or make my way offworld—quickly.

INTERLUDE

"I tell you, Sedly, the creteng was rotten! Have you no sense of smell?"

Morgan leaned in the shadows of the back entrance to the restaurant, beneath the discreet sign reading: *Claws & Jaws, Complete Interspecies Cuisine,* and listened to the one-sided argument in the kitchen with a rare sense of homecoming. He shifted, easing a lingering sore spot on his upper back, loath to move further and be noticed. The med unit had done what it could for his injuries and exhaustion during the trip to intercept Plexis. His face was almost normal, and breathing no longer sent jabs of agony through his middle. Morgan curled his hands into fists, experimentally, then winced. The knuckles would take a while longer. Premick's tough hide had won the battle over Human skin.

A shame he couldn't have afforded being unconscious—a day or so under tranks might have helped settle the maelstrom in his head. *At least it would have postponed it,* he thought wryly. But he hadn't trusted the space he traveled, nor his own mind if released from knowing control. So his thoughts persisted in tumbling over each other in confusion, like the rising voices beyond the door.

One was definitely winning the war of volume. "It doesn't matter if Humans can't smell it either! That's why they're still emptying their stomach pouches, you idiot." A sound like castanets landing in a pot. "What did you think would happen if you left the casserole on the counter all afternoon? It's dead fish, not a jar of pickled nicnics!"

Morgan shook his head. He'd better go in before the *Claws*

& *Jaws* needed a new cook—and its irate owner had to bribe his way out of another assault charge.

The spectacle in the steamy kitchen was about what the conversation had led him to expect. A dozen assistants were pretending to work at their tables, sneaking quick glances at the two in the center aisle beside the huge stove with its load of bubbling pots and skillets. From the looks on those with readable faces, the cook deserved every word.

Whether the unfortunate being deserved his present situation, suspended overhead by a massive claw surely restricting the natural movement of blood through his torso, was another matter.

"You know you always feel sick after you lose your temper," Morgan said calmly, walking up to the owner of the claw: the respected, the successful, and the infamously short-tempered owner of the *Claws & Jaws,* Huido Maarmatoo'kk.

"Morgan!!" the giant Carasian bellowed deafeningly as he whirled about, ponderously agile despite outmassing the Human three-to-one and moving on pillarlike legs that ended in balloonlike pads rather than feet. At the same instant, Huido enthusiastically flung both sets of his asymmetrical, clawed arms out in greeting, completely forgetting about the cook formerly grasped in his lower left handling claw, said cook immediately flying through the air with an awe-inspiring shriek. Fortunately for the cook, a miserable-looking Ordnex, two of the kitchen assistants had moved into catching range with the speed of long practice, saving the being from a landing on either the floor or the surface of the stove. "Morgan!" Huido repeated. "My brother—"

"Watch the ribs—" that worthy cautioned, too late. Morgan grunted as he was swept from the floor in an embrace sure to add a new layer to his bruises. But it felt good to hammer his better fist against the cool black armor his friend called skin, to look down into dozens of warmly focused eyes and know he was safe here, without need for explanation or argument.

Mind you, the ceiling was a bit close for comfort, he decided.

Huido set him back on the floor, his smaller, more flexible, handling arms steadying Morgan with tender care. Black and glistening, the Carasian stood as tall as the Human, his shoulders and bulbous back bulking much wider. His huge head, like a pair of saucepans from the kitchen placed one atop the other, pulsed vertically in a slight rhythmic motion, the black shadow between them dancing with the gleam of those independently mobile eyes, each on its own short stalk. At the moment, most of these eyes were scampering about, as if searching for something missing in the room.

Morgan shook his head. "Sira's not with me."

Huido's eyes settled on him and the being heaved a sigh that rattled his body plates. "You aren't just here to deliver my truffles and celebrate my newest house specialty with hours of delightful gluttony, I take it." He rolled one eye to check on his cook, currently being soothed by the assistants. "Assuming I should discover unexpected competency anywhere in this place—" the Carasian growled meaningfully.

"Your truffles?" Morgan repeated, wincing involuntarily.

"My truffles," Huido echoed with an ominous click of his largest claw. "You did bring my truffles with you—"

"Had to sell them locally," the Human said quickly. "Forget the truffles, Huido."

"Forget the truffles? Do you know how many of my clients are waiting for a taste of fresh Poculan merle truffles, marinated with a hint of anasa sauce—hideously expensive, but absolutely essential to bring out those understated musky highlights in the flavor—and served standard room temperature with only the finest Denebian port?" Huido's voice rose until it approached the roar it had been during his harangue of the Ordnex cook, who, Morgan noticed, was now nodding with satisfaction as someone else was bearing the brunt of the Carasian's ire.

Morgan found himself speechless. Rather than say anything he'd regret later—and Huido would doubtless remind him of for years to come—he pushed past his friend and walked to the door leading to the living quarters adjacent to the restaurant, keying in the code with the ease of long practice. "I need to talk to you," he said without looking back. "Now."

"Where would she go?"

Morgan dipped his fingers in the churning salt water and hesitated. They were in Huido's inner sanctum, a totally Carasian maze of pseudo-rock shelves and artificial pools. The air was moist with salt spray as the deepest pool experienced its high

tide, waves splashing with credible realism against the surrounding edges. It was, Morgan knew, a privilege to be allowed
here. Crescents of shiny black dotting the white surf marked
where Huido's twenty or more mates, barely sentient beauties
totally besotted with their husband, floated their eyestalks so
they could watch the Human.

He'd asked Huido once what the female Carasians thought
of him, the only alien permitted here. Huido had been amused,
replying merely that he'd make sure they were always well-fed
before allowing Morgan to enter, a comment which did help
explain why the *Claws & Jaws'* safe was located in this room.

He brought himself back to Huido's question, staring down
at the cluster of eyestalks marking where the Carasian momentarily bobbed deeper in the water beside him. "I don't know
where she'd go," he admitted when Huido rose.

"Would she return to her family?"

Morgan tasted Sira's rage within his thoughts and had no
doubt of the answer: "The Clan? No." He stretched his legs on
the floating mattress, careful to keep out of the water; even
though all of the wives seemed to be in the other, larger pool,
there was no point offering temptation. "I'd hoped she'd come
here, to you, until I checked Plexis' itinerary. You're too far
from the Poculan System now. Way out of range, even for
Sira."

"So where will you look?"

"I'm not." The Human closed his eyes tightly, then opened
them again. "I can't go after her. I have—other business."

Huido nudged the mattress, making Morgan grab its edges in
reflex. "What kind of business? I thought better of you, Brother.
Your mate is hurt—"

"I can't let them get away with this," Morgan snapped. "You
don't understand."

"But I do," Huido stated, tapping Morgan's leg for emphasis.
"You blame yourself for not protecting her."

Morgan's eyes flashed dangerously. "Shouldn't I? On what
level didn't I fail her?" He used his hands to propel the mattress
to the nearest rock and climbed off. He stood there, breathing
heavily, and went on: "I let her leave the protection of the
Haven. Instead of bringing her back to it, I get drunk and jealous,
picking a fight like some lovesick kid with a being I called my

friend. I abandon her so she's alone and helpless when they come. For all I know, they *needed* the distraction I made."

Huido clambered up beside him, water pouring from a dozen joints as he settled himself on his feet with a noisy shake. "So find her. Look after her now."

Morgan shrugged. "Sira wouldn't have left Pocular without a good reason, Huido. She could have reached me on the *Fox* if she needed me. Sira can look after herself," he paused. "You don't know how powerful she is."

"Ah."

Morgan looked at Huido suspiciously. "What do you mean, 'Ah'?"

"To prove your worth, you will bring Sira the head and hide of her enemies," Huido said as though suddenly comprehending the Human's mysterious motivations in a way that satisfied his own nature. "I will join you in this honorable hunt."

"No," Morgan said, gripping the claw tip of Huido's smaller arm. "I want you to find Sira, make sure she's safe."

"I thought you said she could look after herself."

"I don't want her to be alone," Morgan said, but added with brutal honesty to himself: *And I don't need any witnesses to what I may have to do.*

Chapter 16

THE Judgment Hall of the Drapsk was, well, a transport terminal.

We'd arrived, the bowlcar sighing to a stop amid a crowd of several hundred others—some occupied, some not. This observation was somewhat delayed on my part. I'd had to climb after my companions from the claustrophobic curl of the bowlcar, a process made possible by extrusions appearing in one side of the machine. Once I was at the top of the side, however, I could see quite well.

We were definitely in a transport terminal. I could see no evidence of any meeting place or even a doorway, just ranks of waiting bowlcars and much larger transports lined up and receiving passengers. Closed buildings surrounded the area. It was roofed, but with a transparent material revealing the darkening of the sky beyond the soft glow of the structures around us. The bowlcars fluoresced as well, I noticed, distracted, their surfaces slightly green.

"How far away is your Judgment Hall?" I asked, nudged into motion and into thinking by Maka's gentle tug on my elbow.

"This is it," said the tall Drapsk before Maka could answer. "Here you will join your Skeptic and proceed."

I thought seriously of digging in my heels to hold my little troop in place, but given we were immediately being carried in some direction by the floor itself, and that journey was through a confusing mass of vehicles disgorging their passengers to join us, I decided to go along. For now. I firmed the locate of the bridge of the *Makmora* in my thoughts and promised myself a trip back there at the first sign of trouble. Then they were welcome to try and convince me to step out on Drapskii again.

I was already tempted. "Proceed to where?" I demanded, trying to keep it polite. "Really, my good Drapsk, this is asking a bit much of me."

"You have been assigned to Skeptic Copelup," the hitherto silent orange-plumed Drapsk announced in remarkably high-pitched and precise Comspeak. "Hurry, Fem Morgan, or you will miss the last transport. Time is of the essence. Maka, you would leave such matters of import to the very last possible second."

"We had no idea she had accepted," that worthy protested. Another Drapsk, I wasn't sure which, joined the argument. Suddenly all of my little hosts were communicating verbally, all at once.

A shame it was in a place where it was impossible to catch more than every other word. I glared down at them, quite sure this abrupt switch to vocal communication had little to do with satisfying my questions and more to do with the difficulties of private conversation by olfaction in a crowd of what appeared to me to be every Drapsk ever born. I stuck to my escort in self-defense.

They were herding me toward the nearest transport, a long, sleek affair looking more like a beached whale than a vehicle. Since the strangely mobile flooring ended at an ankle-high ridge just before the transport, I braced myself for the step onto solid ground. Still, it took a second to readjust to having to move my feet to get anywhere.

I moved them. It was that or be trampled as the side of the transport opened and a chorus of Drapsk flooded down and out a broad ramp. This group consisted of two types of Drapsk, most identical, to my eyes, to the Makii, and the others all carbon copies of the tall, turquoise Drapsk now urging me up that same ramp. The overlapping layers of tossing yellow-red and purple-pink plumes were quite striking, especially when one added the ring of bright red tentacles around every mouth.

Once they were gone, I eyed the dark, apparently empty maw of the transport. *Enough was enough.* "I'm not going until you explain where you are taking me and why."

Immediately, all five of my Drapsk grasped some part of my anatomy or clothing and began to tug me forward. It was all gently done, as though I was being encouraged to overcome some fear. Nevertheless, I pulled back, getting ready to put some muscle into it if they continued.

A solitary cone of light appeared at the top of the ramp. A single Drapsk stood within it, yellow-streaked plumes rigidly aloft, a portable fan in one hand. I felt the breeze from the fan on my cheeks at the same instant as my escort stopped their poking and prodding. I didn't look at them, though from the sucking sounds I knew what they were all busy doing.

"Since they can explain nothing, Contestant Morgan—" the Drapsk on the ramp said in perfect Comspeak, his tone amused, "—and I can explain everything, I suggest you come aboard and allow this vessel to keep to her timetable."

"Skeptic Copelup, I assume?" I said, ignoring the last little urging pats from Maka, but finding myself climbing up the ramp anyway. "Frankly," I told him when I'd reached the top and entered his circle of light, "an explanation of anything at all would be a welcome change at this point."

"I am at your disposal."

To be more exact, Skeptic Copelup wasn't so much at my disposal as my time was supposedly at his.

As far as I could tell, we were the only passengers on the transport, which left almost immediately after the ramp had withdrawn and the side wall had closed. As in the bowlcar, there were no seats, but Copelup induced the floor to produce two of the stools I'd first seen on the *Makmora*.

"Your first question," he then said confidently, "is where are we going. I answer it. We are going to the remote border town which is home to this daring, this flamboyantly courageous Tribe of Makii. You must be isolated during your Judgment in order to prevent interference from other Tribes."

I opened my mouth, then closed it as the Drapsk waggled all eight fingers at me playfully. "Your second question, I also know. You want to know what purpose is served by going to this place. Yes?"

I nodded, mute with surprise at finally meeting an informative Drapsk.

"Ahh," intoned the Skeptic happily. "But I can't tell you that until you have passed Judgment."

I found myself grinding my teeth.

* * *

The Makii border town turned out to be a series of low, characteristically curved buildings set down along the edge of an expanse of grain fields for no particular reason I could see, other than it might be the right distance from every other border town we'd passed on the way. The transport hadn't waited for us, spitting us out on the sidewalk and rapidly folding itself back up before whooshing away. It wasn't quite an aircar, I could finally determine, but didn't travel on the surface either. The black interface between its base and the roadway looked remarkably like a crease in the M'hir. With the cheerful, talkative Skeptic at my side, and Drapsk—all visibly Makii—moving about on their business nearby, I kept my curiosity in check again.

While I'd renounced my own kind long ago, I spared a moment to acknowledge I was probably the only Clan who would—or could—function without constantly resorting to power. It had been a harsh lesson I'd arranged for myself, but that now had an unexpected value. No other Clan could have stepped on this odd world without exposing their connection to the M'hir at every turn. A pity I didn't plan to share whatever I learned with any of them.

Copelup had told me we would catch our final transport here. As we waited, we were caught in a little wayward storm—the kind that sends down heavy drops of rain almost as an afterthought, and never really wets anything. I held out my hand to intercept one of the single-minded drops before it disappeared on the hot pavement.

There, I had one. It was larger than a drop should be. And it had two eyes that regarded me without blinking.

"It's a fish!"

My companion bent over my palm, plumes waving, then straightened. "It's a fish," he agreed placidly. "What were you expecting? A sagecow?"

"I was expecting plain water," I said, tilting my hand so as to better examine my odd catch. Its eyes only appeared large because of the magnification of the drop that held it. The tiny body was curled around a whitish yellow yolk sac.

The water drop was shrinking as I watched, squeezing the hatchling into a tighter and tighter curl. It resisted with the occasional writhing motion. But there was nowhere to swim on my hand. "What do I do with it?" I asked.

My Drapsk chuckled. "What do you normally do with fish? Eat it!"

"Normal fish don't fall out of rain clouds," I said, avoiding this culinary suggestion.

"Then drop it on the street, Contestant Morgan."

I closed my fingers protectively about the cold speck of life. The Drapsk pointed to a crew of other Drapsk working at one end of the street. They were hosing down the barely wet pavement, sending rivulets of water into the channels along the street, and in the process quite tidily collecting all the fish before they could dry.

I turned over my hand and nothing happened. The fish was now firmly stuck to my skin. The Drapsk was making a rather dismal effort at controlling its amusement. I gently submerged my hand into the water now passing by my feet and shook it gently. The fish twitched once, then again, then was off and swimming to freedom.

"And you hunt for magic to bring to your world?" I said to my Drapsk guide, wiping my hand on my tunic. "Raining fish seems a fairly magical event."

Skeptic Copelup, rocked back on his heels in the way of someone insufferably pleased with himself. "No magic. No such thing, Contestant Morgan," he opined generously. "I'm here to prove that."

The sky was still spitting baby fish, so I backed under the roofed yet open framework I presumed functioned as a shelter for those waiting for transport. There would be terrible carnage—and a smell to match—on the town's rooftops unless the rain picked up enough to wash those unfortunate fishlings trapped there down to safety. "This happens a lot?" I asked doubtfully.

The Skeptic pursed his tiny mouth then answered me by reciting what had to be an encyclopedia entry. "The desert minnow lays drought-resistant eggs. When the streams and ponds dry, as they always do, the eggs are safe. They wait, in the sand, for the next rains, whether next season or the next decade. They wait, and wait, and wait."

I opened my mouth, thinking he was done. The Skeptic quelled me with an arrogant twitch of his plumes. "If a windstorm should happen to strike the desert, both sand and eggs will be whirled aloft. It does not take *magic*," this with scorn, "to explain what occurs when those eggs arrive in a moisture-laden storm cloud. And such storms track from the desert up to this area, and rain on the town."

"Here comes our transport," my Drapsk announced, quite cheerfully. I followed it, stepping carefully so as not to crush such well-traveled fish, and held my hands over my head to keep them out of my hair.

INTERLUDE

Even warmed and well-lit, as now, the cargo hold of the *Silver Fox* was not a comfortable part of the ship. Neither, Morgan thought, was this conversation.

"I'm not arguing, Brother," Huido said, a suspiciously saber-like click of his great handling claw hinting otherwise. "I merely state the difficulties. Where do you suggest I start looking?"

Morgan—busy unpacking the cases Huido had brought, by-passing Plexis' Port Authority being much easier for a station resident—glared at his friend. It was growing harder to restrain his anger, to keep from lashing out at random, especially when he was tired, as now, and frustrated, as always. A nightmare-haunted sleep spent trying to find Sira's body in a larger, darker, jungle hadn't improved his state of mind. "Ettler's Planet."

"Ettler's? Why there?"

"We'd planned, if anything happened to separate us, to meet here or on Ettler's. I wanted a rendezvous, a place with a lot of traffic and few regulations, somewhere two people could travel easily without being noticed." Morgan's voice trailed away as he remembered Sira's own interest in Ettler's, to complete the passage she'd negotiated from him during their first meeting on the *Fox,* when she'd been a desperate fugitive. She was curious about everything.

Grunting approval, Morgan unrolled the packaging that both protected and hid the several hi-tech and restricted objects within: Plexis being the best place to buy such equipment and conversely, one of the most difficult to smuggle it through. This had more to do with a desire to collect the appropriate taxes than to adhere to any particular Trade Pact regulations. He anticipated no problems; the *Fox*'s hold had a few unusual and well-proven hiding places of its own. He'd meant to show their secrets to Sira, but hadn't.

Odd. It was easier to remember Sira-of-the-past than focus on the present. His purpose continued to cloud her face in his mind. He forced himself to picture it, to see those gray eyes, sparkling with intelligence and warmth. He needed to know she was safe—at least, part of him did.

He needed Huido.

"I don't like Ettler's," that worthy grumbled as if on cue, plate sliding over plate with an irritated hiss. "It's a ball of dust. Why can't I go with you?"

"You won't have to go hiking in the dunes. You've got the list of meeting places we'd arranged—"

One of Huido's mobile eyes peered over the rim of his lower head plate to better examine the sheet of plas he held delicately in one clawtip. Two other claws were busy negotiating the passage of a mug of beer. Then the claws hesitated in midair, the beer only half-poured.

"Something isn't right," Huido stated, an ominous shudder under the words. Suddenly, all of his eyes riveted on Morgan. "Something about *you* isn't right, Blood Brother."

Morgan's hands tended to curl into fists these days. He deliberately flattened both, palms down on his knees, before asking: "How so?"

Huido turned down the tip of one claw, a gesture meaning a foul taste or a warning of poison. "Your *grist*. Now I smell it clearly. And it carries the taint of another's."

"You know Sira gave me some of her strength—" Morgan found himself beginning to explain.

The Carasian's broad head tilted, all eyes disconcertingly stayed level within the shadowed gap. "I have scented you since that time, Brother. This is different. Have you been attacked by one of the Clan?" A pause, then a repeat of the saber-rattling sound. "Would you know?"

I know, Morgan thought sadly, but to himself. Huido's suspicion only added evidence to his own, that Sira had unintentionally imposed her rage, her need for revenge, on top of his when she sent him after her enemies. "What you sense about me is not from an attack, Huido," he said slowly, struggling to find an explanation for the non-telepathic being. "When we parted, Sira—gave me more of herself. She knew I'd need it to deal with her enemies."

"A gift?" Huido growled. "It smells to me like a curse."

Morgan whirled angrily, fists raised. "You know nothing about it—nothing! Are you going to help me or not?"

The echoes of his shout filled the cargo hold, curling around the edges of bulkheads, knocking at open cases of weaponry—legal and otherwise—before sighing to silence over the hoard laid out for inspection on the low table between them. Morgan made himself drop his hands, unclenching his fists, shuddering with the effort to regain his composure.

The Carasian might have been a carving, save for the movements necessary to continue pouring beer into the orifice at the tip of his top righthand claw, then to tuck that claw tip into the dark boundary serving him as a face. Clearly, he chose not to take offense, however justified.

"Huido," Morgan began unsteadily. "I'm sorry—" His control of the rage wasn't as tight as he'd hoped. More reason to get away from anyone he cared about, where he could be free to loose it. He made himself sit back down.

A satisfied slurp. Then Huido said ponderously: "Something about all this, about you, my Blood Brother, reminds me of long ago."

"I don't know what—"

The raising of a large claw silenced Morgan's protest. "When we met, Brother. Then you owned such anger as this."

Morgan remembered. *How could he not?* "Different times, Huido," he countered wearily, running one hand through his hair as though it would soothe the ache there. "I was hardly more than a kid."

"You had been betrayed."

"The past doesn't matter."

"You had been betrayed," Huido repeated, eyes converging to focus completely on Morgan, an unnerving amount of attention. "And you wanted revenge. I had never seen such rage in a being before, nor since. Until now."

Morgan sighed. "I take it you have a point?"

Huido said slowly: "Only that you be careful. Your rage almost destroyed you once. You are not that young Human, granted, but now you have even more power, more anger. I would not see you turn it on yourself."

"No chance of that, my Brother," Morgan said almost lightly. "This time I have a target within reach."

Before the Carasian could respond, the Human changed the subject. "Now, let's go see if Hom K'tar has filled my order yet, shall we?"

Chapter 17

"HUMANS?"

Copelup nodded his blind head, yellow plumes waving. "There is no Embassy for your kind here," he reminded me unnecessarily. There were no Clan Embassies on any world, Trade Pact or otherwise.

I gazed out the windows of the local transport, grateful for the chance to see my surroundings for once, and asked the obvious: "What's an Embassy of any species doing in a border town? They belong on Embassy Row, near the shipcity."

"Embassy may not be the correct term," he said apologetically, after hesitating a moment. I suspected the precise Drapsk was embarrassed. "I believe the Humans maintain this building and staff in order to exchange agricultural knowledge with the Makii. They have always been an adventurous Tribe—good traders, if prone to bringing home just about anything."

Since that last seemed a dig at me, I ignored it. I was learning to enjoy my sparring conversations with the Skeptic. He was opinionated, clever, and—whether deliberately or not—often funny. For my part, I seemed to supply him with all the openings he needed to make his point. *If only,* I sighed to myself, *the being were a bit more forthcoming on the information I needed.*

What he did tell me was that I was to stay in the home of Madeline and Cory Brightson, a Human pair apparently overjoyed to host one of the Contestants for the upcoming Festival. Possible Contestant, as Copelup would doubtless remind me. I wondered if the Humans knew any more than I did. I also wondered if I could enlist their aid to get off Drapskii before becoming a Contestant at all.

* * *

As I'd expected, though friendly and pleased to have another Human for company—a small and convenient deceit I noticed Copelup allowed me without comment—the Brightsons were as ignorant as I about what being a Contestant entailed. On the other hand, they were far more excited. This year's Festival, it seemed, would be their first and was touted as the high point of the Drapsk calendar.

"Only happens once every two years," Madeline had assured me as she showed me my room, a cubbyhole off the main agrilab, but with refreshingly angular Human furniture, including a comfortable-looking bed without a curve to be seen. "We hadn't been assigned here in time for the last one, but the Murtrees told us all about it."

Before I could ask for more details—and more importantly, begin negotiations about my primary goal, to leave—a small voice called impatiently and furiously from somewhere down the long hallway. "Mom, there's no grats left. Linda ate them all!"

Madeline smiled apologetically. "Kids. You know how they are." Actually, I didn't, not having met more than a handful of Clan offspring in my lifetime, and no Human children beyond those avoided underfoot in crowds. *Children.* I found the entire concept more foreign than the Drapsk.

"Supper's at five, Fem Morgan. We operate very casually here. Just use the com if you need anything. Coming!" she shouted, moving away at a rapid pace that suggested whatever trouble was ahead had better look out.

I eyed the com panel. As well announce directly to Copelup that I planned to evade him.

During the flurry of introductions in the front office of the Humans' research facility-cum-residence, I'd been showered with names, duties, and relationships I knew would be impossible to keep straight. The Skeptic had stood silently to one side, plumes atwitch. He was staying as well, somewhere, an accommodation within the overwhelmingly Human-scented building I suspected must be difficult for the Drapsk. I would have also suspected him of being amused by my slight cringing during the effusive welcome from the Brightson family, if it hadn't been for the tentacle slipping inside his mouth for some discreet, troubled, sucking.

So despite the warmth of the welcome, the confusion and foreboding of entering a mass of excited humanity, and the honest exhaustion I felt, there was room for troubling thoughts. Whatever was going on here was important to the Drapsk. *And what was important to them,* I suspected glumly, *was going to interfere nicely with my plans to leave.*

"More dessert, Sira?"

"No, thank you, Cory," I said quickly, discovering no room left for what I'd already eaten, let alone space for more. Then I covered up a yawn. I'd tried for a quick nap before supper, but that attempt failed when Copelup showed up at my door interested in my opinion of several music tapes. I hadn't been sure if he wanted to test the limits of my hearing or simply drive me mad. The bell announcing this meal had been rescue indeed.

Or would have been, I thought, *if supper with the Brightsons had involved more eating and less competitive vocalizing.*

Between the bedlam of fifteen adult Humans and their six variously-aged offspring, I found myself seriously wondering if Copelup had tested my hearing to see if I could survive this.

There was one advantage. I'd been given a seat thoughtfully away from the youngest children, whom I observed needed to physically subdue their food before consuming it with owl-like looks of satisfaction. This arrangement put me beside Grant Murtree, the very same person I'd been told had attended the last Festival. Copelup sat with another Drapsk at the end of the table—its placement near an open window surely meant as kindness in a room redolent with food aromas and warm mammal. The Humans politely wore no perfumes, but there was a certain tang to the air even I noticed. After a comment from one of my Human hosts, one of the younger Murtrees was removed, not without a wordless howl of complaint, from the room.

I could feel Copelup's attention on me throughout the meal, but I thought he was too far away to hear any conversation. Regardless, I kept my voice low as I continued pumping my table companion for information.

"You were saying, Grant, the Festival is attended by offworlders as well as representatives from all of the Tribes?"

Like the Brightsons, and almost all of the Humans at the table, Grant Murtree was short, slightly rounder than most Humans of my acquaintance, swarthy of complexion, and tended to squint fiercely. I found out later this resemblance was due to most of the agricultural staff being selected from the same Human world, Ladin 5, in order to provide the Drapsk with a physically similar Human Tribe. Humans could be very accommodating to local custom when they wished.

Grant's voice was soft and well-educated, the only accent to his Comspeak a rather charming tendency to lengthen his vowels. "Allie's the one who really pays attention to the social details here," he admitted, as if this were a lack I'd find reprehensible. "My specialty is plant engineering. You should ask her, Fem Morgan."

Since Allie was the Human who'd removed her odiferous offspring moments before, she was unlikely to be back soon enough to answer my questions, but I didn't bother to point this out. "Call me Sira, please," I said.

"Sira," he acknowledged with a nod. "But you're a Contestant. Surely they've told you all about it."

"You'd be surprised," I said darkly.

The Human chuckled. "Maybe not. Working with the Drapsk frequently involves, shall I say, unpredictable gaps in information?" He offered, then poured me more sombay. The noise level was dropping as children vanished from the room, but I trusted it would still keep most of what we said private. "Take the Festival," Grant continued. "A great deal of it is similar to celebrations you'd find on any Human settlement: lots of food and drink, music, entertainment. There's an exchange of gifts, but we were advised not to participate."

"Why?"

Grant smiled. "We suspect the gifts are along the lines of betrothal exchanges. Not exactly within the scope of our arrangements here."

Betrothal? "Then the Festival has something to do with their," I paused delicately, "reproductive processes?"

Madeline had been leaning over, listening to this last exchange. "We're not sure about that," she interjected, with an involuntary glance at the Drapsk at the other end of the room. "Norm's made a few discreet inquiries—he's our animal physiologist—but they've been very—reticent about their biology."

"Many species are," I noted dryly.

She colored. "Well, naturally we didn't pry further, but from what Allie told us, the Festival does involve some kind of selection or sorting process."

"We think that in some way they use the Festival to determine the numbers within each Tribe for the upcoming generation," Grant added. "After the last one, the Pardii Tribe doubled—at the expense of the Tookii, who went from owning mines in the foothills to working on farms near here."

"They doubled in what sense?" I asked, puzzled. "More offspring?"

"We've never seen an immature Drapsk," Madeline volunteered, again with an uneasy glance at Copelup, who was now thoughtfully sucking most of his tentacles as he sat aimed in our direction. "It's not something you can ask about, you know."

Grant explained: "I can't say if they doubled exactly—Norm thinks so, but we don't have any stats to back it. But within weeks of the Festival, there were Pardii wherever one went in the foothills, and they'd been rather rare before."

All this was fascinating, and information I would definitely pass along to Morgan, but it wasn't helping me. "Grant. Madeline. I need to get to the shipcity and leave Drapskii. Tonight, if possible."

Both smiled wisely and shook their heads—not exactly the reaction I'd expected. "Please don't worry, Sira," Madeline said in a gentle, humoring voice. "Copelup's told us how nervous you are about competing. He said you might panic a bit as it approached. But it will be all right. You'll see."

"And it's very important to them, you know," Grant added seriously, as if there could be no doubt of the significance of what the Drapsk wanted.

"Oh, I know," I replied glumly, glaring down the table at Copelup. Another plan scuttled. I found a smile somewhere and asked brightly: "So, what can you tell me about the actual Competition?"

These Humans had been on Drapskii too long. "We couldn't

tell you even if we knew, Sira," Madeline answered. "The Drapsk were very specific in what we can talk about with you."

I waved at Copelup, who was coming my way as supper unofficially drew to its conclusion—most of the Humans rising with mutters of tasks to be done. "Why am I not surprised by that either?" I said, but not accusingly. These were my hosts, after all.

And apparently in charge of my entertainment as well, for no sooner had I stood to return to my room, when Cory Brightson reappeared at my elbow, beaming from ear to ear. "We're leaving for the game in about thirty minutes, Sira. Okay?"

"Great," Grant Murtree spoke up before I could so much as open my mouth. "This will take your mind off the competition," he added with a meaningful look. "Just what you need."

"Can't wait," I said weakly, wondering what I was in for now.

INTERLUDE

The group had met in secret, made decisions without her, and left this message planted in the mind of her servant. Rael waved one hand in dismissal, having pulled the information from the young Denebian's thoughts with the subtlest of touches.

It paid to have good help.

Find Sira. Larimar following Morgan. Enlist Pella's aid for the cause.

The message, such as it was, bore the taste of Ru di Mendolar's sarcasm. Or perhaps it was Rael's own interpretation of the likelihood of success for any of its components.

Find Sira? Rael upended her case on the bed where a servant would find the pile of clothing and unobtrusively deal with it. If Sira didn't want to be found, she wouldn't be. Simple as that.

Larimar following Morgan? Rael kicked off her shoes, sliding her toes, with their floral stencils, into a pair of slippers. No one could say she hadn't warned them. Setting a tracker on the Human was about the surest way she could imagine to bring their group—and its aims—to his attention.

Enlist Pella? Rael walked slowly to her balcony, drawing the delicate scent of night-blooming flowers into her nostrils, gazing up at the dusting of stars overhead. The air was, as always, warm and caressing on her skin. She would talk to her sister, for whatever good the group thought it might do. There was little risk; Pella was no more fond of the present Council than any of them and wouldn't bother to betray them.

But enlist her self-centered, self-serving nature to the cause—or to any purpose that wasn't of immediate benefit to Pella herself?

Rael thought it more likely the Denebian sun would rise at the snap of her fingers.

Chapter 18

IT was, beyond any doubt, the strangest thing I had ever seen. And while I hadn't traveled Morgan's great distances across the known galaxy, I'd lived a good deal longer than most of my kind—having waited unChosen and unchanged for the better part of two generations—so I could truthfully say I'd seen my share.

But this?

I sat on the hard bench, my feet barely fitting on the floor before the back of the next row in front of me, my breath coming out in frosty puffs, and pulled my borrowed coat more tightly around my shoulders. Below me was a perfect oval of white ice; above was an arching roof, well-insulated against the daytime's remaining heat.

We were here, I'd been informed proudly by Copelup, to watch a game introduced by the Humans and taken up with a passion by the Makii Drapsk. It was called hockey.

"Hot sombay, Sira?" A cup was pressed into my numb fingers and I accepted its promise of warmth gratefully. Madeline Brightson sat down beside me, tossing a corner of a thermal wrap over my knees before tucking the remainder over her own lap.

"Th–thanks, Madeline," I stuttered. The oval of ice was surrounded by a ring of benchlike seating, about twenty rows in total, at the moment almost completely filled by Drapsk. As they were all of the Makii Tribe, with the exception of Copelup on my right, the effect was that of a giant eye, pupiled in white within an iris of purple. The tiny cluster of Humans and other non-Drapsk around me hardly dented the pattern.

"Best to warm up now," my guide advised, turning on the

wrap. Lifesaving warmth began creeping around my legs. "If you get chilled, it's a lot harder to be comfortable."

Feeling chilled already, I turned guiltily to Copelup. "Did you want to share some of this?" I asked, not quite sure how far the material would stretch. If necessary, I supposed the Drapsk could sit on my knees.

He dipped his plumes to touch my hand briefly. "My thanks, Contestant Morgan, but this temperature is not a hardship to my kind."

A Human elbow nudged my rib cage. "If you think this is cold, just wait until the Drapsk turn on their system."

I sat between the Human and the Drapsk, neither about to answer any truly useful questions, and wondered with a shivering yawn how much of this I had to endure before being allowed back to my room. And that lovely-looking bed.

"Here they come," crowed Allie Murtree, tapping me on my shoulder as she leaned over me to point at the row of figures moving on to the ice. They were, I observed with a sense of complete confusion, balancing on what looked to be knife edges. As I watched intently, it was obvious these edges were giving each of the figures remarkable traction on what had to be a very slippery surface.

Judging from the stafflike weapon each carried, and the abundance of body armor covering all but the plumes of the Drapsk participants, I resigned myself to some sort of gladiatorial game, thinking much less of both the Drapsk and the Humans.

"There's Linda," Madeline announced.

I readjusted my thinking, finding it unreasonable the pleasant woman beside me would allow her young daughter to battle for spectators.

"Perhaps you'd care for an explanation of the game before it begins, Contestant Morgan?" Copelup intruded slyly.

I weighed the potential embarrassment—and boredom—of remaining ignorant against having to put up with Copelup's doubtless unending rounds of self-congratulation. Curiosity won.

"So," I said, minutes later, not sure if I'd made a good bargain after all, "both teams compete for the puck. The team that retrieves it successfully makes an attempt to put the puck into the other team's net. Each net entry is called a goal. The team with the most goals wins. That's it?"

Madeline had been enjoying my lecture from the Drapsk immensely. There was a feather of laughter in her voice as she said: "You'll learn it faster by watching, Sira. They're about to start."

Starting involved an ear-shattering buzz, a roar from those around me who vocalized under excitement, and a furious bout of synchronized plume fluttering by the Drapsk. I paid no attention to my neighbors, instantly absorbed in the action below.

I'd been warned the players were not professionals. In fact, several were the children of the Humans from the agri-lab, the adults playing separately so as not to risk harming the child-sized Drapsk who, Madeline informed me, had formed a substantial waiting list for a chance to strap on skates, equipment, and grab a stick.

They may not have been experts, but to my eyes there was an immense amount of skill being exhibited by all concerned. To move quickly in a straight line on ice was one thing—I was reasonably sure with a sufficiently vigorous push, I could do the same. But to stop in a cloud of snow, to whirl and dodge past opponents? The Human players, all lanky limbs and prone to tumble for no reason I could detect, kept pace with the slower but sturdy Drapsk and their advantage of a low center of gravity. I forgot all about my numb toes.

"When does it go in the net?" I asked after a furious passage of puck from stick to stick to stick.

"Now!" shouted everyone around me as the small black object soared past the well-protected head of the Human goalie.

Madeline distracted me by immediately yanking the thermal wrap up to our chins. From the feel of it, she'd also raised the temperature. I was about to protest, when a sudden roar overhead explained her precaution.

The Drapsk system she'd warned me about was now in full gear. A series of fans directed a virtual storm wind down our necks and over our shoulders. Just as I was trying to decide whether they meant to kill us by hypothermia or deafen us all, the fans stopped.

"What was that for?" my question rang out regrettably loudly in the relative silence. Several Humans coughed or chuckled. "Cheering," Copelup said from beside me. "It is a time-honored part of sports, Contestant Sira."

I grew accustomed to the cold, including the galelike cheers of the Drapsk, and understood the game sufficiently by its end to appreciate some of the better moves. It ended in a tie, a score greeted with more enthusiasm by my immediate neighbors than I'd expected from their partisan commentary throughout. Perhaps I didn't understand the game after all.

I certainly didn't understand the motivation of the Drapsk, something that kept me silent and in thought as we marched from our seats.

"You are puzzled, Contestant Morgan," Copelup stated, reading me correctly.

I nodded. We waited by the arena's doors for the Humans to obtain their vehicles. Fortunately, the Drapsk and I would go back to our residence immediately, while others waited for their respective offspring to shed their hockey gear. I was tired enough to lean against one Drapsk-smooth wall. "Yes, I'm puzzled, Skeptic Copelup. Any chance you'd answer questions about this sport?"

He waved a four-fingered hand in amusement. "Ask!"

"The fans carried your cheers to the ice surface, where they could be detected by the Drapsk players, correct?"

"Correct," he agreed. "It would otherwise be very difficult to communicate. The air tends to rise in the arena."

"And you said it was 'cheering.' "

"Correct again, Contestant Morgan. You have grasped matters well."

I raised an eyebrow for my own benefit, watching his ring of six fleshy tentacles for want of a better clue on that eyeless globe of a face. "I'm not entirely sure I have, Copelup. Your people 'cheered' regularly, at exactly the same intervals following the first goal. Was I missing something?"

"No, no. That is correct, too. You are most observant."

"Then you often cheered when there was nothing worth cheering for, and failed to cheer when there was—unless I missed the key strategy of the game," which was, I confessed to myself, possible.

Copelup rocked back and forth on his feet, a sign of thoughtful consideration. *Maybe.* "You are not the first to question this," he said at last. "While I do not understand how this confuses other species, I will attempt to explain the obvious. We perform the *empakii*—cheer—to inspire effort, not as appreciation for some outcome or skill."

"That seems very well-mannered of you. And hardly confusing," I agreed.

"Of course," Copelup said more quietly, looking around as if in fear of eavesdroppers, "we are careful to ensure that only those who understand the game are in the arena, so all know when to provide *amapka*—the discouragement—to the appropriate team."

"Discouragement?" I echoed, somehow sure the Drapsk was about to dispel any understanding of their nature I foolishly thought I might have gained tonight.

"Surely you noticed that the Drapsk of both teams were Makii, Contestant Morgan."

"Yes," I said warily.

"The Tribe is the unit of our society," he recited seriously. "We do not approve of winning within the Tribe any more than we approve of losing, Contestant Morgan. So we must provide amapka to the team in the lead, or else they might exert themselves and attain a position of superiority over the other team."

"So it was no accident the game ended in a tie."

Copelup stretched himself to his full height, saying proudly, "All games within a Tribe end in a tie, Contestant Morgan. It is the only satisfactory resolution."

A passing Human herding a young player still in equipment, carrying a bag bigger than himself, overheard this last comment and winked at me. He held up four fingers, then pantomimed a yawn, adding: "No matter how many overtime periods it takes."

When I was finally granted the asylum of a dark room, closed door, and warm bed, perversely, I couldn't relax. Sleep was out of the question, even if my eyes ached unless shut. My thoughts milled around, attempting to force sense from the bits and pieces I'd acquired about the Drapsk and what lay ahead of me.

I still had no idea if I was being judged whenever Copelup and I were together, or if there remained some day of reckoning to come. If so, I hoped he was mannerly enough to inform me when it arrived.

I'd made some progress toward my escape, in a way. I'd managed to find out where I was. Drapskii wasn't too far—by translight—from the planet Auord, a world I'd visited before and so could locate through the M'hir. That distance, however, was considerably beyond what I'd ever attempted, and I seriously doubted there would be pathways of power leading from Drapskii to aid me. It was an effort I'd make only if given no other choice. There were other, more mundane options, starting with the shipcity and its starships.

I seriously thought about 'porting to the walkway near the *Makmora.* The locate was crystal clear in my mind. However, less clear was what I could do once there. I had no way to pay for passage. Could I sneak aboard a ship loading cargo? A hundred schemes ran through my mind, each less practical than the last.

And what about the Drapsk? There was something about the little beings, something uncanny enough to tangle my thoughts whenever I considered leaving. How could I compete for a species that refused to permit winners or losers? What did they want from me?

I turned over the pillow and gave it an unnecessary punch. I knew what I wanted. I wanted to find Morgan.

And say what to him? I asked myself. The fresh surface of the case took some of the heat from my flushed cheek. "Hello, Jason," I muttered into it. "Found any bits of me yet?"

I rolled on my back and stared up in the dark. "I don't care about them anymore," I said softly, surprised it was true. I no longer even cared much about my enemies, though I'd been contently fanning my anger against them throughout the past year.

Then what did I want? Tired, lonely, and alone, there was only one thing. I couldn't stop myself from throwing all the power I possessed into one urgent sending, one plea into the seething turmoil of the M'hir.

Perhaps I should have cared who might overhear. It didn't matter. Nothing mattered suddenly but making sure Morgan was all right, that he knew I wanted him back with me and not out there.

It was a dangerous extension of myself. I risked sanity as well as my grip on the body lying in that bed in the Makii border town on Drapskii. But I dared the heart-search, pouring everything into my image of Jason Morgan, the other, missing, half of myself.

... *darkness* ... I floated, drifting in a landscape of energy pathways and nothingness, myself the brightest object until, at a distance, I spotted something familiar. I pushed myself toward it, reaching desperately for contact, until I touched ... *a tiny core of light surrounded by madness, guarded by rage* ...
... and was flung back into myself.

I knew that rage, that overwhelming anger. It wasn't Morgan's, not wholly. What I'd tasted around his consciousness, blocking me out more effectively than any shielding I'd taught him, had come from me.

What had I done to him?

My body shivered as though I was still at the Drapsk hockey arena. I realized without caring I'd probably come close to life-threatening convulsions as I'd drained myself, although I would have regretted causing my hosts the distress of finding my corpse.

Everything—my thoughts, my surroundings—clarified and grew still.

I would leave here in the morning. I would find Morgan. I would remove the poison of my hate from his mind and return it to my own.

Where it belonged.

INTERLUDE

"Your air tag, Hom Sarc?"

Barac kept his distaste to himself, smiling graciously at the Human female operating the tag point. He leaned forward, anticipating her next request.

"Do you accept responsibility for the air you share on Plexis?" she asked. At close range, she gazed up at him through her tinted lashes and returned his smile. When he nodded, she tapped his cheek once lightly to affix the tag to his skin.

The Clansman backed away as quickly as possible without being obvious. *Humans,* he thought with disgust. He'd experienced such reactions to his appearance frequently in his various roles as spy for the Clan. It didn't make it any easier to tolerate. As if any of their Talentless females could attract him.

He slipped into the flow of foot traffic entering the mid-range shopping concourse, deliberately walking close behind a mixed group of Humans—Denebians from the revealing and expensive cut of their clothing. This was familiar territory to the former Clan scout, his tension soothed by the very inconspicuousness of being one more in the crowd. Humans made excellent camouflage, even if they could be annoying.

And dangerous in numbers, Barac reminded himself, feeling a new tightness in his throat as he gazed ahead. The concourse was carpeted with Humans and other aliens, the occasional stilt-like servos and their draperies of packages rising above the heads like bizarre furnishings. This was the most popular level of Plexis, the massive station stuffed with the shops and merchants from a hundred Inner planets, though Barac knew the remaining levels would be just as packed. It had been a brilliant idea, to bring the marketplace to the customers. Those in the Fringe were eager to spend their credits.

Barac found the rampway he sought, leaning nonchalantly against its railing as the device, with its endless ranks of passengers, carried him down. He maintained a watchful presence in the M'hir. Once this had been his habit in order to spot those of his kind he was to contact. *Now,* he acknowledged grimly to himself, *it would warn him.* As self-proclaimed exile, he was fair game, outside the few laws held by his kind. And Plexis was reasonably popular with the Clan, particularly the upper floors with their quietly exclusive shops.

He checked the address on the sheet of plas in his hand. The place was sublevel 384, predominantly a wholesalers' district, and 1/3 spinward, a section of restaurants and other entertainments; Barac could ignore the remaining coordinates until he was closer to his destination. He wasn't at all sure what he'd say to Morgan, if the Human were there. Rael had secrets? Hardly likely to surprise the Human, even if Barac himself found it hard to believe of his luxury-loving, self-centered cousin.

"Sorry, Hom."

Barac grunted with surprise as the being, a Human, knocked him sideways just as the ramp reached the next level. A nearby guard stirred, ready to intervene. Given the customer gold of Barac's tag and the "here-on-business" blue of the clumsy Human, it would be the Human shuffled off to give an explanation.

Barac waved the guard away, glancing briefly at the Human—thin, bearded, and dressed in nondescript once-white coveralls, his work belt stuffed with gadgetry the Clansman couldn't identify. "No problem," the Clansman said graciously, fighting the temptation to check his own clothing for grease stains.

As he started to walk away, the incident forgotten, the Human caught up to him. "Sorry. Sorry, Hom. My foot slipped. Sorry." His voice was an irritating whine, like a machine overdue for lubrication.

Unwillingly, Barac found himself drawn into responding; anything less would have been more noticeable than what had happened already. "Think nothing of it, Hom," he said firmly. "Good day."

Three quick strides into the flow of traffic put the Human out of sight behind a troop of Ordnex musicians and as easily out of Barac's thoughts.

Chapter 19

MY sending to Morgan had had an unexpected but, as I thought to myself with disgust, perfectly predictable result.

I had been Judged.

My first intimation of a change in my status came when I woke and went to breakfast. The building was oddly quiet, no thunder of small feet, no reassuring drone of adult voices from the labs I passed on the way to the dining area. The place appeared deserted.

Full of my own determination to leave, I saw this only as a bonus. There would be time to grab a quick bite—I was starving after the night's exertions at the arena and in the M'hir—before trying my luck at finding transport offworld in the Drapsk shipcity. If the Humans had left their building for some reason, their timing couldn't have pleased me more.

The long table where we'd sat for supper was again loaded with plates, cutlery, and platters of food. I helped myself to a sweet roll, only then noticing the plates were half-filled. Steam curled above a cup of sombay near my hand. Chairs were pulled back as though their inhabitants had jumped up and run. *From what? And why?* I sank my teeth into the roll, capturing a second one as I looked around. If there'd been an emergency—whether biologicals loose in the lab or fire in the kitchen—surely they'd have come for me, too. For some reason, I was still not alarmed. It wasn't that I didn't care about the Humans; it was more, I decided numbly, as though my decision to leave meant I had no ties left here.

So be it. Their disappearance would have to remain a mystery. I swallowed a too-hot mouthful of sombay from the nearest cup, then formed the locate I'd chosen: a branch of the walkway near the *Makmora*. *I pushed . . .*

And found myself staring at the abandoned table, reeling with the impact of power thwarted against a familiar prickly wall.

"Are you ready to go, Contestant Morgan?" came a voice I knew too well from behind me. I whirled to glare down at the Drapsk. "Don't worry about the Humans. They ran outside to greet the transport bringing the plussard chicks—"

"What have you done?"

Skeptic Copelup looked insufferably pleased with himself. His plumes were bright yellow and spread wide enough to fill the doorway, his red tentacles fanned out in a perfect ring around his bud of a mouth. "It is what you have done, Contestant Morgan—forgive me—O Mystic One. You have succeeded in your quest."

"What quest?" I growled, ready to use some of the sharper implements behind me if the small being didn't get out of my way.

He raised one hand, holding out a small boxlike device I hadn't noticed until now. "Right off the scale. Most impressive. Simply the strongest readings I have ever recorded."

I felt an inner shock as I finally, stupidly, understood. The Drapsk did know about the M'hir. They knew enough to use technology to monitor it, to somehow measure my sending to Morgan last night. They were capable of blocking my movements through it at will, whether on the ship or here.

Their search for magic took on an entirely unamusing and threatening light. "Why do you hunt magic, Copelup?" I asked, suddenly sure this was the right question.

"Ours has been lost," he answered promptly, if cryptically, hurrying forward to take my unresisting hand in his smaller, warmer one. "Now come. Ask your questions as we go, O Mystic One. It's time we returned to the city. The Festival is about to begin." He paused and I felt a feather's touch on my cheek. "You have a vital place in it. The Makii were quite right about you, quite right," he muttered, pulling me with him. "You may just be the one."

Predictably, my promotion to Contestant and confirmed Mystic One hadn't loosened the Drapsk's tongue on anything of major import. As we endured the windowless return trip by an identical transport to the one which had brought me to the Makii border town only yesterday—at least heading in the direction I wished—he told me about the scheduling of the Contest, in two Drapskii days, but not what the Contest would be. He assured me it wasn't dangerous, then sucked all of his tentacles for an alarming amount of time. And, finally, I learned who I was supposed to compete against.

Or rather *what*. "The planet?"

"There will be other sapient beings competing for this privilege, selected by Tribes less fortunate or perceptive than the Makii. But yes," Copelup admitted, "for you, the main competition will be Drapskii itself."

I mulled this over for a moment, distracted by a growl from my stomach. Not enough breakfast and far too much secrecy. "You aren't," I asked suspiciously, "proposing some kind of outdoor endurance test, are you?"

Copelup hooted, a new sound from a Drapsk. As he continued doing this, loudly, for some time, I decided to ignore him, standing and pacing around our featureless compartment.

Finally the hoots were replaced by what sounded remarkably like hiccups. "My profound apologies, Mystic One," the little being gasped. "I had no idea you had such a sense of humor."

"Neither did I," I replied, despite knowing any sarcasm was wasted. "You could answer my question."

A single hoot made its way out before Copelup gained control of himself. "No. It is not a physical trial, Mystic One. All will begin and end within the city. You'll see."

I ran my fingers over the smooth, soft wall of the compartment, wondering if I dared remind the Drapsk I had no intention of participating in its competition or Festival. Morgan was out there, somewhere, being driven to recklessness and danger by the rage I'd shoved into his helpless mind. I had no time or desire to entertain these creatures at their Contest.

No, I wouldn't bother with words. And there were other ways to leave a world than through the M'hir. This transport would take me conveniently near them.

Given I could make my way through a city of Drapsk.

INTERLUDE

Morgan took his time, checking the goods displayed on the countertop in front of him as though the relative quality of antique table linens was the top priority of his day. Finally, he chose four at random and waved his ident disk at the proprietor of the small store, who blinked all three eyes in apparent surprise at having made a sale. By the dust, the linens had been there since Plexis opened for business. "Deliver to this address, packed for vacuum stowage," Morgan ordered. Then he took a few steps and started the same process again before a towering stack of used footgear. Behind him, the proprietor crooned to itself, a happy sound punctuated by the occasional cough as its tentacles stirred up more dust. Whirtles were sensitive to particulates. This one probably wore a respirator when its store lacked customers.

There.

His lips pressed together in satisfaction as Morgan caught another glimpse of his tracker in the corner of one eye.

Big, humanoid. He'd make no assumptions about species. Spacer coveralls, but with a gold customer patch on the cheek. The coveralls had sharp creases along the leg. Brand new, then. "Two dozen pairs," Morgan announced calmly, sending the proprietor into obvious ecstasy. "Same address. I know a collector."

As the Whirtle humped forward to start dismantling a display that likely hadn't been touched since it was first prepared, Morgan continued casually: "Do you have any more?"

The Whirtle hugged itself. "In the back room, perceptive and wise customer. There are crates and crates and crates." It realized this might have sounded more of a complaint than opportunity and amended: "All very rare. All pieces exclusive to this shop. Would you—would you care to view them?"

"Absolutely," Morgan announced, giving the being a gentle push in the right direction when it seemed paralyzed with joy. "Lead the way."

And out the corner of his eye, he watched a big, humanoid figure in spacer coveralls fade back into the crowd outside the store, becoming just another silhouette in the night-dimmed concourse.

Chapter 20

MORGAN had never explained to me the source of his more arcane skills. For instance, I didn't know why a trader with his own ship would need to know how to open other being's locks. I was only grateful he'd bothered to show me.

The Drapsk, for all they loved architecture without corners or visible technology, still needed doors within their buildings—especially, I thought dryly, in buildings they intended to use as prisons. Oh, the suite of rooms was luxurious enough, and no one had so much as implied I couldn't leave when I wanted. But there was the small matter of the locked door.

A locked door had a mechanism I could deal with—maybe.

I didn't know how long I'd have before the Drapsk returned. On our arrival in the city, Copelup and I had been greeted at the transport terminal by the same trio of unnamed Drapsk who had delivered me to him. The Makii, Captain Maka and his officer, Makoori, were conspicuously absent. I found I missed them, granted they were unlikely to sympathize with my desire to desert their Tribe.

My escort had taken me to what might have been the Drapsk version of a hotel. Certainly the main floor had walls that bulged outward to hold what appeared to be a series of restaurants, all deserted, and odd little cubicles I thought might accommodate biological necessities as on the *Makmora,* but which turned out to be communication pods.

We'd taken a lift to the floor I was on, a process I watched as closely as I could without making myself obvious. The controls were simple to operate; the trick was discovering how the Drapsk coaxed the panel from its hiding place inside the wall. I memorized the short sequence of rapid taps the creature gave, hoping there was nothing more sophisticated than the code. A biosensor would stop my flight in an instant.

First, however, I had to pass through this door. I'd tried the M'hir, very carefully and with a disquieting sense of exposure. I had no idea how sensitive their devices could be. It was irrelevant. However they locked me from the M'hir was as effective here and now as before.

But the lock on the door was another matter. I rapped experimentally on the wall around where the door had been— Drapsk-doors tending to vanish politely and with disconcerting completeness when closed—and was rewarded with an open panel within seconds. The switch and lock were, as I'd expected, inconveniently free of ways to access their underlying mechanism. No matter. *That's what plumbing is for,* I recited Morgan's instructions to myself as I swung the length of metal I'd detached from the workings of the fresher in the bedroom stall, smashing right through the remarkably fragile material of the switch.

Fortunately, this was an ordinary room, with an ordinary lock meant more for privacy than prisoners. I'd counted on that. As my second assault caused an arching and burning-plas stench, the door sighed open, the lock quite rightly set to release as a safety measure in the event of power failure or fire.

I didn't care which, the result being the same. I grabbed the bag of supplies I'd scrounged from the room during my hours there, before peering out the now-open door into the hallway. *Empty.*

The Clan part of me hesitated, longing to release a tendril of thought, to confirm what might wait around the corner leading to the lift. The Morgan part of me decided this was silly, since I couldn't sense the Drapsk anyway, and propelled me forward in a bold, confident stride that would hopefully confuse any being looking for an escaped prisoner.

I made it to the lift, its door opening automatically as I approached, although my heart leaped into my throat as I expected to see Copelup and several of the taller Drapsk march out. I didn't know what kind of physical restraint the Drapsk would be willing to use to keep me here, and I didn't intend to find out. I liked the annoying beings and was disturbed to imagine harming one, even in self-defense.

The controls responded to my tapping, assurance the Drapsk hadn't bothered to install species-specific biosensors. This implied either they felt no need for such security against non-Drapsk, something their care with the Scats didn't match, or that this building regularly housed non-Drapsk, making such sensors more of a problem than an aid.

I found myself stopping the lift.

Were there other Contestants locked in rooms in this building?

My Clan instincts told me to restart the lift, to hurry away while I could. My newer, Human-influenced side worried and fussed.

In the end, I gave in to the colder, saner argument. After all, I had no reason to suspect the Drapsk of intending to harm the Contestants. Judging by the gifts Maka had tried to shower on me back at the Haven, there could be a substantial profit for those competing. *Who was I to interfere?*

My reasons for leaving were my own.

On some worlds, Morgan had assured me, a cloak and a hunched posture could allow one to pass inconspicuously among the most bizarrely nonhumanoid species. I had no hope of that here; not only did the Drapsk not wear any clothing, let alone cloaks—the hockey players had been the only dressed Drapsk I'd seen—their senses were hardly likely to be fooled by mere fabric.

So I'd had an idea. If I couldn't be inconspicuous, I'd be as conspicuous as possible.

I made it from the lift, past the now-busy restaurants and compods, and out the front door to the moving walkway before hearing a shouted: "Wait, Mystic One!"

Without turning to see who was calling me, I tossed one of the objects from my bag on the pavement, hearing it land with a most satisfying shatter. Then I jumped the marker step separating the firm surface from the yielding flow of the walkway and began to run.

There was instant confusion. Which was just as well, since running on the moving surface was about as effective as running on ice. With every step forward I took, I felt as though I was about to fall on my face. But glancing about, I could see I was making rapid progress away from the chaos I'd left behind me.

Drapsk were literally climbing over one another in an effort to retreat from the scene. One bolted right into the side of the building, just missing the hotel door, which was already jammed with fleeing Drapsk. But no one seemed to be hurt.

I shook my bag, satisfied with the clicking sound within. The bedroom of my suite had been furnished for Human use, complete with a selection of toiletries having, as I'd expected, only the mildest of scents, barely detectable to my nose. But the Drapsk had provided me with a generous platter of local fruits and cheeses. I'd experimented until I'd produced an absolutely vile-smelling mix of fruit pulp, cheese, and lotion. Emptying out every tiny container in the bedroom, and refilling them with my mix, had definitely—as I'd devoutly hoped—provided me with something I could use to occupy the Drapsk.

I made sure I had another jar in my hand, ready to toss. Next stop, the shipcity.

What I'd do if and when I reached it, I had no idea at all.

INTERLUDE

"He might have been a spacer. Legit."

"And I might be a Human with an odd taste in accessories," Huido rumbled. "I don't like this, Brother."

Morgan's lips twitched, though his blue eyes remained glacial. "I do. If someone's set a tail on me, at least I'm bothering them. Which is the least I plan to do."

The Carasian clicked reluctant agreement. "Are you going to talk to this lurker in the shadows?"

"Not yet," Morgan decided, stretching his arms over his head and sliding farther into the soft depths of the chair. The pace of the last two days was taking its toll, but he begrudged even this much rest. "Did you find anything?"

Huido poured them both a beer, maneuvering his bulk into a seat designed for him, the claw tips of his lower, and larger, two arms resting comfortably on the floor. "Yes and no. The name you gave me, Baltir, is an ingredient in my father's unlamented meatcakes and part of a few thousand place names. One thing it didn't do was generate a match in any Trade Pact records for Retians. You're sure about the species?"

"He's Retian. Barac saw him on Camos; he was brought there, as I told you, by one of their Council," Morgan said slowly. "A Retian with an unknown name. That's very odd."

"I agree. The toads are fanatical about records and genealogies. An alias suggests a strongly asocial being indeed," Huido clicked triumphantly. "I did turn up something else. A newly arrived Denebian crew was doing the bars last night. They were tossed out of a couple, then ended up in Keevor's—you know the place."

Morgan did, quite well. Keevor's was about as low as you

could get on Plexis, a place where you went knowing or oblivious to the high cost of watered-down drinks and risk of creatively-spiked drugs. Keevor itself, an alien of truly obnoxious personal habits, was also somewhat of an epicure. It considered Huido's kitchen to be the only one worthy of its business. Fortunately for the other clients of the *Claws & Jaws,* Keevor preferred takeout.

"Keevor picked up on this crew. They were half-gone, grumbling about Pact regulations, the usual. With a couple of Keevor's 'Specials' under their belts, poor beings, the Denebians complained about an Enforcer shakedown right after lift. From Pocular. Keevor knew to contact me."

"When."

"Time's right." Huido's slurp of beer was altogether smug. "Interestingly, despite the free drinks and their condition, the crew was not forthcoming about any passengers or cargo. Keevor said they were thoroughly spooked."

Feeling himself tense, Morgan took a slow, relaxing breath. It wouldn't be this easy. "Where were they going after Pocular?"

"Ret 7."

He was on his feet before he was aware of the movement. Huido's eyes focused on the Human, expression impossible to decipher. "Shall I take care of your follower?" the Carasian asked mildly enough. "Before I leave for my penance on Ettler's?"

Morgan knew he had to plan, to do the right things in their proper order or fail. But he trembled, speechless with a resurgence of rage. Rage that suddenly seemed to have an accessible target.

"I will," he answered, when his lips would move again.

Chapter 21

I'D made it to the shipcity, skipping around the driverless bowlcars, avoiding—or temporarily fumigating—any Drapsk foot traffic that came too close. I actually moved as quickly as the cars, an exhilarating, nerve-racking progress as the walkway itself determined our speed. No organized pursuit showed itself, not that I was sure I'd recognize the Drapskii version. Perhaps it involved Tribe politics of some sort—whatever delayed them was fine by me.

The most difficult and dangerous part of my travels had been leaving the walkway to reach the ground itself. I'd discovered the Drapsk didn't see any need for permanent access; ships must request connecting walkways when ready to move passengers or crew up or down to the main system. I'd looked in vain for such a connection until literally stumbling into a cargo loading area. Here the walkway was supplemented with antigrav lifts, launched from a central point. After watching for a while be sure there were no automated, or fanged, guards, I'd boldly hopped on the next set of crates heading downward, jumping off again short of the cargo bay doors.

I'd known better than to try and enter any ship that way. There were reasons few ships bothered posting guards. If one could pass the servos watching for vermin traveling in either direction, there'd be an inventory screen just inside. Passing that was conceivably possible, but surviving a trip in the hold was not. Having handled cargo myself, I knew such a move was a fast way to suck vacuum, not a cozy home for a stowaway—unless one had a spacesuit and a gambler's approach to life, neither of which happened to be mine.

Instead, I ducked behind a handy docking tug, considering

myself incredibly lucky to have made it this far and feeling a likely unwarranted optimism in my ability to get even farther. I looked up at what little showed of the sky past the ships and walkways. I couldn't see the stars, but they were there. My destination.

Given I could get inside one of these ships. Memories swirled around, placing another sky overhead, the taste of a different atmosphere, rain-washed and cold, on my lips. I'd done this before, been hunted, sought escape from a world.

And had found Morgan.

I shook away the past, grimly aware that finding Morgan would not be as straightforward this time.

There were few Drapsk in this section of the shipcity. I walked, or rather slunk, around the ramps and fins of predominantly Human vessels; yet another piece of unexpected luck. These would be outbound ships; more traders' lore I owed to Morgan.

Drapskii exported various agriculturals and cultural artifacts. I thought ruefully I could add mind-shields and other devices sure to panic the Clan to that list. In turn, the Drapsk imported a wide range of items, from certain rare metals to Human literature. However these they usually obtained themselves at the source, preferring to send out their own ships. So most of the non-Drapsk starships around me here would be on-loading cargo.

The problem was, traders hoping for cargo were at the low end of their profit cycle. Taking on potential Drapsk-trouble such as an illegal passenger could mean a minimum of losing their cargo and deposit here, as well as failing to meet the expectations of waiting customers. Few traders of my acquaintance could afford either consequence, let alone both.

Could I bribe one? I doubted it. I had no proof of credit with me. Tapping into the Drapskii planetary system to verify my funds would have meant immediate exposure—however minimal those funds were beyond the former ownership of a shabby bar on a fringe world.

Which left, I realized, two options: someone dishonest enough to tap into the system for me, or someone powerful enough to take my side against the Drapsk. This realization came without much thought, since once I reached the end of the next row of docked starships, I found myself staring up at two very different vessels indeed.

The *Nokraud* herself was one, her bulk looking slow and unwieldy squatted on pavement, as though protesting innocence of any predatory abilities in space.

And the pirate happened to be docked uncomfortably close— and likely by no accident—to another, smaller ship, one that made no attempt to look other than it was.

A Trade Pact Enforcer, patrol class.

There hadn't been much of a choice. While the Enforcers might have been sympathetic and interceded with the Drapsk— I thought they'd at least listen: despite the Clan not being a signatory of the Pact, Morgan and I knew some names and were owed some favors—they might equally have believed the Drapsk claims of the innocence of their Festival, considering me a nervous Contestant who got cold feet and wanted a free ride home. To explain my need to find Morgan would involve a great number of revelations about the Clan and my own abilities, something I wasn't prepared to do. About the only thing I held in common with my kind was the need to preserve the secrecy of the M'hir.

The pirates were a known and possibly lesser risk, Scats being dangerous but predictable. If I could offer them something they wanted, I was sure they wouldn't hesitate to fracture any number of regulations on my behalf. I thought I could play on their curiosity about the Drapsk and why they'd brought me to their world.

As plans went, it was as reasonable as anything else I'd accomplished today.

"Ss–so, you wisssssh to leave Drapssskii," Grackik said, her thin black tongue whipping out to capture a bit of foam from the corner of a long front fang. "Without quesstions–ss."

"I'll make it worth your while," I repeated. Getting on board the *Nokraud* had been the easy part. I'd simply snuck around the side of the ship away from the Enforcer and waited for someone from the pirate's crew to notice me waving insanely at the remote vids.

Dealing with my own reactions had been somewhat more

difficult. I'd been imprisoned and almost been killed on such a ship. This one was larger, newer, with different species making up the crew. But there was an aura about a pirate I'd learned to identify: equal parts dread and the satisfaction of causing it—something I'd forgotten in my urgency to leave the Drapsk. It had been a mistake to come on board, I knew now, but too late for the knowledge to do me any good.

Outwardly, all was civilized. We sat in a proper Captain's lounge, sipping iced drinks—those of the Scats being a black foam they thankfully didn't offer to share—and served finger foods by a silent Human. I hadn't known their species liked anything that didn't squeal as it met their teeth, but these two were patently enjoying the Drapskii delicacy of fried cheese and grains. I didn't assume this meant anything tamer about their natures.

Rek, again I thought with deliberate malice, held her drink in one hand and her choice of treat in the other, waving both to collect the attention of her one-armed comrade as she spoke to me. "It would add confidence–ss to this–ss dis–sscusssion if you could be more—s–sspecific—about our rewards–sss, Fem Morgan."

"Do you prefer to carry party favors?" I asked, putting an edge to my voice. These were not beings from whom it was safe to retreat. "And have Drapsk ships clamp explosive grapples to your hull in thanks?"

"Profits–ss come in different s–shapes–ss." I saw Grackik pick up the witchstone I'd left on the black polished table between us. She held it between two claws, raising it to her large yellow-black eye and turning the stone from side to side to catch the light. "More of thes–sse would be of interes–sst to our buyers–ss, Rek."

"One gem hardly pays–ss for the trouble this–ss will s–sstir among the Drapsssssk."

"What they don't know . . . ?" I suggested.

"True," a deprecating wave of a drink-encumbered hand. "But willing dec–ss–eption adds–ss to the cos–sst."

Since I couldn't pay what they'd already mentioned as a starting point, adding to the cost wasn't an issue. So I was able to shrug carelessly. "Whatever it takes."

"Why do you want to leave this–ss world with us–ss?" Grackik demanded with a snap of her heavy jaws. "There are liners–ss, regular flights–ss, even a trader will take on a pass–ssenger. No, Fem Morgan. I think you wis–ssh to leave because you have offended our hos–ssts–ss in s–ssome way. Perhaps–ss murder?" The last word was drawn out as if it left a special taste within the Scat's mouth.

"Or theft?" added the second Scat, her snout turning to face me, eyes taking an identical predatory fix.

Theft? I thought guiltily of the bottles and containers in my bag. "I hardly expected a trifling brush with the authorities to bother you two," I said with all the confidence I could manage. "Or did I judge you on reputation and not on fact?"

"You mis–ssunders–sstand, Fem Morgan," Rek said calmly, still with that unnerving focus on my face. "We merely s–sseek to be clear with one another."

"Then be clear. Whatever is between the Drapsk and me is private. Will you take me offworld or not?"

"Most assuredly not, Contestant Morgan," the Drapsk said primly, entering with the servant. "You must stay until after the Festival."

This wasn't any Drapsk I'd seen before. It was rounder, slightly wrinkled around the mouth as though from too much tentacle sucking during its growth. The plumes of its antennae were a mottled green and gray. I leaned back, still eyeing the Drapsk, and crossed my legs. "Was I mistaken in who Captains the *Nokraud?*" I asked the room in general.

The Scats hissed to one another, their sibilant language splattering the furnishings as well as the Drapsk and myself. The Drapsk, I was gratified to note, sucked in all six tentacles and was rocking back and forth. I could wait.

The pirates didn't want me. That was plain. But by shaming them in front of their guest, the Drapsk—with my help—had neatly boxed them in a corner. To accept the Drapsk's authority over their property, as I was sure they thought of me or whatever profit I could bring them, was an admission they were subservient to the clawless little alien. Not an admirable image for a species that advertised itself as the scourge of the galaxy. However, to take me in defiance of the Drapsk would put them at odds with a species who, while known as polite and civilized, also tended to react to insults in groups, the smallest unit of which was the considerably formidable Tribe.

It would have been quite amusing watching the two Scats squirm, if the outcome hadn't mattered so much to me.

INTERLUDE

"Saving the Clan? You didn't really believe I'd be interested, did you?"

Rael took a sip of her wine before answering: "Of course not."

Pella sud Sarc, youngest of the daughters of the Joining between Jarad di Sarc and Mirim sud Teerac, raised one lovely eyebrow. "I detect disapproval, Sister."

Rael measured the voice against the deeper presence of the other Clanswoman in the M'hir touching both their minds. There was a resonance under the words, a flow of some unidentified yet uneasy emotion. She politely didn't probe deeper, though it would have been an acceptable use of her greater power—Pella barely a Third Level Adept in spite of her di heritage. *Ability,* Rael thought to herself, *did matter.* "How can I disapprove?" she said aloud instead. "As you said, I didn't think you'd join us. It wasn't my idea to come."

By custom, the outermost layer of their thoughts lay open to one another. It allowed the gentle testing to reaffirm relative strength. It supposedly reduced falsehood. *Supposedly*—Rael thought wearily and didn't bother to conceal it—*because the first thing one learned was how to lie mind to mind.*

Pella had been easy to find. She kept to her summer house in the mountains at this time of year, disliking the noise and excitement of the Humans in their cities as the winter relaxed its grip and spring roared through the hemisphere in a vast unstoppable wave of change. The Clanswoman would return for the theater season, quick to tire of her isolation. But for now, it was her preference.

There was nothing of Sira in her, Rael observed. It wasn't

only the power she lacked. There was a petulance to the full lips, perhaps a narrowness to the dark eyes. The hair matched her own, dark, heavy, and glossy. Only Sira had the red-gold of their father's youth, its thick fall another mark of her body's unusually-timed Commencement: their sister having matured in response to the Human's power instead of following the Joining between two Clan. Now Sira was some half-thing, Clan in power but not Clan in form, not truly. Ica had been right to warn her.

"Why are you thinking of her?" Pella asked out loud, her mind closing rudely. "What has this group of yours to do with Sira?"

Few Clan outside the Council knew exactly what had happened. Rael had told Pella most, but not all. Now she looked at her sister appraisingly, then asked: "Do you remember learning to play?" As she spoke, she stood as if restless, moving over to the elaborate music stand before the windows.

Pella followed her as she expected, pointedly pushing shut the lid of her keffle-flute as though afraid Rael meant to touch her beloved instrument. "Of course I remember. Sira taught me. Make your point, Rael."

"She doesn't play anymore. She's forgotten how."

"Oh," Pella whispered, her face averted to look out the window. She ran her fingers protectively over the case. "I didn't know."

"It was the stasis. When her own memories were blocked on top of it—well, it's more surprising she recovered as much of herself as she did. Though by her actions since, one could doubt . . ." Rael let her voice trail away.

Pella turned to stare at Rael. "What are you saying? What's happened to Sira? Where is she?"

No, she hadn't told her all. "I thought you would have heard by now, Pella," Rael said, eyes wide. "Sira went into exile—to be with that Human."

The case and its precious contents dropped to the floor. Rael didn't enjoy the shock on her younger sister's face, but she was relieved to see this much reaction. She had been the one close to Sira, heart-kin with the glorious older sister living out her years isolated from any unChosen in the Cloisters. After fostering, Pella had come to join them until her own moment of

Choice, a time of music, peace, and a rare sense of family. In the following years, they'd grown apart, as was proper for the Clan, but something special had existed between them.

It was all gone now. In her deepest thoughts, Rael believed the new Sira had lost her memory of their bond along with her music, replacing everything that had mattered to her before with the Human, Jason Morgan.

"Let me tell you about Ica's plans one more time, Pella," she coaxed.

Chapter 22

It had been worth a try, I decided the next morning, stretching within the warm comfort of my Drapsk-made bed, proportioned to humanoid norm but oddly softer at the edges than the middle.

And I'd possibly gained something out of it. The Scats had accepted the truly awe-inspiring bribe, euphemistically called a reward, urged on them by the Drapsk. But their frills had pulsed with anger. I thought I might just be able to convince them to side with me, next time.

If there was a next time. I was back in the same room. The fresher stall had been repaired, the toiletries replaced, and the doorplate made thoroughly tamper-proof. The huge platter of useful fruit had been pointedly replaced by a bowl containing one mild-smelling musk melon, its seeds already removed.

"Well, they're serious about this competition," I said to the ceiling, not particularly concerned about eavesdropping.

I wondered what the Drapsk would do when I refused to compete.

"That's not possible, O Mystic One," Skeptic Copelup assured me in a warm, soothing voice, the merest hint of anxious rocking to and fro in his stance. "Just not possible at all."

"And I assure you it is," I replied calmly, pulling the sheet closer to my chin. My staying in bed had perturbed the Drapsk who brought my breakfast. That worthy had sucked a couple of tentacles as it considered the situation.

When I announced I wouldn't get up until they let me leave, the poor being had scurried for help.

Help had arrived within minutes, in the form of the Skeptic

accompanied by two Makii Drapsk, one I was relieved to recognize by the ribbon faithfully tied to his tool belt as Captain Maka. *A Human reaction to the familiar,* I scolded myself, knowing full well none of the Drapsk was likely to be in favor of my leaving—especially not the one who'd brought me here in the first place.

"You cannot ignore the needs of the Tribe," Copelup went on, as though this was the ultimate argument. "Unless you are unhealthy, you must rise, O Mystic One. Eat your breakfast and come with us to meet the other Contestants."

Curiosity tempted me, but not sufficiently to abandon what was beginning to look like a worthwhile strategy. I snuggled farther down, nothing loath to get more comfortable in the process. "Maybe I am unhealthy," I offered in a weak voice, careful not to commit myself until I knew how the Drapsk might react. "Or maybe you've exhausted me. All this stress and running about," I continued. For all I knew, claiming illness could get me locked away in some med area for weeks while they searched in vain for a malady to cure. Then I had a brilliant idea. Maybe. "Take me to the *Makmora.* I'd like to see Med Makairi. He's been caring for my injury."

"I am Makairi, O Mystic One," said the Drapsk wearing Captain Maka's ribbon.

"Oh," I blinked. "Glad you are here," I added, while wondering what on Drapskii the med was doing wearing Maka's tag. But any delay could provide opportunity. "You should examine me. I may have strained something—"

"This is the Captain of the *Makmora,* O Mystic One," the remaining Makii Drapsk broke in, obviously trying not to inhale its tentacles. Its plumes were erect and tense. "Why should you wish him to examine you?"

The Med was now the Captain? I sat up, forgoing my feigned weakness in surprise. "Where—or what does Maka do now?"

"I am Maka," said the ribbonless Drapsk, rocking back and forth in unison with Captain Makairi. I was upsetting the creatures without knowing exactly how. I thought they knew I couldn't identify individuals.

Or wasn't that the point? They hadn't put on ribbons to identify themselves, I understood suddenly. They had put on ribbons to identify their shipside roles for me. I'd needed to know who was the Med, not who was Makairi.

Which didn't explain why Makairi now wore the Captain's ribbon.

Copelup was the only Drapsk not distressed. In fact, he waved his chubby little hands around in amusement. "Calm yourselves, Makii," he said with what had to be a chuckle. "You are not offended by the gripstsa occurring without you, are you, Contestant Morgan? It was overdue on the *Makmora*—the crew was becoming quite fatigued waiting for your return."

"How can I be offended or not when I don't know what *gripstsa* is?" I replied reasonably, working to copy the guttural roll of the new word as I wondered if they'd ever clearly explain anything to me.

This occasioned a sudden silence. Judging by the directions of the antennae, and the slow rippling of their plumes, I was being excluded from some conversation again. "Copelup," I warned.

A yellow antenna tip bent my way. "Yes, Mystic One. Our apologies. Just a moment."

I pulled the sheet right over my head and growled to myself. They ignored me. When it grew too stuffy underneath, I poked my head out again. There'd been no movement by any of the three I could detect. Were they arguing, resting, or being briefed in some new way to deal with this ever-difficult Mystic One? Maybe, I hoped, they'd decide I was just too much trouble to keep around.

"Copelup?" I hissed, reminding them I was still in the room.

The three moved immediately to stand in a line, so close I could have touched the nearest, Maka, had I wished. Their body postures were identical, tentacles forming rosettes of determined red. Some decision or other had been made, I thought uneasily.

"We will show you gripstsa," Captain Makairi stated firmly.

"But not perform it, of course," Maka, whose new rank they hadn't bothered to tell me, added as if this was vitally important.

"Proceed," order Skeptic Copelup impatiently. "The Mystic One has no time for your blathering."

I disagreed, but to myself. If it gave me any inkling what to expect from the Drapsk, Maka could blather for another hour.

Still, what was happening was intriguing. The former Captain and his replacement took up positions facing one another, moving together until they could touch. Their tentacles disappeared into each others' mouths in a gesture at once intimate and surprisingly dignified, while their plumes fell over their backs as if avoiding any chance of contact. Their eyes closed.

"If this was true gripstsa," Copelup said in a hushed, respectful voice, "each would exchange—" he searched for a word, then raised his hands in exasperation. "—the nearest concept in this language is 'experience with the outside world,' but that's completely inadequate, you understand."

For no reason I could later remember, unless it was a Human-like hunch, I opened the thinnest of cracks between my own consciousness and the M'hir. I was astonished to detect the merest breath of a potential connecting the two Makii—less than a pathway but far more presence in that space than I'd detected before. Almost instantly, all three Drapsk broke their tableau, turning to face me with plumes pointing in my direction. I waited until I felt the potential fade from the M'hir before withdrawing my own sense from it, confirmation if I needed any that these beings did what I'd thought no other species but mine could do: push some of their consciousness out of normal space, into that otherness.

While they'd obviously responded to my presence in the M'hir, all Copelup said was: "True gripstsa is essential before members of the Tribe can exchange duties, O Mystic One. Do you comprehend now? This ritual permits each individual to learn what it must about the role of the other."

"So following gripstsa, everyone on the *Makmora,* all the Drapsk crew I met there, have different jobs now. And they can all perform them as well as their predecessors."

"Naturally."

Fascinating. No wonder it was advisable to address every Drapsk one met offworld as 'Captain.' Eventually, it would be true. "How often do you do this—this switching about?" I'd been about to say "reprogramming" but recognized that as my own prejudice—I'd become familiar with the Human model of promotion: rising by accomplishment through the ranks of a ship's crew. *Different ways,* I reminded myself. That of the Drapsk must work; their ships were models of efficiency.

The Captain answered: "Gripstsa has no schedule or pre-dictability, O Mystic One. It may follow a stirring event—such as your arrival as Contestant for the Makii—or a period of long inactivity. Both of these tend to make individuals less content with their place and wishing for change. Gripstsa preserves harmony within the Tribe."

I had a too-vivid image of being on a ship full of Drapsk who suddenly and simultaneously abandoned their duties to grapple with one another in a frenzy of gripstsa. One hoped there were adequate automatics.

I also felt guilty. The Drapsk had been generous and kind, if overwhelming, hosts. "My coming set this change happening on the *Makmora?* I'm sorry if I disrupted—"

A soft touch on my hand from the plumes of the newest Cap-tain. "It is an honor to gripstsa from the knowledge of great things to come for all, O Mystic One," he said warmly. "It is our duty to thank you for this."

Skeptic Copelup harrumphed. "I think that is all the Mystic One should hear about the matter, don't you, Captain?" He spread his short arms as wide as they would go. "Now will you please get up?"

"Please?" added Maka. "It is so important, O Mystic One."

The three of them stood motionless, waiting for my answer. I sighed, more annoyed with my own inability to resist them than with their persistence.

"For breakfast," I offered. "Then—then we'll see."

INTERLUDE

It never paid to ignore the details, Barac thought to himself with disgust, half-minded to turn around and confront his pursuers. But that confrontation, though appealing emotionally, made no sense at all when one was outnumbered.

Outnumbered and uneasy. Barac touched the M'hir more firmly this time, sensing nothing but the currents of energy typical in a place visited by Clan, left behind by the passage of thought or matter. He was tempted to *push* himself elsewhere as well.

But then he wouldn't know why they chased him.

There were five at least. He'd stopped in front of an art dealer, the polished metal surface of a frame's edge giving him an inconspicuous mirror. Human males and scruffy-looking ones at that.

One was the Human who'd collided with him at the base of the ramp, supposedly by accident. *Details.*

Barac kept walking, staying carefully in the midst of the crowd but now heading opposite to his original direction. No point leading them, whoever they were, to Morgan. Unless it became necessary, he thought, amused.

The thought of Morgan triggered another, and Barac slipped his hands into the pockets of his coat, searching as unobtrusively as possible for anything that shouldn't be there. Morgan had planted a tracking device on him once before. Typical Human trickery. The Clansman didn't know whether to be relieved or otherwise to find nothing unusual.

He crossed into one of the night-zones, portlights dimmed to imitate stars, the floor and passing customers streaked with lights of various colors and intensities from the establishments on either side of the concourse. It was immediately noisier, with the bass sounds of percussion vibrating through the flooring and his brain. Barac sighed. He was fond of dancing.

Right now, however, his dancing was around those moving too slowly in front of him. Somehow he doubted those behind were after his credit chip. He needed to lure them into a place of his choosing. One hand had stayed in his pocket, caressing the stock of the one piece of technology Barac kept with him at all times, his force blade.

"Excuse, Hom? I believe you dropped this?" A soft voice from behind, female. Barac stopped and turned, knowing it for a trick, but willing to face them here if that's what they wanted. What could they do to him in a crowd of hundreds? Besides make a scene sure to rouse the ever present security guards?

It was the Human female from the tag point, smiling as she held out a small bag, like those carried by almost every other shopper passing them. They might have been enclosed in some force shield, the way the crowd split mindlessly around and past them.

Barac tasted foreboding and ignored the sensation. He'd already noticed the other figures coming closer, stopping to make a semicircle to either side of the female, the one who'd bumped him earlier farthest to Barac's right. Six to his one. Not bad odds, he thought.

"You know that's not my bag. What do you want?" the Clansman asked mildly.

"You're Barac sud Sarc, aren't you," a dark-skinned Human stated rather than asked. "One of the Clan."

Barac scowled but didn't bother denying it. He hadn't hidden his identity to board Plexis—lazy perhaps, but he'd been in too great a hurry to take the time to arrange an alternate credit account. There was usually almost no bureaucracy tainting his travels, but Plexis asked proof of solvency for its gold patches.

"I repeat, what do you want?"

The Human from the ramp was wringing his hands together, visibly agitated, though by what Barac wasn't sure. "We want you to come, come, come," the Human said suddenly, drawing startled glares from his comrades. "We do. Yes. Now, come with us."

"I don't think so—" Just as Barac began to concentrate, feeling the time to leave these crazy beings was long overdue, two of the males lunged forward and grabbed his arms. Horrified by the contact, and definitely not willing to take them along into the M'hir, Barac started to struggle. *Where was security?*

There was another way. He gathered his Talent, aiming a mental blow at the Human holding his right arm. It was turned aside.

Barac stopped fighting to free himself. Those holding him nodded approval and loosened, but didn't release, their grips on his arms. He stared at them, reaching out with his deeper sense for any part of their thoughts.

Not the blankness, the unsettling emptiness of a mind-shield. He'd encountered that with the Enforcers and knew the sensation too well. No, what protected these minds from his power was innate and well-trained.

"*All* telepaths," he gasped, watching the six nod one by one. He hadn't known there were so many Human telepaths in this quadrant, let alone expected to see them in one place. Weaker than the weakest Clan, unable to touch the M'hir—or at least ignorant of its existence and potential, they had enough strength to resist him for a while. Not invulnerable *and they know it,* he decided, tasting a leak of anxiety from someone. He could likely overcome any one, given time. But, perhaps, not all six. Humans had a regrettable tendency to band together. "What do you want with me?"

"Come with us, quietly," the one holding his left arm replied. Barac didn't need to pull to judge the broad, bearded Human's physical strength was greater than his own. It didn't matter. No matter what these Humans thought they wanted with him, he wasn't about to waste time with it. There were other, simpler ways.

He opened his mouth to call out, just as a needle pricked the side of his neck. "Never underestimate the value of a good gadget," he could almost hear Morgan's scolding.

The hands on his arms became the only things keeping Barac upright as the world around him dimmed. A face appeared, directly before his, harsh featured, with puckered scars framing cold and curious eyes. It moved closer, so close he took in warmed air with his next breath, so close Barac knew he'd never forget this Human.

Could no one in the crowd see what was happening? Perhaps they saw nothing alarming in friends supporting a being who'd had one too many at the nearby tavern. Barac felt his head spinning and desperately tried to push himself elsewhere. He couldn't concentrate . . . couldn't hold a locate . . . they were pulling him away.

"Barac! Glad I caught up with you!" The hearty voice penetrated through the fog dimming Barac's perception of himself and his surroundings. His supporters seemed to vanish into the mist, his body falling almost to the floor before a new set of strong arms took his weight. "You have been misbehaving, haven't you? Let's go tell the Chief all about it, shall we?"

Barac rolled his head on his shoulder and desperately tried to concentrate. That careless grin and flint-hard eyes could belong to only one being.

A shame the trank was going to knock him out completely before he could say hello to Constable Russell Terk, Trade Pact Enforcer and personal assistant to the Sector Chief herself, Lydis Bowman.

A shame indeed.

Chapter 23

IT was, I had to admit, fun.

The urgency to find Morgan, to stop him before he foolishly risked himself, beat constantly in the back of my mind.

But at a moment like this, even that need could be tucked to one side. After all, how many beings could say they'd been given their own parade?

I rode with the Skeptic and an escort of four Makii in a bowlcar almost filled with flower petals. If we hadn't stood the entire way, we'd have been invisible beneath them, despite the regrettable gaudiness of my Festival dress. I'd hoped, in vain, they'd forgotten about that. Our bowlcar drifted behind a stately procession of well over a hundred others, each bearing some dignitary or other. I'd lost track very soon after Copelup had proudly begun announcing each name and affiliation. Not all were Drapsk. Some were ambassadors or other offworlders invited to the Festival.

Behind us stretched a seemingly endless series of longer, lower bowlcars, these bearing what I was told was the entire living population of Makii—Copelup adding in a discreet whisper that in reality about fifteen percent had had to stay at various essential tasks, but I wasn't to mention it. No flag or standard was necessary. It was like drifting along a river of purple and pink feathers.

We paraded along the broadest walkway I'd seen yet in Drapskii's Port City, passing platform after platform lined with Drapsk of other Tribes. I'd been told there were only three Tribes competing this Festival; the evidence overwhelming as we reached the area where walkways from other quarters of the city crossed. There was another parade, predominantly white-plumed, passing overhead while underneath I could just make out a third, this followed by a stream of bowlcars carrying blue-green Drapsk.

I found myself humbled by a system that could assemble and move this many individuals so smoothly, and it wasn't only the technology that impressed me. The Drapsk were like some tidal force moving through their buildings; a gentle, immense migration. *How did I ever think I could avoid being part of this,* I asked myself soberly.

I hadn't met the other Contestants, seeing them only as distant specks amid their own flower-filled bowlcars. My delaying tactics had shuffled breakfast and courtesy schedules completely offtrack, something I suspected pleased Copelup; meeting the other Contestants might have answered more of my questions.

The watching Drapsk waved their arms and plumes as I passed, prompting me to wave back even though I felt totally foolish waving to a crowd without eyes. I'd braced for more windy cheers, but the air stayed unusually calm. I presumed there was no need for the Drapsk to share their emapkii or amapka, since the only being who would benefit from such encouragement or discouragement couldn't detect the scent.

The mood of my escort was jubilant to say the least. "Is this not marvelous?" Copelup asked for at least the tenth time since we'd started, plumes twitching almost fiercely in unison with the others in the bowlcar. The resulting draft kept the top layer of flower petals constantly stirring about my waist.

I nodded in agreement again. Then I asked, "I assume the parade from the last Festival was larger?"

"No, no, O Mystic One," Maka answered hastily. "This is the most hope-filled Festival of all our lifetimes. Everyone wishes to touch the Scented Way as you pass—"

"Hush!" this admonishment from Copelup. Still, I was satisfied to glean even a bit more.

I was even more satisfied by what I'd left behind me in the hotel, and waved with genuine enthusiasm at the next platform of Drapsk.

Somewhere behind me, a Drapsk was placing my order for the feast day to follow the competition, a meal in which I was assured I could have anything I desired, at any expense, including my favorite dish: rare merle truffles, found only in the wild jungles of Pocular, prepared as the new specialty of a certain restaurant.

If that order in my name made its way to the right ears, I thought cheerfully, catching a fleeting glimpse of the other two parades ahead winding their way around the buildings, *I might even bring myself to eat the truly disgusting fungus.*

Parade's end. The anticlimax as we milled about at our final stopping point brought a return of all the tension I thought I'd controlled rather well up until now. But there was no escaping what was ahead—whatever that might be—not by any means remotely at my disposal anyway.

I think the Drapsk anticipated this moment of panic, a couple of them moving close beside me as we stepped down from the bowlcar, shedding flower petals like flakes of dead skin. They stroked the backs of my hands lightly, wisely not offering to hold them. In my current state, I doubted I could have endured any further sense of restriction.

The bowlcar had deposited us alongside a vast slope, made of the same material as the walkways, its surface covered with the Drapsk it already carried like a sand dune whose grains tumbled upward instead of down. It rose from my feet to the top of a monolithic building, a structure that must be the tallest in the entire city. Like all Drapsk architecture I'd seen, it was windowless. Unlike those other structures, this one bore elaborate markings up its rounded sides. The markings were like overlapping plumes, I realized, millions upon millions of them in a pattern spiraling well over our heads.

Here, for the first time since the parade started, I felt one of the manufactured winds. It sloughed down the slope to explore our faces, spilling more flower petals from the bowlcar behind us, creating undulating waves among the plumes of the Drapsk ahead. "What does it say to you?" I asked Copelup, holding my hands in its way for a moment, my hair resisting the efforts of the breeze to lift it.

"Welcome," the Skeptic answered contentedly, standing straighter, his yellow plumes ruffling. "Welcome to all, and especially to the Contestants."

I can do this, I told myself, and surprised my escort by stepping onto the rampway first, leaning slightly forward involuntarily as if to compensate for the angle, although the dimpling of the strange surface underfoot actually made me feel as if I stood on level ground. *I couldn't help Morgan any faster by resisting what the Drapsk had planned,* I thought.

Having finally convinced myself, I found I was curious about what that might be.

INTERLUDE

Hunting in a space station like Plexis had a great deal in common with the same pursuit in a jungle, Morgan thought idly, half-sitting on the edge of a planter filled with ornamental shrubs and the inevitable litter. His icy blue eyes swept the passing streams of customers, never lingering on any one face.

You couldn't wander aimlessly about in hopes of surprising your prey. No, you had to know where your prey was likely to go and wait, as he was doing now.

From where he sat, in the shadow of a shrub more alive than most, Morgan could see the entrance to the *Claws & Jaws* as well as the fronts of three restaurants spinward and the multiple doorways of the much larger, if untrustworthy, Skenkran cafeteria on this side of Huido's establishment. Later in the stationday, the number and relative wealth of those lined up to enter each of these eating places would provide ample evidence in support of Huido's boast of providing the best food in the quadrant.

At the moment, however, there was only the steady, unending flood of customers on their way to other levels and activities, making it occasionally difficult to see right to the entrance.

Morgan was patient. His follower would want to find him again. Anyone who knew him would know his affiliation with the Carasian. The Human had toyed with the idea of waiting near the *Fox*, then decided against it. The parking levels were simply too easy a place for the hunter to become the hunted.

Something captured the corner of his eye. Casually, as if by coincidence, Morgan turned his head to the right. *There.* A head of red-gold hair appeared and then disappeared in the throng. Heart in his throat, he lunged to his feet, pretense forgotten. *Sira?* he caught himself in time to stop the sending, knowing that was the single most dangerous thing he could do.

As he stood, the crowd opened to completely reveal a woman burdened with packages, her hair close in color to the heavy, strangely alive locks he remembered warm and soft against his cheek, this hair bound tightly to frame a face nothing like the one in his dreams. Or nightmares.

Morgan subsided, turning his attention back to the restaurant entrance. As he waited, he felt his mind slipping from whom he waited for or why he was being followed. Instead he found himself savagely examining and reexamining every minute of that endless night, playing *what if* scenarios over and over again until what really happened almost began to blur. Then one thought solidified, cold and hard, just as his eyes fixed on a tall figure standing right outside Huido's front door.

What if he hadn't found Sira? What if they'd succeeded in leaving her to die?

He took a slow deep breath, outwardly calm, inwardly fighting to control the impulse to free the knife from his sleeve.

And test the color of his target's blood.

Chapter 24

"NO. No. No!"

"It's all right, Maka," I soothed the outraged Drapsk, finding I had to keep a firm grip on his concave shoulder to hold him safely at my side.

"But, Mystic One—"

"I can wait," I said firmly, tipping my head to try and see through the forest of purple-pink plumes in front. My—supporters, I supposed—had created a wall with their own bodies around me. It wasn't helping me figure out what was happening on the floor of the amphitheater. "I really don't want to be first."

The journey to the top of the towering building had been truly awe-inspiring, affording a panoramic and potentially terrifying view of the Drapsk city. Distant mountains lost all perspective, appearing similar in size to the gleaming tips of starships marking the shipcity and port, edged by the setting sun. There were no transports or ships in the air—further indication of the importance of the Drapsk Festival.

Fortunately for my peace of mind, the surface of this moving rampway had been markedly more adhesive than I'd experienced before. It had taken all of my strength to pry up one foot and replace it, suggesting we wouldn't be blown away into the distance if the Drapskii weather decided to become creative.

As if it wasn't enough to build to such heights, and to enter from the outside, another shock awaited me when the ramp had reached its final destination. The building was hollow.

Well, I temporized, looking up at what I could see of my surroundings, *not quite hollow.* But we'd poured over the lip of the building's wall like flotsam passing over a dam. I'd had an instant to reach the sickening conclusion that the Drapsk had brought me to their world in order to join them in mass suicide before realizing we were drifting down in a field very similar to any anti-grav lift—albeit a larger one than I'd ever heard of being constructed. A unique way to enter what was, after all, an elegantly shaped amphitheater.

For such polite, quiet little beings, the Drapsk had an unsuspected knack for the dramatic.

"O Mystic One?" A delicate touch on my elbow drew my eyes back from the darkening sky overhead. There was no perceptible chill in the air, something I attributed more to the thousands of warm bodies surrounding me than to anything technological.

It was Captain Makairi, holding up a disk-shaped device about the size of my hand for my inspection. "Will this be of help?"

I took it, bemused to recognize the device as a remote vid. Before I could open my mouth to ask where the image collector was, Makairi tossed a second, similar object into the air. It hovered noiselessly over our heads, before disappearing beyond the wall of Drapsk plumes.

"Your thoughtfulness is—" *overwhelming,* was the thought that crossed my mind. I chose another word: "—appreciated, Captain." I keyed on the vid, immediately dizzied by the perspective it displayed. There was something about soaring over a featureless panorama of moving purple plumes.

Then the image, or rather the plumes, cleared, showing a central oval of plain white stone that had to be at the focal point of this amphitheater. I sank without thinking onto the stool pressing against the back of my knees, then looked up, startled again.

Stools had appeared conveniently behind every Drapsk I could see, and not in straight rows. I eyed the floor beneath my feet suspiciously before looking back at my tiny window on what was happening.

A Drapsk identical to Copelup was standing in the opening beside what appeared to be a tall, white-haired, male Human. The Human was surrounded by several boxes, each of these decorated with an eye-confounding pattern of stars, spirals, and other astronomical symbols. Although there was no air moving that I could detect—the Drapsk themselves making excellent weather vanes—he wore a midnight blue cloak that floated up and around him, snapping to a nonexistent wind. An unannounced toss of his fingers upward freed a handful of starlike dust to soar above all our heads.

The Drapsk had found themselves a magician, all right. I grinned, recognizing the Great Bendini from Morgan's entertainment tapes. A shame that what the Human practiced was as far from real magic as one could imagine.

Yes, this could be fun.

"How could he have won?!" I shouted at Copelup two hours later. "There hasn't been any other Contestant up yet! I haven't—" I closed my lips over what might sound like an eagerness to put my own reputation on the live in front of most of this city, substituting: "I didn't expect your people to be this gullible, Copelup. They were tricks!"

Great tricks, even I had to admit. The magician had spared nothing from his repertoire: sawing Drapsk in half and reattaching the parts; making an entire row of Drapsk float in midair; producing ribbons, fruits, furniture, and wildlife that appeared and disappeared at his whim. While I couldn't see how he'd done any of it, I knew there was nothing fantastic about the illusions. *And the Drapsk were falling for this?* I thought angrily, glaring at my so-called Skeptic.

Copelup pried the container of whatever he and most of the Drapsk were drinking from his face in order to answer me. It made a small popping noise as the suction was broken. "We know, O Mystic One." He began hooting, a revoltingly cheerful sound several of the nearby Makii seemed to find in poor taste, at least that was how I interpreted the suddenly stern angle of their plumes and their deliberate leaning away.

"Then—" I went speechless, shaking the vid at him as if Copelup needed or could use the screen. He must know what was happening below us: the Great Bendini receiving a huge gem-encrusted trophy, and what looked to be an endless line of equally valuable offerings, each borne by a member of his supporting Tribe, the white-plumed Niakii. The Skeptic beside the Human bowed and accepted each gift into his own hands, showing it to the triumphantly beaming magician before passing it to a row of other Drapsk filling up a series of grav-sleds with his loot.

"What makes you believe this is how we treat a winner, O Mystic One?" Copelup said, recovering sufficiently to speak instead of hoot. "Do you not see how the gifting is one way only? That the poor Niakii must impoverish themselves—symbolically, of course—while having received nothing in return from their Contestant?"

"The Human thinks he's won," I objected, not sure I accepted Copelup's explanation at face value.

"The Niakii know better, O Mystic One," Captain Makairi said somberly, one finger resting on the vid screen in my hands. "Observe for yourself."

At first, I didn't see what he meant, assuming the Drapsk overestimated my ability to read their state from visual information alone. Then I saw how the white plumes of each Niakii Drapsk drooped down over their shoulders as they turned and left the central oval. They formed two slow lines, one leaving the amphitheater through a floor level exit I hadn't seen before, the other returning to their seats. "What's going to happen to them?"

Copelup's voice was still amused; I supposed because his Tribe wasn't at risk during this Festival. "Half go to the Niakii holdings. They own a great deal of property within the City and operate several essential services. Most of this will go to the Tribe whose Contestant succeeds today, so they prepare for *lar-gripstsa,* the transfer of place."

I looked around at my innumerable chorus of Makii Drapsk. If my hold on the vid became more of a clench than a grip, I thought they might not notice—though I couldn't do anything about their ability to read my organics, given they understood such information. Personal embarrassment in front of thousands of aliens? What was that compared to the loss I saw taking place before me? And the Makii thought I could prevent that? The consequences of failure here were beyond anything I'd expected.

"How could the Niakii have chosen so badly?" I said, pleased my voice was steady anyway. "I thought you Skeptics judged each Contestant."

Copelup sucked all his tentacles at once, refusing to answer.

Maka spoke up from in front of me, his chubby fingers waving skyward in emphasis. "The Human arrived on his own, seeking a sponsor. This happens. The Niakii were greedy."

Out popped Copelup's tentacles. "They didn't listen to the wisdom of their Skeptic. It was evident from the onset the creature had no true magic to offer."

"They listened," Captain Makairi disagreed. "They knew. The Niakii took the chance of no true Mystic One entering. That has happened all too often during our Festival, Contestant Morgan," he went on to explain in a most un-Drapsk moment of revelation. "In such a case, there is no winner. The Tribe the Skeptics judge to have the most successful Candidate is still permitted to move into ascendancy over the others. But today, the Niakii already know they will lose. You are with us."

"And are not the only one. While I discount their Contestant's ability to match our own, the Heerii have found a Mystic One—" Copelup spoke up.

"Having neglected their trade routes and spent resources belonging to others." This interruption from Maka was as close to a snarl as I'd ever heard from a Drapsk. I raised my eyebrows.

"In order to do what?" I asked, trying to will the Drapsk to continue talking. Out of the corner of my eye, I watched the tiny vid screen. Events in the center were wrapping up, literally, as Bendini collected the last of his loot and began moving from the stage.

Copelup answered, Maka apparently too distraught to continue. "The Heerii have long believed there were Mystic Ones beyond the boundaries of the Trade Pact and its member systems, Contestant Morgan. They have explored farther than many would dare—at, as Maka rightly notes, considerable expense. But they did find a worthy Contestant."

I drew in a slow breath, as if, like the Drapsk, I could decipher knowledge from molecules floating in front of my face. So a Tribe of Drapsk had gone voyaging and found another Contestant. The Skeptic believed in this being's abilities, meaning quite clearly it possessed some Talent within the M'hir.

Was it possible? I thought with a dizzying sense of foreboding. *Had the Drapsk found the Clan Homeworld?*

My ancestors, the M'hiray, had been exiled from the Homeworld during the Stratification, a genetic cleansing to rid the species of a new mutation in the Talent—the troublesome and dangerous Power-of-Choice that on one hand allowed Joined pairs to link through the M'hir and on the other acted to destroy any weaker male. Whether the exile had been willing or not, or indeed whether it had been effective in ridding the Homeworld of the threat, had never been revealed to us. After taking up discreet residence among the similar-appearing Humans, even the location of our original home was blocked from Clan thoughts, accessible—so rumors went—only by certain members of the Council. I was reminded of the vision I'd had in the M'hir when I'd left Pocular for the *Makmora:* the image of a gigantic pathway etched in power. It could have been a clue to the location of the Homeworld. It could have been my imagination.

I'd had no reason to wonder until now. No other M'hiray had joined us since that day. None, save a fanatical few obsessed with reclaiming some mystic heritage, even paid attention to the half-forgotten and neglected stories of our home.

Until I stood on this planet of aliens, and wondered if I was about to come face-to-face with my own kind's past.

And what I would do, if I did.

INTERLUDE

"Hello, again, Hom sud Sarc," said the voice from his past, piercing through the fog starting to lift from his brain, leaving behind it a vast throbbing pain that bode to make waking up no bargain at all. "Why is it I always seem to find you like this—"

"Chief Bowman," Barac gritted through his teeth, eyes still closed. He suspected opening them to the light would only make matters worse.

"Med."

A searing, pungent aroma filled the Clansman's nostrils, making him jerk upward in offense. As he glared at his surroundings, which included a familiar pair of Humans and an unfamiliar Ordnex, Barac realized his head was no longer trying to separate from his neck and relaxed back into the pillows. "Thanks, I think."

"That'll be all, Med Talruo." The Ordnex left.

The Human female who had spoken regarded Barac with keen interest. She was wider than some, shorter than many, and wore her uniform carelessly, sleeves pushed up her thick arms and the neck open as if she hated anything tight. A worm's trail of a scar wound around the back of her right hand, a disfigurement Barac always found disturbing, given it could be so easily removed. Sector Chief Lydis Bowman, virtual head of the Trade Pact Enforcers stationed here and throughout this part of space, an intelligent being who had made the Clan her personal project, despite the lack of interest from other members of the Pact. Always dangerous, Barac remembered glumly.

And with her, Terk. That worthy stood staring at Barac as though deciding how best to take the Clansman apart for investigation. No need to tap the M'hir. Both of these Humans had risked the mind-deadening implants. They might have been servos or ghosts for all the taste Barac could have of their thoughts.

Barac shrugged, cautiously, and when his head didn't implode immediately, sat up again and swung his long legs over the side of the examining table. "I owe you my thanks, Terk," he admitted, making the effort not to sound grudging. But he'd learned from experience these two were the most likely to interfere with what he, Barac, considered private Clan business.

"Something more substantial would be nice," Bowman suggested. "Along the lines of some information."

Barac took a sip from a cup of—*yes, it was* plain *water,* he shuddered—before looking up to meet Bowman's curious and determined look. "I'd like to know why I'm here—and why he," a nod to Terk, "made such a timely entrance at my kidnapping."

"Sounds as though we have a bargain," Bowman announced cheerfully. "Information for information. And over lunch, if you feel up to it, Hom sud Sarc. I'm sure my galley is ready."

"Fair enough," Barac said, standing cautiously and surprised when he felt quite normal doing so. *As far as information went,* he added to himself, *he'd like to know about the drug used to subdue him and this miraculous cure in Bowman's possession.*

He was, after all, suspicious of Humans by both nature and training.

Chapter 25

I'D tried to convince Copelup to take me closer to the stage, using every argument I could come up with: the ache behind my eyes from staring at the tiny screen, which was true; my desire to spy out the tricks of my erstwhile opponent, which was, I thought, at least plausible. None of this swayed the Skeptic, who must have had his own reasons for keeping me as far away as possible without tossing me back over the wall.

At least the sun had set, making my portable window on the world a bit easier to see. The Drapsk seem to need light, if not much; the amphitheater glowed from its floor, rather than from any source on the walls. The soft illumination emphasized the roundness of the Drapsk bodies, turning my neighbors into rows of white repeating curves, so much like their architecture I might have sat within a miniature of their city, the arching plumes an echo of the purple dusk overhead.

A city pulsing with excitement. The failure of the Niakii's Contestant and the rumored quality of the Heerii's seemed to ignite endless speculation—some of it vocal and politely in Comspeak. I grew increasingly uneasy. The Drapsk, my Drapsk, were totally convinced I'd win. Since I still had no idea what they expected me to win with, I thought this unreasonably confident of them.

Servers moved through the crowd during the delay of about a standard hour between the removal of the Great Bendini and his treasures—and the dismal exit of the Niakii Drapsk—and the arrival of the next Contestant. The servers were of the orange-plumed variety. I didn't catch the Tribe name, but they certainly were a fine choice from my point of view, their lurid plumes standing out like tiny sails as they passed among the ranks of seated Drapsk. I found enough appetite for a roll of some type and a hot drink, Copelup checking both for me with quite alarming haste. When I'd asked, jokingly, if he suspected the Heerii of trying to poison me, he hadn't been amused.

Which had given me yet another reason to wonder what the Drapsk hoped to gain from this whole exercise, if it was worth this much to them.

"The Heerii Contestant," Copelup whispered in my ear, pointing to the vid screen. His antennae and its plumes, along with those of every Drapsk I could see, were fully spread and erect: a closeness of attention I hadn't observed for the Great Bendini. *They did know the difference,* I thought, feeling just a little sorry for the triumphant magician.

The oval space at the center of the amphitheater was empty at first; the only new feature I could see being a long rectangular dais affair, put together from separate box-like pieces and draped with what appeared to be issa-silks, white of course. Then I saw what had already captured Copelup's attention.

A small procession of several blue-green Heerii Drapsk, their yellow-plumed Skeptic in the lead, was entering the opening from the side nearest to us and opposite their own section of the amphitheater. Two of the Drapsk towed a floating litter on which rested a large irregular lump of something, covered in more of the white silk. A long flaccid arm, more like a fibrous tentacle than a limb, hung over the side of the litter to almost touch the floor.

Not Clan. I wiped my hands surreptitiously on my Contestant's gown—sparing an instant to remember to ask the Drapsk why they'd insisted on making me wear the hideous thing when the other Contestants seemed to dress as they pleased—and refused to think about whether I was disappointed or relieved by what I was seeing. I hadn't realized how much I'd expected the new Contestant to be one of my fabled cousins. *Or had I feared it?* I shook my head. It was irrelevant.

There was little else to see of the being the Heerii escorted so tenderly to the center and eased onto the dais. I assumed it was either infirm or fragile, perhaps suffering from an unfamiliar gravity. The draperies slid this way and that over its surface, as though beneath them was a form less solid than most. The limp arm had been withdrawn, as though its owner was dismayed by having revealed even this much of itself.

A stronger contrast to the flamboyant showmanship of the Great Bendini wasn't possible, I thought, approving. This mystery being was far more intriguing. Of course, I wasn't sure I'd notice whatever magic he/she/it was doing, the Drapsk not using any verbal broadcast to enlighten those of us olfactorily-deprived.

Luckily, Copelup was feeling poetic. "Behold, O Mystic One. The first brave Rugheran to leave its homeworld."

"The only Rugheran to leave its homeworld," corrected Captain Makairi. I'd noticed the former med had lost nothing of his blunt bedside manner in his promotion.

"And where's that?" I asked, eyes on the screen but my attention on whatever information I could squeeze out of these two. Morgan would love to be the first Human to know about a new intelligent species. I had visions of exclusive trade in whatever Rugherans did and new fittings for the *Fox*'s starboard thrusters.

"The Heerii will, of course, reveal such valuable information only to their own Tribe—or to the Tribe which reaches ascendance today. A role the Makii confidently believe you will gain us, O Mystic One."

Great, I said to myself, glaring at the smug creatures. Toss another piece on the growing pile of bets on this table.

"What do you—" I was about to say "expect" when something *happened.*

I sensed it at the same moment the Drapsk reacted, the entire multitude surging to its collective feet, plumes of all three Tribes rising to point at the motionless lump on the stage. It was as though a wave passed through the M'hir, sliding against my awareness of that dimension before fading away again without a trace.

Not quite without a trace. I felt dampness on my cheeks and wiped away tears. The wave tasted of sorrow, of longing. It carried more: now I knew—and suspected all the Drapsk knew as well—the creature below was dying. This demonstration for their Contest had been its last testament.

I didn't think. I didn't plan. I was just suddenly, gloriously, angry. Without hesitation I *drove* myself through the M'hir . . .

. . . Though I was surprised when it actually worked and I found myself on the oval space, a step away from the failing Rugheran.

I went to it, not letting its huge size and odd shape beneath the silk interfere with what I knew was right. The Drapsk had gone too far this time, trapping this poor creature here. The Drapsk in question were maintaining a comically frozen posture, none appearing to even breathe. Just as well. I wasn't in the mood to be coaxed or forced.

Gently, I lifted one corner of the silk. All I could see underneath was a pulsating mass, so dark its color was impossible to determine, here and there glittering with perhaps moisture or perhaps scales. It was hard to tell. I considered where best to touch it, but the question was answered for me as the tentacle-arm reappeared, waved at my eye level for a moment, then dropped to rest with truly staggering weight on my shoulder. I had to brace myself to stay upright, needing both hands to keep my abruptly enthusiastic hair from lashing me in the face.

But the contact was all I needed. I opened my sense to the M'hir, finding the flickering light within it that was all that remained of the Rugheran. It was ready to give up its existence, traumatized almost to insanity by the probably well-intentioned ministrations of the Drapsk. But it needed others of its kind to touch and support it. This close to its musical thought patterns, that need was enough to make me sob with my own emptiness.

There was only one cure. It suggested what to do, pleaded really, and I agreed.

I collected every bit of power I possessed, and *pushed* the dying being into the M'hir, extending my senses with it as it sought the way home. Silk sighed down around me and I felt myself drop to my knees as I lost the burden on my shoulder.

This was not how the Clan or I traveled, I thought, keeping my other sense with the Rugheran. Rather than dissolving or struggling, the being seemed to me to gather strength from the power around us both, to prepare itself, then, suddenly, I lost all sense of it as it plunged into the blank darkness like a fish into an ocean.

I pulled myself free, returning my consciousness to the amphitheater, my palms flat on the floor as I panted with the aftermath of my effort.

I could hear my breathing and nothing else.

I looked up through the cover of my still-twitching hair at several hundred thousand colorful, motionless, and likely quite shocked Drapsk.

Somehow, I didn't think Copelup was going to be impressed with his Mystic One.

INTERLUDE

"I'm impressed. You came all the way to Plexis just to talk to me." Morgan was sure his voice was smooth and expressionless, but Huido swiveled two more eyestalks toward him, as if reading more into the sound than the polite disbelief the Human intended. He raised a brow at the Carasian—an "I know what I'm doing" gesture—confident their guest would miss the exchange.

"That's right, Captain Morgan." Their guest, when accosted, had willingly identified himself as one Larimar di Sawnda'at of the Clan. He'd agreed to join them in Huido's private and eavesdropper-proof apartment—appearing relaxed and confident. If true, Morgan was equally willing to have him continue with this error in judgment.

Morgan smiled thinly, attracting yet another pair of eyestalks. "And you were following me—?"

"As I told you. I wished to be sure of your identity before speaking to you. And you were buying such—interesting— things. Have a customer planning a private war?" Solidly built, Larimar had coarser, more blunt features than most Clan Morgan had met, though well within the standard considered handsome by most Humans. His eyes were the flaw: cold, pale green, and brimming with the superiority all Clan but one in Morgan's experience appeared to feel in the presence of Humans. Morgan was willing to let the Clansman cling to that error in judgment as well.

The Human ignored the question. "Well, now you're sure. Why so careful?"

Larimar shrugged, adding a charming, not quite Human smile.

"We all know the attention of the Council hasn't left you, Captain Morgan. I don't wish it drawn to me as well."

"I see," Morgan said noncommittally, walking to the sideboard. His back safely to the Clansman and the overly observant Carasian, he watched his hands shake as they reached for the bottle of Huido's private stock of Brillian Brandy. He stopped the movement, staring at his palms, forcing calmness through every part of him until his fingers were rock-steady once more.

Morgan's smile as he turned with a tray was a shade too friendly, but he knew Huido wouldn't comment—yet, anyway. "So what did you want to ask me, Clansman di Sawnda'at?" He knew the House name well enough. There had been a Sawnda'at at the head of the Clan Council on Camos; for all Morgan or any of his contacts knew, there still was. No news where they'd moved their meeting place after being ousted from the Human world of Camos; nothing about their activities at all.

Until Pocular.

The Clansman took the brandy, sniffing it appreciatively. Huido's body armor clattered and rumbled as he shifted unhappily—his idea of hospitality to any Clan but Sira had more in keeping with his wives' notions of entertaining—but Morgan quelled further complaint with another meaningful look. There was more brandy, and here was an unexpected chance for information. "There are those," Larimar began, "who do not approve of the direction in which the Council would take our kind."

"Rebels?" Morgan asked in polite disbelief. "You aren't serious."

"Of course not. Say, rather, those who would prefer our current Council consider other paths, other ways." Another slow swallow and a considering look from those pale green eyes. "Unfortunately, there are few safe ways to make such suggestions."

"I can imagine," Morgan said dryly. A governing system based solely on which individuals possessed the greatest abilities within the M'hir, rule by Power, wasn't inclined to look downward in its population pool for ideas. "So what do your politics have to do with me, Clansman?"

"You are the Chosen of Sira di Sarc," Larimar said, as if Morgan were feebleminded as well as Human. "Clan politics have everything to do with you."

Morgan's vision seemed to cloud over as he heard Sira's name in the Clansman's deep voice. He made himself gaze into the golden liquor in the glass between his fingers, seeing how it stayed level, striving for the same equilibrium within himself. The rage inside demanded violence, craved vengeance. He knew exactly how to remove Larimar's tongue, where to cut through the muscle and skin of the throat. He knew exactly how satisfying it would feel to carve her name from the Clansman's mouth.

Some of this must have stayed in Morgan's eyes as he looked back up at the Clansman. Huido snapped his handling claw, producing a deep, bell-like sound. A stern warning. Perhaps a hint leaked through into the M'hir, though Morgan knew his shielding was superior to anything this Clansman possessed, since those green eyes widened suddenly, as though startled.

"*We,*" Morgan stressed the word, "do not have anything to do with Clan politics. If that's all you came for—"

Larimar had recovered his composure, though Morgan thought there was a shade less confidence and a touch more caution in the look he received. "You don't understand. Sira di Sarc could take a Council seat at whim. From what I've been told, she could rule it, without any questioning her right to do so. She could change the—"

"She could be left alone. That's all we've asked." This time Morgan knew his voice was threatening, but didn't care. "You're wasting your time, Clansman, if you've come thinking I'll persuade Sira to follow any course that puts her back among the Clan. You, or Rael di Sarc."

"Rael?" Larimar's brows raised a bit too high. "I know Jarad's second daughter by reputation only. Why do you mention her?"

Not a good liar, Morgan said to himself, knowing he'd scored. "I thought Rael might share your sudden interest in Sira's future—and mine. My mistake."

The Clansman frowned, hesitated, then said as though testing: "There may be others. I don't say I know who they may be or their intent regarding you. You would be wise to be careful, Captain."

"Oh, I'm always careful, Clansman," Morgan said mildly, sipping his brandy and hoping Huido would continue to imitate a piece of furniture while the Clansman was being so forth-coming. He opened his awareness a crack to sample the emotions the Clansman was involuntarily broadcasting. Anger, definitely. Impatience. But also, Morgan recognized with a thrill of wariness, a strong thread of satisfaction. Why?

The Clansman seemed unaware of Morgan's perception—or didn't care. "Where is Sira? I would like to pay my respects." When Morgan didn't answer immediately, Larimar went on almost glibly: "Come now. Surely you are aware that her Talent is superior to mine. I am the one at risk, should she be displeased."

The Human turned his glass, as if admiring the reflections. "You know, Clansman di Sawnda'at," he said thoughtfully. "It's been my experience that the Clan aren't very comfortable talking about such things around me. Now, why is it that you are so accepting of Sira's Choice being Human?" Morgan's eyes snapped up to meet the Clansman's. He was not surprised to see pure hostility. He was surprised, and not pleasantly, to see how quickly Larimar controlled the expression.

"It is not my place to dispute Choice," the Clansman said, his Comspeak gaining more of an accent; perhaps his self-control came at a price. "Especially that of the powerful Sira di Sarc."

"The powerful Sira *Morgan*," Morgan corrected, deliberately baiting his opponent. "That is the name she uses now. A Human custom."

The green eyes narrowed to slits. "I have been polite, Human. Do not push me. You will regret it." Morgan felt a pressure on his shields, the merest hint of force.

"So I'm to believe you have no opinion about Sira's Choice with a Human."

"My opinion," this between gritted teeth, animosity in the open now, "is irrelevant. Joining cannot be undone, even if I were to—" The Clansman's big hands clenched and unclenched, as though he'd have liked to put them around Morgan's throat. Huido snapped a claw in warning.

Then Larimar raised one hand, moved it as though tracing the outline of the Human's head and shoulders in the air. Huido rumbled threateningly. Before the Carasian could act, Larimar clenched his fingers and dropped the fist, done.

Morgan tilted his head. He'd felt nothing. "And that was—"
There was pure triumph on Larimar's face. "An experiment,
Captain Morgan. Confirmation, if you like. I believe I needn't
waste any more of my time here." He put down his empty glass.
"My thanks for the excellent brandy. If you see Sira *di Sarc,* give
her my respects." A grim smile: "You will see me again, Human."
Air sighed into the space where Larimar had stood.

"Couldn't you have stopped him?" Huido asked, plates
sliding over plates with an annoyed hiss. Recently he'd developed a general dislike of those who didn't use doors.

"Yes," Morgan said. Sira had taught him that, how to hold
someone from the M'hir; it was a skill demanding more in
technique and control than power. She'd been pleased when
he'd mastered it, yet unsurprised.

"Why didn't you?"

"He'd stayed too long already," Morgan turned and looked
at the gleaming darkness of his friend, eyestalks clustered in
worry. "I should have realized what he was up to—"

"What?"

"Larimar di Sawnda'at was sent to follow me, to see me. Not
Sira. Why? Because I survived the testing of their most powerful Chooser. They're becoming desperate, Huido, desperate
to find out how we did it. That business at the end, the hand
gesture? He was testing me somehow. I believe Larimar knows
there was no Joining."

"Why does this matter? I thought you told me this was for
your protection. And Sira's."

Morgan picked up the Clansman's empty glass, then threw it
at the nearest wall before he'd recognized the desire for violence. He held his empty hand before his eyes. Sira had taught
him many useful things, he realized, shaken by the deadly potential he sensed in himself, stirring as though it awaited only
an excuse to take control.

"It matters, Brother," he said wearily. "If he spreads that information, Sira could lose the rights the Chosen enjoy within the
Clan. The Council has kept the secret—to avoid confessing
their guilt. Even though she calls herself an exile, it's that status
which protects her from outright interference." Morgan found
himself pacing and forced himself to sit instead. "If the Council

has to admit we aren't linked through the M'hir, it's back to the way things were before. No one on her side but us."

"What more does Sira need?" Huido boasted, with a cymbal-like snap of his handling claws in emphasis. "We shall defend her!"

Morgan looked up at his friend, feeling a welcome resurgence of his own rage. "Easier done if we prevent the problem." He stood. "Leave Larimar to me."

He'd deal with Rael later.

Chapter 26

I DON'T remember how long my Drapsk audience and I regarded one another. Long enough for me to decide to stand up, the crouch turning out to be both uncomfortable and somewhat demeaning when you were the focus of attention for thousands of beings. Long enough for me to then, eventually, turn completely around, so I could be sure every single Drapsk was also standing, antennae pointed straight in my direction.

Mercifully, an isolated spot of movement appeared, high up on the wall bearing the rows of Makii. I kept my gaze on it, quite sure it was my Skeptic and escort bestirring themselves to come down at last.

This process consumed sufficient time that I tired of the whole concept and would have tried to leave myself, but for one thing. I was, as their Mystic One and Contestant, at least partially responsible for whatever became of the Makii's fortunes now. I thought it at least polite to stay and try to explain what I'd done.

If I could.

"O Mystic One! O Mystic One!"

Well, I reassured myself, *Copelup sounded happy.* I watched the Skeptic practically tumble his way down through the last rows of mesmerized Makii, several willing hands making sure this passage was more figurative than painful. Captain Makairi, still faithfully wearing his ribbon, followed close behind, with a third Drapsk trailing whom I blindly assumed to be Maka.

"O Mystic—One," Copelup landed with an *oomph* of breath at my feet. I stretched out my hands to catch him, but he steadied immediately on his own. He took advantage of my gesture to capture the fingers of my right hand in his, squeezing them with most un-Drapsk vigor. "You did it!"

Fully aware of the rapt attention of the witnesses forming a veritable forest around us, I leaned forward and whispered: "I sent the Heerii's Contestant home. Isn't that—cheating?"

The Drapsk had excellent hearing, or else Copelup passed along what I whispered in some other fashion. Captain Makairi answered for him, at normal volume. "It would be cheating if you'd harmed or killed the other Contestant, O Mystic One. The Skeptics frown on those methods of eliminating the competition."

"So if I'm not in trouble, what happens now?" I asked, avoiding the effort of working my way through that particular nest of Drapsk ethics. Pushing the Rugheran into the M'hir had been, to put it mildly, a strain on every resource I had. My wounds, almost healed but still sore, were also reminding me how desirable a good night of sleep would be.

Copelup and the three Makii each inhaled all their tentacles, sucking pensively, antennae twitching in synchrony. I frowned at them, after a quick glance upward to be sure the remaining chorus of Drapsk were still quiescent. Thank goodness it wasn't a Human crowd.

"What's next, my good Drapsk?" I asked again, growing more suspicious. "You may not know this, but my abilities are not limitless. Neither's my patience, of which I've given you a considerable amount since coming insystem. What do I have to do in your Contest?"

"You'ff whon."

As this was from Maka, spoken around his tentacles with the requisite and sizable amount of drooling, I wasn't convinced. "If I've won," I said, directing my attention at Skeptic Copelup, "and I have no idea how that's reasonably possible—but believe me I won't argue the decision—does this mean I can leave now? Are the Makii," *what was the word?* "in ascendance over the others?"

"MAKII!!!"

I was almost knocked off my feet by the unexpected roar of agreement from the hitherto silent crowd, especially when that roar was accompanied by one of the Drapsk's trademark winds. My escort rocked happily to and fro in the breeze, plumes aflutter, tentacles now wide in a ring of contentment. I pointedly went over to the dais, tugged my heavy skirt out of my way, and sat down on an untidy pile of silk.

Even I could tell when a celebration was forthcoming; I just hoped it wouldn't take too long.

It was pleasure closer to agony. I stretched my toes, rolled my ankles one at a time, flexed my knees gently, twisted my hips until my spine thanked me, then slid my hands up and down the smooth sheets. *Alone at last.*

Not a bad day's work, I congratulated myself, feeling quite ridiculously satisfied considering I'd accomplished nothing for myself. I'd saved the Rugheran, a being whose thoughts had left a warm, happy presence in mine—if completely incomprehensible beyond its need for its kind.

And I'd given the Makii, my tormentors and friends, everything they'd hoped for from their Mystic One. As far as I knew, their Blessed Event was still underway. Thank goodness, Captain Makairi still recognized a bona fide state of collapse when he saw it, ordering me sent back to this room before I had to be carried.

A long soak in the fresher, a quick bite to eat, and here I was, back in the odd softness of my Drapsk bed. *Not a bad day at all.*

The celebration had explained a very great deal about the Drapsk and what this day had meant to them. It was so incredibly vivid in my mind, I could relive it by closing my eyes.

The Heerii had been first. They came down from their seats to pass me, dipping antennae in mute acknowledgment. Then, like the Niakii, they formed two lines, half going back to their seats, half joining the queue leaving the amphitheater.

This took remarkably little time, the Drapsk not prone to pushing or other disorderly behavior. Eventually, the amphitheater was again filled with quiet, motionless Drapsk, only with vacant seats marking where some from the losing Tribes had left.

I hadn't dared speculate during that expectant silence, wanting to believe the best of the Drapsk, or at least to believe whatever they were up to would be something I could comprehend as fair and reasonable, within my humanoid bias.

The lights below brightened, and I heard the first deliberately musical sound I'd encountered among the Drapsk—Copelup's tapes of Auordian croons not being what I considered particularly local. To call the three-note whistle "music" was, I decided, an allowable exaggeration, since the Drapsk began to sway to its arrhythmic beat in perfect unison. They were dancing; so the sound was music. I just hoped it wouldn't go on too long.

It hadn't. The music stopped, but the swaying continued as if the Drapsk had used the sound to set themselves into some desired pattern of movement. Then the first rank of Makii moved forward, still swaying, and approached the first ranks of remaining Niakii and Heerii Drapsk.

When Grant Murtree had told me about last year's Festival, and how one Tribe diminished in numbers and wealth while another increased, I'd made certain assumptions. I'd been wrong.

The clue, gripstsa, had been given to me, but had been too alien to understand.

This, then was the lar-gripstsa, the exchange of place taken to a new level. For each Makii Drapsk chose one Drapsk from another Tribe, holding hands, and bending forward until they could gently take each other's tentacles in gripstsa.

I *felt* it. I couldn't avoid the echoes within the M'hir as more and more paired off, each creating a true, if temporary link, the whole a latticework that included the inner part of me as surely as each other.

For a brief moment, I endured it in order to savor the resonance of energies, to cling vicariously to a sense of completeness that I instinctively knew would be so much more in a full Joining. Then the temptation was too great and I pushed myself free, clamping shut every protection I had.

It had been wonderful.

And, as a final surprise, there was more happening in front of my eyes than the Drapsk exchange of information and self-knowledge. For as I watched, the plumes of Niakii or Heerii within each gripstsa-entranced pair slowly lost their characteristic color, fading to drift almost clear in the slight breeze, only to bloom again with the rich purple-pink of the Makii.

Who were happily and, seemingly very politely, now in complete ascendancy within the amphitheater of Drapsk.

* * *

But they hadn't used the fireworks, I thought, suddenly less comfortable with both my bed, the night's memories, and my situation. *Why?*

They'd gone to a lot of trouble—potentially running afoul of the Trade Pact Enforcers—to obtain them.

There had to be something else about to happen.

Copelup had told me my true competition would be Drapskii itself. He had never explained what he meant.

I tested the M'hir. As I'd expected, the Drapsk had restored their barrier. I was sure it had only come down in the amphitheater so I could demonstrate my "magic." Although I hadn't bothered confronting the Skeptic, I suspected Copelup of deliberately placing me last in the list, knowing somehow the plight of the Rugheran would make me do something his kind would consider ample demonstration.

And, having proved what I could do, now they wanted something else.

For some reason, I shivered.

INTERLUDE

"No, I wasn't followed. Don't you think I'd know?" Barac kept his voice down, fully aware he couldn't budge the massive Carasian by any means other than persuasion. No question of any use of the Talent. The mind somewhere in that pulsating tin pot of a head was too bizarre for comfort.

Just as Huido's stubborn protectiveness of the Human was too ingrained to be other than a perfect roadblock now, holding Barac at bay. "Why do you want to see Morgan?" Huido repeated, clicking his lower handling claw as if contemplating the feel of a Clansman in its grip.

"Can I come in while we discuss this?" Barac glanced over his shoulder. This was about the busiest time of day for the restaurant district—perfect, he'd thought, for an inconspicuous chance to slip into the *Claws & Jaws* and catch up to Morgan. Perfect, except that Huido had rumbled out like a delivery servo and confronted him in the midst of the line of beings waiting to enter. To say they were drawing attention was an understatement.

Enough was enough. Barac could see the entranceway past Huido's hump of a back. He focused on the spot right behind the door and *pushed. . . .*

. . . Crash. He'd materialized with impeccable timing, scaring the waiter and sending a probably irreplaceable delicacy toward the ceiling. *Damn.*

Huido burst through the door an instant later, everyone from well-gowned customers to tray-laden staff scattering out of his way. One person elected to dive head-first into a large ornamental shrub. A Carasian in a hurry, and an unhappy Carasian at that, was guaranteed to disperse most crowds.

Barac stood his ground, though he looked around in hopes of finding Morgan and kept his mind firmly within the M'hir in case more significant dodging proved necessary.

Huido slammed to a halt so close to Barac that the Clansman could see his face reflected in several dozen pupils. Then the eyes parted, and a pair of exquisitely-sharp jaws protruded to press ever-so-lightly against his cheeks. Barac stopped breathing, but stayed where he was.

As suddenly, the huge being drew back, swinging one of his smaller arms around Barac's shoulders in bruising comradeship. "I approve of your *grist*. You want to see him this much? Come with me."

The noise level in the restaurant foyer began to return to its normal muted mix of voices, from a variety of vocal cords and implants, as Barac let Huido push him toward the private dining area in the back. *Grist?* Barac had no idea what the being was referring to—and decided as long as he had a good one, he wouldn't ask. Their progress was halted at the entrance by a waiter hurrying up to whisper in the Carasian's elbow.

Huido's claws made a sharp click, as though the Carasian were startled. More than half his eyes began searching their surroundings, while the rest kept a steady stare at Barac.

"What is it?" Barac asked, somehow sure this had to do with him—or with Morgan.

"Come," Huido ordered, lurching into motion while electing to keep several eyes on the Clansman.

The waiter led them down the hall from the eating area. He was Human, older than the others Barac had seen, perhaps Huido's personal servant. The Clansman reached for his thoughts, lightly, cautiously.

Nothing but a deep, formless anxiety. The Human had seen something upsetting—no, Barac corrected himself, refining the impressions he'd gained, the Human had seen something horrifying.

Their destination was the kitchen. Beyond the sound of a bubbling pot, the room was utterly quiet, at least until Huido arrived; staff huddled in one corner. The door to the freezer was ajar, puffs of frost drifting across the shining floor.

"We found it when Resy called for more iced prawlies," the

servant burst out as if the sight was too much. "We didn't know what to do, Hom Huido."

Barac stayed at the Carasian's side as he rumbled up to the freezer, so the two of them saw what had so disturbed the staff at the same time.

He wasn't too surprised by the dead body tossed in the back corner of the freezer—there had been overtones of death from all the readable minds in the room as they'd come in—or shocked by the plentiful and messy evidence of how the being had died—he'd seen the work of force blades before—but Barac was surprised to recognize the being lying like one of the sacks of frozen fish.

"What is Larimar di Sawnda'at doing in your freezer?" he asked the Carasian with real curiosity.

"And where is Morgan?"

Chapter 27

WHATEVER faced me next among the inscrutable Drapsk, at least I wouldn't have to endure it while clambering about in their ceremonial dress, I was relieved to discover in the morning. The spacer coveralls they'd found for me on the *Makmora* had been cleaned and laid out for me to wear, and a small box had been left as well.

I dressed and ate first, having learned to be suspicious of unexpected gifts. I wore the Ram'ad witchstone around my throat now, there being no further benefit to pretending I belonged to that unpleasant sisterhood. I'd snatched it from the Scats when our bargaining was interrupted. My hair hadn't liked the restriction of the leather thong around my head in any case, pulling itself free at every opportunity.

I wrapped a piece of the thick stuff around my fingers as I took a second look at the box. It looked expensively simple, with a rich gleam to the wood's finish suggesting either loving age, superb craftsmanship, or both.

"Well, the Great Bendini took his loot," I said out loud, reaching for it.

I'd expected jewelry or some exquisite ornament. I hadn't expected a tiny vial to be nestled inside, by its elaborate seals and mechanism exceedingly high-tech protection for what appeared to be a dull tawny-colored powder.

The thing was smaller than the tip of my little finger, blinking to itself with almost imperceptible indicators. It was—I hefted it on my palm—oddly heavy. I wasn't tempted to open it. In fact, I quickly replaced it in its box and shut the lid.

I had no idea what the Drapsk had given me. I was only sure

that anything so well-packaged was either illegal, hazardous, or both.

"Illegal? Hazardous? I'm shocked you would think such things, O Mystic One," Copelup protested when he arrived. "Shocked."

I picked up the box and waved it under his antennae. "Then what is it?"

His plumes flattened down his back and not only did Copelup inhale his tentacles, he covered his tentacle-stuffed mouth with both hands.

I looked down at him, tapping the top of the box with one finger. After watching gripstsa, I no longer considered this behavior to be comparable to a Human seeking pseudo-maternal comfort from a thumb. Instead, it appeared more likely to be the Drapsk equivalent of reviewing its immediate past, of replaying what it knew in order to make better sense of some new, confusing event. Such as me.

Copelup gradually unfurled himself, the plumes, I noticed, being the last body part restored to a relaxed yet alert position. "Forgive me," I said quite sincerely. "I meant to cause you no distress, Skeptic."

A wave of chubby fingers. "No. No. We value your curiosity as well as all else about you, Mystic One. It is just that I am unworthy to speak of this treasure to you. Please believe me when I assure you there is no greater gift we Drapsk could have placed in your keeping. Later, you will meet with those who can tell you more."

"Later?" I repeated with a sinking feeling, putting the box back on the table with care. "Copelup. I can't stay on Drapskii indefinitely. I must leave, and soon. I've told you—"

"This time tomorrow you may go wherever you wish, Mystic One."

There had to be a catch, a Drapsk "*but . . .*" buried in that smug voice.

"I can leave tomorrow," I said, stressing the last word. "Tomorrow as in one planet-day or as in one Pact Standard day?"

Copelup gave a delicate hoot. "As they differ by only three

tenths of a Standard second, Mystic One, I will leave that decision to you. And now it is time for us to go."

Go? A flood of almost unendurable impatience seized me, as though knowing I would be allowed to leave, it had to be immediately or I couldn't bear it. I took firm hold of that weakness, controlled it. There was more to deal with—I knew it.

"What happens between now and tomorrow, Skeptic?" I asked, pleased my voice came out with the right touch of nonchalance as I planted my feet firmly in place on the carpeting.

The Drapsk had started to urge me toward the door, his hands making little excited shooing motions, as though wherever we were going or whomever we were to meet wouldn't wait a moment longer—as impatient to have things done as I was. "The Contest, Mystic One. It's time for the Contest!"

I put my hands on my hips, wishing for a moment the outfit had come complete with its tool belt and preferably a small hand weapon. "We've been through the Contest," I reminded him. "I won. Didn't I?"

He'd hurried ahead to the door, yellow plumes trailing back toward me as though they might sense more than my words. "Won? Yes, Mystic One. You are the Competitor. You won the chance to enter the Contest."

"The Contest," I said slowly, then remembered what Copelup had told me. It still sounded crazy. "Against the planet."

The Skeptic drew his hand away from the door panel and turned to orient in my direction—facing me not being quite the term I'd use. He came back two steps and stopped. "This is not for show or entertainment, Mystic One," the Drapsk said with unusual bluntness, as though it was finally time for some honesty between us. "Our magic is gone; our world lost. Festival, the finding of competitors—whether of worth or not—and our search for magic is all to this purpose: to find the one who can recover what was squandered in our past; to restore our place in the universe.

"You are the first hope we have had in a very long time, Sira Morgan."

"What if your hope is misplaced, Copelup?" I answered as

plainly, my mouth starting to go dry. "I don't know what you want from me."

"That's all right, Mystic One," the Drapsk said with remarkable calmness. "Neither do we."

INTERLUDE

The air was heavy on his lips and methane-tainted to his nostrils. It could rain again at any moment, Morgan decided, peering up into the dull gray cloud that passed for a sky. As if it needed to; his feet sank in mud at every step, a momento of the morning's drenching.

A typical summer day on the northern half of Ret 7. Morgan had made sure the *Fox* was sealed tight. The atmosphere was significantly corrosive to metals even in the drier winter months.

His multi-terrain vehicle, complete with hired driver, waited ahead, bobbing slightly as though to prove there was real water beneath the layer of flattened reed grass passing for a shoreline. More of the open craft dotted the flat landscape as far as the dim light permitted one to see, cutting swathes of mud and water in every direction. Easy to see why they were better known as mudcrawlers.

Or can-of-toads, if one were so inclined, Morgan thought uncharitably. He'd traded with Retians for years, finding them profitable clients, if predictably cheap when they could get away with it—a trait which also encouraged a willingness to deal with small independents such as himself. They were at the same time more prejudiced against non-Retians than any offworlder could possibly be in return. Fortunately, this was a bias they rarely bothered to exhibit, feeling it sufficient to bar those not born here from any ownership of land or other property. To each their own. Very few had shown an interest in living on this mudball as it was.

Huido, for one, hated the place, Morgan reflected, grabbing the moisture-slicked handle to pull himself and his bags on board.

Which was logical in a being whose idea of paradise involved rock, salt spray, females, and cold beer.

"Destination, Hom Captain?" The driver's Comspeak was flawless, a valuable commodity around a shipcity. Morgan glanced back over his shoulder. Shipcity? On Ret 7, it was a strip of pavement to keep the ships out of the mud and little more.

"Jershi. Malacan's Fine Exports," the Human said, moving toward the back of the long, almost rectangular mudcrawler. It wasn't so much the potent odor of native Retian—traders learned early to ignore, or endure, differing biological realities as much as possible—as it was experience. Morgan propped himself as close to the bulky rear-mounted engine as he could manage, pulling out a large square of water-repellent plas and wrapping it around himself and his bags.

The driver watched with interest, one eye blinking, then the other, lips a wavy line of blue. The color was startling against the mud gray of wrinkled skin. There was a very long and not very polite joke about the difficulties experienced by Retians attempting to find one another in their natural habitat.

Morgan tucked himself within his wrapping as the driver, satisfied his passenger was settled, released the holds anchoring them to whatever might be solid beneath the surface. The mudcrawler pulled away from the shore and headed into the marsh itself. The sound of the engine was almost deafening, but he was out of most of the spray. The Retians didn't believe in shields, having nictitating membranes over their protruding eyes and relishing the feel of their damp environment on their skin. It wreaked havoc with off-world tech, but that only increased the frequency of trade.

Morgan wasn't interested in trade this trip, though he'd been careful to post a small list of reasonable cargo. No sense alerting Port Authority that the *Fox* was here on personal business. Information entering the official channels was as hot a commodity here as any other goods.

No, Morgan thought grimly, *no sense making himself obvious, especially when his business involved one Retian in particular.*

Chapter 28

I'D sought out the Drapsk for my own ends: a means to flee the complication of Rael's arrival; later, a place to heal. I hadn't thought at all about what my coming meant to the Drapsk. *Had I done so,* I realized with a sickening, familiar guilt, *I doubt I'd have cared.* I'd used the little aliens as willingly and carelessly as I had Morgan.

Sira Morgan was fully in charge of my emotions and responses now, events of the past days having finally overwhelmed what remained of Sira di Sarc's Clannish self-absorption. Or maybe, to be kinder to that other half of myself, my inner selves had at last found common ground. The Drapsk had a problem achingly similar to my own.

And here I sat, as I had for what seemed hours, listening to a chorus of Drapsk debate what I could do about it.

"There is no alternative but to use the 59C-3 interspanner we developed as part of the measuring process before going too far," the two turquoise Drapsk said together. They were Doakii, a Tribe relatively rare in this city I'd been informed, but dominant in the southern hemisphere due to a streak of inspired luck providing the winning Contestant there several Festivals in a row. The two of them seemed most comfortable speaking in unison and sat with the tips of their plumes in contact. I wondered, but didn't dare ask, if this was affection or a way of passing private messages.

There were also three Skeptics present in the group surrounding me, all inclined to stand and pace when the discussion—as now—sank into technicalities, presenting me with the unanticipated problem of repeatedly losing track of which individual was Copelup.

We were in the same building where I'd slept, in a large, almost round room shaped and furnished as a miniature replica of the amphitheater from the night before. I had the seat of honor, or at a minimum was the focus, having been urged into the center of the space beneath the two ringlike rows of Drapsk.

It didn't seem to be a government meeting. Orange Drapsk, who I assumed must own the restaurant and catering business in the city, scurried about politely offering various delicacies and beverages. I'd declined all so far, too nervous and too much the center of attention to want to fight my way through a flaky pastry or deal with sticky foam.

It didn't have the happy expectation of last night either. These Drapsk sat quietly on their stools unless expressing an opinion or offering an idea. There were thirty in total, a group comprised, another detail from Copelup's typically patchy briefing, of members from each of the currently viable Tribes on Drapskii. I didn't know what constituted a nonviable Tribe and again, didn't dare ask.

They'd stated in the beginning, when I first walked hesitantly into the room with Copelup and Captain Makairi, that all conversation would be in Comspeak. The Scented Way was not to be deliberately invoked, a courtesy I appreciated, though one I couldn't confirm for myself anyway.

These, then, were the Drapsk who could tell me about the dust, though they hadn't chosen to as yet. I could feel the box in the side pocket of my coveralls where I'd slipped it for safe-keeping, Copelup having a mild fit at the idea I might leave it behind in the room.

"This talk of spanners, sensors, and other gadgetry is pointless if she can't do it!"

I snapped to attention, my mind having drifted free from the occasionally raucous debates that ensued over the oddest-sounding things. I certainly agreed with the owner of that indignant voice, one of five Niakii sitting companionably with the Makii's four representatives. Some of the latter, I thought idly, could well have been white-plumed Niakii themselves before betting on the Great Bendini. It was an interesting system, to say the least.

"What does the Mystic One say?"

I could hear someone's impatient tapping in the expectant silence following this helpful suggestion from the Makii.

"I," I coughed and started again, wondering how I could stand in front of the powerful Clan Council and feel less nervous. "I should probably just give it a try. Whatever it is."

Even the tapping stopped.

I rose to my feet, firming up my voice. "I've come here because I'm willing to attempt your Contest." I paused and turned to look them all in the, well, in the mouth. "It sounds as though you don't know what to expect either. How can I promise what may be impossible? But I'll try. If—" I paused again. "If you promise me that no matter what happens, I can leave Drapskii tomorrow."

Despite their earlier assurances, enough plumes began waving after this ultimatum to generate a small battle of breezes flowing past my face. Tentacles disappeared then reappeared in rapid succession, making each Drapsk face seem like a miniature vid screen with flickering images.

I sat back down. This could take a while.

INTERLUDE

"You're not serious," Barac demanded, feeling queasy not only because he couldn't help trying to meet the gaze of several dozen whirling eyes.

Huido clicked disagreement. "It solves the disposal question."

"No," the Clansman said, shaking his head for emphasis. Ideal to have *pushed* the body into the M'hir—it was what the Clan preferred to do with their dead anyway. Unfortunately, being only sud, he couldn't push a scrap of plas through without borrowing strength.

But the Carasian's solution, if sincere and not just the being's way of baiting him, was equally impossible. "You can't add him to the menu," Barac repeated firmly.

Four arms lifted and dropped in an impressive and noisy shrug. "He can't stay in the freezer," Huido argued reasonably. "There's no room. And the mess upsets my staff."

They hadn't made any progress in other, far more important issues either, such as how and why Larimar di Sawnda'at had ended his life as part of the *Claws & Jaws'* provisions. As for who had made that decision for him, well, they'd avoided any discussion of that detail. Both of them knew very well who wore concealed force blades as a matter of course. And both were aware of Jason Morgan's present disposition toward the Clan, even if Barac, for one, hadn't expected anything quite so brutal as this, so soon. This was a conclusion the Clansman knew better than to express to the devoted and easily angered Carasian.

"Maybe we can slip him out in the waste stream," Barac offered.

Neither of them had mentioned contacting Station security or the Enforcers. Barac had his reasons, primary among them being a deep-seated reluctance to involve non-Clan in what was definitely a Clan matter. This was more than his training as a Scout: it was self-preservation. The Council would take a very dim and likely hostile view of his exposing the Clan's internal business.

Of course, there was the peculiar difficulty of how the Clan, particularly the Council, would treat the death of a Clansman already declared dead. For Larimar di Sawnda'at was one of those reportedly lost years ago in the explosion of the liner *Destarian,* along with Yihtor di Caraat. The last time Barac had seen Larimar alive, he had been on the jungle world of Acranam, hiding with others of his kind and beliefs in Yihtor's enclave to escape the Council's tight-fisted rule. That Yihtor planned to start his own Clan empire from this humble beginning was, from what Barac knew of Larimar's ambition, probably a bonus.

So what was one of Acranam's rebels doing on Plexis, in Huido's freezer? He'd been following Morgan. Why? Barac didn't believe for an instant that Larimar had come to ask Morgan to convince Sira di Sarc to enter the struggle to rule the Clan Council. What would he, or whomever he represented, hope to gain? Every Clan knew Sira cared nothing for her own kind and less than nothing for the Council. She had, Barac knew, every right to feel so.

More likely Larimar had hoped to find Sira for some end of his own. *If he had,* Barac thought with a certain grim satisfaction, *it would explain the Clansman's current state.*

"This is Plexis, Clansman. The waste stream is monitored," Huido continued his argument. "That method has been tried too often. I still say my way is best."

The Carasian, Barac knew, had only one simple motivation for finding a secure way to dispose of the inconvenient corpse, one that had nothing to do with politics or the nerves of his staff.

Huido would do anything necessary to protect his blood brother, Morgan, from any threat at all. Including hard questions from Station Authority.

Even if Morgan did—as Barac believed—dump a body in Huido's kitchen, undocking the *Silver Fox* late last night—that much was on record—and leaving without a word of warning or explanation. It was, Barac thought, a measure of their relationship that Huido accepted this without any of his characteristic temper.

The Clansman sighed. Whether Morgan was guilty or not, they had a more immediate problem.

"If we do it your way," he said reluctantly, fighting the rising gorge from his own stomach and vowing never again to eat at the *Claws & Jaws,* "I want your promise Larimar won't end up on the humanoid side of the menu."

Chapter 29

HELD up to the daylight coming in through the window—a rare feature in Drapsk architecture—the powder was a leather-like brown, with brighter, almost golden specks within it. Dirt, I'd have thought, if I hadn't been told otherwise. But the reality was so daunting, I found myself asking for the third time:

"This came *from* the M'hir?"

"Yes," Levertup said proudly. "From the Scented Way; what you call the M'hir. It has, as you can see, physical substance." He was senior among the Skeptics, distinguishable only in that his was the voice trying to convince me of this, among other unbelievable ideas. The others sat quietly, plumes nodding occasionally as if in agreement.

I stared at the tiny vial. *I was holding some of the M'hir in my hand?* I'd have been less astonished if the Drapsk insisted I was holding last night's dream. I opened my awareness, feeling only the familiar blackness and turmoil, seductive energy and warning lifelessness. *What was there to touch?*

Disconcertingly, the Drapsk reacted to my inner exploration with a bustle of instrument consulting, a collection having been brought to the amphitheater on trays by the helpful orange Drapsk, an event which made me revise my estimation of their role in this society from caterers to possibly all-purpose messengers.

I smiled, and knew it wasn't pleasantly. So much for the much-vaunted Clan ownership of the M'hir and the abilities it gave my kind. These aliens had an understanding and knowledge of the M'hir beyond what any of our scholars could imagine. And, from the look of things, the Drapsk owned the technology which could spread that knowledge to others.

Knowledge, but they also had need of what I could do. I sat a little straighter, putting the vial back in its box along with any consideration of what its contents meant—I'd need quite a while to comprehend that, and I doubted such comprehension would make a difference in what I was to attempt anyway.

"Let's give it a try now, Levertup," I said, proud of the confidence in my voice if sure it was nonexistent anywhere else.

Another moment of bustling with instruments and gadgets. Some of the Heerii were occupied at a long, complex console that had appeared from the smooth wall—a not-uncommon trait of Drapsk machinery. As I understood it, these were all monitors of some type, to let the Drapsk know if I were successful.

As to what I was to do, all they'd been able to tell me was based on a song, chanted to two notes, and important enough to have been passed down through the generations within every Tribe. I hummed it to myself, now, having listened to it through several, thus far meaningless, repetitions.

> *"Once upon a silent planet,*
> *Drapsk did come to sing and play.*
> *Playing on a silent planet,*
> *Drapsk did find the Scented Way.*
> *Tribe to Tribe the Way did lead us,*
> *'til its magic passed away."*

It rhymed. That was about all I could say about it. The Drapsk were no better at explaining, except to add that they hadn't evolved on this planet. They'd colonized Drapskii, moving their entire population here, because of the strength of the Scented Way they discovered, implying the planet itself had some connection to the M'hir. There had been some kind of golden age. Then, a few generations ago, this connection had become tenuous, then was lost completely. The Drapsk had suffered ever since. They didn't elaborate on how they had suffered, but felt strongly enough about it to have curled into dismal balls of upset for several minutes after these details were revealed to me by Levertup.

I was to reconnect Drapskii to the Scented Way. How, they had no idea. Since I didn't know either, I thought I should verify one important detail.

"I'm leaving tomorrow," I reminded them. "No matter what happens."

I took the inhalation of tentacles as a yes.

As Sira di Sarc, I'd studied more than most of my kind, at first in order to uncover some way out of my dilemma as unChosen, but eventually because I found my curiosity about anything unfamiliar to be an itch constantly in need of scratching. My time as Sira Morgan had only added an innocent wonder to my interest. So I'd experimented within the M'hir, testing and probing; it was never safe there, but I'd found ways to explore its potential. I was perhaps better prepared than any of my kin to attempt what the Drapsk wanted, not that any of them would.

The Drapsk had, at my suggestion, coaxed a long low couch-like bench from the floor. I stretched out on it now, the three Drapsk I considered my friends, if the word meant anything comparable to them—Captain Makairi, Maka, and Copelup—taking positions beside me. They dipped their antennae until I could feel the feathery tips on the bare skin of my lower arms and hands. "Remember, You must not risk yourself, Mystic One," the two Makii said in harmony. "Return to the Makii, your Tribe."

I closed my eyes, opening fully the other vision I possessed, *pushing* my consciousness from this place and this body, into the black heart of the M'hir. . . .

I was the center of the universe. Power coursed toward me, spinning me about, tempting me to stay with its seductive, unheard voice. This I knew and dismissed, looking deeper.

The Rugheran had been a clue, its ability to move within the M'hir, instead of through it, sufficiently different to guide me now. I sought something other than the ever present crackle of energy, some of it my own. Something solid, like the grains of powder I'd held up to the sunlight.

There.

I flung myself back, thoroughly startling my Drapsk companions as I sat up. It would seem to them I'd only just closed my eyes, but there was a limit to the subjective time one could spend in the M'hir. I knew better than to linger without returning. "I've found it," I said triumphantly, breathing heavily as though I'd climbed stairs at a run, grasping tightly to my own sense of self.

There were machine hums and purrs overlaying the quiet murmurs of the Drapsk. Maybe they hadn't needed the announcement, I said to myself uneasily, laying back down. For a second time, I *pushed* . . .

Knowing my target let me focus more quickly. I had no physical sense of what it was I'd found, but I recognized it on some level as belonging to the Drapsk, a *something* similar to the flavor of the potential I'd sensed between the individuals during lar-gripstsa—immensely stronger. Perhaps it was the planet.

Whatever it was, it was slippery. Even as I *reached* for it, a process indescribable in any other terms but definitely not part of my body's repertoire of movements, the something I thought was Drapskii faded, becoming stronger at the edges of my perception.

Maybe I shouldn't reach *for it,* I decided, dreaming a little, riding the waves of dark and terrible beauty around me. Sure enough, as I drew away, the sense of Drapskii increased, falling toward me with increasing speed.

As should all here, I dreamed, knowing myself the core, the center. This was my rightful place, my palace . . .

Pain!

INTERLUDE

Secrets. They were her business to uncover and expose—to those who should know. There was no question of this. Yet the Watcher hesitated, for once in conflict with her purpose. She should alert the Council, send warnings to the other Watchers. Then again, she could wait. She could Watch. And find out just what the daughter of di Sarc was doing.

Secrets within secrets. Faitlen di Parth, knowing full well that the best secrets bestowed power on their possessor, cherished this one close to his heart.

And protected it deep in his thoughts. Jarad di Sarc's was the greater power—so far. No point taking any chances.

Faitlen also knew others thought him weak willed, easily led. It was true, in part. He had always been painfully aware his Talent alone could never make him first—or even close to first—within the Clan. Until now, he'd approached that goal by clinging to those who did rise. Now? There were other ways.

Five lay in the boxes arrayed in front of him, their delivery precisely timed and as precisely arranged to avoid notice. It had taken months of planning and funds moved with a deviousness only a Queeb could appreciate. Faitlen ran his hand over the nearest box. "You are the future of the House of di Parth," he whispered, though alone in this receiving hall. Elsewhere, technicians busied themselves with preparations. "Soon you will know the honor I have granted you."

He moved from one box to the next, greeting its unconscious occupant, until he stood between the final two.

There, Faitlen pressed his hands flat on both, bowing his

head briefly. His thin features were resolute—this was a decision made long before, the final payment for the future glory of di Parth. "Sleep, daughters," the Clansman said softly. "You need never know."

Nor, he devoutly hoped, would the Watchers. And so, Jarad.

Chapter 30

"MYSTIC One?"

I waved one hand feebly, pushing away whatever was tickling my face in the process, realizing too late it was someone's appendage. "Sorry," I mumbled. My head felt stuffed with feathers as well. "What happened?"

"She wakes!"

I blinked involuntarily, having opened my eyes as breezes fought their way over me, relieved the Drapsk were happy— though I wished they could express it in a less drafty manner. I shivered and someone, a Niakii, thoughtfully pulled a sheet up to my chin.

I was still lying on the couch in the center of the small amphitheater, still surrounded by ranks of gadget-fascinated Drapsk of every possible color. Nothing had changed.

It didn't have time to, I thought, remembering. Then I shivered in earnest. Like some fool, I'd almost lost myself in the M'hir. These beings had saved my life. And quite simply, I found, examining a red mark on my forearm. "You pinched me," I accused Copelup. Hardly a technological approach.

The Skeptic didn't appear repentant in the least. In fact, he hooted three times in succession.

"And you should be grateful, O Mystic One," he said when able to speak. "We wish your help, not your corpse."

"Can you try again?" This in an overlapping confusion of voices as most of the Drapsk bent their plumes hopefully in my direction.

"The readings are most promising," Levertup encouraged, coming closer. "The best we've ever had."

Well, I thought, *it had been my fault I'd skirted disaster, and*

244 Julie E. Czerneda

the Drapsk had been able to save me from myself. I nodded,
closed my eyes, and *pushed* myself from the room for the third
and I hoped, the last time . . .

Drapskii wasn't hard to find now. The insubstantial webbing
my mind labeled as the planet surrounded me when I entered the
M'hir, as if I'd come close to luring it from the M'hir with me.

Was that what the Drapsk hoped?

No, I thought, while holding very tightly to my sense of place
this time. *What's wrong here isn't the location of the planet
within this other space. It's the way it is coiled on itself, severed
and independent from surges and patterns beyond.* Carefully,
experimentally, I *reached* for just one tiny part of the webbing,
teasing it free. Once released, it glowed with what I recognized
as power along its length, as though the exposed end were a leaf
collecting radiation from some unknown sun.

It felt *right.*

I began teasing more parts free, watching their neighbors begin
to copy the action on their own, multiplying so that for each one I
untangled, dozens more spontaneously freed themselves.

I held myself together firmly, intent on doing as much as I
could before returning to myself; in truth, so fascinated by my
unsuspected ability to affect this place I was reluctant to leave.

It was this fascination that came close to ending my life. I
didn't sense what approached until it was on me.

How to describe what happened next? It was as if every vein
in my body was being torn open and sucked dry; every emotion
I'd ever felt was being ripped from my mind. Worse was the
sensation of power pouring out of me until I realized in horror I
was about to dissolve.

Pain! Pain!

The Drapsk were fighting for me, too, but it wasn't enough.
Something was *keeping* me in the M'hir.

Why, I was fading, I realized with numb surprise. In another
moment, there would be nothing left to return to the body I'd
abandoned. At least there was no link to pull Morgan to this death
with me.

Morgan. All that was worthwhile in my life. His name, the
rightness of him, coursed through me like a stim. He needed
me. How dare I die?

Very easily. The force, or whatever it was holding me, cared nothing for my sudden struggle, for my frantic efforts to find out what was happening. I'd gained a handful of subjective seconds, if that. I searched desperately for some tool, some escape.

Drapskii. I reached for the nearest glowing tips, aghast as some snapped and died at my touch, but finding I could hold others. From them, energy flowed back into me. More, more. Then, suddenly . . .

It was enough.

I opened my eyes, aware of three things at once.

I was surrounded by Drapsk, bending over me so all I could see was a rainbow cloud of feathery plumes. My body was, I felt myself hastily, completely intact, despite the sensation of having been torn apart for some feast.

And my arms were covered with small pinch marks, already sore.

"Dear Drapsk," I think I said, before everything went peacefully blank.

INTERLUDE

"How much longer?" Morgan asked, fuming.

His driver waved his hand, the poison spur at the base of the thumb a warning glint of white against gray. Morgan had a healthy respect for this natural armament, enough to have updated his antivenom supplies, taking a shot before coming insystem. "Who can say?" the Retian answered peacefully, both bulbous eyes closed and webbed feet dangling in the water to one side of the mudcrawler.

Morgan's glare was wasted on both the relaxed Retian and the source of the mid-marsh traffic jam, a straggling herd of migrating brexks complete with outriders. He'd seen vistapes of the Retian food beasts, but not until now appreciated their size.

Or stink. The Human added a second filter pack to his breather, seeking some relief for his burning nostrils and mouth. *It wasn't a smell,* he said to himself, eyes watering. *It was an all-out assault.* An outrider scooted past, controlling its skidder—a one-rider version of the mudcrawler and as agile as its name suggested—with practiced insolence. Morgan ducked under his plas blanket in time to miss most of the resulting spray of mud and water.

Morgan was impatient with any delay. His destination was in sight past the distant ring of muddy dike works. Ahead lay the lumpy buildings forming the outer edge of Jershi; just within that edge was the All Sapients' District, where the Retians rented space to offworld entrepreneurs. And on one of the few high and dry spots—fortunately considered marginal real estate by the amphibious Retians, was the storefront of Malacan's Fine Exports.

Morgan found himself grinding his teeth and deliberately relaxed his jaw. Malacan Ser was his only reliable contact on this world. That didn't guarantee Malacan's cooperation or that he'd have any useful information, but it was a start.

Except that between them was a line of over two hundred mud-splattered, grumpy-sounding, smelly beasts, each easily three times the size of this or any of the other mudcrawlers floating in wait.

Another skidder plowed through the marsh dangerously close to them. Morgan prepared to duck, then spotted his driver slithering over the side. He disappeared with a plop in the dark water just as a second skidder appeared coming from the other direction.

Morgan reacted instinctively, pulling himself clear of the waterproof and motion-restricting sheet. There wasn't much of a side rail on the vessel, but he found what cover he could beside the engine mount, flipping open the holster of his sidearm. He didn't draw it yet. This could all be more Retian fun in the water; Human-baiting was a popular sport.

He licked his lips as the skidders came near, tasting sweat, mud, and a psychic tinge of foreboding. *No joke,* Morgan abruptly knew beyond doubt, no more than the crossing of the herd in front of his mudcrawler was a coincidence.

Morgan lunged for the controls. They were simple enough: a switch flipped up to engage the engine's drive, a lever aimed and controlled the resulting force to steer the mudcrawler. He toggled the switch and leaned the lever full ahead in time to send a surge of wake into the path of the nearest skidder. It flipped, spilling its rider, who began swimming toward him almost as quickly.

Without thinking, Morgan swung the lever hard left to deal with the second skidder, holding on as a loud thud marked his success. His lips stretched over his teeth in a predator's grin, but Morgan resisted the temptation to make sure of his pursuers. Instead, he aimed the mudcrawler at the herd of slow-moving beasts.

Time to see if they had the sense to get out of his way.

Chapter 31

"COPELUP?" I called, padding barefoot down the long, empty hallway. The flooring, though soft to the touch, carried a faint echo of my steps. The lights were dull—night-dimmed, I assumed. "Any Makii?"

I'd awakened in my bed, as tired and sore as if I hadn't truly slept. Perhaps I hadn't. There had been other times I'd come close to exhausting my resources, to pushing my Talent too far. The resulting weariness had been nothing compared to what I felt now.

But it didn't matter. What did was discovering what had happened to Drapskii. My most vivid memory was of breaking threads, stealing energy to save myself. *From what?* I didn't believe in monsters. What I did believe was that I'd personified my own failing strength and weakness, used some hallucination to goad myself into surviving at any cost—even their planet's connection to the M'hir.

My misjudgment. I feared the result. So I'd left my room, hardly noticing the door was no longer locked, and began searching for my Drapsk.

After a while, I began to doubt I'd find any at all. The entire floor was deserted. Rather than head down in the lift in my nightshirt—another gift from the Drapsk—I went back to my room and dressed.

"Might as well pack, too," I said out loud, remembering with guilty relief the Drapsk's promise to allow me to leave today. They'd given me a boxlike carrier for my things, few as they were. I folded up the ceremonial dress, smiling as I imagined the look on Morgan's face when he saw it, and put it inside. Then I picked up the small box.

I noticed its odd weight, one puzzle among many. How had the Drapsk brought a bit of the M'hir into this existence? *And why?*

Slipping the box into my pocket again, I pulled the dress out of the carrier and dropped it on the bed. I couldn't leave, I admitted to myself, not without knowing what had happened and if they still needed me. Sira Morgan's decision: the part of me who—despite the urgency to go to Morgan—knew full well what Morgan's own choice would have been.

I took the lift to the main floor with an eerie sense of retracing my steps. The open area, with its bulblike eating rooms, was as deserted as the hall upstairs. From all evidence, I was alone in the building. I found myself half-running to the doorway leading out, beginning to suspect I'd done something truly dreadful to the Drapsk.

After one step out the door, I was convinced I had. The dark sky above was ablaze, as if set on fire, while the platform and walkways were literally stuffed with Drapsk of every possible color, all dashing to and fro as though they'd lost their senses. Fortunately, the walkway wasn't flowing and the bowlcars sat abandoned, or there would have been some tragedies in front of my eyes. *Had they gone mad?*

"The Mystic One!" The cry sprang from a thousand tentacle-ringed mouths at once. The sky went black at the same time, throwing off my vision just when my horrified eyes saw most of the Drapsk turn to start coming my way.

I stumbled back through the hotel doorway by feel. As I started to close it, panic-stricken at the thought of the mob, the sky lit again. Immediately, the Drapsk stopped and fluttered their plumes.

"Fireworks?" I said in disbelief, staring upward as I stepped back outside for a better view. "They're sending up the fireworks."

"There you are!" Captain Makairi and four other Makii detached themselves from the near edge of the crowd and hurried toward me. When they were close enough, all five of them reached out to pat me gently, as if checking I was real. "We've been worried, Mystic One. Copelup said you would wake in your own time. Are you recovered?"

"Tired," I said, hearing the truth of that in my own voice. I found myself patting them lightly in return, a gesture they didn't seem to mind. "And concerned, Makii. What happened? Do you know if I succeeded at all?"

The five began to hoot uncontrollably. It wasn't quite the reaction I expected, though it was, I thought, reassuring in a way. Captain Makairi recovered his equilibrium first, saying: "Come with us, Mystic One. We're on our way to one of the Makii Houses—just behind this building. We will tell you how very, very well you did for all of Drapskii."

As I should have guessed, the Makii House turned out to be the Drapsk version of a tavern. I let them herd me inside to where I stood waist-deep in purple and pink Makii. I looked in vain for a seat of any kind, noticing that most of those who'd been here a while had containers of various shapes and sizes firmly affixed to their mouths, their tentacles making this a very reasonable way to carry a drink. One result was a most unfamiliar absence of sounds, despite more of the bitonal music and the irregular thudding of feet as individuals milled around one another.

"Make way for the Mystic One!"

This shout from Captain Makairi—in Comspeak for my benefit and backed by the no-nonsense hand fan he produced and aimed around the room—had the effect of opening a wide expanse of floor in front of me and totally disrupting the party atmosphere. I felt as conspicuous as a disbeliever among Turrned Missionaries.

It didn't help when the Drapsk began bowing in great waves, drinks still clamped to their mouths.

All I could do was to hurry to where Captain Makairi had found an actual table and chairs along one back wall—perhaps ready for aliens such as myself. Each Drapsk I passed brushed me lightly with their fingers, as if I were irresistible yet fragile. Since I felt the latter at least, I sank gratefully into the nearest seat, trying to ignore the scrutiny of every being in the room.

"Sombay, hot, with those spices she likes," another Drapsk barked an order into the air. "Biscuits, Mystic One?"

Already drooling at the thought of the sombay, I nodded mutely, only now spotting the name inscribed in Comspeak on this one's tool belt. "Maka. I'm happy to see you," I said, delighted my own Drapsk were keeping track of me.

The Drapsk indicated gratitude with a quick touch from his antennae. "This pleases me also, Mystic One. We of the *Makmora* hold you in our souls. We never doubted you."

"Where's Copelup?" I asked, craning around in hopes of spotting those yellow plumes. None were in sight.

"The Skeptics . . . study . . . argue . . . Niakii . . . their numbers . . . results . . . speculate," two other Drapsk answered in a confusing overlap of voices. "No fun," they synched at last.

"Maybe I should go and talk to them," I offered, weakening as the sombay was delivered steaming hot and with a fragrance promising it was exactly the way I'd come to love it. The Drapsk always did their homework. To complete their effort to pin me in place, a plate of fresh biscuits arrived, already split and filled with my favorite sweet spread.

"Then again," I decided around a mouthful, "I could stay here a while." I sank deeper into my chair. "Especially if you can tell me what is going on."

INTERLUDE

Barac shook his head, convinced he'd lost his appetite forever. "You go ahead, Chief Bowman," he said graciously. "I've already eaten."

Bowman raised one eyebrow. "Must have been early," she commented, helping herself to another spoonful of some green cereal. "Thought I was an early riser. Didn't sleep well? Or don't Clan sleep?"

The Clansman had to smile. Was there ever a moment this Human didn't pry for information? Even now, when Plexis and the ships tucked in her sides were still an hour from stationday, the Enforcer's eyes were bright and interested. "We sleep," he gave her. "From the look of it, more than you do."

"Hmmph," was all she answered, busy eating. Barac looked over at the third member of this breakfast group.

Terk, leaning up against the galley wall, didn't seem to have an appetite either or else, as Barac sometimes suspected, the Human was actually a servo and needed neither food nor rest. His appearance did nothing to belie the impression, Terk's uniform having to cope with a barrel chest and unusually wide shoulders. His hair was pale and limp above features that, to be generous, looked like a sculptor had forgotten to finish them properly. His eyes, currently fixed on Barac and apparently not needing to blink, were like chips of stone.

All in all, Barac decided, *not the look of a diplomat.*

Nor the manners. Terk, seeing his commander occupied, asked abruptly: "So where did Morgan light off to? Didn't Huido know? Or wouldn't he tell you?"

"Didn't the *Fox* file a destination?" Barac shot back.

Bowman patted her lips with a napkin. "There is an interesting tendency on Plexis to withhold information on departures, Hom sud Sarc," she answered with a glint of real annoyance in her eyes. "They don't consider themselves to be a spaceport, you see, and feel this should grant them unusual latitude in how they deal with us."

"We don't pay bribes," Terk clarified, his normally deep voice a growl.

Barac knew better than to grin. "In answer to your question, Constable, no, I don't know where Jason Morgan went. His friend, the Carasian, may know, but you'd have better luck with Plexis." He tilted his head, considering the two Humans. They couldn't know about Larimar. *Why the sudden interest in Morgan?*

"You told me you were investigating the telepaths who attacked me yesterday. What does Morgan have to do with them? Besides being one himself," he added, quite sure these Enforcers knew this much and more about Sira's Chosen.

Bowman pushed aside her plate, though it remained half full. She nodded once at Terk, who went to the door and locked it. Barac merely raised a curious brow. The Humans knew he could leave any time he chose, so this precaution wasn't against him. "I don't want interruptions," Bowman answered, her perception, as always, uncomfortably close to that of a true mind reader.

"I'm becoming convinced we have a problem, a serious problem, Clansman Barac sud Sarc," she continued, steepling her fingertips together on the table and regarding him with those keen, miss-nothing eyes. "But first, are you able to—what's the word?—block any telepathic eavesdroppers?"

Barac started, automatically checking his shields. In place and properly so, despite there being no conceivable threat to his thoughts here. "Human eavesdroppers?" he guessed and was rewarded by her nod. "Yes. Of course."

Her lips twitched, amused perhaps by the involuntary superiority in his voice. "Forgive the question, but it's become an issue lately. Terk? Why don't you give our guest some of the background to our—investigation?"

Terk tossed a sheet of plas covered with notations to land on the table in front of Barac. "Human telepaths have been disappearing," the Human said bluntly, pointing at the sheet. "We've lost seven from our force in as many weeks. There are rumors, hard to confirm or deny, of civilian disappearances as well. The most solid are there."

Barac pulled the sheet around so he could read the precise script. It was a list of two dozen names and systems, one link immediately obvious. "All male. I thought your females were as likely to have some Talent." The Clansman was proud of the way he said that, as though Humans could have anything like the abilities meant by Talent among his kind; Morgan, he hoped, being the exception.

"We've noticed."

The Clansman frowned. "So what are you implying? That this is why I was attacked? Someone is kidnapping male telepaths— Human and now, with the attempt on me, non-Human? I don't recommend the practice."

Bowman shook her head. "No, I doubt Sorl and his group had the same reasons for their attempt to carry you off with them, Hom sud Sarc."

"You know them?" Try as he might, Barac couldn't keep the outrage from his voice. "Then have they been arrested?"

"Not unless you filed charges with Plexis," Terk said with a straight face. "We only deal with Trade Pact species, remember?"

"You persist in reminding me."

"Homs," Bowman interjected smoothly, as Barac and Terk kept glaring at each other. "We do have crimes enough to work with, if you don't mind."

Barac gestured appeasement and Terk pulled back a chair to finally sit. The atmosphere eased slightly. "Better," Bowman approved. Her voice hardened. "Now, we have missing Human telepaths. We have a really quite desperate attempt to kidnap you, Hom sud Sarc, by the few Human telepaths left in this quadrant. To me, this suggests a possible cause and effect."

"You think your telepaths are blaming the Clan," Barac stated, turning the idea over in his own mind. "Do that many of them know we exist?" he wondered out loud.

"You know what they say. What you tell one telepath, you tell them all," Terk said with a crooked grin. Bowman glowered at him and he subsided.

"As far as I know, telepaths don't share information," she explained. "They don't share much of anything, except a tendency to mental illness if untrained. But this threat has united those who know one another. Do they know about the Clan?" Bowman repeated. "There have always been rumors, hints circulating here and there. If they wanted to learn about you, it wouldn't have been difficult."

"If you are going to ask me next, is their suspicion the truth?" Barac said calmly, "I can't tell you."

Terk's big hands flattened on the table. "Can't or won't?"

"Can't," Barac said, stressing the word. "I've told you. I'm exile. Even if I weren't, you of all Humans know the Council doesn't reveal its planning to others—especially *sud*." He met Bowman's eyes, wishing he knew how to convince her he was telling the truth, for once. Among Clan, it was so much easier to communicate. "For what it's worth, I can't imagine why the Council would become involved with your telepaths at all. They have less strength than the least of us. They are not a threat, nor an asset." *Beyond,* Barac added honestly to himself, *being the easiest of minds to control if need be.*

"Well, it may take more than your opinion to convince those on Plexis. You'd better be more careful, Hom sud Sarc."

"I intend to be," Barac said fervently. "Is this all you wanted me for?"

Bowman hesitated a moment. When Terk would have spoken, she held up a finger to keep him silent.

"Well?" Barac prompted. "You said an exchange of information. I regret I have so little to share, but then you don't seem to have a lot to offer in return. I repeat: I was too late to catch Morgan before he left Plexis, and I know nothing about your problem of vanishing telepaths. My thanks again for your rescue, Constable. So. Are we done, Chief Bowman?"

"Not quite." Bowman's eyes sparkled. Barac knew that look: half pleasure and half predator's fix. "Tell me. What do you know about a species called the Drapsk, Hom sud Sarc?"

Chapter 32

LOOKING back, I'd probably let the happiness of the quasi-intoxicated Drapsk blind me to certain—potential consequences—I might have paid close attention to otherwise. But by the time I'd been in the Makii House for several hours, receiving delegations of the small beings who only wished to touch their Mystic One in adoration, it was difficult to keep in mind these were the same creatures who'd kept me prisoner until I'd agreed to help them.

It was much the same social climate that has led otherwise sane beings to have the names of transient loved ones carved in their skin.

It had led me to this moment. Rings of silent, expectant Makii Drapsk surrounded me, plumes waving in encouragement. Little hands patted me constantly, urging me onward. I stared down at the plate in front of me and wondered if I were insane.

"Hurry, Mystic One," someone said. "They don't stay fresh for long."

Well, nothing ventured, I thought queasily. I picked up the first of two bright red tentacles, kindly shed on my behalf by Captain Makairi—a temporary sacrifice: nubby replacements had already sprouted since he handed me the plate. After being shed, each tentacle had shrunk to about the size and shape of my thumb, but remained, I found, disconcertingly warm. I closed my eyes and popped it into my mouth, the room instantly roaring with chants of "Makii! Makii!"

No worse than unripe nicnic, I decided, though the taste could be improved. The texture was rubbery enough to challenge my teeth, but I was only to chew several times, then spit it out anyway. Trying to ignore where the object I gnawed so dutifully had originated, I opened my eyes and nodded reassuringly at my companions.

"Next!"

I removed the morsel as daintily as possible, putting it on the plate without looking too closely. I did notice the red color was gone. Knowing what to expect, the second tentacle was easier.

When I was done, the plate was mercifully removed, and I gazed at my cheering hosts with a triumphant sense of really breaking through the interspecies barrier. "Is that the end of the ceremony?" I asked innocently.

Maka produced a pair of what appeared to be Drapsk scissors from his tool belt, while Captain Makairi coaxed a stool from the floor on the other side of the table from me, a new and empty plate brought and placed before him. I tucked my hands in my lap, rolling my fingers into protective fists. "You aren't proposing to cut off part of me, are you?" I asked with what I thought commendable composure. "I can tell you now, it doesn't work that way." It was all very well for the Drapsk to want me to take part in this somewhat modified version of their celebration, a way of symbolically welcoming me into their Tribe, but I wasn't prepared to sacrifice anything irreplaceable.

"A piece of hair will be quite sufficient."

"Oh," I said wisely, as if I knew this all along. From the subdued hoots in the background, the Drapsk were perfectly aware what I'd worried about. I found myself grinning. It took two of us to hold a lock of the indignant stuff in place—the hair of a Chosen Clanswoman tended to have a significant amount of motility, particularly, I found, when scissors were in the offing.

Captain Makairi's plumes dropped perceptibly as he contemplated the small mass of fine red-gold tendrils on his plate. I was sympathetic, having likely looked similarly thrilled by his offering on mine. This didn't stop me chanting with the rest: "Makii! Makii!" until the poor being had to shove the hair into his mouth and chew. From the speed with which he did so, and spat the little wad back out, I assumed he found my taste as foul as I'd feared his would be. *There was,* I thought smugly, *some justice in the universe.*

* * *

Copelup's antennae came to attention, then folded to point straight at me. "What have you done?" he shouted, mouth tentacles splayed out in an equally rigid ring.

I'd been hoping for an explanation of exactly that, having found the Makii more interesting in celebrating than making sense, but it seemed something else had upset the Skeptic the moment I'd been ushered into the indoor amphitheater. The other Drapsk, all Skeptics, Niakii, or Heerii, turned from their various machines and devices to orient in our direction. One by one, their antennae snapped into the same posture as Copelup's.

I had a sudden bad feeling about all this and turned to look at Captain Makairi. His tentacles, including the two still shorter ones, were tightly clamped in his mouth. *Oh dear,* I thought. "What have I done?" I asked reasonably.

The Skeptic pushed Makairi to one side, an atypical use of physical force among the Drapsk, with the exception of the hockey game. Then he patted me gently, while his plumes touched my face and shoulders. "Well, it's done, isn't it?" he announced in a decidedly grumpy tone, moving away from me and returning to the console he'd left in order to greet me. The other Drapsk remained at attention.

"What's done?" I demanded, my voice regrettably loud, suspecting anything and everything at this point.

"You're Makii," one of the Heerii explained in a matter-of-fact way. "You did perform the *ipstsa*. We can all tell."

I felt myself blush. "Well," I confessed, feeling as though I'd committed some as yet unknown crime or lewd act, "there was a celebration and a ceremony of sorts—no one told me the name." I looked down at my hands, expecting to see a hint of tentacle red or Makii purple-pink. "How can you tell?" I asked suspiciously.

Captain Makairi hooted, possibly, I thought glumly, still under the influence of whatever intoxicant he'd been using at the Makii House. "They are all jealous. You bear the taste of your Tribe, Sira Morgan of the Makii, as you will throughout your life. They wish they had thought to do ipstsa with you first. But now all Drapsk will acknowledge your place within our Tribe."

Great, I said to myself, wondering how I'd possibly missed deducing the consequences of ingesting molecules from such an olfactory-oriented species as this one. Still, I was fond of the

Makii. If they wanted to claim me, I wasn't about to argue—even if I could at this point.

The remaining Drapsk in the room appeared to be immobilized by the Makii's daring. Only Copelup muttered away to himself, back deliberately in my direction. Ignoring the others, I walked over to him and reached out to touch his arm.

"Skeptic Copelup," I said softly. "You of all beings understand that I didn't do this in order to slight any Drapsk. The Makii were celebrating and this—just happened. If I had known—"

Copelup gave a small, forlorn-sounding hoot. "Yes, Mystic One. You do tend to precipitate events." His antennae struggled up into a relaxed, more cheerful position, one I was glad to see the other Drapsk in the room emulate almost at once. "As you have here, you know."

Ah. "I've been very concerned about what happened," I admitted, sitting beside Copelup on the stool that courteously nudged the back of my legs. "The Makii have not told me anything beyond the fact they—and what looks like the entire city except for those," I waved my hand around "in this room—are celebrating some victory." I gripped my knees tightly. "I don't recall a victory, frankly."

Levertup had joined us, the remaining Drapsk returning to their work. Captain Makairi had found a seat near the door and was humming to himself contentedly. "To the Tribes as a whole, and to many individuals, you achieved more than we'd dared hope, Mystic One," the second Skeptic said soberly. "And at a terrible risk to yourself."

"What have I achieved?" I remembered the linkages I'd formed between Drapskii and the M'hir, and those I'd shattered in my escape. "What do you think I've done?"

Levertup raised his arms, spreading his fingers wide, then pulling them back down as if collecting something unseen. Accurate enough, I thought. "Our devices show the reconnection of our world to the Scented Way," he confirmed unnecessarily. "It is not complete, but it is sufficient to allow the Tribes to once more attain the—" the word he said in Drapsk was too difficult for me to catch entirely. Gripstsa was part of it.

"She doesn't know what you're talking about, Levertup," Copelup interrupted. "You're being too theoretical again. I keep telling you to stick to the implications, not the details."

"I'd like either," I reminded them.

Copelup pursed his round mouth, then went on: "As you've observed, within a Tribe is gripstsa, roughly: the changing of place. After the Competition, there was lar-gripstsa, in which members of various Tribes are given the opportunity to join a Tribe in ascendancy if they choose. But at the core of our society, what was lost from us with our magic, is something much more. It is the Joining of Tribes. Now, for the first time in generations, all Tribes can intermingle while remaining true to their own." He and Levertup sighed deeply in unison. "It is the most wonderful, beautiful thing of being Drapsk, and you have restored it to us." A short pause. "If temporarily."

"The threads I broke," I said with regret, guessing this much. "But I sensed there needed to be only a few more and the rest would connect on their own. I can—" as I spoke, I could hardly believe what I was saying, but I knew it was right "—I can try to finish it."

"No!" This from more than the Skeptics. The others moved closer, as if to protect me. I'd agitated them all, especially Captain Makairi, who pushed his way to my side and took my wrists in his chubby hands.

Their reaction seemed a bit extreme. "I'd be more careful," I said soothingly. "I overextended myself, that's all. I know what to do—"

"No!" from Copelup, who fairly bristled with alarm. "You cannot return to the Scented Way near Drapskii. It will be waiting for you this time."

I blinked, looking around at the featureless faces. "It?" I repeated numbly, not understanding. "You know? How could you—it was only a hallucination—"

A third, emphatic "No!" from Copelup. "Come here," he added in a kinder voice, leading me over to a table filled to overflowing with various instruments. He selected one, a tube with a flattened disk midway up its length. The disk was polished and reflective, like an inactive vid screen. "Hold it thus," a Heerii ordered me, placing my hands so that I held the tube with the disk centered at my eye level.

The tube began to vibrate lightly. That wasn't why I came close to dropping it. Through the cold, then warming metal, I could sense the M'hir. Not the way I usually did, as an exten-

sion of my inner self, but more distantly, as though I observed
it through some other's perception.

The disk remained blank, but images formed behind my
eyes, lines of fire and ice, globules of pure energy that pulled
themselves along those lines, dark flashes moving almost too
quickly to hold in the mind, tearing through the globules yet
leaving them unaffected. There were other things, so stomach-
twistingly strange I found myself without the words to describe
them, but recognizing one thing beyond any doubt.

They *lived.*

INTERLUDE

"You could have brought a steak or two."

Morgan rubbed the last dampness from his hair in the dry hot air from the fresher and shouted back: "I didn't plan to stick around that long, thanks." He stepped out, catching the robe thrown at him with one hand and avoiding the reflex to dodge out of the way. *This was,* he reminded himself sternly, *as safe a place as any on Ret 7.*

This safety was primarily due to the thin, wizened Human leaning in the doorway, artificial eyes, Retian-made, blinking as though having trouble with the vapor-laden atmosphere of the bathhouse. Malacan Ser was a powerful being in this place, in part because of his business skills and in part because he was one of those rare individuals who actually liked it here.

Including having a taste for brexk-steak, or liver, or whatever morsel was available. The Retians didn't allow many to be slaughtered, prizing, it was rumored but not confirmed, the products of living brexks for their tables.

"I only hit one, anyway," Morgan said, shrugging the robe over his shoulders and wincing slightly as the movement pulled muscles already sore enough for one day. The mudcrawler had just clipped the head of the incensed bull brexk—a freakish, split-second collision during which Morgan had fervently wished—not for the first time—that he'd reached the point in Sira's teachings where he could move himself through the M'hir.

But all was well, if not for the brexk, which had dropped beak-first into the muddy water as though shot, occasioning a reflex milling by the grieving herd which had in turn provided Morgan with a most effective barrier against pursuit. He'd settled the now-dented mudcrawler into a lawful pace and there had been no further interruptions until reaching Jershi. He'd even found a groundcar to take him to Malacan's right away, the Retian driver delighted to convey a passenger who'd been up close and personal with Ret 7's mud.

"Well, if you couldn't bring a steak," Malacan said in his precise, dry voice, "you did solve one problem for me."

Morgan felt himself brought on guard by something in his host's voice. He covered the reaction by tying the belt around the robe and tossing his mud-soaked coveralls into the fresher. His other belongings, including some interesting items from Plexis, were safely dry in their bags.

"And what small problem might that be, Malacan?" Morgan carried the rest of his things with him as he followed Malacan into the other room, stepping on a layer of rugs easily ten thick at this end. Being Retian in design, the underlying floor was deliberately uneven. Being Retian-owned, the building couldn't be modified in any way. The leveling of the floor with rugs was one of several ingenious compromises Malacan had devised to keep both himself and his landlord happy. *To each his own.* Morgan, looking around at the plas-coated and windowless mud walls, found himself missing the clean, crisp lines of the *Fox.*

"Have a seat," his host urged, sitting cross-legged on the carpet. There was a squeaking sound as he did so that Morgan knew not to remark on—the adjustment points on Malacan's artificial leg were inclined to complain of the dampness. It was a common occurrence with most offworld mechanics.

At the thought, Morgan tugged a long, sealed container from a bag as he joined Malacan on the carpet. "I did remember your order for more synth tubing," he said. "Though if you keep using up the stuff, Bowman will think you're running a still in the basement again." One of the difficulties of being an agent for the Enforcers was a certain restriction in one's allowed commerce. Malacan frequently complained, to no avail, that he should be allowed to conduct his business—all his business— without interference as long as it didn't break Trade Pact laws. Bowman had, characteristically, insisted that if she caught him breaking any law, local or otherwise, she'd arrange for an extremely rapid and unpleasant transfer.

"The Chief knows about my mold problem," the older Human

said primly. His eyes, normal enough until their flat surfaces reflected at just the right angle, focused on Morgan.

"So. What other problem did my coming solve for you?" Morgan ignored the dark inner voice reminding him why he shouldn't trust anyone to the point of sitting unarmed and relaxed.

"Why, finding you, my dear Jason," Malacan answered. "Bowman's been firing up comlinks throughout the quadrant. There was even a hint you'd been, well, kidnapped or disposed of. Most regrettable. I'm quite relieved to see you here and whole."

"Really," Morgan said, with a deliberate shade of boredom to his voice. "Well, you know how rumors spread."

"Yes, I know." Malacan Ser, the sole individual on Ret 7 Morgan even remotely trusted, reached into an oversized pocket to pull out a highly illegal and very menacing-looking nerve disrupter. As Morgan stared into the weapon's ugly muzzle, his host added pleasantly: "Then again, why don't we make this one come true?"

Chapter 33

I DROPPED the tube and covered my eyes. "A trick!" I heard someone shout in utter repudiation, then recognized the voice as mine.

A breath in my ear. "We would not trick you, Mystic One. What you saw was real."

"No!" I said, pressing my lips shut over what could have been a sob, my sense of the M'hir closed so tightly I might have been Human again. This was impossible. These creatures were trying to destroy everything I knew to be true. They had brought me here to ruin me.

Warm feathers tickled my throat and ears. "Would you like to sit, Mystic One?" a soft, troubled voice asked.

Others called out various suggestions: "Get her something to drink!" "Call the meds." "Does she need gripstsa?" "Copelup, this is all your doing!"

At the angry condemnation in this last voice, I opened my eyes, spilling tears to run cold over my heated cheeks. "It's not his fault," I said faintly, groping for and finding the stool someone had produced behind me.

A small, oddly-shaped hand curved itself to fit comfortingly in mine. "We thought you knew the Scented Way had life of its own, Mystic One. Please forgive us."

A sigh dragged itself from the very bottom of my lungs. "There is nothing to forgive, dear Drapsk. Unless it is three generations of appalling ignorance. My people have existed as part of your Scented Way without ever suspecting this truth you've shown me. We thought it was ours; perhaps even something our power produced." I felt my lips twitch at the quickly silenced hoot this elicited from someone safely distant in my audience, but couldn't smile. Not with the shattering of all I'd believed echoing through my thoughts at every level.

There was worse. I stared in my mind's eye at the memory of being held, being sucked empty in the M'hir, and understood at last it had been real. "What—what attacked me when I tried to reconnect Drapskii?"

Levertup rocked back and forth beside me. "We haven't seen such a thing before, Mystic One. Not one so large or so strong. It is possible the power you used summoned it."

"Yes," Copelup agreed. "There is an attraction between the Scented Way and this existence." One chubby hand waved around the room. "At least some of the entities there are able to—gain nourishment from such intrusions."

I pulled out the box containing the tiny vial of brown powder. "This isn't dirt, is it," I said.

"We trapped something, or a piece of something, during one of our many attempts to try and reconnect Drapskii on our own. When it entered this existence, it became as you see it, dust. But it was our first proof of the physical nature of the Scented Way. A nature others," Levertup dipped an antennae negligently at Copelup, "were slow to accept."

"Evidence," Copelup muttered to himself. "There needs to be evidence."

I considered the tiny vial. With my thumb, I triggered the release, the powder cascading over the lip of the opening to puddle in my palm. I didn't look at the Drapsk, but I could hear enough tentacle sucking to know they were observing me anxiously.

I tilted my hand, watching the M'hir dust slide around. It stayed with itself, not sticking to the dampness of my skin or filling the lines of my palm. It reminded me of the raindrop with its tiny imprisoned fish. I concentrated and *pushed* . . .

The powder was gone. I didn't linger in the M'hir more than the flash needed to send it, having developed a certain repugnance for some of my neighbors. But I imagined I saw a streak of something pale and glistening, sliding away into a fold of darkness as a fish into a pond.

The act, probably meaningless to the dust and as likely very upsetting to the Drapsk, was important to me. It restored an inner balance I'd lost with the Drapsk's revelation about the nature of the M'hir. It might be filled with life—of what sort I still couldn't imagine—but I could affect it. I remained in control of my own destiny within it.

As long as I was careful.

The Drapsk were not, as I'd feared, upset. They were puzzled. "You realize there is no other sample, Mystic One," Levertup said in a tentative voice. "Should you wish to repeat this, ah, experimental procedure, we could not supply you with more. We have been unable to duplicate the occurrence."

"I don't need to repeat it," I said, brushing imaginary dust from my hands before standing. "What I need now is to go."

Antennae drooped, but not to shoulders. My announcement wasn't a surprise, then.

I smiled at them, feeling much younger than my years or responsibilities.

"Perhaps you'd like to come?" I asked.

There was more to it than that, of course. As the Drapsk debated and discussed, I excused myself from most of it, content to go with Captain Makairi back to the *Makmora*—a ship which not only felt like home after my time on Drapskii, but which I discovered was mine, in a sense.

"Explain this to me again, Captain," I asked one more time, just to be sure I understood.

"You are now marked as Makii," the Drapsk repeated happily, as if he enjoyed every bit of the explanation. The rest of the bridge crew seemed equally entranced, blatantly ignoring their stations to come up in turn to pat me lightly and sometimes stroke their plume tips over my skin. "The *Makmora* is the flagship of the Makii trading fleet. We take her to new markets, to explore new opportunities, to—"

"To find magic?" I suggested.

Maka, standing behind the Captain, gave a brief hoot.

Captain Makairi ignored him. "Just so. You are our Mystic One as well as Makii. It is our duty and delight to take the *Makmora* on whatever path you choose for us."

I made myself think the matter through objectively, as Morgan would have me do. I'd hoped my invitation would have been accepted by Copelup and a couple of Makii. They could have brought their instruments and helped me convince

Barac, and then possibly others. A small start in correcting the
way the Clan viewed the M'hir, but a vital one. Deep in my
thoughts, suspicions were taking root and growing: suspicions
about the real reason so many Clan had dissolved in the M'hir.
It could be mistakes: flaws in judgment or technique. It could
be our nature. Or it could be something else. And, worse, why
did the remaining member of a Chosen pair go mad at the
instant of the partner's death? These were questions that had to
be answered.

That was only part of my reasoning. The rest concerned
Drapskii itself. If the world was to be fully reconnected, something I knew the Drapsk devoutly wished, it might be safest if
done by more than one Clan at a time. I couldn't at the moment
conceive of an argument or threat which could persuade any
Clan I knew. But that didn't mean I wasn't going to try.

But this, this immense ship at my command? This was far
more than I'd ever expected from the Drapsk. But I shouldn't
have been surprised. I was Makii and Tribe was everything. A
refreshing change from the Clan way of thinking.

At a rough estimate, the *Makmora* was crewed by over 400
Drapsk, all biochemically certain of my identity and right to be
here. The reputation of the Drapsk as taking care of their own
was well-known and well-deserved. I already knew this ship
and crew were capable of controlling a pirate and keeping me,
the so-called most powerful member of the Clan, thoroughly
harmless.

"The Skeptic and his equipment are on board, Captain," one
of the crew called out, plumes stirred by a downdraft from the
com system.

"We're ready to call the tug and prepare to lift, Mystic One,"
Captain Makairi said proudly. "Do you have a course for us?"

I chewed thoughtfully on a knuckle. *That was the next
problem, wasn't it?*

At least I did know what I wanted to find first.

A certain Human.

INTERLUDE

"It's been confirmed, Chief," Terk began on his return, then stopped, scowling pointedly at Barac. The Clansman smiled and waved from his graceful slouch in Bowman's extra chair. Barac knew exactly why Terk was annoyed. The Human was convinced Barac was untrustworthy, an opinion Barac hardly begrudged him. On the other hand, Bowman was convinced he might be useful, an opinion Barac cultivated with care. Without the resources of the Clan behind him, without Morgan, he really had no other allies. *Well,* Barac corrected to himself, *he had the Carasian, if only because he knew the main ingredient of the newest entrée.*

"This concerns our guest," Bowman said, nodding for the Constable to continue his report.

" 'Whix lifted from Drapskii yesterday morning, Station time. The *Nokraud*'s already gone outsystem. 'Whix sent this vid."

Another nod. Barac could hear Terk grinding his teeth as he obediently inserted the disk and activated the viewer.

Then he forgot all about the pleasures of tormenting the Enforcer, transfixed by the image showing Sira di Sarc, his cousin, moving—no, her posture was definitely that of someone sneaking—around the fins of a docked starship. "Sira?" he asked in disbelief, regardless of present company. "What's she doing on Drapskii?" Then Barac recalled his bothersome and expensive companions the first night in the Spacer's Haven: Captain Maka and his crew. "She went with them after all," he breathed. "Clever."

"Went with whom?" Bowman asked silkily. "The Scats?"

Barac looked at her, startled. "What are you talking about? Sira wouldn't go near them. Not after Roraqk."

"The *Nokraud* is a Scat vessel. Your cousin boarded her and stayed for some time before exiting again with several Drapsk," Terk informed him. "There was no sign she was being forced to do so, or 'Whix would have intervened."

"We hold your cousin in very high esteem, Hom sud Sarc," Bowman said frankly, her eyes curious but sober. "I know what she risked for Morgan's life. There are standing orders— my orders—to watch out for her when we can."

Barac chose to be equally frank. *Why not?* "Once I'd have objected to your interference, Sector Chief Bowman," he admitted. "I'd have taken any hint of her needing Human help as a personal offense. Now—I'm grateful. Sira has enemies who appear to care nothing for her power." He sat up straighter in the chair. Finding Sira, knowing these beings watched over her, made a difference to all of his schemes.

"What enemies?" This from Terk, who wrapped one large hand around the viewer. "Scats?"

"I don't know how they are involved. They may not be."

Bowman's eyes narrowed. "Something happened on Pocular, didn't it, Barac sud Sarc? Something pulled Morgan here, away from her. Something drove Sira to hide among the Drapsk. Care to tell us about it?"

Barac found himself on the edge of a precipice. This wasn't the cultivated trust he'd planned, the carefully coached revelations of just so much and no more he was accustomed to playing out with other species.

Bowman might have read his thoughts again. "Barac. You're exiled from your own kind. Space knows, we never had reason to trust one another, but this time it's different, isn't it? This time we both know there are dangerous currents stirring. The telepaths. This trouble on Pocular and Ret 7—"

On the verge of agreeing completely with the Enforcer, and telling her everything he knew, Barac froze. *Baltir,* he thought, no longer in any doubt about where Morgan might have gone. No wonder Huido hadn't told him; the Human must be out of his mind to confront the Retian on his homeworld. He asked aloud: "What trouble on Ret 7?"

Terk seemed to relish being the bearer of bad news. "Our

contact there, Malacan Ser, was found murdered in his room last night. Someone used a force blade to separate him from his artificial parts. And Morgan's insystem there—at least the *Silver Fox* is docked, bold as you please—but he's not responding to his com. No one's seen him. He may have been attacked as well."

Did they not know their fellow Human at all? Barac asked himself. *Or was this concern a lie?* If ever there was a being capable of taking care of himself, it was Morgan. If ever there was a being with the means and motive for murder—Barac stopped there, his silent musings having made him the target of Bowman's crystal-sharp gaze. "I tend to prioritize finding those who harm my people," she said. "Do you know something about this, Clansman?" she asked with deceptive softness.

Here was help and protection such as no Clan would offer him. Here was a powerful ally and equally dangerous foe.

Barac smiled with regret. "Nothing you'd want to know," he said, before *concentrating* . . .

As he materialized in Huido's office, Barac said to the empty room: "Morgan, you'd better be able to explain all this."

Unlike Huido, he doubted Morgan could.

Chapter 34

THE harsh voice hadn't changed, hadn't softened; its message remained equally implacable: "Join with our Choice for you."

The darkness around me was crowded, filled with nightmare shapes that leaped at me with teeth oozing venom and smoke. I eluded them desperately, shouting: "I have made my Choice!"

The round globe of a Drapsk face floated past me, oblivious to the threats on every side. "No, you haven't. No. No. No." His voice trailed away, then came back as a whirling, confusing echo. "There's been no Joining. See how you bleed? How you bleed? You bleed?"

I twisted but couldn't see myself. What I did see was a stream of crimson, pouring away from me. It split into thousands of tinier, seeking rivulets, each hardly wide enough be visible, almost all lapped up by tongues belonging to the dark.

A new voice, with the sound of a campfire behind it. "What will he do when there is nothing left? Do you think he will survive you?"

I sat bolt upright, breathing in ragged gasps as though still fighting off the creatures in my dream. Without thinking, I looked around for Morgan, stretched out to him in my thoughts. Nothing. No presence to offer warmth, no comfort.

Of course, I chided myself. *I was alone.*

I may have been alone, but it was a state I endured only within the cabin the Drapsk had made for me. Elsewhere on the *Makmora,* I was a magnet for whatever crew were in my vicinity. I'd have been more flattered by the attention and outright adulation if I hadn't known how much of it was chemical. Still, it eased something inside me to have the small beings accept me as theirs. It wasn't Clanlike, I knew.

It wasn't Clanlike to regret past actions either, but I did—every minute—whether herded through the ship by my chorus of adoring Drapsk or by myself at night. No doubt where the nightmares came from now. There was no way to turn back time, no second chance to stop myself before sending Morgan into danger. I understood enough of his depth of feeling for me to know I'd only freed him to do what he himself wanted to do. But I could have stopped him, held him by me until we could tackle the Clan together. Now that the *Makmora* was underway, I felt a return of the burning impatience I'd experienced earlier. I wouldn't be too late to help him. I wouldn't.

We'd needed a destination. Feeling very silly, but hopefully not showing it, I'd ordered the Drapsk to take their immense and beautiful ship two days' translight to check on my order for truffles.

Simplicity itself to convince the Drapsk this was necessary. I thought guiltily they'd probably send the ship straight into the Drapskii sun if I told them it was essential. Where I found my conscience truly suffered, however, was observing the anguish of several of the Drapsk, including Captain Makairi. They took the implied failure to please me very personally because I had, it was true, missed the promised celebratory feast and so the truffles. Since that had been because I'd happily slept through it didn't seem to console them at all. Copelup, who knew exactly how little the feast and the truffles meant to me, nonetheless cheerfully aggravated matters by suggesting the Makii could have postponed the feast until after I awoke.

So nothing was going to stop them from providing one for me now. As I'd slept my innocent, if nightmare-ridden, sleep, the *Makmora* had flung herself between stars in pursuit of truffles while her crew scrambled to plan the finest celebration possible.

I really could have tied Copelup's antennae into knots. But at least we were on track for Plexis.

And, I hoped, Morgan or Morgan's trail.

"Plexis-com is requesting docking information. How do you wish to respond, Mystic One?"

"They were able to do this before I arrived, weren't they?" I whispered to Copelup.

The Skeptic sucked a tentacle pensively. "I assume so," he said back as quietly. "They really are showing you the most extraordinary courtesy. Perhaps your Makii scent is unusually potent."

Great, I thought, glaring around at my usual ring of devoted crew. "Captain Makairi, could I speak to you in private, please?"

"What about Plexis-com, Mystic One?"

"They can wait," I assured whoever had spoken, looking over my shoulder to be sure Captain Makairi was following me. So was Copelup, but I'd learned days ago he considered the word "private" to mean the two of us plus someone else.

Actually, privacy on a Drapsk ship wasn't much. There was a spot on the bridge Copelup had told me was kept free of the airborne com signals. The Captain could retire there to rest or perform eopari, depending on the circumstances. I'd looked that one up on the vidtapes. Eopari was the term for tucking oneself into a tight ball, with antennae retracted and curled in for protection. The reference concerned proper safety precautions if caught in extreme weather conditions, which didn't quite explain the incidences of this behavior I'd seen so far. Why the Captain might decide to do this on his bridge was something I couldn't find in the tapes and somehow didn't think polite to ask.

But this area was to one side of the crewed portion of the oval bridge, and it gave me the illusion at least of speaking to only two Drapsk instead of an awestruck audience of a dozen.

"Would you like to sit, Mystic One?" The Makii had tried to show me how to summon a stool from the floor, but this, as well as certain other modifications to the surfaces of the ship, required either some biochemical signal from a Drapsk foot or a form of mental contact which so far had eluded me. So they were always quick to ask if I'd like the service performed for me.

"No, thank you," I said, then went on quickly to forestall any more delaying courtesies—Plexis wouldn't wait that long. "Captain, I appreciate the way the Makii are responding to my every need—"

"But of course we are. Have we missed something? Offended you?" As I'd feared, his first reaction was to fuss.

"No. I'm delighted in every way. I'd be even more delighted if you would contain your enthusiasm, especially when we arrive on the Station. What I mean is—"

Copelup hooted rudely. "What the Mystic One means is you are all acting like a bunch of gripstsa-starved idiots. And I agree. Nothing's getting done properly. Next, you'll starting asking the Mystic One for permission to clean your plumes! This is no way to show respect and gratitude to someone of your Tribe!"

"Is this true, Mystic One?" the Captain asked miserably, the plumes in question seriously drooping.

"I wouldn't have put it quite so firmly," I said, distressed in turn. "You've treated me well. It's just that—"

"Yes, it's true," Copelup interrupted again. "The Mystic One has too much patience with you. I would have spoken to you myself if I'd thought it would penetrate."

"What should we do, Mystic One?"

I touched the back of his hand. "If the Makii on this ship would treat me with the fine and gracious courtesy they accorded me before I became a member of your Tribe—without locking me in my room, you understand—that would be more than sufficient. I don't need to be involved in running the ship, Captain Makairi. I'm not qualified to make these decisions for you anyway. Just take me where I must go."

I glanced over at the suspended chaos around the com console. "And you could reassure Plexis-com for starters. Without," I suggested as the Drapsk's plumes struggled bravely upright again, "letting them know you have a passenger."

The plumes shot ceilingward. "No one shall know of your presence, Mystic One. I swear it."

Copelup inhaled two more tentacles to suck as he listened. I didn't bother to explain.

I'd just realized what docking at Plexis meant. I was back into the part of space regularly used by the Clan.

My self-imposed exile was officially over.

INTERLUDE

All Clan. Rael surveyed the group of conspirators, still mildly surprised how well her sister Pella fit in, and waited for Ica di Teerac to finish her liptus tea. Ru looked impatient. Only Larimar was missing, which was just as well. Those from Acranam wisely avoided any chance of direct confrontation with the Council.

Camos was a familiar world, Rael thought; more, despite its Human population, it remained a Clan world. She wondered if the Humans really believed the Council would abandon Camos. So what if their secret meeting hall was discovered beneath the Humans' government building? There was too much here of value to the Clan—not in replaceable property, but in the invisible lacework of passageways forged through the M'hir around this place. More Clan lived or visited Camos than anywhere in the universe—save, perhaps, the mythical Clan Homeworld. This was both the source of the passageways and the reason for the continued Clan presence. This was as close to a home as their kind now acknowledged.

Making it the most dangerous place in the universe to plot against the Council, whose Watchers kept their senses probing the M'hir as much for suspicious activities by their own kind as for alien intrusion. The group in this room kept their thoughts shielded and their voices low. Rael's own pulse tended to race whenever a servant opened the door or a shadow flickered on the opaque window screens.

None of this affected their hostess, it seemed. "Welcome again, Pella sud Sarc," Ica said after delicately patting moisture from her pale, thin lips. Her hair stirred, its heavy locks slowed by age but retaining the rich dark amber of her Commencement. "Your courage was—unexpected."

Rael thought Pella's smile a bit forced. "Thank you, First Chosen," her sister said graciously enough. "But there really wasn't any other decision to be made, was there? The Council," her smile faded, "the Council would lead us into perversion—destroy the Choosers and our way of life. We can't allow it."

"Exactly," Ica approved. "See, Rael? I told you our cause would attract others. It is only a matter of time."

"Time is what we don't have," Ru di Mendolar snapped, her lean features drawn and gray-tinged. "Forgive me, First Chosen. But events have begun without us. The Council must be about to move against the Choosers. They've started with Sira di Sarc. Where will they stop? Who knows what they plan? What can we—"

The ancient Clanswoman shook her head. "Calm yourself, Ru," she admonished. "Hysteria will not help. We are—" she drew her fingers in a sweeping gesture, "many more than meet here. Just because you do not know or see all that is happening, does not mean we sit idle and wait for disaster."

Ru leaned forward, eyes brightening. "Do you have news for us, First Chosen?"

Ica's gaze moved from one to the other, stopping briefly at each. Rael, meeting those expressionless, light blue eyes, retested her own shielding.

"I will not reveal all of our works to you," Ica said sternly. "For safety's sake, even my mind does not hold all of our secrets. But it is time you knew more.

"Tell us, Rael," she continued in her paper-thin voice, "how Sira was able to gain control of the Power-of-Choice."

Rael blinked in surprise. "I don't think she did—not completely."

"Come now," Ica said, as if humoring the Clanswoman. "She was a Chooser yet did the unheard of: she was able to contain her instincts, to hold herself from Testing your cousin, Barac, as well as Yihtor."

"Sira wanted to protect—" Rael closed her lips and changed what she was about to say. There were advantages to speaking aloud instead of mind-to-mind. "Sira had been practicing for years; she's incredibly powerful. Who else would be the first of us to control the Power-of-Choice?"

"She did it to protect that Human." This scathing remark from Pella, who glared at Rael. "I don't know why you can't admit it. You know what she's done. You know she's Chosen this perversion." With a more respectful glance at the other two, as Pella remembered her place as sud, she went on: "Sira's mind was damaged. She didn't know what she was doing until it was too late. First Chosen, our sister hasn't regained her true nature. We must help her. Rael has told me all about it."

"More, it seems, than she told us," Ru said darkly.

Ica raised one slender, gnarled finger, an order for silence obeyed without question. "Sira's fixation on the Human is not what is relevant here."

"I don't understand, First Chosen. Why not?" Pella burst out, then sat back as though to take herself out of range. Rael carefully smoothed an imaginary wrinkle from her skirt, as careful not to show any reaction, wondering furiously how she could have so misread her sister. Perhaps, she thought, the hurt of Sira's honest anger and her own guilt had blinded her. Pella had been too easily convinced to join their group—her motive not to save their kind's future, but to change Sira's.

Rael found another wrinkle to ease away, also aware she'd underestimated their grandmother's knowledge. Neither boded well for her own future as a conspirator.

Ica had continued, "Larimar confirmed what I suspected. There has been no Joining formed between Sira and the Human."

Pella's cry of triumph died as Rael glared at her before turning back to Ica. "That's not possible, First Chosen," she denied. "They underwent the ritual of Choice—the Testing and Joining. The Council witnessed it. Barac was there—"

"A Testing in which any unChosen of our kind, and certainly the Human, should have died," Ru broke in. She looked savage, her power boiling at the edges of Rael's shields. Less able to keep out the emotion, Pella covered her face with her hands.

"Not a Joining. Something—different," Ica said with satisfaction. "Sira spoke these words before she left with her Human: 'The Power-of-Choice hasn't been matched in contest—I'm rid of it!' " Ica paused for effect. "Then she said what has haunted me ever since I was told: 'Haven't you scanned him yet, in your arrogance?' "

"Morgan? Sira was able to *give* the Power-of-Choice to him? Without Joining?" Rael said, at first with utter disbelief, then with a rising hope she saw reflected in the eyes of the others. Ru was nodding—this was not news to her, Rael realized, her heart sinking into her stomach.

"It was confirmed. My source on the Council felt the power floating around the Human in the M'hir—not part of him, of course, but safely contained nonetheless. Think of it, my kin," Ica urged. "To be able to end the destruction of our kind during Choice. To free our Choosers of this urge to battle in the M'hir, to drag the unChosen to their deaths. What if this can be repeated?"

"I must find Sira," Rael said numbly. "You should have told me this before I went to Pocular. Why did you wait until now?"

"We suspected. We weren't sure. And if we could accomplish this feat without disturbing the firstborn of Sarc, even better and safer. You of all of us know she wanted to be left alone," Ru replied, then the corners of her mouth drew downward as if in distaste. "The time hasn't been wasted. There were tests to be done, experimentation. Even the First Chosen doesn't know all of it."

"Nor wishes to," Ica said with a refined shudder.

They all jumped as a soft-footed servant entered the room, depositing a tray bearing a single sheet of plas on the table. Ica waved the servant away impatiently, ignoring the message.

"What kind of tests?" Rael asked, when they were alone again.

Ru and Ica exchanged looks, no more, not so close to the Council's stronghold. "We recruited suitable male telepaths," Ru began. "There were several Choosers willing to—"

"No!" Pella shouted, struggling to her feet from the depths of the armchair. Not a dramatic move, but her expression of loathing was powerful enough. "Tell me you're not talking about Humans," her head swung from one to another of them. "You couldn't have tried with Humans."

Ica was unperturbed. "Of course, Humans. We didn't want to harm our own. That's the whole point."

Sira had seen this coming, Rael thought, her mind crystallizing in opposition to everything she was hearing. Pella's hatred of Humans was wrong. Their group's use of Humans was worse. No wonder Sira had taken her beloved Morgan and hidden him in the jungle of that fringe world.

"Sit down, Pella, or leave. I have no patience for fools. This is life and death, do you understand me? And not just yours," this last in unmistakable threat.

Pella stood perfectly still, looking down at her grandmother. "I understand, First Chosen," she said faintly, easing back down into her seat. From the look on her face, there would be no further outbursts.

"Good. Now, Rael, you can see our difficulty. There must be something more Sira did—something we haven't been able to duplicate. So we need to talk to her."

Rael was careful to keep her voice calm and her expression willing, no matter what she was thinking. "I've been trying to find her, First Chosen, but without success."

"No matter. Sira will come to us," Ru said confidently.

"Why?" Rael stopped, then answered her own question: "Larimar. He's found Morgan—and he's to bring the Human here, isn't he? To use as bait for Sira."

"Her attachment to the Human is well-known," Ru confirmed unnecessarily.

"You can't believe Larimar will succeed."

Ica reached for the message on the tray. "I do. This should be from him, in fact. A barbaric but, sadly, more secure method of communication." She lifted the sheet and read quickly. Emotions raced across her face: disbelief, rage, and finally, reluctant respect.

"It's from Acranam. Prin sud Teerac was granted mercy. They thought I should know."

"Larimar's Chosen," Ru said for Pella's benefit.

They were silent. If Prin was granted mercy, it could only be for one reason. Her mind had been pulled into the M'hir; her body left an empty husk.

Because Larimar was dead.

"The Human," Pella said in a high-pitched voice. "He's killed one of us. I told you, Rael—"

Rael stopped any further speech from her sister with a flick of power, uncaring what the others thought. "I don't believe it—" she began.

"Isn't he capable?" Ru spoke quietly, all trace of emotion gone from the M'hir.

Unwillingly, Rael pictured the scene on Pocular, relived the violence of Morgan's reaction to Sira's wounds. She'd accused him of complicity in the attack, knowing at her core she was wrong, that it was her jealousy, her prejudice trying to sever the Human's hold on Sira, to turn her sister back to her, Rael, for comfort. Though unJoined, Morgan's feeling for Sira was beyond anything Rael could imagine. So she knew the answer. "Capable? Yes," she said reluctantly. "But only in self-defense." Adding to herself: *or if Morgan realized Larimar was a threat to Sira.* As all here had become.

"What of Sira?" Pella said abruptly. "How will we find her now?"

One by one, they all looked at Rael.

Chapter 35

PLEXIS. The *Makmora* was nosed in to the underbelly of the most famous shopping concourse in the Fringe. And I wasn't going to be able to explore it this trip either. *One of these days,* I swore to myself, *I'll travel where and how I choose.*

Not today. Today, I kept my shielding impeccably in place and let my Drapsk do the searching, no matter how it tore at my heart to think Morgan might be within reach of my thoughts. The risk of alerting a Clan Watcher in the M'hir here was too great.

All of this being true and sensible did nothing to improve my temper. "If you have the address," I asked the comtech on duty irritably, "what's taking so long?"

The Makii looked miserable. "There is a difficulty, Mystic One. The truffles delivered to Drapskii for your celebration did not come from the location you recommended. I've checked the records. The order was rerouted to a more local source in order to save time. We have come to the wrong place if you wish your delicacy in time for this evening's banquet."

"No, we haven't," I explained, counting under my breath before doing so. "It isn't the truffles that matter. I don't like truffles."

The comtech inhaled all his tentacles and didn't move.

I sighed. "I've told you. The order is a way to attract the attention of the right person without having to use my name. The restaurant where you must place the order is the *Claws & Jaws,* the owner, Huido Maarmatoo'kk."

"You don't want the truffles, Mystic One?" came a mumble around the tentacles, followed by a bewildered line of drool.

"But I do want you to order some. Just place an order for

truffles—to the *Claws & Jaws* this time—and have them contact the ship to confirm delivery time. Make sure the owner delivers them in person."

I stood and walked away. The Drapsk would manage better without further confusion from me. I'd learned to give them time to rationalize in Drapsk terms why I wanted certain things done, a step that seemed important to them and fortunately wasn't usually time-consuming. The Skeptic, who apparently didn't need to second-guess me, reported various Makii efforts to me with obvious delight. His favorite so far was the crew's understanding of why I wanted to sleep within walls and a closed door: because a Mystic One such as myself dreamed within the Scented Way and shouldn't be interrupted by the scent of others.

I didn't share Copelup's amusement. Dream within the M'hir? Move one's subconscious into that other place without any control? An easy way to never wake up.

"You are troubled, Mystic One." Copelup trotted up beside me.

I nodded, inviting the Drapsk to join me in the lift with a gesture. "How much do you sense of the Scented Way, Copelup?" I asked him as we rode to the next level. I'd almost mastered the orientation of the *Makmora*. If only I'd dare ask them to color code the halls, I'd have been fine.

"Our instruments are capable of very exacting measurements—"

"Not with technology. On your own."

This produced an unusual silence in my companion. I let him think about it, unsure if I was approaching some species' taboo or merely providing him with an interesting puzzle to worry over. I'd grown to have a great respect for the intellect packed into the round little body walking beside mine.

"Why do you ask, Mystic One?" the Skeptic asked finally. "Is this important for you to know?"

"I'm not sure," I answered, pausing to get my bearings. "But I would like to believe what I did on Drapskii makes a personal difference to these Drapsk, to you. It all became very abstract back there."

"Ah." He pointed to the left corridor with one plume, the other busily sampling whatever information was blowing through the air just above the top of my head. "It is like explaining gripstsa to a Drapsk who hasn't participated yet. What you have done, the reconnection, will enable entire Tribes to commit gripstsa with one another, to the betterment of all Drapsk. But," he gave a charming little shrug, "it is still abstract to us, too, at least until it happens. Suffice it to say we feel better knowing it is again possible. Does this help, Mystic One?"

"Maybe. Yes, I suppose so." I took the next right, for no reason but to show some decisiveness. "There is another matter, Copelup. It's quite likely we'll meet those who'll try to interfere with me. Other Mystic Ones. I may need your help."

He hooted.

I glared down at him. "I'm serious. You have devices which can keep my kind from the M'hir. And I know perfectly well you can detect any Clan activity there. Would you be willing to use them if I asked?"

Copelup restrained himself with a small hiccuping sound. "My apologies, Mystic One. You ask a reasonable question, from your point of view. It only sounds silly to a Drapsk."

"Why?"

"There may be other true Mystic Ones, something I personally doubt, but you are as much ours as we are yours. Whatever you need, we need as well. You are of Drapskii now; of the Makii. There is no question."

Well, I said to myself, *so much for worrying about whom they would support in a conflict with the Clan.* He'd been right to accuse me of thinking like Clan. We were the ones who would automatically switch allegiance to the one of greatest power. The Drapsk idea of loyalty had much more in common with Morgan's, an unexpected gift.

We were still walking, passing the occasional Makii crew on their way somewhere or busy with some panel or other. I was thoroughly lost, of course, and suspected Copelup knew it, but I wasn't going to be the first to mention it.

Copelup, naturally, thought it time for questions of his own. "Why do you wish to know if we can sense the Scented Way without our instruments, Mystic One? Does this matter?"

"Right now, Copelup," I told him, "I'm just collecting information. I touch the Scented Way at will, unless your devices are shutting me out. I detect it as a potential, a link, between those in gripstsa or lar-gripstsa. I want to understand how you

sense it—how your perception may differ from mine." I shook
my head, admitting: "I'm still amazed."

"The Clan did not think they would ever meet another species
with this ability. That was," Copelup paused and searched for the
word he wanted, "That was nearsighted of your kind."

I shook my head. "Not really, Copelup. Just—greedy."

"They didn't have any truffles, Mystic One. But there is a
famous seafood dish available as a substitute."

Counting was no longer working. I spoke between teeth that
really wanted to grind together. "What else did they say?"

The bridge, I'd just been shown, opened into a second bulb
of space as large or perhaps larger than itself. This was currently filling with Drapsk bearing trays and bowls of all manners of food and drink. There was enough lined up on smooth
round tables to feed an army of epicures and the deliveries
didn't seem to be stopping.

"The person in charge—" antennae drooped, "—seemed inefficient. There wasn't any other message, Mystic One."

"Did you ask to speak to the owner, to Huido?"

"As you suggested, Mystic One," the Drapsk said sadly. "The
owner was not available."

So much for subterfuge, I thought with disgust and a certain
relief. "I'll be right back," I promised, and *pushed* . . .

Seeing the food-laden tables of another, more familiar setting form around me. I moved immediately to one side, disappearing within the crowd of beings of every shape and type. I
knew my way around the *Claws & Jaws,* better than around the
Makmora at any rate. With this many customers, Huido should
be splitting his time between the lobby and the kitchen. I'd bet
on the kitchen.

"Where's Huido?" I asked, pushing through the doorway.
Several kitchen assistants pointed at the same time to an Ordnex,
perhaps the head cook, none of them bothering to look up from
their tasks to see who was asking.

The Ordnex's nasal opening flared, giving me too clear a
view into its rosy-veined sinuses. Politeness came in numerous
shapes, I reminded myself, attempting without much success to
flare my own. "Huidopackedandleft," the being droned helpfully. "InchargeamIhelpyou?"

"Where did he go?" I asked, disappointed—it would have been nice to have things work out neatly—but not surprised. If Morgan needed him, Huido would go. *It wasn't comforting, I realized, to think Morgan had.*

"WiththeClansman."

I took a second to be sure I'd heard that correctly, feeling as though I'd been hit in the stomach. "What Clansman?" I demanded, stepping closer and lowering my voice, although it wasn't necessary. The pots on the huge stove beside me were bubbling and seething like a miniature orchestra. At least the contents of the largest had stopped whining. The heat brought beads of sweat to my face, the heat and formless apprehension. "Was Captain Morgan with them?"

"NoTheCaptainleftbeforeExcusemeFem." The cook flipped up a lid and added spices to a simmering mass, his other hand busy on the heat controls: a feat of coordination commonplace in a being with significantly more joints in each arm and hand than humanoid-norm.

"Without Huido?" I muttered. Louder, "I need to talk to you. Can someone take over here for a moment?"

You'd have thought I'd asked him to give me the heart of his fifthborn offspring. The nasal opening closed to an insulted slit below its broad compound eyemass. "Cannotleavemymasterpiecesnow.Ruined!"

"Fine," I said, grabbing a metal stool from under the counter, and placed myself where the being could work on his masterpieces, but not leave without climbing over me. "Then I'll talk to you here." He still looked offended. "Look, I have a right to know what's been happening. I'm Sira Morgan. Jason Morgan is—" I hesitated, not sure what word to use, then settled for the simple truth. "The other half of me."

INTERLUDE

Morgan used two fingers to make a tiny opening in the window slats, peering cautiously at the building across the lane. Malacan had been helpful, if at first reluctant to cooperate. *But,* the Human thought, *there were definite advantages to knowing your opponent's habits.* Morgan had not been surprised by either Malacan's attempt to cash in on the offer for his, Morgan's, preferably living hide, nor Malacan's quick decision to accept a better offer.

Mind you, using a flick of power to freeze Malacan's trigger finger hadn't hurt negotiations a bit.

Unfortunately, Malacan insisted he didn't know who was offering such a handsome number of credits for Morgan. The bounty was simply something being spread around. There was a contact number and an amount. That was all.

It wasn't important, beyond being an explanation of sorts for the attack in the Rissh Marsh. Morgan had sufficient enemies of his own, a few sharing this atmosphere with him at the moment, to account for any number of attempts on his life or credit chip. Though the amount Malacan mentioned had given him pause. He really didn't think he had enemies that desperate or that wealthy. Implying the Clan.

He stepped back from the window, lips stretched in a humorless grin. *Fine.* If they were resorting to posting a bounty for him among the scum of any port, they must be worried. It was a peculiarly satisfying notion.

As was his proximity to his target. Morgan took his bag to the soggy mat passing for a bed in this Retian version of a hotel room, dumping out its contents. He'd laid the waterproof sheet over the surface first, keeping at bay the vermin doubtless swimming inside. No offworlder comforts here, the landlord had warned, and no refunds.

Morgan didn't intend to stay long anyway. It had taken the better part of a sleepless night and day to follow the leads Malacan had given him, three turning out to be worthless before the last had brought Morgan here. Baltir hadn't turned up as a personal name because it wasn't. It was written in Retian business script beside the doorway Morgan had been watching these past hours.

"A research facility devoted to humanoid biology," he repeated to himself. "Now won't Bowman be interested in that." Convincing Malacan to make a properly full report to his contact in the Enforcers had taken a bit more of Morgan's nonexistent credit. He'd worry about the forged ratings and other book-keeping details later.

He picked up an innocuous-looking plas ball from among the devices spread before him, twisting it until it opened into two. Sira had taught him how to open his inner sense, to carefully explore nearby minds in order to identify those which might be touched. She'd also taught him a very healthy respect for the trigger-sharp response of a Clan adept of any strength to such a touch. He didn't plan to try it.

This little beauty, he thought, checking a sequence of fine adjustments before twisting the halves back together, *would have to do.*

Then he sat, his hands and the device in his lap, ignoring the foul smell coming from the mat as his weight pressed air through the moisture, remembering. He'd shown one of these to her once. *Sira.*

The rage was there, in front of her memory, a prism of darkness bending her image in his mind into something tormented and confused: sweet longing coupled with anger; the feel of warm, willing lips tasting of his own blood; despair.

Morgan rubbed his free hand over his face, pressing the fingers into his eyelids as though that might clear his inner vision. This wasn't right. He should be worried about her. He should be frantic to know where Sira was, how she was. *Did she need him? Was she safe? Did she think of him?*

He dropped the ball on the floor and buried his face in both hands. A broken sound tried to force its way up his throat, but couldn't.

Sira had made him into the weapon of her vengeance.

At what cost to them both?

Chapter 36

THERE were few things in my life I was absolutely sure of, so few I could tick them off on my fingers.

First on the list? Morgan could never be a murderer.

It was, however, the consensus among Huido's too-talkative staff, starting with the cook's confession to me and seeming to have moved translight through everyone else at the *Claws & Jaws*. I wondered if either Huido or Barac had paid any attention to the number of ears and other listening organs in attendance at their conferences. Probably not. Barac had not yet overcome his Clan arrogance around lesser species, and Huido likely didn't care.

I could ruthlessly remove the memory from three of the thirty-or-so beings involved. Perhaps I could talk, bribe, or threaten the notion from another twenty. That still left more than enough potential witnesses to embroil Morgan in an investigation if and when the Law discovered the crime. It wasn't particularly relevant to me whether that Law was Clan, Enforcer, or Station security.

Mind you, they had disposed of the body. The new dish had been such a hit on the Rillian menu the cook waxed positively poetic about the possibility of more. I assured him I thought it quite likely there'd be another Clan corpse available, an assurance easy to give whenever I thought of my sister.

I'd scanned Barac. His motivations were understandable and plain: justice for his brother's death, a chance for a future. I wasn't pleased to learn he'd chased after Morgan, but didn't suspect any darker motive than a charming tendency to interfere.

Rael? I wanted to believe we were truly heart-kin, and that here was a Clan who cared about me. I'd been wrong. And if it was a mistake that harmed Morgan, I promised myself, she would be the first to pay.

"Have you decided on a course of action, Mystic One?" As he waited for an answer, Copelup lifted his container of nicnic juice to his mouth, all six tentacles whipping around to hold it in place. His plumes angled slightly toward me.

I'd told the Skeptic everything. If the Drapsk were to continue helping me, they had to know the risks they might share. Not much had surprised him, or else I wasn't as good at reading Drapsk expressions as I thought.

It had been the right decision. Copelup had listened, asked only a few questions, then hurried away to give several rapid orders to the Makii, in Comspeak for my benefit. So as we sat in the *Makmora*'s main galley, a chorus of Drapsk moved through the Station ostensibly looking for trade goods, but actually hunting for answers. They were, I'd noticed, remarkably adept at subterfuge for such a conspicuous bunch.

Other Drapsk were set searching computer records, Captain Makairi suggesting I wouldn't want the details of how they proposed to find out the departure logs from Plexis' notoriously tight-lipped, or whatever, Port Authority. I was happy to agree.

"A course of action, Copelup?" I repeated, sipping my own beverage without tasting it. "Find Morgan. Undo what I've done to him."

The cup was pried free. "And then?"

I narrowed my eyes at the Drapsk. He used that innocent tone, the one meaning he was driving at some point, though what I couldn't guess. "I hadn't thought that far," I confessed. "It seems enough to accomplish, don't you think? Go somewhere safe from the Clan. Morgan—Morgan will know what we should do."

"Morgan is not Clan, Mystic One. He is not of your Tribe," Copelup stated, affixing the refilled cup to his mouth with a smug slurp.

I controlled a flash of temper. Copelup simply stated facts as he, a Drapsk, viewed them. "This does not affect my commitment to him, Skeptic."

I waited while Copelup finished his drink. "I do not suggest that it should, Mystic One," the Drapsk said. "My meaning is that he does not share your species' peril. Only you perceive that. So only you can help them."

"The Clan?" If two baby-blue eyes had appeared somewhere on his smooth head and winked, I'd have been less surprised. "Why should I care about them?"

"How can you not, Mystic One?"

So straightforward for the Drapsk, I thought, bonded with their Tribes and now, through their world's reconnection, bonded among their Tribes into one focused unit. They were individuals comfortably nestled in a framework of unity and purpose. I found myself gripping my cup more tightly than necessary. The Clan was a bickering, dangerous collective, driven by ambition and governed by fear.

"It is not the same for us, Copelup," I found myself explaining, to myself as well as the Drapsk. "We don't have a home like Drapskii to link us. We don't even enjoy each other's company. I think," I hesitated, then knew with a shiver of cold certainty I was right, "we are a dead end. A mutation about to fade from the universe."

Copelup inhaled a tentacle, as if mulling over what I said, then spoke around it. "Life survives. Your people want to survive. How can you deny this?"

I stood, pacing away from the table, basically a long, low version of the stools produced by the floor. As temporary as the Clan in the larger scheme of things. "Survive? We're a disease within the Trade Pact, Copelup. Powerful, deadly. Unrestrained. A bacterium attempts to survive, to reproduce, but at what cost to its host? We've interfered with others—kept the Humans from learning about the M'hir. I hate to think what the Council will conclude about you and your Scented Way. There is," I concluded heavily, "nothing good about us."

Copelup hooted softly. "There is you, Mystic One."

"Is there?" I said, thinking of Morgan, thinking of Yihtor and all the unChosen I'd threatened by my mere existence.

"Yes," he replied sternly. "And I don't think you can be the only one."

I shook my head. "The price of our survival is too high. I'm not willing to pay it. As far as I'm concerned, the M'hiray strand of the Clan can end with this generation."

"So, Mystic One, while avowing you care nothing for your kind, you make this decision for all?"

I stopped pacing and looked at the wise little being. "I can only make decisions for myself, Skeptic."

"Ah, but if you refuse to help them, are you not imposing this choice?"

The word—Choice—resonated through my thoughts, disturbing what I'd been about to reply in rebuttal, shaking free memories of those decades spent in study, desperate years looking for a solution to the Power-of-Choice. In one sense, it had been a typically selfish, Clannish search, since I looked for a means to end my personal dilemma, but had it not also been a striving to find a solution for every Chooser, to prevent what had appeared with me from being the end of us?

"No," I denied furiously. "I owe them nothing. I gave them everything I could and they tried to betray me, to kill Morgan, to *use* me. When I fought them and won, they stole what they wanted. How dare you even think I should help them! Let them help themselves!"

The Skeptic pursed his round, small mouth, tentacles a brilliant red ring like petals on some flower. "Because, Mystic One, it is what you want to do. It is what you've always wanted to do. They just haven't let you."

I couldn't see him very clearly; my eyes had filled with burning tears. Something tumbled away inside, some unknown wall between the Sira-I-had-been and the Sira-I'd-become. I'd believed in my kind once. Like the Drapsk, my place and my role within the Clan had sustained me. The actions of a few—not all—had destroyed that belief, setting me adrift and alone, my love for Morgan a saving anchor. He had taught me how to care for another individual, to accept that a stranger might one day be more.

The Drapsk, it seemed, had another lesson for me. I was part of a larger whole, willingly or not. And that whole was my responsibility.

"I can't forgive them," I said bitterly, wiping away the tears with a rough hand. Then, with shattering clarity, I knew what I must do. "But—I'll save them if I can.

"Once Morgan is safe."

INTERLUDE

"They must have followed you. They certainly didn't follow me."

Huido snapped a claw in irritation, but quietly. He was the one on watch, it being simpler to look around corners if one owned eyes on stalks. A pair of those eyes angled back to see the Clansman where he sat on a plas crate. The alleyway offered several such seats, though none strong enough to support Huido's bulk.

"It's still your fault. You know those two. Bowman only uses them when she's after the Clan."

"True," Barac admitted, keeping his voice down. He was sure they'd spotted the Enforcers before being seen themselves, but it still begged the question: what were Constables Russell Terk and his partner, the Tolian P'tr wit 'Whix, doing in this part of the All Sapients' District of Jershi?

Not being inconspicuous, that's for sure, he thought to himself, as if Terk could ever hide in a crowd. And Tolians, while common elsewhere, were disgusted with Ret 7's almost perennial dampness, preferring to barter for their exports through hardier species. To see one of the lanky, feather-crested beings stalking along Jershi's streets, three-clawed feet fastidiously avoiding puddles, was sufficient to stop traffic.

Barac had also heard that the Tolians distrusted the Retians' ability to distinguish their sentient selves from the local farm stock, but like all such rumors, one had to judge the source.

So these two weren't sneaking about. "The question remains, Huido, did they follow us or beat us here?"

"Irrelevant," rumbled the Carasian. "We will find my brother first. We must tell him about the murders—warn him. The killer may be hunting him even now." A muffled click as Huido expressed his feelings with a threatening wave of one huge claw.

Barac no longer bothered to argue. The Carasian's belief in Morgan's innocence was unassailable, although it was based on a conviction that if the Human wanted someone dead, he would do it with more discretion and finesse. This implied an expertise Barac found most unsettling in a being he'd thought he understood.

Unsettling? There was more to it than that. Barac glanced around, suddenly uneasy. They were alone in the short, dark space between the two warehouses. Alone except for some repulsively mobile native fungus, the Retian version of rats, busy adsorbing a pile of food waste. He shook his head, not dismissing the premonition, but uncertain what it meant.

"With Bowman advertising her presence, the port scum will head for their holes," Huido said thoughtfully, swinging all his eyes to gaze out into the street. "I know a couple of likely spots. Are you ready? They're out of sight."

Barac understood the true threat the instant it was too late to fight it. He opened his mouth to cry a warning to his companion, the alleyway fading from sight around him as someone else's power *pulled* him into the M'hir . . .

When there was no reply, Huido's eyestalks swiveled around, one at a time, until all had followed the first to stare back at the alleyway.

An alleyway in which he was quite alone.

Chapter 37

MY legion of feather-headed spies reported in just before the celebratory feast which, Drapsklike, had to occur or the Mystic One would be offended. Since this was the feast I'd unwittingly abandoned by 'porting to the restaurant and spending the rest of the day questioning Huido's staff, and since I had no interest in more delays of any kind, the Mystic One tried several times to convince the Drapsk nothing was further from the truth. My protests had fallen on deaf hearing organs. No matter how I tried to convince them, over one hundred Makii happily devoted their time to preparing a second wonderful meal.

So I grimly prepared to enjoy it, intending to do so visibly, unmistakably, and in front of all the Makii and one amused Skeptic, in order to move the immovable and get the *Makmora* offstation.

But the reports came first. Most were supplied nonverbally and, I was intrigued to witness, simultaneously. The Drapsk stood in a circle around Captain Makairi, plumes shivering toward him. I could feel soft puffs of air where I stood watching from the doorway to the bridge.

Copelup, predictably, was eavesdropping. "There's a rumor about some disappearing Humans, Mystic One," he warned. "And a group of other Humans looking for them."

"If you are going to scent," Captain Makairi said dryly as he came over to us, the reporting process apparently over, "at least do it well, Skeptic. I have your information, Mystic One," he added more formally. "It's not as much or as specific as we hoped to give you. We sincerely apologize for our failure—"

I cut him off, sensing another round of mutual graciousness

as lengthy as the pre-feast debate. "I'm sure the Makii have done all possible."

Copelup had to jump in: "The Mystic One can't tell you how good the information is, Captain, unless you give it to her. The feast awaits."

"By all means, don't delay the feast," I hurried to assure the Drapsk. "What did they find out?"

"Not all of the reports were based on reliable sources, Mystic One. The Makii cannot vouch for their truthfulness or intent."

A stool nudged the back of my legs suggestively, and I sat instead of bursting with impatience. I knew better by now. "Then let's go through it all and decide for ourselves, Captain," I suggested with what I considered remarkable self-control.

The Drapsk had learned several things of interest, some very odd and useless facts, and at least one item that made it next to impossible to enjoy my feast. I shoveled in bite after bite regardless, comforting myself with the idea that when I'd stuffed myself to the limit, the Drapsk would be satisfied and leave Plexis.

Sector Chief Bowman herself was on-station, an acquaintance I was tempted to renew, but on second thought I realized that could become a serious complication if she learned about the source of the *Claws & Jaws'* latest entrée. Her own motives for being here were suspect: her people were asking questions around the Station about Humans, but not just any Humans. They were asking about Human telepaths.

In any Human city, I thought, rubbing an old, fading callus on my left hand, you could ask around and find a master-class keffle-flute player. They might be rare, but not impossible to find. You could round up a dozen or so very good ones. And doubtless locate hordes of beginners torturing the ears of their brave instructors.

Just so with Human telepaths, except, unlike professional performers, they tended to make every effort to avoid notice, this effort increasing with their Talent. Few could do more than feel an uneasiness around other minds, leading most to be solitary, reclusive individuals. Some, like Morgan, found space a kinder environment, away from the weariness of screening out millions of other minds. Many went mad to an extent, a sad waste of even minimal Talent.

Then, as Morgan had told me, there were those who were lucky—or unlucky—enough to have both Talent and a mentor to train them in its use. Of course, there were two kinds of mentors, split neatly by the ethics they applied to the use of mental abilities: those with some and those without.

Morgan hadn't told me about the Human who had trained him, though it was obvious from his skill he'd had good instruction at an early age. I was not prone to asking him about his past, not being interested in remembering my own.

Bowman's Enforcers weren't hunting telepaths, though there were certainly enough on the other side of the Law to make such a hunt profitable; the Enforcers were collecting information about missing telepaths. Word was, they had lost several of their own recently.

From rumors the Drapsk heard, it wasn't only law-abiding, well-protected telepaths disappearing. Crime syndicates, including the Grays and Blues of Deneb, and the local Plexis underground had lost telepaths as well, posting huge rewards for their return.

I wasn't sure how all this fit into the timing of the attack on me, the dead Clansman in the freezer, or where Morgan, Barac, and Huido had gone. I was sure I didn't like the sound of it. Premonition might be a skill I lacked, but it didn't take the taste of trouble in the M'hir to know who might be interested in Human telepaths and why. I didn't doubt the same thought had crossed Bowman's mind: the Clan Council. They'd forbidden my Joining with Morgan on the grounds of species' purity. Yet they'd been willing to use him if it brought my body into its reproductive state.

Who better to blame? The Council had motive, and they certainly had the ability to overpower a Human telepath. I thought only Morgan would be able to withstand them—and that only long enough to flee.

I reserved judgment. The Council made almost too easy a target. If they were responsible for the attack on me, which I didn't doubt, why hadn't they taken Morgan? I still believed it was because, to them, he didn't matter.

No matter who was to blame, it concerned me. If someone was hunting Human telepaths, Morgan could be next on their list. I sent a few Drapsk back to their contacts; holding our lift from Plexis might be worth it if we could identify this threat.

My spies had ferreted out a plethora of other rumors and facts in the short time they'd been marching through the Station and examining its records. They'd procured an order of Tolian nut-based liqueurs, having coaxed the upcoming rise in price from a dealer. I had lists in my hands of probably every crime occurring over the last five days, as well as every posting of a grudge or bad debt.

One of those was informative. A trip box had been ordered, paid for, and delivered to one of the luxury hotel suites, Level 22 spinward ¾. The owner hadn't shown up to claim his bulky purchase, so the hotel manager had complained to Plexis security. They could find no trace of one Larimar di Sawnda'at, Clansman—hardly a surprise to those who knew about the memorable Rillian dish.

His was a name I knew. Larimar had been one of Yihtor's followers on Acranam, freed from Council rule by the faking of his own death. Why would he want a trip box? Was he involved in kidnapping Human telepaths? The chambers were used legitimately to transport beings with certain medical conditions—including the not-uncommon fear of translight travel—and illegally to transport less willing passengers euphemistically called "recruits." He'd been following Morgan, possibly with the intention of getting the Human into the trip box, but instead was confronted by Morgan, then questioned by Morgan and Huido.

Sometime after that, Larimar had been killed and left in Huido's freezer. I waved the Drapsk with the dessert tray back to me again, having found a tiny spot in my stomach not ready to burst. They did remarkable things with sweets.

Huido and Barac had worked together to dispose of Larimar's body. I examined this from every possible interpretation and could only conclude they, too, believed Morgan was guilty. So instead of having a body to help prove Morgan's innocence, they'd cleverly removed any chance of it giving a clue to the real killer. I wished I'd arrived soon enough to stop the helpful pair.

What made it impossible to fully enjoy the delicacies the Drapsk lavished on me were the departure logs for Plexis. The *Silver Fox*, Karolus Registry, had lifted four days before the

Makmora docked on Plexis. I'd missed Morgan by so little. Her flight plan—another item the Drapsk mysteriously obtained—listed Ret 7 to Ettler's: destinations I hardly doubted.

Huido and Barac sud Sarc were listed as first class passengers on yesterday's shuttle to Ret 7. They'd gained on Morgan—taking advantage of Plexis' own stationday of translight travel, part of her scheduled movements to fresh markets.

And, to round out the cozy fleet, Bowman's own cruiser had lifted shortly afterward, no destination filed. But I had no trouble guessing.

Time we joined the crowd.

"Well, Captain Makairi, my heartfelt thanks to you and all the Makii for my feast," I said as jovially as I could manage, given the state of my mind and the swelling of my stomach.

Makii oriented toward me, a rather perplexing assortment of containers stuck to their faces. It had been a feast worth sharing. All of their plumes were upright and quivering. A happy bunch, I thought, hoping my digestive system could cope.

"We are pleased to have given you a satisfactory feast at last, Mystic One," the Captain said gratefully. "Are you certain you don't want anything more? Perhaps we can still obtain your truffles?"

I choked back a laugh that was close to something else. "No. No. I'm perfectly satisfied. Any more and I would lose—" my feast, I thought to myself "—my ability to stay awake and savor the moment!"

Copelup had stood up at the same time. "The feast is over," he announced proudly. "The Mystic One is satisfied."

There would have been a round of cheering as well as a joyful breeze in my direction had more Drapsk not had their faces full of feast. I went on before this occurred to them. "My dear Makii. While I hate to ask more of you after such a tribute, your Captain knows I must. I have learned our destination. As soon as those Drapsk on-station return, the *Makmora* must leave Plexis as soon as possible for Ret 7."

There was, of course, no objection from the dear Drapsk.

There was, equally of course, a delay due to the dear Drapsk, as Maka informed me in my cabin later that shipday.

"What do you mean, a visitor?" I squeaked at him, still

fuzzy-headed from the nap my overindulgence at the feast had demanded. Then I thought: *Morgan!* And without thinking how improbable this was, I sent out a blaze of questing thought.

A sense of pain, not mine, someone else's. I pulled back instantly, realizing at the same moment the Drapsk had not brought me Morgan but another Human telepath.

And not just any telepath. The mind I'd slammed into like a rock against ice had reacted to my demand for Morgan with immediate and clear emotion.

Recognition.

INTERLUDE

"Keep interrupting me, Sister, and we'll never find her," Rael snapped, restraining an angry lock of her black hair.

Pella didn't quite pout. "Ica wants to know if you've made any progress. It's been hours."

Feels like it, Rael said to herself, stretching some of the tightness from her shoulders. Aloud she said: "If any of them cares to augment a heart-search through the M'hir, let them. Otherwise, leave me to my work."

Pella stepped completely into the bedroom, closing the door behind her. They each had rooms here in Ica's house. It wasn't said or thought, but Rael knew better than to try and leave her own without results.

"Ru doesn't believe you are trying to find Sira at all. Why would she say such a thing?"

Because I'm not, fool, Rael wanted to shout. She wanted several other impossible things as well, including the chance to shake some sense into her younger sister. But Pella was convinced they had to save Sira from herself and had thrown herself completely into Ica's scheming as the best way to do it. Rael couldn't wait until Sira had a chance to discuss matters with Pella in person.

Of course, that opportunity would come only if Rael found Sira and could convince her to come, both events she was working diligently to avoid. How much longer she could delay success was anyone's guess. The heart-search was tricky. She could hardly be blamed for failure. But there were others under Ica's sway who could taste power in the M'hir. If Sira spent much time there, she could be traced.

There was, Rael thought to herself, with melancholy pride, *no way to hide such brilliance in the darkness.*

Chapter 38

I'D asked the Drapsk to raise the level of lighting. They'd happened to bring my so-called visitor in the midst of shipnight and I had no desire to meet anyone while fumbling around in near darkness. I did trust the Drapsk to take care of any hazard the stranger might pose. Any ship equipped with explosive grapples could manage one Human.

Even an older, but very fit-looking, Human, I thought as two Makii brought my guest to the *Makmora*'s trading lounge. The lounge, a luxury afforded by only the largest trading vessels, was a beautifully appointed and carefully species-neutral space reached easily from the air lock and much less easily from within the ship. It would require more explosive to break into the rest of the *Makmora* from here than to penetrate the outer hull. As I'd noticed about the Drapsk, they took care with their clients.

I didn't know the face. Since meeting Morgan, I'd made an effort to learn Human expressions and features—a pastime considered meaningless among the Clan, who preferred to share emotion through the M'hir. My visitor's face reminded me of a battered warrior, a fighter knocked down once too often before realizing his time was over—if he'd realized it even then. The features were too angular, too harsh for any beauty; even his short-cropped hair was retreating from his face. The lips came closest, full and sensual. A shame, I decided, the brown eyes within their frame of puckered scars held so much bitterness.

He was dressed in casual work clothes, Station issue. I dismissed them as camouflage. This Human did not work for anyone but himself. I had tested the edges of his shielding very lightly when he came into the room. There was considerable power here, well-honed and carefully protected.

"Who are you?" I asked, stifling a yawn. The Drapsk hurried to coax me a stool. I noticed they didn't provide one for the Human and stifled a smile at the same time.

I felt a tendril of thought touching my own. I faded back, but instead of an impenetrable shield, hid myself behind a trace of seemingly open consciousness that would tell him nothing, lead him to suspect nothing of what I was.

His face revealed nothing in return, a control of expression that reminded me suddenly of the polite mask Morgan assumed so easily. "My name is Symon. Ren Symon," the man introduced himself. His voice was low-timbered and smooth, his Comspeak accentless. No clues there. "These Drapsk asked me to come and tell you what I knew." A pause to raise an eyebrow. "The information isn't free."

Captain Makairi spoke up, anger in every fierce twitch of plume. It was an effective display, especially as it was copied in matching rhythm by the other ten Drapsk in the room, including Copelup. "We warned you not to speak to the Mystic One of payment. That will be taken care of by the *Makmora* should your information please her."

Ren Symon was a big Human, muscled but not heavy, his movements graceful despite his size. I estimated he would top Morgan by a head and he certainly towered over my Drapsk. But there was something about knowing the way Drapsk reacted as a Tribe that tended to keep a respectful expression on most sane beings. This Human was no exception. "My apologies, Mystic One." His lips quirked over the title.

Let it amuse him. I had no intention of sharing my name with strangers. "What is this information, Hom Symon?"

"You're looking for a trader, Jason Morgan of the *Fox*. I can take you to him."

A dangerous Human, I told myself, forcing back every response but caution. He was fishing, I decided, having sensed my attempt to contact Morgan but probably unsure it had come from me. What story had he originally concocted to gain the interest of the Drapsk?

Or the Drapsk could well have mentioned Morgan's name. I hadn't forbidden it. Maybe I should have.

"Morgan? If he's a practitioner of magic," I replied in my smoothest voice, "then we would very much like to meet him. I've been commissioned by these fine Drapsk to find reputable magical beings for their next Festival. They did tell you our purpose, didn't they?"

A few tentacles hit the mouth at this, but the Drapsk weren't uncomfortable with a lie or two. Copelup gave a strangled hoot the Human could interpret how he chose.

He chose to ignore it, smiling a disturbing, assessing type of smile, as though he savored something about me. I knew some Humans, including Morgan, responded to the innate power of a Clanswoman the way an unChosen male of the Clan might do. Or perhaps he was one of those affected by a female's appearance. *It was,* I thought coldly, *only another reason to be cautious.* "No, they didn't mention it," Symon answered at last. "But I should have guessed on my own. The Drapsk are reputed to know their—magic." Did I imagine the hesitation before the word, as though he really did understand what the Drapsk had sought to find?

"Where is this Morgan, Hom Symon?" Copelup asked for me, perhaps aware I was wary of asking more myself. "What is your relationship to him? Are you his agent on Plexis?"

"Jase and I go way back," Symon claimed. "I'm not his agent. I just know what's good for him, that's all."

I met his dark brown eyes with a jolt of understanding. He was the one—I was suddenly sure—the mentor Morgan had never told me about, the one who had taught him the rudiments of using his Talent. I didn't need to be told that this was also the one who had driven Morgan to seek solitude in the *Fox.* What had Morgan said? That the telepaths he knew worked for or against the Trade Pact. I didn't need to ask which type faced me now.

I stood slowly, reestablishing all of my shielding, pressing outward with an edge of power until I saw him stagger and wince, eyes wide in surprise. *Good,* I thought. Let him know who and what he deals with. "You didn't come here to help us find Morgan," I said scornfully. "You came here hoping we would help you find him."

"Sira di Sarc," he breathed, nostrils flared with triumph. "Yes, I'd hoped to find Morgan, but to find you? This is much better.

Much." It was as if he now talked to himself, face reddening with excitement, oblivious to what his rapid words revealed. "You know, I'd thought maybe removing those memory blocks from Jodrey's empty head would be as big a waste of time as his life. But curiosity was always my greatest fault. And here you are. In the flesh. Tell me, is it true? Can your kind pass your power to us? Can you? I'd pay—"

It was as if I'd turned over a piece of crystal and found a dirty slug underneath. "I'll show you what I can pass along," I said. The Makii on either side of Symon drew away quickly, guessing what I was about. "Be careful you don't cross my path again, Ren Symon."

I formed the locate, *pushed* . . .

And air slithered into where he'd been.

I hoped they checked the freezer at the *Claws & Jaws* regularly, or there could be a very cold telepath in there by morning.

Not that I cared.

INTERLUDE

Delivering the stalker had been simplicity itself. Understanding what it showed him was not. Morgan toggled and spun various controls, coldly patient, trying to bring up a scan that made sense.

Just before dawn, Morgan had made his way to the roof of the hotel, careful to avoid the lumps of sleeping ort-fungus draped over most of the vents—no wonder the air inside was so stale. The orts were harmless pests, but their tendency to climb up pant legs in search of food left in a pocket was a nuisance at the best of times.

Standing several paces back from the edge, Morgan lobbed the sphere in his hand in an arc clearing the narrow street below to land on the opposite roof. Then he put a pair of nightviews to his eyes and watched; stalkers were hideously expensive on Plexis, restricted items everywhere else. If he missed with this one, he'd have to steal another or resort to a riskier tactic. Under the circumstances, theft from the Retians didn't strike Morgan as particularly amoral, but there was no question he'd be better off avoiding complications with the local law.

Ah. The sphere rolled slowly until it came against an upright piece of ductwork, then stopped. Morgan stepped up the magnification on his lenses in time to see the sphere crack itself open in several places. Long, delicate-appearing legs protruded, lifting free the stalker itself: a dull brown mechanical body no larger than the tip of his finger, its core packed with sensors. Beneath it, meanwhile, the discarded outer case performed its final function, dissolving a tiny hole through the roofing material as it consumed itself. After a moment, the stalker lowered itself into the cavity and vanished from Morgan's sight.

So it was back into the musty hotel room, to sit on the water-proof sheet and watch for results.

Morgan tried another adjustment. *There.* The viewpoint was upside-down, the stalker preferring the ceiling where it could avoid auto detectors as well as feet. It was scanning infrared to produce the image he was interpreting, at least when the stalker wasn't crawling over lighting fixtures, a move which resulted in a shocking blaze of bright reds across the screen.

High tech, Morgan mused, gradually piecing together a sense of the building's interior. None of the Retian proclivity for moisture or mud in here. These walls and floor were pristine, flawless.

A splash of light pinks, body-shaped, massed together along one section of wall. As programmed, the stalker paused to collect more information. Morgan tapped the order to continue. It must be a pod of junior Retians, packed shoulder-to-shoulder into a pocket or closet in the wall, dozing until needed for some menial task. While young, the beings were capable of a light state of hibernation—a convenient way for their elders to deal with a stage of Retian development in which brains were less than functional and behavior varied between meaningless repetition and absolute distraction. Given detailed direction, the juniors were useful workers. There were likely several such pods, none of concern in his present search.

Morgan had his sketch pad on his knee and jotted down a rough map as the device passed closed doors and side corridors, marking areas of potential interest with a quick circle of black. By the time the stalker's power source failed, and he'd straightened up with a groan and stretch, he had covered ten sheets with detailed notes.

And, he thought with grim satisfaction, *he'd found what he was looking for,* circled twice on page six.

A room with a locked door but offering access to the stalker through a ventilation grille at the top. Within the room, boxes glowing with the infrared signature of incubators held at humanoid norm.

And, as a bonus, a sleeping form in a side chamber of the

same room—a sleeper with a body temperature well above that for a Retian, but well inside the range for Clan.

Morgan began repacking his bag, pausing first to check the fit of his throwing knives in their sheaths on his wrists.

With any luck, he'd found the robber along with the spoils.

Chapter 39

"PORT Authority has given us clearance to land. We are thirteenth in the docking schedule, Mystic One. You have time to rest, if you wish."

"Thank you."

The door closed behind Maka. I drew up my knees, wrapping my arms around my legs to hold them tightly against my chest. There was only a slight initial discomfort in my abdomen, quickly fading to no more than a pulling sensation. *Fit for duty,* I told myself, shying from any thought of what might have been altered within.

I dropped my forehead to my knees, my hair sliding down to close me off from this cabin, its fresh-washed scent a touch of my own, non-Drapsk, reality. *Things would happen in their order,* I vowed to myself. I would no longer lose control. No matter how much I longed to send that sliver of thought along the path to Morgan's mind, no matter how easy it would be to disappear from this place and find myself in the comforting familiarity of the *Fox,* I would do neither. The risk was too great.

There were Clan here. As on Plexis, I could open the tiniest slit in my awareness of the M'hir and sense the power crackling through its blackness. The pathways were not numerous, but they were burned into place from frequent use. I knew of no Clan who lived here. No offspring would have been fostered here to create a link to his or her absent parent. So what I tasted around me had been forged to a purpose. To come and go from Ret 7 without other species being aware.

Secrecy was a good sign, I assured myself, licking dry lips and straightening up. It meant this was the right place, something I'd taken for granted given Morgan had chosen to come here. I lowered my legs, rubbing my abdomen not so much to ease the memory of soreness as in promise. I may have forced my anger into Morgan's mind; it didn't mean I had none left of my own.

Copelup, while overly free with his advice on most occasions, hadn't been able to offer any suggestions about how to proceed on Ret 7. I'd turned to the Makii instead, formulating the beginnings of a plan. The *Makmora* had never traded with the Retians until now, this system apparently belonging in some sense or other to another Tribe. This didn't preclude the Makii from dealing here, I was informed, as long as any profits, including valuable information, were ultimately shared. It was, Captain Makairi told me, inefficient but acceptable.

My part was easy to remember, if increasingly difficult to perform. I was to sit in this cabin, being completely unobtrusive, while the Drapsk did my looking for me.

I pulled up my knees again, considering the movement a useful bit of exercise, and worked on my patience.

The Makii's patience turned out to be worse than mine. "Bargain hunters, Mystic One," Captain Makairi snarled within a day of our landing. "That is what one contends with on these isolated worlds. Bargain hunters!"

Having worked on a trade ship myself, I did sympathize—sympathize, even as I felt a familiar frustration with my always literal Drapsk. "We aren't really trading here, Captain," I reminded him gently. "Has there been any success contacting the," I stumbled over the name, "the *Fox*?"

The Captain had three Drapsk monitoring the intership chatter, as well as recording those messages in languages he'd need to run through a translator later. Other Drapsk were listening intently to Retian news and religious broadcasts. I was beginning to see how the Drapsk earned their reputation for knowing their clients exceptionally well. Former Captain Maka answered my question from his comtech post. "Port Authority routes all calls to the *Silver Fox* through an answering service listing requests for samples of local artifacts and a few specific pharmaceuticals. There was an insignificant offering of cargo, already purchased but not delivered. We were quite circumspect in contacting this service, Mystic One," he added quickly, rightly gauging my mood.

"I didn't think he'd be on her," I said more to myself.

"We have heard from the *Nokraud,* Mystic One," another Makii called out helpfully. "She has docked safely and awaits your communication."

The pirates from Drapskii were here? I turned slowly to stare at Captain Makairi. "You didn't contact the Scats," I said with disbelief, mouth dry. "Did you?"

His plumes dropped almost flat. "Mystic One. How could you think we would do such a thing without your instructions? This communication originates with the *Nokraud,* not any Drapsk."

"They scent profit," Copelup offered from his seat beside mine. "It's not an uncommon strategy for the Sakissishee to follow a freighter into port, hoping to pick up scraps of trade."

"They followed us to Plexis and then here?"

"Certainly not to Plexis, Mystic One," Copelup said with a hoot. "Plexis has recently banned the Sakissishee—quite against Trade Pact regulations forbidding discrimination by species. No, I think it more likely the *Nokraud* waited at a distance, until certain of our course here."

"Do not let this possibility alarm you, Mystic One," Captain Makairi said hurriedly. "We are keeping a close watch. But I do wonder what communication they expect from you. Did you make some arrangement with them during your time on the *Nokraud?*"

I felt my cheeks growing warm. "They may believe I want to purchase transport on their ship. I don't."

"Should we relay this message for you?" Makairi asked with some concern.

I shook my head. The Drapsk convince the Scats I no longer wanted to flee them? Not likely. "I think that had better come from me. Tell them I'll be in touch. Anything else I should know before we leave?"

The bridge grew silent; too silent, I thought, considering how many Drapsk were crowding around me. There was a fair amount of plume waving going on, indicating a debate in progress. "What?" I demanded.

Predictably, Copelup answered. "The Makii have—concerns—about your safety away from the *Makmora,* Mystic One. As the Captain said, this is a world of bargain hunters. The Retians are famed for their ability to spot a valuable commodity—" he paused.

"Such as myself?" I finished with a resigned shrug. "I appreciate your concern, Copelup, but there's only so much I can do hiding in here. We'll take all the precautions we can." I smiled without amusement. "And this time on Ret 7, I do believe I can take care of myself."

It was finding Morgan without using my power that daunted me.

"This will do nicely," I said, forestalling the attempt by my new personal tailor, the former comtech Makoori, to pull yet another article of pilfered clothing from his collection. The tailor's room, the usual Drapsk bulge off a main corridor, had become a most unusual miniature warehouse. Luggage ranging from plain crew duffels to ornate—and well-locked—grav-free pieces made artificial walls almost head high. All of it, alas, stolen property.

Of course, the Drapsk had paid for it, not being a species that engaged in thievery. But I'd wormed out of Makoori the fact that they'd bought the assortment of luggage from the *Nokraud* at the same time as the fireworks, suggesting a less-than-legal origin to this wealth of Human clothing and personal belongings. Since they'd done it for me, I didn't ask further, nor did I want to know. If I'd had the time or inclination, I would have been quite horrified.

I had neither and so was quietly grateful when Makoori found me a set of humanoid rain gear which both fit well and looked reassuringly commonplace—some of the clothing we'd gone through had been definitely meant to help the wearer stand out in any crowd, or perhaps even in the dark. I put my hands in the pockets, pulling out a selection of hair clips from one. I caught myself staring down at them.

"My apologies, Mystic One," Makoori said, virtually snatching the clips from my fingers. "I thought I'd cleaned all of these articles thoroughly."

"It's all right, Makoori," I replied, hoping these were merely stolen clothes, their owners somewhere in a line, complaining about their missing things to a hapless clerk or impervious servo.

What I knew of Scats didn't support that hope at all.

I'd contacted Grackik and Rek before leaving the bridge earlier in the afternoon. They had, as I'd guessed, offered me alternative transport. It was a halfhearted offer, though, without any effort to convince me to leave the Drapsk. I declined their services firmly—and I hoped, unmistakably—but was left with the impression they hadn't followed me at all.

I shook my head and gathered up the carrysack of other items Makoori and I had prepared. What the Scats were really doing here was none of my concern. The Drapsk could handle them in space, and Port Authority—even on Ret 7—would keep a worried eye on them while grounded.

The Drapsk who would accompany me off the ship were waiting in the lounge. I was about to leave and join them when Makoori stopped me. "Wait, Mystic One." His purple plumes were fully erect, sampling the air flowing over our heads.

"What is it?" I knew it was a message, or possibly even a two-way conversation. I had yet to be sure of the limits of Drapsk olfaction.

"You have a visitor." Makoori inhaled his tentacles as he oriented his plumes toward me, shaking them as though he wanted to tell me in his own way before saying: "A visitor who has asked for you by the name Sira di Sarc."

I put down my case with care, removing my rain gear and laying it neatly on top. For a person who was supposedly traveling inconspicuously, was there anyone who didn't already know I was here?

At least my visitor was as concerned as I was with keeping my presence somewhat of a secret.

"It is genuine, Mystic One," Copelup said glumly, handing the ident back to the Human. The Drapsk had subjected it, and my latest guest, to an impressive series of scans and checks. They weren't happy with the results and neither was I. "We have verified that this being is Constable Miles Ekkurtan, presently assigned to Sector Chief Bowman's staff."

Constable Ekkurtan nodded politely. He'd sat comfortably

on a Drapsk stool while all this went on around him, looking like anything but an Enforcer. His outfit was identical to any number of the mid-category spacers currently fin-down on Ret 7—or any other spaceport for that matter—not-quite shabby blue coveralls, clean and maintained to suggest a trader careful of his deals yet poor enough to take risks. He was a small Human, dark, with tight curling black hair and a warm, easy smile. I tasted the M'hir near him and felt nothing. Protected by an implant. The final proof, if I needed it, that this was one of Bowman's most trusted officers.

The Makii were mortified. First the *Nokraud* had followed us and now, it seemed, so had the Enforcers. How was what I wanted to know, which was why I was going against all the Drapsk's good advice and leaving the *Makmora* with the Constable. Sector Chief Bowman, my former acquaintance, had invited me to join her for supper in the nearby city of Jershi. We would travel surreptitiously, of course. The kind Constable had come to the *Makmora*'s air lock in a covered groundcar, a true luxury when traveling on this damp, soggy world.

But I didn't abandon all caution. I let the Constable take the lift from the lounge, then turned to the Drapsk forming a morose semi-circle behind me. "I'm not expecting any trouble," I told them, causing already drooping plumes to sink further. "But how good is your sense of smell out there?"

One by one, as I explained what I wanted, plumes rose to the ceiling in what I thought was pleased anticipation.

INTERLUDE

Pounding his fists on the door hadn't helped.

Though it was an improvement over the pain in his head, Barac thought ruefully, rubbing the back of his neck. He'd thrown himself at the M'hir as well as the wood, straining to break through the sphere of power restricting him to this cell-like room more surely than the locked door and surrounding walls. It had been a futile attempt. Whoever—or whatever—wanted him here was powerful enough to insure he stayed.

The list of those capable wasn't short, the Clansman knew, giving up at last and leaning on one wall. He'd lie on the floor before touching the one item of furniture—a soggy reed-and-mud mattress, half-curled in one corner as if startled into the position by his arrival. No, there were plenty of his kind with more power and almost as many with fewer scruples in its use. Not to mention the alarming devices the Humans seemed to be developing, of which he glumly suspected the mind-deadeners were only the start.

But why? Barac's fingers rubbed the comforting warmth of the bracelet around his left wrist, a gift from his brother Kurr. Not robbery, he thought, since the pre-Stratification relic was probably the most valuable thing he possessed, despite the faintness of the designs in its plain, dull finish.

No matter how Barac puzzled at what was happening, he couldn't pull it together. First Rael had shown up on Pocular, supposedly to visit her sister; his instincts and training said that was a lie. Then Larimar, however briefly, had dogged Morgan's footsteps on Plexis. What little Huido had been willing to repeat of their conversation had been enough for Barac to conclude Larimar was lying as well. Two liars. Separate or together?

Now this, his own kidnapping. Why?

The dampness, though warm and musty, was already raising gooseflesh under his thin jacket. Barac sneezed miserably, glaring up at the one dim light fixture overhead. What ventilation there was came through a grille in the ceiling, a grille half-covered in fungus. With his luck, it would be the mobile variety, able to drop down to visit if and when they turned out the lights.

He hadn't been scanned or questioned. There'd been no touch in his mind beyond the pull to bring him here, which was information in itself. Whoever was responsible didn't want him for what he knew, however little that might be. No, there must be something else.

Barac shivered. Whatever it was, he didn't think it would be to his benefit.

Chapter 40

"SAY what you like about Retian cooking, they know what to do with fowl," Bowman pronounced with satisfaction and an absence of tact, given the Tolian's presence at the table.

I grimaced apologetically at 'Whix. The glinting emerald curve of his left eye was angled my way—an apparently compulsive behavior that started the moment Constable Ekkurtan had delivered me to the restaurant and this discreet back table. That was all the subtlety Bowman had bothered with in our meeting: both she and her companion were in full uniform. 'Whix and I had shared a platter of some small, sauce-drenched crustaceans. Having a beak was a distinct advantage in its enjoyment, I thought, trying to unobtrusively remove yet another tiny leg from between my teeth.

Bowman's plate was covered by a pile of much larger legs. She contemplated it with the look of someone trying to decide if it would be worth asking for seconds, before pushing her plate to the center of the table. "Now, Fem di Sarc," she began in a more businesslike tone, having been unwilling to discuss anything but menu choices (few) and the weather (pouring rain) until now.

"Morgan," I corrected softly. "My name is Morgan, Chief Bowman."

"So," she said, her curious gaze meeting mine. Whatever question lit them at the moment was discarded, her expression turning serious. "You are probably wondering how we located you."

I pushed my own plate away, reaching for my glass of wine. It was an excellent vintage, definitely offworld, and left an expensively pleasant aftertaste on the palate. No sense wasting it. *Or more time,* I decided. "I'm interested in why you wanted to meet with me," I said bluntly. "This—" I saluted her with my glass, "—is hardly what I'd expect if you were after me for some crime against the Trade Pact. So?"

"After you?" Bowman shook her head, gesturing at 'Whix. He produced a strip of plas and a vistape from a pouch on his belt, attached between two large, accessible, and very visible hand weapons. As I recalled, the Treaty gave the Enforcers considerable latitude in their behavior insystem or out. I preferred my armament less obvious, but there was no point reaching for the minds of these two.

I reached instead for the plas when 'Whix proffered it, glancing at what was a simple list of names.

After I read the first few, my hand tightened involuntarily, crumpling the strip into a ball.

"You do know these individuals." It wasn't a question and Bowman's voice was no longer friendly.

I looked up at her, seeing not the Retian restaurant and a justifiably suspicious pair of officers, but a table with a comp interface and a steady stream of data passing under my fingers. "Yes. I should," I told her. "I wrote this list."

It had been two years ago, I explained. Bowman knew the outcome—she'd witnessed it—so I saw no harm sharing its past with her.

A past before Morgan, when I'd been solely Sira di Sarc. I'd lived in voluntary isolation on Camos, chasing numbers and ideas as I sought any means to satisfy the cravings of my Power-of-Choice, to solve the crisis my being the most powerful Chooser alive had caused. One of my efforts had involved searching for some solution outside my kind. I'd looked at the other humanoid species boasting some hint of the Talent, and decided on Human. Simply because, I remembered too clearly, they were so common.

"I made a request to a few of my kin, those I knew could be relied on to actually complete a task—not all are reliable," I admitted to Bowman, knowing the irony. After all, hadn't I proved the most unreliable in the end? "Whenever they encountered a Human telepath, a specific type of telepath—"

"Male and adult," 'Whix interjected in his cool, precise, and artificial voice, iridescent throat feathers lifting ever-so-slightly over his implanted com.

"Yes," I agreed, feeling cold inside. "Male and adult. The age of our unChosen males, no younger, no older. They were to test them for strength as well, cautiously, not to create alarm or notice. I didn't tell them why I wanted the names and locations. Because I was Sira di Sarc, they did not question me." I straightened out the strip. "This is the list, but there was more. Rankings by strength. Personalities. Preferences—" My voice thickened suddenly, and I paused for another sip of wine. "You have to understand. We'd never paid attention to Human telepaths before. Not like this, systematically, in detail. Only the odd chance encounter or conflict, perhaps a business arrangement. Here, for the first time, I could hold up proof you were stronger than we'd hoped, that there were more telepaths among you than we'd imagined in our nightmares. It wasn't a happy discovery."

"Why not?" Bowman asked. "I thought the Clan preferred using mental abilities. Surely dealing with Human telepaths would be easier for you." Her eyes were fixed on me, her hands restless on the tabletop. "Why would you care if all of us were telepaths? We've never matched your capabilities. I'm sure we don't even know them all."

"It's not what is here," I said, raising a finger to the side of my head. "Or what we can or cannot do. We are not many and we are becoming less, while you Humans are filling up world after world." Bowman and I both ignored 'Whix's sudden fit of choking. "And you have another strength we lack. Your kind work together," I said grimly. "The Clan can readily picture a future in which bands of Human telepaths hunt us down, one by one, no matter where we try to hide."

"But that's not why you collected these particular names."

"No. These were—" I took another hasty sip. "These were the possible Human candidates for my Choice."

"Including Jason Morgan."

I nodded, mute, not needing to read it all to find his name. That Morgan had become my Chosen, through his own wish as well as mine, didn't absolve me from the crime of having plotted to force him or any of those others into attempting that Choice without knowing if a Human could even survive it.

My past wasn't important at the moment, so I shook it away impatiently. "Where did you get it?" I demanded. "Who gave it to you?"

Bowman's smile was as hungry as any Scat's. She took the list from me and smoothed it on the table, before plunging down one blunt finger to hold it in place. "What's really interesting about all this, Fem Morgan, is that I made this one up myself."

"W–what?" I couldn't control the stammer in my voice. "That's my list—I know those names—"

'Whix replied for his Chief. "This set of names is based on an ongoing investigation into the disappearance of several Trade Pact citizens, all Human, all male, and all telepaths. These disappearances have occurred in this sector of space, within the last three standard months."

"Jason?" I asked, lips gone numb. "Why did you say his name, then? He hasn't disappeared—the *Fox* is docked, cargo requests posted."

That finger moved down the strip, stopping as if at a name. "Morgan? You're right. He hasn't vanished like the rest. Not yet, anyway. In fact, your Morgan has left a trail a Skenkran could follow in the dark." The hand raised, the pointed finger making a dagger's thrust in my direction. "And why might that be, Sira Morgan? Is he leaving this trail for you? Or to keep someone from you?"

I didn't know what to say.

"No matter," Bowman continued. "He's gone to ground—or rather to mud—but hiding a Human on Ret 7 is almost impossible, even for him. And when I find your Morgan, I'll have sufficient questions to keep him out of circulation for some time."

"Has he communicated with you, Fem Morgan?" this from 'Whix. "We know he wasn't on Drapskii with you."

"How?" I asked, dazed as much by their questioning as by the implications of the list. "How did you know about Drapskii?" Then I shook my head. "The Enforcer sitting in the dock. It had surveillance on the *Nokraud.* I should have known. You saw me there."

'Whix held up the vistape. "It was my ship," he explained

matter-of-factly. "We did record your entry into the *Nokraud,* to what purpose we do not know—"

"I was," I said unsteadily, "trying to find a way back to Morgan. The Drapsk wanted me to stay for their Festival. I was desperate enough to try almost anything."

"You could have come to us," Bowman said. I glanced up at her and shook my head.

"Perhaps. I won't say I was thinking clearly. Anyway, the Drapsk would have been prepared to counter anything I tried. You can't imagine how important their Festival was to them." I raised a hand to forestall her questions. "Ask the Drapsk to explain it, Chief.

"Were you following the *Nokraud*?" I continued warily, looking at 'Whix, my fingers smoothing the fabric of clothing that was definitely no bargain if it came from a pirate raid these two were investigating.

"Not this trip, Fem Morgan," he answered dolefully, as though the high-risk pursuit of pirates would be a vast improvement over any time spent on Ret 7. I could agree.

"We aren't after them," Bowman confirmed, then surprised me by adding: "I'm here looking into some Pact business—and tracking down Morgan. 'Whix has been following you since Pocular."

"With the exception of your stop at Plexis," 'Whix corrected carefully. "I was ordered to change course to Ret 7 instead."

"Pocular?" I said. "Why? And how?"

Bowman didn't misunderstand me. For the first time since I'd known her, she looked uncomfortable, delaying her answer to wave over a waiter and ask for sombay.

I drew my own conclusions, and didn't like any of them. "You've been watching us, haven't you?" I accused her once privacy was reestablished. "All the time, since Camos. Morgan and I thought we were being left alone and in peace. But that was a lie, wasn't it?"

"You believed you'd be left alone. Morgan—" she sipped her sombay, "—Morgan knew better. He was worried about you, about the Clan Council and how it might retaliate against you for standing up to them. So he—called in a debt, you might say. At the time, I told him no. But in reality, we shared an interest in your safety, Fem Morgan." A sober look. "I've been keeping an eye bent your way. We've been watching."

My world narrowed to a focus consisting of the Human across from me and no more. If I'd been able to use any power against her besides simply *pushing* her into the M'hir, I would not have been able to restrain myself. As it was, I felt a thrill of pain as my unresolvable fury tore at my inner controls. My hair squirmed on my shoulders as if it could reach out and wrap around her throat. With a prudent movement, 'Whix shifted as far from me as his chair permitted.

"So you were watching when they attacked us and killed the villagers," I snarled in a low voice, careful of listeners even now. "You were watching when I was ripped apart. You were watching when Morgan almost killed himself trying to find me. And you were sitting, just sitting and watching when I sent him into hell alone." I gripped the table edge until my fingers went white. "How dare you admit it!"

The Chief Enforcer for this tumultuous sector of space was as calm and collected as I was inflamed. I might have imagined her discomfort of a moment ago. She added spice to her mug before saying evenly: "You overestimate the closeness of our scrutiny and dismiss its good intentions, Fem Morgan."

"Good intentions," I growled.

"We did not wish to bring attention to your presence on Pocular, Fem Morgan," 'Whix said, panting oddly as though he at least felt stressed by the hostile turn of the conversation. *Good,* I thought, still glaring at the imperturbable Bowman. "Our surveillance consisted of adding an extra pass through the system by certain ships, such as mine. Our contacts planetside were to keep their eyes and ears open, but there was no use of vid equipment or remotes."

"One of our contacts is fond of gambling," Bowman clarified. "So we did know when Barac sud Sarc, your cousin, arrived. We also," she paused to consume a sweet, "we also heard reports about the Drapsk ship, the *Makmora,* and how her crew were routinely making fools of themselves in attempts to have you with them." Then her voice deepened, and I saw what might have been outrage in her eyes. "We found out about the village and the attack *after* you'd left. Sent in some meds and equipment to help the village. Tried to turn up some information on the attackers. But our main witnesses? You and Morgan? Nowhere to be found. Even Barac was gone."

And so you never saw Rael, I added, but just to myself. *Where did you go, Sister, after I'd left? What did you do?*

'Whix's panting had improved, but still affected his voice. "Several of our ships became involved at that point," he said, "mine being first. I'd been stationed in orbit, under the guise of conducting standard contraband checks on outgoing ships—" Bowman's impatient wave sent him past this digression. "I was ordered to follow the *Makmora.* It was reasonable to conclude that if you had voluntarily left in any way other than through the use of your—abilities—it would have been with the Drapsk. An hypothesis I was able to verify."

"What matters is the present," Bowman said accurately. "I didn't know you'd been injured. What happened? Are you all right now?"

I blinked at Bowman, startled by what might have been honest concern in her voice. I wasn't about to jump to that conclusion. She had more than my health to worry about, starting with that list lying between us and ending with an entire sector of beings who would not be pleased by the latest Clan activities in their space. "I've healed enough to get around, thanks to the Drapsk." I considered, then added: "Someone performed surgery on me. Whether there's permanent damage—I don't know. Once all this is resolved, once Morgan is safe again, then I'll find out."

"Surgery? What type of surgery?" Bowman's voice had the snap of an order.

"If I knew—"

Bowman reached up to her face, tapping her left eyebrow sharply with two fingers. It appeared an absent gesture, but I knew by the sudden concentration in her eyes it meant something more. "What is it?" I asked.

"You haven't been examined by a humanoid med—or even gone into a Human-based med unit, have you?"

"No. I told you, there's been no time. But I'm all right. The Drapsk took good care of me." I leaned forward in emphasis. "We were talking about finding Morgan. I hardly think this is the time—"

She looked at 'Whix, who swiveled both his eyes to meet

hers, then returned his left eye to its stare at me. "Fem Morgan," Bowman began, and there was no mistaking the note of concern, "I want you to come back to my cruiser where you can be examined by my med staff. Please—"

Her voice and my alarm over what they intended faded from my immediate concern. Just behind Bowman was a half-wall, meant to provide privacy without blocking the movement of air through the restaurant. It was topped by a metal latticework, encrusted with the lichens and mosses Retians considered houseplants.

In each of the bottommost triangular openings in the lattice, a bright, black, and glistening eye looked back at me, making a row of about ten. Once I'd spotted them, they disappeared below the solid part of the wall.

I wasn't going to have to keep my Drapsk hunting for Huido, I realized with a relief so deep I was almost shaking with it.

He'd found me.

INTERLUDE

A guarded flash of light let Morgan check his bearings on his homemade map. The next right-hand corridor should lead to the ramp down. He closed his hand back over the lens, dousing all but the minimum glow he needed to see the floor in front.

It wasn't the Retians' fault the emergency lighting hadn't kicked in the moment the building's illumination went dark, necessitating the evacuation of the few beings still at work inside. Morgan checked his wrist chrono. It should take a while to find any repair specialist at this hour of the night, let alone one capable of deciphering the reprogramming he'd done to the environmental controls, assuming they were able to spot his tampering in the first place. And he'd timed his intrusion to take full advantage of a night when all he knew of Retians suggested most would be—fully occupied.

In the interval, he had the building to himself, dark and vid-free. There were some skills too useful to leave behind in one's past.

Down the ramp, this one set with regular steplike treads, as if designed for use by non-Retian feet. Morgan slipped down them, moving noiselessly but rapidly to his target. *There.* The door was just where he'd marked it on the map.

Through it and he was in the final corridor; it was below ground level and damp, despite what were, for Retians, heroic efforts to scrub the air of excess moisture. Morgan risked removing his hand from the lens completely for a moment, training the full beam from his light on what lay ahead. Nothing but bare walls and locked doors.

Another check of the map. It was the third door on the left he wanted. Morgan switched off his light, using his fingertips against the wall to feel his way along.

Past one closed door. Smooth plaster, broken only by the outline of an inset cupboard. The stalker had shown him one cubbyhole stuffed with dormant Retians on this level, further along. That didn't mean there were none packed behind the doors. Regardless, they weren't a concern without an adult to awaken them.

Morgan's fingers encountered the second door. As they passed over the rim marking the frame and reached the panel itself, it was as though he'd touched a live circuit. Morgan reeled back, startled.

As quickly, he returned to the door, tucking his light into his belt so he could place both hands on the panel. His eyes closed as a further aid to concentration.

The stalker hadn't tried this door; knowing its batteries were low, Morgan had sent it to the most promising of the three. Now he regretted the lapse, forced to rely on a more intimate and dangerous method. He reached out with the utmost delicacy, sending a questing tendril of thought, no more than a wisp, past the panel to seek what had called to him.

Power. Strangely familiar. Morgan took a deep, steadying breath, then opened his inner sense to the M'hir as Sira had taught him, just the thinnest crack.

Three glowing masses in the darkness, dimly lit, like embers banked on a dying fire. Brighter lines he somehow recognized as restraints.

Morgan pulled his mind back from that awareness, his fingertips leaving the door panel and seeking the controls to open it instead.

Then he stopped himself, standing there in the dark, his head turning to look where he knew the other door stood locked and waiting. Beyond that door might be what had been stolen from Sira, what she'd asked him to recover for her. Beyond that door might even be the thief. His hand twitched as though around a throat.

Why should it matter to him or to his purpose if the Baltir also contained three unconscious and power-bound Clanswomen?

It shouldn't, his rage answered for him, impatient so near its target. They were strangers—not even his species—likely her enemies and his! There was no guarantee the Retians wouldn't restore their lighting and security systems at any minute. He'd be a fool to be distracted.

Morgan shuddered once, then turned on his light so he could find the tools he'd need to open the door.

So he was a fool.

It wouldn't be the first time.

Chapter 41

I SUPPOSED Bowman and her constables had meant well. I supposed, on sober reflection, I may have been too extreme in my urgent desire to be left alone, so I could join Huido and find out where Morgan was. But that was the kind of thinking that follows, not precedes, an impulse.

Such as the one which had almost certainly ruined the restaurant behind us. "Will you hurry, Sira!" Huido rumbled, clattering along beside me like some wagon loaded with loose pots.

"I hope no one was hurt," I said wanly, looking over my shoulder at the flames now roaring skyward with remarkable enthusiasm, given the pouring rain, the chronically soaked building walls, and the efforts of several firefighters already on the scene. I truly hadn't expected merely 'porting a bottle of brandy into the business end of the stove—the kitchen door having been conveniently ajar for me to see it—would result in quite so much chaos. It had had the desired effect of allowing me to give Bowman and 'Whix the slip, the two of them hurrying toward the "accident" as rapidly as the rest of us exited the scene. Huido had been waiting outside and snagged my arm with a claw as I ran out with the other panic-stricken customers.

"I just hope we make it off this road to somewhere less conspicuous," my companion grumbled. He didn't ask me to transport us—a lack I knew had more to do with his dislike of the M'hir than with any caution about attracting attention. Since our earlier adventures together, in which I had somewhat freely hauled him back and forth through that other space, Huido had grown of the opinion that the M'hir was responsible for a decline in his poolside performance for some weeks afterward, something I hardly wanted to debate with him and which Morgan found vastly entertaining.

I had to admit, running with a Carasian through the foot and wheeled traffic of a busy city had its entertaining side as well. There were few Retians, or other beings for that matter, willing to stand their ground before an onrushing armor-plated behemoth, claws snapping erratically in the air as though this helped Huido's thick legs scuttle faster, and eyestalks whirling in an absolute frenzy. Retians were not quick, graceful creatures by any stretch of the imagination, being well-suited to their muddy world and placid lifestyle, yet these individuals were moving out of our path in a combination of death-defying leaps, desperate rolls, and last-minute dives to either side. The pouring rain and huge mud-filled puddles underfoot everywhere just added to the effect.

It was, I was ashamed to confess, hilarious.

Mind you, the wheeled traffic was a bit more of a concern. Not so much to me, because the drivers of the small and mid-sized groundcars allowed in this portion of the city were just as anxious as the pedestrians to avoid the Carasian—possibly because he outmassed most—but the pedestrians themselves were at risk from the wild movements of the vehicles. If Huido had wanted to broadcast our route to the Enforcers, he couldn't have done a better job with weeks of advance planning.

"In here." My giant partner didn't wait to see if I was complying, a reasonable assumption as he hadn't released the claw locked firmly around my arm since the restaurant. There would be, I was sure, an interesting bruise as a souvenir.

Huido's "here" was an alleyway, or rather an overflow channel between buildings, at the moment filling nicely with the water running from rooftops as well as from the street behind us. His sponge-toed feet found anchorage easily. Perhaps recalling the fragility of my species, he kindly opened his claw to release me, but I found I needed both hands gripping his arm to keep upright as he continued to thunder forward at a gallop, spraying me from my head down with oily, muddy water.

No one, I thought, *positively no one would recognize me through all this.* There was the minor complication that anyone with partial vision would spot Huido. Escapes, I'd noticed, frequently had some such flaw.

We weren't being followed, I realized a heartbeat or so later, gasping for breath. The channel had taken a quick turn left, then right again, meeting smaller channels only wide enough for a being my size, its flow deepening with each junction. We were constrained to it, at least for now.

"Slow down, Huido," I shouted to make myself heard over the pounding rain, spitting out as much water as sound. "Stop!" I planted my feet in the ankle-deep stream as best I could and resisted his tug.

He stopped. Three eyestalks rolled over to look at me, the valves of his head almost closed to keep out the rain. I remembered Morgan saying Huido didn't care much for fresh water.

"Where is he?" I shouted, putting my mouth closer to his arm so he could hear me. "Where's Morgan?"

There was a settling clunk as he turned his massive body to face me, all eyestalks converging to watch my face, a glittering line in the shadows. "I was hoping," Huido muttered in a deep, distressed bass, "you knew."

For an endless time, I stared at him, my own hope washing away to leave me shivering and exhausted. Then I licked rain from my lips, not surprised to taste salt in it. "Well, then," I said, wearily, "we'd better keep looking."

I drew a small device from my pocket and activated it. I didn't need the purring sound over our heads, Huido's mutter of surprise, or the relieved greetings of the half-dozen soaking wet Drapsk leaning precariously out its open doors to know when the aircar I'd arranged to shadow us through the city had arrived.

I'd just hoped I'd have another destination for it than the *Makmora,* and better news than none at all.

As it turned out, we did have another destination. Huido told me about Morgan's search for Baltir—a name I remembered all too well—and I'd immediately had the Drapsk use the aircar's com to contact the *Makmora.* While they didn't find the Retian in question in any records, they found enough to divert us to another ship altogether, a decision which just happened to bring us out of the rain without alerting any potentially interested parties.

"I'm fine now, thanks, Maka. I'll call if we need anything else." The Drapsk inclined his plumes, once to me and once, adding an odd flutter, to Huido. The Carasian responded with a subdued click of his handling claw. I didn't ask.

Just as Huido had politely refrained from asking any of the thousand questions he must have at the moment, uttering only a brief, noncommittal: "Nice ship," when we boarded the *Nok-raud* under the cover of rain.

I hadn't realized the Drapsk would continue in my absence with the tasks I'd assigned them on Plexis, namely searching for information on anything remotely connected to the Clan, telepaths, or, hopefully with more discretion, Morgan. I should have known, since they were prone to a certain level of inertia in all things. But in this case it had been far more than a waste of time. In addition to what I'd asked them to do, they'd been in contact with every source they could find, including, it seemed, the pirate vessel.

The Enforcers were definitely watching the *Makmora*. No question they were watching the *Fox*. But, the Drapsk reported cheerfully, the pirates had lodged a harassment complaint against Bowman and her crew upon their arrival, being quite convinced the Enforcers had followed them to Ret 7. The complaint was taken at face value, since no charges were up against the ship or her crew at the moment. Port Authority obligingly docked the *Nokraud* at the far end of the shipcity, well out of the Enforcer ship's sensor range.

This, of itself, was no reason to knock on the ship's port of such opportunists and expect anything more than a huge bill, if not worse. But something in the Drapsk's information requests had apparently jogged Captain Rek's memory. She'd heard, it seemed, rumors of clandestine research being done on Ret 7. Research of a type the Trade Pact would not approve. Would the Drapsk pay to learn more?

For the Mystic One? There was no price too high—as long as bargaining was allowed.

Fortunately the Drapsk in the aircar were so enamored of Huido they hardly fussed when I ordered them to take me directly to the *Nokraud*, so I could negotiate for this information in person. They merely insisted on making a precautionary call to the *Makmora* first.

The results, I thought, looking around the lounge, were impressive even for the Drapsk. Before our aircar had reached the shipcity and made its less-than-direct approach to the *Nokraud*'s dock, crew from the *Makmora* were already boarding the pirate. Whether by bribe (probable), threat (possible), or extortion (highly likely), they'd managed to place their own people throughout the *Nokraud*'s key stations without protest from the Scats.

It took a great deal of the disappointment from my day to see Grackik and Rek being oh-so-polite to the dozens of little Drapsk swarming on their decks.

So now, I pulled the cover closer around my thoroughly chilled but dry legs, regarding my surroundings with a sense of déja vu. It was in this lounge the Scats had been faced down by the Drapsk. It would not be wise, I was convinced despite all the Drapsk precautions and confidence, to gamble that humiliation would have been forgotten no matter how much profit was involved.

But as a temporary haven from the rain, Enforcers, and Ret 7 in general, it would definitely do.

"More beer, Huido?" I asked. The Drapsk had torn the back from one of the couches, making a padded bench affair Huido seemed to find quite comfortable. His massive claws rested on the floor, while the smaller ones moved restlessly about, making a soft, rain-on-leaves sound. I shared his impatience.

I'd asked the Drapsk and pirates to leave us alone for a while. The Carasian had been a silent hulk during my discussion with Rek, festooned with adoring Drapsk who apparently considered physical contact with him irresistible. In turn, having the smaller beings climbing over his claws, limbs, body, and head didn't seem to bother Huido. He'd stirred only when the second Scat entered unannounced, then settled down.

The Scats had been remarkably, unsettlingly cooperative: handing record disks to Maka, describing to me what they knew—by rumor only, of course—of Retian experiments with alien biology, particularly Human biology. Since using intelligent beings for research was forbidden under the Trade Pact, the Retians relied on volunteers, willing to sacrifice themselves for the future good.

Grackik had chittered at this, the chilling laugh of her kind that produced a scalding foam from her saliva, a foam she collected carefully with her long, thin tongue.

They denied knowing any Retian named Baltir. There wasn't much more, not that they'd admit anyway, although I didn't doubt some of those "volunteers" arrived in trip boxes in the *Nokraud*'s dark hold. While their willingness to be gracious hosts lasted, I decided to impose on it, judging that with almost a hundred armed Drapsk throughout the ship, we should be able to keep them out of trouble for the present.

After our discussion, which concluded with a round of Drapsk bargaining that would have shamed a Denebian into honesty, the *Makmora* agreed to pay in cargo and future business for the information obtained, anything further learned, and the use of the ship as a temporary haven. The Scats appeared content, even sending a large number of their crew on shore leave—not an easy prospect on Ret 7 for any offworlder—in order to free up cabins. Their ship, it appeared, was temporarily ours.

I wondered when we'd find out what they were up to, but didn't bother the Drapsk with suspicions I was quite sure they shared. I had someone else's suspicions to counter as soon as we were left alone.

But first, there was a little matter to have explained. "Huido," I began the moment we were alone. "The Drapsk seem unusually—fond—of you."

An amused chuckle. "They have good taste."

"I'm fond of you," I countered. "So's Morgan. We don't climb all over you to show it."

"Good. You're too heavy."

"I'd like an explanation," I said. "Our little friends are mysterious enough, thank you, without your adding to it."

Huido shrugged, a rocking movement of his wide head resulting in a series of almost melodic clanks. "My *grist* is considered very attractive among my kind—a pity you are not equipped to appreciate it, Sira." This with definite innuendo. "The Drapsk, on the other hand, are extraordinarily sensitive to such things."

"Meaning?"

"They can't help but love me. It is a harmless obsession. Don't let it bother you."

"Oh," I said, then looked at my companion, a mass of shining, opinionated black armor more like a stripped-down ground-car than a living thing, and didn't even try to imagine what the Drapsk felt. At least, I thought, they were happy.

"Huido," I said evenly, waiting until the attention of more eyestalks meant he'd noticed my change of tone. "It's time we talked about Plexis. I know what you and Barac did to hide Larimar's body. And why."

"You do?" A castanet sigh. "It was my staff, wasn't it. They're all fired."

I put all the earnestness I could into my voice. "Huido. Morgan didn't kill the Clansman."

"Of course he didn't." All of Huido's eyes converged on me. A massive handling claw half-rose from the floor, but then he thought better of snapping it.

I should have known. Which didn't explain anything. "Then why dispose of—him? What were you and Barac thinking?"

A hiss as plates shuddered over one another. "That the murderer left the corpse to cause trouble in more than my kitchen. Perhaps to delay Morgan with an investigation. Perhaps to inflame the Clan against him." He paused, eyes whirling. "Or perhaps the killer missed his true target. I do not like the pattern I see forming, Sira. First Larimar talks to Morgan and dies. Now Malacan Ser—"

"Mal—" I stopped, remembering the name from what seemed a lifetime ago. "That's the Human on Ret 7, the exporter Bowman uses as her eyes and ears insystem. What about him?"

Huido's voice became slow and grim. "Murdered by the same method as Larimar. And only three standard days ago. Morgan planned to see him."

"You think the murderer is following Morgan," I said numbly. "And Bowman's here looking for Morgan. She must know about Malacan, if not Larimar. But she can't suspect Morgan—"

"Why not? Your worthless cousin believes it," he said with disgust. "He was so convinced of Morgan's guilt, the creteng deserted me the first chance he got."

"Barac doesn't know Morgan's nature as we do," I said, better able to see Barac's viewpoint, if not inclined to forgive it either. "Or he'd know Morgan couldn't be a killer."

The Carasian threw up both his massive handling claws, snapping them closed with an ominous cymbal-like sound. "Yet," he rumbled darkly.

I sat up straight, feet together on the floor, blanket clutched between my hands as I stared at him. "What do you mean? Morgan will defend himself if he has to—"

"There's a difference between reacting to violence and seeking it." Huido's head carapace tilted forward, eyestalks milling aimlessly back and forth. "With what you've done to him, my brother could cross that line at any time. If he hasn't already." His sudden air of dejection was all the more inexplicable, considering his passion of an instant before. My heart began to beat more heavily, as if preparing for flight. But Huido's next words seemed harmless enough: "Has Morgan told you how we met? Has he told you of his youth?"

"No. What does this have to do with today, now?"

Two smaller arms swung up, as if gathering air, then came together. "We are today what was begun in the past, Sira Morgan. Sira di Sarc. You should know this if anyone does."

I curbed my impatience to be looking for Morgan. If I'd learned anything from the Drapsk, it was to never underestimate what other beings viewed as important. And, perhaps because Barac had abandoned the Carasian without warning, I owed him a member of the Clan who would listen. "Tell me, then."

Morgan, so Huido's story went, had been the youngest in a family of farmers, living in the foothills near Karolus' shining new shipcity, in sight of the bright lights marking the colony's future. He'd had his Talent even when young, sufficient to encourage a boy to be a loner, to enjoy long walks deeper into the wilderness, away from the clustered busy minds of family and stranger alike.

Had been the youngest. Just before Morgan's twelfth birthday, Karolus had been lapped up in a civil war between neighboring systems, its modern shipcity a prize tempting both sides to invade.

Morgan had run home one afternoon, pulled from his wanderings by a dreadful foreboding to find his home empty, his family dead or missing, their crops in flames. The shipcity itself was a fireworks display in reverse, streaks of eye-stabbing light raining down as both sides fought to keep it from one another.

Morgan's Talent, though he didn't know it then, drew him from the destruction to where his uncles had fled into the hills with what remained of the valley's adult population. The sturdy colonists, well-accustomed to fighting nature and chance, took on the role of reclaiming their world with typical single-mindedness.

There were years of guerrilla warfare, made worse by having no clear enemy. A victory against one foe merely opened a doorway for the other to move in; caught in the middle, Karolus slowly choked to death, her population dying as often by mistaken fire as by planned attack. Young Morgan survived his uncles, gaining a reputation as being lucky as well as a skilled saboteur. He and those with him counted their successes in days survived.

The day came when one of the offworld forces claimed total victory, its foes turning over their bases on Karolus as part of the spoils. The planet's original colonists had been almost forgotten, their ineffectual raids blamed on the defeated enemy. But now the attention of the victors turned to them alone.

Morgan and those with him were sick of a war they couldn't win, that wasn't theirs to begin or end. They were ready to surrender, and might have succeeded in doing so if there hadn't been a change in the conflict. Colonists, fighters or not, were no longer being captured or killed. Instead, rumors spread like wildfire of atrocities, of the collection of the living for sale offworld. There was a certain group of offworlders responsible, went the story, hunters with the task of cleaning up the Karolus problem once and for all.

It was at this time that a stranger walked into the caves where Morgan and his dwindling band of guerrillas were hiding, a charismatic Human brought to them by the representatives of two other families. A born leader, they called him. Able to spot enemy installations in the dark. Lucky as Morgan, boasted someone. At this, the new leader had reached out his thoughts, unerringly finding Morgan where he stood well back of the others, touching and soothing the chaos and confusion that was Morgan's Talent fighting to be expressed, granting the comfort only another trained telepath could give.

I'd known the name before Huido'd said it, known it with a sick certainty. Ren Symon.

Symon was an inspiring leader, daring and smart, brave but interested more in results than glory. Many of the surviving colonists flocked to his side, as charmed as Morgan. It was the only place with hope, as daily more and more disappeared or died. Morgan became Symon's protégé. The older telepath showed him how to keep out the thoughts of others or how to read them, how to interpret the sensations of warning, and how to lend his strength when needed.

It was impossible for Huido to imagine what that must have been like for Morgan, but I knew. To be able to control the voices in your mind, to realize it as a gift, not a madness—above all to communicate freely with another mind, giving and sharing. It was the best of what we could do.

It was also the worst.

There were times when Symon left them, to lead raids by other bands. Morgan was told to remain behind, his Talent serving as an early warning too important to the dwindling numbers of survivors to risk.

One night, Morgan didn't stay. He was startled from a light doze at his guard post by a terrible premonition of disaster, catching himself stumbling through the dark after Symon before he'd realized his intention to follow. So be it, he'd thought. If Symon was in danger, this time he'd be there to help.

Morgan's shields, as I could testify, were naturally strong. So he was able to follow Symon undetected, down to the valley floor, right up to the end of the battered shipcity where he ducked behind the wreckage of a starship. If he could have called a warning without being overheard, he would have. Some instinct kept him from calling mind-to-mind.

It was just as well. Moments later, he stared in disbelief as Symon reappeared walking with an officer of the enemy, taking a bag from him before giving a casual salute.

Morgan knew what loss was; he'd had practice. He closed down all emotion, any reaction except cold curiosity, and kept following, determined to find out the truth. It wasn't a long journey. Symon led him farther through the field of wreckage to where a force field marked the edges of a camp. Morgan didn't dare approach any closer. There would certainly be detectors set around the perimeter.

There was another way, a way Symon had taught him. Morgan found a place where he could hide, then tucked himself into a ball and closed his eyes. He sought outward, carefully, carefully, sending out a tendril of questing thought, avoiding the lodestone of a mind he knew as Symon's, seeking someone else, anyone else.

There. A susceptible mind. Morgan's eyes snapped open in shock. It was a girl, a prisoner. She wasn't alone. Through her eyes he could see dozens of colonists, chained together, some injured, most unharmed. There were trip boxes stacked to one side, ready to receive their cargo. A Scat made its stalking rounds nearby, its heavy snout moving from side to side as though testing the air. *Roraqk,* whimpered the girl's thoughts in Morgan's. *He has the ship.*

The rest of the camp was a jumble of shadowy moving figures, all armed, most Human. The enemy's cleanup squad, Morgan guessed, not needing the fearful confirmation from her thoughts. He felt a surge of rage, a hate so deep it startled him. It wasn't only his, it was hers as well. It was their world's.

How had it been possible?

Through the prisoner's ears, Morgan heard a familiar voice. "Well, are you ready or aren't you? They aren't going to sleep forever—not without our help, anyway!" Raucous laughter echoed through the camp.

It was Symon, armed to the teeth in the enemy's camp, a terrible look of anticipation on his face as he urged the others to follow him. He was their leader, too, Morgan realized with a shock that echoed into the girl's thoughts and made her gasp. He disengaged himself, leaving behind a promise of vengeance.

Somehow, Morgan had kept ahead of the swiftly marching troop, using every scrap of knowledge he possessed about his home to gain a step here, avoid a slower patch of treacherous rock there. He was pursued by more than the threat they posed. Symon was with them, his emotions leaking through his shielding just enough for Morgan to feel them like nightmares breathing down his neck: a dreadful anticipation, a lust for pain and power, a need like poison to drink from the suffering of others.

This was the mind Morgan had let into his own, had allowed to shape and teach him.

Betrayer! Morgan barely held in his own thoughts. He retched as he ran, holding his hands across his mouth to muffle the sound.

Symon's thoughts became more vivid as he neared his goal. Morgan felt his name in them, not in a calling but as an understanding of what Symon planned for them both. Morgan was to be spared from the recruiters, kept safe from any weapon fire. He would be with Symon always, a source of strength if he was willing—the most delightful of victims if he were not.

Fatally distracted, Morgan misjudged his leap across a streambed, landing awkwardly so that he hung unbalanced, grabbing at air, then dropped backward onto the rock. It was all he knew for a long time.

It was daylight, too late, when he opened his eyes. Everything Symon had wanted to happen, had craved to have happen, was done. The only victim he'd missed, Morgan, lay with his own blood drying on his face, and wondered why he should even try to live any longer.

Then, slowly at first, the reason came to him. It was rage: deep, utter, terrible, and dark. Symon would pay. They all would pay.

"I met him a few years later," Huido finished. "He'd eventually escaped Karolus in a stolen scout ship—teaching himself to fly it on the way—then tried to smuggle himself onto Plexis in a shipment of pickled creteng. My pickled creteng. I'd never met a being so full of anger, like an explosive waiting for its fuse. Nor had I met one who smelled so much like dead fish. He—I will spare you the details, Sira. Morgan chose to remain with me.

"Years passed. He became a trader and bought the *Fox*. We traveled together at times. When we became blood brothers and shared our pasts, he told me what I've told you, Sira. I didn't ask what happened after he uncovered Symon's treachery, and he never told me. With luck, he killed the monster. But I think Morgan found even he couldn't fight a guerilla war by himself. I think he recognized the risk of becoming what Symon was if he tried. I do know there are none of the original colonists left on Karolus."

I let out a long shuddering breath. "I can tell you one thing. Morgan wasn't a killer then, either, Huido. Ren Symon came to me on Plexis just after you and Barac left. He was looking for Morgan. And he was looking for me."

As Huido clashed and rumbled in the Carasian version of swearing—or was it cursing—I rocked back and forth, not fighting the waves of emotion pouring through me. Anguish for Morgan's youth and its pain was part of it, but not a large part. I knew the adult he'd become. If it had taken such a forge, the result was still pure and wonderful.

What I felt the most was grief for what I'd done to him. Huido had been right to tell me this.

Morgan had learned to control the pain and anger from his youth, to push aside those feelings until they were no longer part of his consciousness.

Until I had thoughtlessly given him my rage as well, throwing Morgan's control so far out of reach that even Huido had sensed it in him.

But did that mean I'd turned him into a killer?

I probed at the missing part of me, the place in my thoughts where Morgan belonged. It was not the shape of evil, or of someone who would willingly harm another—no matter how provoked.

I gazed at the still-agitated Carasian. "Morgan won't cross that line, Huido," I promised him, myself, and Morgan. "Whether because I repair what I've done to him—or because, in the end, he's who he is."

INTERLUDE

Midnight on Camos, at least here in the northern lake region of Nisneae, could send shivers down one's spine, Rael thought, her arms wrapped around her body as much to comfort her soul as to hold tight the heavy robe she wore. The air nipped, this close to the end of summer. The evening birds—their boisterous songs a source of good-natured complaints earlier in the season—had left for their winter homes, leaving behind a waiting silence. The sky was clear, its stars overlaid by the running lights of personal aircars as the gamblers and theatergoers headed back to their estates. Rael watched them pass, troubled—as she seemed to be more and more these days—by the thought of Humans.

Pella's viewpoint was simple enough: Humans were part of the landscape, convenient producers and builders of the material things the Clan needed and enjoyed. Like many, if not most of their kind, Pella was disturbed by any consideration of Humans as individuals and thoroughly offended by any mention of Humans as beings of power.

Rael left the terrace and went back into her room. Ru, she pondered, broadcast the opposite attitude, the cause of no little friction in their group whenever she and Pella locked horns in disagreement. From what the Clanswoman revealed, be it only in hints and reactions, it was plain she had few if any compunctions about the blending of Human power with theirs, if it could free the Choosers from the Power-of-Choice. Rael suspected, but kept the thought to herself, that Ru would even support a more physical hybridization, if it could be made possible.

She shivered again, despite the warmth indoors. *Was it possible?* Humans could and did produce offspring with two other humanoid species; to her knowledge the effort required extensive medical intervention, rarely worked, and when it did, the offspring were sterile.

Whether possible or not, it was an abyss she doubted the Clan would cross, no matter what Ru might think. Where would be the benefit? What would become of the M'hiray, if they were drops amid the vast ocean of humanity?

Ica certainly wouldn't allow it. Rael made herself climb into bed, sighing with relief as it responded to the chill of her skin and heated immediately. She lay back and wondered about her grandmother, keeping her shields impeccably locked, as always, against eavesdropping.

Ica's ultimate goal, the one Rael shared from the beginning, had been to learn how Sira had mastered the Power-of-Choice, Commencing her reproductive maturity without harming any Clan or her beloved Morgan. This secret, whatever it was, was key to their survival as a species. The Council's alienation of Sira, their methods, had only succeeded in driving that vital secret and its owner away from them. Worse, the Council's every move had been to eliminate the free will of Choosers, to manipulate and use them in any way possible to control the power of future generations. *Well,* she told herself grimly, *Sira was right.* There'd be no future generations if the Council continued on that path. Breeding for increased ability would be their doom. Ica and the others were equally convinced of the danger.

The one goal no one else seemed to share with her, Rael told herself miserably, curving her body into a ball under the covers, *was to protect Sira's own free will and Choice.* Pella wanted her sister "cleansed" of the taint of Human. Ica wanted Sira's cooperation at any cost and would willingly use Morgan to obtain it. And Ru?

Rael shuddered. She didn't know what Ru intended for Sira or her Chosen. She only knew it wasn't what Sira would want.

Maybe it was time she tried the heart-search in earnest, if only to warn Sira to hide from them all.

Chapter 42

WAS Rael the key?

I couldn't take my eyes from the message in my hand. It was a reply to one I'd asked the Drapsk to send—life with Morgan having removed all of my Clan prejudice about technology. I read it again, whispering the words aloud as though that would help me make sense of them. "To Sira di Sarc. No one has asked permission to use your computer interface. Should I expect such a request? By the way, Pella and Rael are visiting your grandmother in Nisneae. Were you coming home, too? Please stop by and see me if so. Signed: Enora sud Sarc, First Chosen."

Rael had sought me on Pocular, a sign of concern I'd taken at face value because I'd wanted, I knew now, to believe in her. Pella? I hadn't touched mind-to-mind with our youngest sister in years. I remembered her as self-absorbed and frankly afraid of change. As I'd told Rael once, I thought Pella would never willingly leave her home unless summoned by the Council to her Chosen to begin the offspring required for her lineage. *And maybe,* I nodded to myself, *not even then.*

Yet now, both my sisters were on Camos, the Clan stronghold, with Ica di Teerac, a Clanswoman I watched grow old without wasting a moment of her long life on those with lesser power. Certainly she'd never shown an interest in hosting family gatherings until now.

Which meant, of course, it was nothing of the kind. So Rael was indeed the key to something happening among the Clan, but not, I suddenly suspected, part of the Council.

I folded the message carefully, then put it into the galley's disposal unit. I set the controls for demolecularization and vented the elements once the machine had done its task. I wished I could do the same to the data I'd left behind on Camos. It was a legacy I had never imagined would matter.

Had Rael stolen the list of Human telepaths from my comp? Enora did not have the Talent to sense any entry into my rooms. *No,* I decided, *not Rael.* My sister knew nothing about such systems. I remembered trying to explain the equipment to her once, only to quickly change the topic at the pained confusion in the M'hir between our thoughts. And I found, despite all evidence, I wanted to keep thinking the best of Rael, as I did of Morgan. It was likely the Sira Morgan part of me being a fool.

That left two equally interesting candidates for the theft: Ica—or some lackey of hers—or the one person I'd sought hardest to erase from my thoughts this past year. Jarad di Sarc. My father, High Councillor of the Clan, and the mind behind my almost ruin.

If I tried, I could imagine his face in the polished metal of the cupboard in front of me, lined with age yet vital, dominated by fierce eyes over a hawk's beak of a nose, an expression of disappointment and pity as he considered what his firstborn had chosen to be. Only I, and later Morgan, knew what he was capable of doing to achieve his personal ambition. Power—his, mine, the Clan's—was everything to Jarad, a terrible purpose that had led him to justify setting up a private kingdom of discontented Clan on Acranam, with Yihtor to be my Chosen and the means of preserving the di Sarc bloodline no matter the price to me.

Acranam. Larimar di Sawnda'at had been from Acranam, of my father's doing whether Larimar knew it or not. *Likely not,* I reasoned. Jarad worked in the shadows. He'd been quite ruthless in suppressing even Yihtor's knowledge of his involvement, to the point of hiding a message about me in the mind of Barac's brother Kurr, an unwitting courier Yihtor murdered to keep their secrets.

I saw my own reflection now, eyes shadowed as I leaned closer. Was the same pattern repeating itself here? Had Larimar died because he was following Morgan—or because he posed a threat to Jarad's secrets?

I thought I saw some of the truth. A group of Clan collecting Human telepaths, perhaps for the same purpose I'd intended, to present them to Choosers in place of the unChosen, to see what might happen. Hadn't I Commenced? What I'd fought so hard to bring to a trial, in the end having to try on my own, could now seem possible to others. My own list of candidates, helpfully provided by an unknown source on the Council, would be the perfect encouragement.

The only flaw in the argument? Jarad had done everything he could to prevent my attempt to Join with Morgan, short of murdering the Human. Only when I'd gone too far along that road to stop—and demonstrated my resolve to protect Morgan—had Jarad acquiesced to completing the experiment. So why would he want others to try?

Unless, of course, he could guarantee they'd fail, a demonstration to all the M'hiray that the "Human option" wouldn't work and must be abandoned for his and the Council's methods.

I opened the cupboard, pulled out the cold beer I'd promised Huido, and closed it again.

There was one person who might know.

"This is not good, Mystic One," Copelup huffed. Behind him, Huido stood like a gleaming black wall of disapproval, claws half-raised. I hoped he would be careful so close to the Drapsk's fluttering plumes. "A terrible risk."

"And if you take it, why to reach her and not Morgan?" This condemnation came from Huido. "Morgan must be warned."

"I told you why." I felt myself flush, a sign of emotion these nonhumanoids could interpret how they chose. "The heartsearch is too intimate, too direct. I don't know what might happen. He could lose his shields, his protection from the Clan." *It could trigger the Joining,* I added to myself. *Making Morgan's survival dependent on mine.*

I'd known I'd have to tell the Drapsk what I was doing before attempting the heart-search, but I hadn't expected them to panic. "It's not like a sending," I went on. "There's almost no trace in the M'hir—the Scented Way—to be detected. I'll be perfectly safe."

"You saw the hunters there for yourself, Mystic One," Copelup insisted.

"Hunters?" I shuddered at the memory of that presence. "Maybe they are only around Drapskii, a function of your world," I said hopefully. "The Clan have used the M'hir for this purpose for generations, Copelup, and never seen anything like them."

Out came the tube I'd used before to observe the M'hir, the one which had shown me the disturbing evidence of some type of life there. Copelup contented himself with waving it under my nose. "We've monitored the Scented Way everywhere Drapsk travel, including this world. There is always something to be found."

"Then how do you explain the fact that I haven't seen anything until you showed me? I've been in the M'hir all my life."

Huido's deep voice answered: "You haven't looked." His eyes had stayed fixed on me in that disturbed cluster they'd formed the moment we'd started talking about life in the M'hir. I supposed he was congratulating himself on his better sense in staying out of such an obviously dangerous place.

The Drapsk's fear for me wasn't making it any easier. But it was a place I'd been in more times than I could possibly count, a place that was literally part of me. I couldn't afford to fear it, too. I said as much.

Copelup, understandably, didn't agree. "You think you know your M'hir, Mystic One," he said with what sounded like frustrated anger. "I don't think you have listened to what we've tried to teach you at all."

"I've listened—"

"Then you haven't understood!" This was close to a shout, shocking me silent. I blinked at the outraged being. "You are part of the Scented Way. Not users. Not visitors. Your power *feeds* them."

I sank back down on the couch. "What do you mean, my power feeds them?" Somehow, I didn't think the Drapsk was talking about the draining I'd felt when caught near Drapskii.

Copelup turned around completely, as if he needed to be sure he'd sampled all of the air in the room. There were only the three of us in the lounge. I'd thought the place ideal while I tried the heart-search, there being no way to predict how long the process might take. Now I was wondering how long it would take until I could start.

The Drapsk looked at the floor in mild dismay—I was sure he'd planned to summon a stool before realizing we were still on the less cooperative *Nokraud*. He leaned against Huido instead, the Carasian having settled himself on the modified couch. The sight made me want to smile, even in my present state: the feathered and delicate white Drapsk tucking itself quite casually and precariously among the Carasian's formidable natural armament.

"Your power—the Clan's power—feeds them the way sunlight feeds the fields on Drapskii," Copelup stated, as if explaining something to a child—assuming the Drapsk passed through any comparable stage of development.

"When I enter the M'hir, those things we saw consume some of my power?" I heard myself ask, as if this made complete sense.

"It is not *your* power, Mystic One," Copelup said, plumes twitching as though I'd startled him.

I'd been wrong. It made no sense. "Then whose power is it? I'm the one who makes the effort—it's my mind that pushes me in and out, that holds me intact while I'm there." I felt an instant's vanity, a pride in the strength that was my heritage and curse rolled into one. I quashed it. "I can feel myself tiring," I argued. "How can it not be my power?"

"I believe that is how you must perceive it, Mystic One. That's not what we measure."

I glanced at Huido. "Do you know what he's talking about?" A dip and rise of the broad head carapace—a definite maybe. *Very helpful.*

Copelup stroked the Carasian's great claw with a chubby four-fingered hand. "Carasians are aware of the Scented Way, as are the Drapsk. Remarkable beings. So sensitive, admirable, kindhearted—"

"The M'hir?" I reminded him.

"Yes, Mystic One. I think I see how you are being confused. The power you use to concentrate, to form images of your destination and other minds in order to leave this," he waved his hands around, "is yours. The power you exert within the Scented Way is what you—attract, that would be the best word, perhaps. Attract. Or not. There is some debate among our scientists.

"Imagine, Mystic One," the Skeptic continued in a singsong voice, lost in a lecture that fascinated me as much as it appalled. "Imagine an ecosystem of pure energy, of life-forms enriched by the movement of power along pathways, flowing downhill not as a river from a height, but from a higher potential to lower.

"Add to this system beings who naturally attract and store this power, beings able to send their accumulated energy flashing down these pathways like a surging flood of wealth."

"So when I, or any Clan, travel within the M'hir, we are— feeding—what lives there?" *It wasn't,* I thought, *so bad.* In fact, the concept was a vast improvement over being hunted by some predator within it. Then, for no reason, I remembered my nightmare vision of streams of blood pouring away from me into the M'hir, and wasn't so sure.

"We Drapsk, and the Carasians, believe there are many forms of life here which have their place within the Scented Way as well. Some knowingly, as yourselves, and some without. I trust you'll forgive my saying that the Clan are the only ones we've met who considered they have created it themselves."

I shook my head. "Only one of many misconceptions my kind has to overcome, Copelup. Their enlightenment will be," I paused and felt myself smiling involuntarily, "interesting."

"Interesting, Mystic One?" Copelup repeated. "Is this how you expect them to respond to the knowledge that your kind are being cultivated? I would not have guessed."

"Cultivated. As in—" I swallowed.

"As in farming."

INTERLUDE

At some point, Barac discovered, it didn't matter how filthy the floor or ominous the vermin, you had to sleep. So he had found himself nodding off time and again, despite having propped himself in the driest corner with legs and body arranged for the minimum contact with Retian architecture.

He tried harder to keep awake after the lights turned off—a surprise when, by his chrono, it had looked as though they'd planned to leave it on all night, possibly to keep the restless fungi from investigating the latest offering. A plan he highly approved.

A nearby slobbering sent the Clansman scrambling to his feet. "If these things aren't harmless," he called out, his heart rate speeding to nearly terminal levels, "I suggest you get me out of here or turn on that light."

There was no answer. Barac felt his way to the door, touching only when he must in case more of the things were stuck on the walls. Still locked.

He stepped on something that writhed and pulled itself from underfoot with appalling strength. "Get me out of here!" he shouted, no longer concerned about what anyone thought.

Instinctively, the Clansman threw himself at the M'hir, knowing it was probably still as locked to him as the door. *No,* he realized immediately, *it wasn't!* But before Barac could concentrate and form a locate, there was another presence in his way.

It was beautiful beyond mere words, desirable beyond life itself.

Desperately, Barac tried to hold himself in the cell, knowing what he'd inadvertently found was deadlier to him than any hungry fungus.

But the attempt was impossible, doomed by a need deeper than survival.

Helplessly answering it, Barac *pushed* himself into the M'hir . . .

. . . seeking the Chooser whose power called him to her Test.

Chapter 43

FARMING. It was one way to conceptualize what Copelup told me about the M'hir and the Clan, though like any model of something unknown, it didn't explain everything. Just enough to ring of the truth.

I stood in the fresher, letting jets of foam pound against my face, using one hand to keep the stuff out of my nostrils. Concentrating on the warmth rolling over my shoulders and down my back was infinitely better than concentrating on what I'd learned, but there was no escaping it.

What I really wanted was to talk to Morgan, to have him help me puzzle some meaning from it. I switched from foam to needles of rinse water, gasping as I took away my hand and couldn't breathe for a moment.

Something in the M'hir—Copelup's insistence he wasn't implying deliberation or intent more than sufficient to terrify me by the mere idea of an intelligence there—something was acting on the Clan in order to increase each generation's effect on the power within the M'hir. The Power-of-Choice, as I'd described it to him, was the method; the connections between mother and daughter, between Chooser and Chosen, were the goal.

The Power-of-Choice itself was like some charge built in the M'hir around the presence of a Chooser, a potential growing throughout the Chooser's early years until great enough to forge a permanent pathway to the power of an unChosen male. Looked at without emotional overtones, it was like some mine of precious ore to whatever M'hir-life relied on that movement of power.

Viewed, however, with the knowledge of dead and future-less unChosen, it was an alien curse, applied to us without our knowledge or consent.

I hit the control for warm air, rubbing my hair with both hands though I could feel the heavy locks vibrating to shake off the moisture. Old habits died hard.

As did the habit of considering the M'hir lifeless, a domain peculiarly Clan. But it was a habit not likely to help me, so I tried to keep my mind open to the strange ideas of the Drapsk.

Especially when one of them was a dire prediction concerning my own future. I'd given the Power-of-Choice to Morgan, ridding myself of it forever, I'd thought.

According to Copelup and his instruments, the M'hir was replacing that power, continuing to attach more to the space I inhabited; a buildup of force he saw no sign of stopping until it was again as it was.

And until I was again that deadly, dangerous thing: a Chooser, driven to test the unChosen and kill the less potent.

Including, perhaps, Morgan himself.

I stepped out of the fresher, feeling as weary and soiled as when I'd entered it. *No,* I decided. I felt as worn as when I'd first discovered the truth about myself, about being a Chooser and the threat I'd willingly posed to Morgan.

The Drapsk theorized I'd been attacked in the M'hir by some life-form attracted to me not by what I was doing to Drapskii but by the same imbalance of power that was causing the return of the Power-of-Choice. For this reason, they wanted to forbid me to enter the M'hir until the Power-of-Choice was restored. Copelup feared I would be attacked again any time I lingered in that other place.

A shame I wasn't prepared to wait.

I pulled on the spacer coveralls, too new still, but I'd asked the Drapsk to buy them for me. Squeamishness, but it did feel better knowing mine was the only skin to have been inside them.

Then I made sure my door was closed and locked, one advantage to the *Nokraud* over the Drapsk ship, and lay down on the bed. I didn't know how long I would have before Copelup's instruments would warn him of what I was attempting—I didn't assume they couldn't.

Closing my eyes, I concentrated, forming the image of my sister Rael, adding layer upon layer of knowledge and memory until I could have reached out and touched her in my mind, heard her soft voice. The image left me, became a crackle of energy soaring out into the darkness of the M'hir, carrying my consciousness along with it. The heart-search was uncontrollable and not always successful. *It was,* I remembered dimly as it carried me along, *usually exciting.*

Sira! A recognition in my mind more than a name and a reaction so laced with warnings and fears I could hardly make sense of it. Instead of trying, I grabbed impulsively, *pulling* Rael with me . . .

On one level I knew where my physical form was, could feel the sheets, sense the heaving of my lungs as I fought for strength. On another, more immediate and pressing, I was a sun around which worlds revolved, one of them glowing with its own light and linked to me by the merest thread, lengthening and thinning with every instant.

Dark things orbited me, too: things of unimaginable form and vaporous teeth, recognizable from nightmare visions. I grabbed without hands or arms for the glow that was Rael, knowing suddenly I'd doomed us both if I couldn't pull free before they decided to attack.

I *pushed* with all I had, feeling Rael's considerable strength joining me in that desperate effort to escape. It wasn't enough. Just when I'd knew I'd failed and resigned myself to death, I was *pulled* forward, somehow still clinging to the brightness that marked my sister . . .

. . . and came abruptly back into myself, staring up at the circle of agitated Drapsk and one very noisy Carasian. Rael was crouched on her knees beside me, her hand in mine, looking as though she'd fallen out of her own bed. There was the beginning of a smile on her face, as well as a suspicion of tears. I thought to myself, with vast relief: *here was one time I'd been right.*

Past the forest of twitching plumes I could see all that Huido had left of my door.

"I'd like you to meet my sister," I told my rescuers feebly.

INTERLUDE

All three were lovely, a detail easy to confirm in the glow of his handlight given the transparency of the boxes housing them. They might have been dead, for all the signs otherwise, if Morgan hadn't his other sense to rely upon.

And they were Clan, as he'd suspected. Morgan tiptoed around the small laboratory, irrationally afraid of waking the sleepers, although he was sure it would take more than a clumsy step. Their hair lay lifeless, silken shrouds over their shoulders and breasts; Sira's had moved with her dreams.

The boxes weren't the type routinely used on passenger liners, being more elaborate and, he looked more closely at one, these could be opened at will without affecting the occupants. Morgan didn't dare touch them without knowing their purpose. He hunted for clues, shining his light around the small room. There were lines of script on the various machines, sheets of the same notation scattered about on counters. None of it was Comscript and Morgan's knowledge of written Retian was confined to traffic signs and numbers.

They were not Choosers, as he had come to understand Clan physiology. The bodies of these Clanswomen were mature. He didn't recognize their faces, though the one in the middle bore some resemblance to Rael in the shape of mouth and chin.

He stared at each face in turn, hoping Sira would be able to lift the memory and recognize them. There didn't seem anything else he could safely do for them. They might, though Morgan doubted it, be here of their own free will, seeking some therapy from the Retians.

Time for the next door. Morgan dimmed his light as he reentered the corridor, taking a moment to lock the door behind him.

No sign of any success in the repairs yet, but his lips pressed together in a grim line as he calculated the likely number of minutes he had left.

The next door had a double set of locks, one easily circumvented, the other requiring a scan to confirm identity. Morgan slipped his force blade from its sheath into his hand, triggering the tiny blade. It cut through the plas and metal cover of the door mechanism itself as if through flesh and bone. From there it was the work of a few seconds to thoroughly destroy both locks and convince the door to open.

Mind you, Morgan thought as he very cautiously stepped inside, *it will be much less than a second before a restoration of systems sounds an entry alarm.*

Time and care. He breathed lightly, irregularly, establishing no rhythm. His handlight was off, there being sufficient illumination from the indicator lights on the incubators to show Morgan the outlines of furnishings and walls once his eyes became accustomed to it.

Twenty-four domed incubators filled the center of the room, each no more than an arm's length long and half that wide. Morgan moved to the nearest, examining it intently. Servo arms and other devices filled most of the interior—when he bent to look through the clear sides, he could see a small tray in the midst. He risked a beam from his handlight. The tray reflected it back as though filled with water or a similar liquid, an almost invisible disk of something moist floating on its surface.

Morgan checked the rest, moving swiftly yet soundlessly. All but three of the incubators and their contents were identical. Those, he observed with a sense of foreboding, those three were empty and dark, their servos shut down.

The Human put his free hand on one of the dark incubators, thinking of the three Clanswomen next door; his fingers trembled until he pressed them against the cold surface. He didn't need to be an expert to understand the implications: Sira's missing tissue implanted into willing or unwilling hosts. Anger, he acknowledged, feeling it pounding in his ears, anger for what had been taken from Sira and how it was being used.

But it was more than anger that held him rigid and dismayed, uncertain what to do next. Morgan had given the Clanswoman his love unconditionally, knowing it meant turning aside from other possibilities, including the one represented by this empty box. He'd convinced himself it was only a minor cost against so great a benefit.

Yet here was proof his sacrifice was meaningless, that others might do what he could not, provide Sira with a living legacy. It was like a blow, this realization of how much it mattered to him. He couldn't destroy what was here—he couldn't bring himself to so much as disturb it.

Morgan fought to regain his self-control, to think through his options. Maybe there would be some kind of stasis tube he could use to carry the tissue safely; maybe he could use his Talent to reach the sleeping minds of the Clanswomen, confirm or refute his suspicions. What would Sira want him to do, if recovering what was stolen was patently beyond his abilities?

Too late! The sound of a curtain being yanked to one side was paired to the return of full lighting, blinding both Morgan and that other so that they froze, squinting at one another for a comic instance.

Even as the force blade dropped from its sheath into his waiting hand, Morgan recognized Faitlen di Parth, member of the Clan Council. The Clansman must have valued his experiments enough to stay here on guard.

Morgan's mind was suddenly calm and focused, cleared of everything but his rage.

What might have happened next, Morgan never knew. A scream tore through the air—no, it was unheard, echoing only in his mind. And Faitlen's, as the Clansman put both hands to his head, writhing as if in pain. "No!" the Clansman shouted furiously, turning from Morgan and hurrying back into the room he had just left.

Leaving the Human no choice but to follow.

Chapter 44

THE Drapsk, especially the Makii, had been under considerable strain these few days, starting with my inexplicable truffle chase and culminating in the arrival of a new Mystic One right under their nonexistent noses. A Mystic One, moreover, without Tribal affiliation. They were not, I could tell, happy at all.

If anything, Copelup the Skeptic was in worse shape. My near-disaster in the M'hir had indeed registered, as I'd expected, on his instruments. Instead of pointless panic—he'd saved that for the aftermath—Copelup had activated the machine which collected matter from the M'hir, somehow keying it to the identity I displayed there. I could amply testify to the machine's drawing power, despite having no idea how such a thing could work.

Copelup couldn't explain either. For the first time since I'd met him, Copelup wasn't interested in observations, information, or even my annoying questions. Once he'd seen I was safe, he'd performed eopari and, from what the others were telling me, might stay stubbornly dormant for days.

"Can't they, well, move him?" Rael asked, walking around the ball of Drapsk now forming the centerpiece of my room on the *Nokraud*. The pair of Drapsk repairing the door hooted softly to themselves.

"The Makii," I said with a stern look at the two within view, "assure me this would cause the poor fellow extreme disorientation when he emerges. Some of them find the idea quite entertaining. Since this disorientation might lead Copelup to need gripstsa, and since there are no other Skeptics on Ret 7 to perform this act with him, I find their amusement in poor taste."

Rael looked doubtfully at the Makii crew, then back to me.

Her words formed in my thoughts: *Strange beings. Why are they helping you?*

"Turn around," I told her out loud, watching her stiffen with surprise as she obeyed only to see the Makii with their plumed antennae aimed at her. Then, I added in the inner speech: *They have a connection to the M'hir, Rael. Not like ours, but as you see they can detect our presence there.* The antennae, as I'd expected, switched instantly to point in my direction, even as the Drapsk continued working on the door. I felt Rael's exploring thought reach toward them, shutting down as the Drapsk cooperatively turned their plumes her way again.

I thought Humans were bad enough, she sent, her generous mouth twitching into a smile.

I returned it without the offense I might have taken before we'd shared mind-to-mind. It had been Rael's offer, the first thing she'd said to me after I'd brought her to Ret 7. Traveling through my sister's ordered and open thoughts had been like an antidote to some poison I hadn't realized was coursing through me. I now understood why she had involved herself with Ica di Teerac's plotting and, seeing the depth of her concern for Morgan's fate as well as mine, forgave it. We'd been heart-kin before I'd been Sira Morgan. I found, like an unexpected gift, we could be again.

Unfortunately, it was just in time to face the rest of the family, including a few I'd gladly send to Huido's cook. "Sit, Rael," I suggested. My room was the best the *Nokraud* could offer a passenger. Since it was also designed as luxury for a Scat, I concluded Grackik and Rek had their species' sense of humor. The Drapsk, undaunted, had done a magnificent job in very little time to remove all evidence of that species' preferred lifestyle, replacing cages, sandpits, and heating lamps with a mismatched but comfortable assortment of Human furnishings.

These included a pair of wonderfully odd chairs, the sort that looked hazardous to one's health, yet were seductively difficult to leave once you took the chance. Rael hesitated but followed my lead, her look of surprised appreciation making me laugh. She peered over at me. "You seem remarkably cheerful for someone receiving the news I brought," she commented dryly.

I shrugged. "When you are at the bottom of things, Sister-mine, any improvement is appreciated." Her eyes glistened as I sketched the gesture of beholdenness and kinship in the air between us. "I'm simply grateful," I continued with the truth. "I've been warned about Ica. And you are here."

Rael's face, transparent as always, showed her puzzlement. "Yes. And I'd like to know exactly how I came to be here." She paused and licked her lips. "Not to mention some explanation of what I experienced in the M'hir."

I understood. She'd seen the M'hir life-forms, but I knew she had no context to recognize what she'd seen. To her, they were oddities of the M'hir pathways and what really mattered was the Drapsk machinery. Rather than share the formless apprehension I felt, courtesy of the Drapsk, I pointed a toe at the ball on my carpet and replied: "I'm afraid there'll be a delay. Your answers are in that brain, not mine. Suffice it for now that I don't dare use the M'hir—and not just because of the Council's Watchers."

She winced and shook her head. "The Watchers. Let's hope the power of your friend's device clouded the trace we left, or they'll know you're here, if not why." Then, more anxiously, "You don't suppose the Watchers will react to the Drapsk—"

"Copelup hasn't been concerned about the Watchers," I said, more to reassure Rael than because I was convinced myself. "He said they monitor a different part or frequency. Something like that."

"They think the M'hir has parts?" My sister was startled into a chuckle. "What odd little beings."

"You can't begin to imagine," I agreed wholeheartedly. "We'd better hope he's right—what the Watchers know, the Council knows. And you said Ica has a source on the Council?"

Rael gestured an apology. It was becoming habitual. "I never intended to plot against you, heart-kin."

"And you didn't, not really," I assured her, the feel of her memories in mine more than proof. "To be honest, you were only doing what I should have done myself. It was time for me to come back. I had no right to choose exile, to take my happiness and leave the needs of the Clan behind me."

"They betrayed you—" Rael sounded mystified. "Tried to use you, even kill you."

I glanced at the Drapsk, now reluctantly installing the replacement door panel they'd taken from some other cabin presumably with the Scats' permission. The fewer doors the better, as far as they were concerned. Anything that divided the Drapsk from one another diminished the whole. "I have learned to look beyond that," was all I said, adding briskly: "Now, as far as Ica is concerned . . ."

We talked for an hour or more, sometimes by voice, as often our thoughts and feelings mingling underneath. Rael accepted there were things I chose to keep hidden—I had been this way before I had the secrets of others to protect, I remembered; I'd never been comfortable revealing my inner self completely to others, no matter how trusted, until I'd granted Morgan that right.

A right and a peril, I thought, when we paused a moment in respect for the loss of Larimar's Chosen in the M'hir. Those Joined shared every risk, whether they shared belief in it or not.

"I don't like it," Rael said when we were done exploring plans and actions, all avenues seeming to lead to one possibility. "It's risky."

"Do you think there's anything we can do, including hiding, without risk?" I countered, not particularly pleased with our results either. But there wasn't time to debate or second-guess ourselves.

"So you agree," I went on briskly. "We won't wait to find out if the Watchers are aware of what I've done—we'll grab their attention and turn it toward Ica's group and the Human telepaths. The Watchers will sound the alarm to Council, keeping them both busy while we search Ret 7 for what was stolen from me." *And Morgan,* I said to myself, my priority if not Rael's.

"Pella—" Rael closed her lips over the name, but her concern lapped against my thoughts.

I didn't share Rael's sense of responsibility for our younger sister, having lately grown less patient with fools of any kind. "From what you've told me, Pella hasn't done anything yet but linger in Ica's orbit. If they scan her, that's all they'll find. Maybe she'll learn something from it, but I doubt it."

"You can't trust the Council."

I smiled, completely without humor. "Rael, my dear sister, I trust nothing but their predictability. I know exactly what the

Council intends for me. I have no intention of helping them succeed."

This was a point on which we didn't agree. "I can't believe the Council is behind what happened on Pocular—it makes no sense for them to act against you. At least, not so openly." This last with a reluctant conviction. Rael had lost a number of her illusions.

"How much proof will it take, Rael?" I countered. "I told you what the Scats said about the Retians' experiments. And Huido discovered a Retian named Baltir was involved in the attack on me. Baltir, Sister. The toad brought to the Council by Faitlen di Parth, in order to supply technology to use my mindless body to produce more 'Siras' if I failed to be willing or able to do so. The evidence," I rested a hand on my violated abdomen, "proves they didn't forget that plan."

"After you left, Sira," she argued, "the Council claimed it had no prior knowledge—"

"With shields wide open, no doubt?" I waved a hand, softening my tone. Rael wasn't the enemy, not anymore. "It doesn't affect our plan. We both know how the Council views rebellion. They react to it almost as violently as they do to the idea of Humans in the M'hir. They won't be impressed by Ica's venture into the forbidden." I made two fists and brought them together gently. "We tie both groups up in accusation and counter-accusation until I have Morgan safe." A new thought came to me, and I considered it before musing aloud: "We could add Bowman and her Enforcers to the mix."

"You wouldn't!" Rael said, aghast. "Bad enough they are already sniffing around you and your Morgan."

"It was," I responded mildly, "just a thought." *But not a bad one,* I added to myself, quite willing to use whatever leverage I had against my enemies.

Rael regarded me suspiciously.

I smiled.

INTERLUDE

For all Barac knew, his body was still in the cell, probably crawling with hungry fungi dissolving their way through a feast of clothing, flesh, and bone. The thought was a distant horror, almost forgotten in the surging joy.

She was near.

He was desire.

Nothing else existed but the desperate need for completion, to reach the Chooser, to offer himself for her Testing. Barac flung himself forward, not knowing if he flew within the M'hir or ran across a midnight field. His destination was that light, that radiance.

He gasped, reeling as the Chooser sensed his approach and drove at him with her power. This was her place. He was the intruder. His was a contamination to be pushed aside.

Instinctively, desperately, Barac resisted, knowing this was the Test, the measure of his worthiness to Join her absolute perfection.

He resisted, but knew at once he would fail, that he wasn't worthy of such overwhelming power. Just when he felt himself about to dissolve, crying out his disappointment and feeling her triumph, there was distraction.

Another!

A candidate was never offered to two Choosers at once. Barac experienced the why of it as he hung like a piece of metal suspended in the overlapping attraction of two powerful magnets, unable of himself to move toward one or the other.

Powerful magnets who became aware of each other, their thoughts filling with jealous fury. *Mine the Choice,* they screamed as one.

Barac felt his sanity returning as the attraction of the Choosers transformed into their battle with one another. He fought to free himself from their grip, but was stuck fast.

Helpless, he felt them tear at each other, pulling free pulses of power to bleed into the darkness. Invisible tears cascaded down his cheeks as their beauty weakened, their power faded. They were killing each other, as caught in passion as he had been.

Help me, he screamed without sound, trying to recapture their attention, to pull them from their fatal conflict.

It became more and more difficult to keep his thoughts straight, to understand what was happening. The moment came when Barac imagined the fungi from his cell had entered the M'hir with him, that clumps of it surrounded the doomed Choosers, climbing over their brightness, consuming it in some obscene feasting.

He struggled to reach them, then stopped. Somehow he knew it was too late for the Choosers. It was too late for him as well. Barac felt himself become less and less, spreading so thin he hardly knew where he began or ended.

Then, from the nothing, an outpouring of raw energy, strange yet oddly familiar, encircling what he'd become, collecting and compressing until Barac writhed with the pain of living again. There was a *pull* that threatened to rip his mind apart . . .

. . . until he spun away into a darkness unlike any he had known before.

Chapter 45

OUR plan, like several others I'd made recently, ran headlong into the Drapsk. The Makii, it seemed, had somehow adapted Copelup's M'hir-blocking device to encompass the *Nokraud*. While it probably protected Rael and me from detection by others of the Clan, it also prevented us from using the M'hir to contact the Watchers—or any other Clan for that matter. And there was the parallel and not unrelated business of the locked ship ports. It all began to seem very familiar to me.

Captain Makairi had rushed over from the *Makmora* the moment I'd started seriously shouting. Now, we stood face to front on the bridge of the *Nokraud,* and I felt no closer to a solution than I'd been on Drapskii itself.

"There are other ways to send a message, Mystic One," the Captain was insisting.

"Watchers don't have addresses and comlinks," Rael said impatiently. Not having my previous experience, she was finding it very difficult to accept that the small polite beings were literally holding us prisoner for our own good.

She had a point. There were two kinds of Watchers: those who guarded the unborn and those who guarded the M'hir. The first were posts of honor within a House: Clan assigned to act if a Joining were severed during pregnancy, to attempt to save the mind of the infant despite the loss of the mother's into the M'hir.

The second, those we and other Clan rightly feared, did not know themselves. In some individuals, a portion of the mind lingered within the M'hir waking or sleeping, a portion that formed a complex awareness completely separate from the individual's consciousness, possessing the knowledge of that individual but none of the personality. Some believed the Watchers were the next step in our evolution, beings closer to a true, continuous existence in that other space. Regardless, all Watchers shared a grim protectiveness about the M'hir, a territorial instinct which the Clan Council found very useful indeed. The Watchers never acted on their own, but were lightning-quick to sound the alarm to Council if Clan or alien transgressed borders or behaviors they themselves established. Their thoughts felt strange, almost hollow; their communication left a spectral echo in one's mind, unforgettable and unnerving. I, for one, didn't trust them.

I wondered, mind flitting off on a tangent again, if any Watchers had encountered the M'hir life, and if so, had they reported it?

Rael and the Drapsk were arguing; I put up my hand to stop it, not bothering to follow the details. "Captain Makairi, when will Copelup—reemerge?"

He sucked a tentacle pensively. "Who's to say, Mystic One? Eopari can be a very personal matter. If Copelup is in deep mediation, it could be days as his mind explores connections and meanings, moving into a higher plane of reason. If he is sulking, we could wake him right now with a good kick in the— You get my meaning?"

I smiled. "I most certainly do, Captain."

It had been, as Makairi hinted, a case of sulking. Copelup unrolled himself immediately, giving a shout of outrage that was the loudest sound I'd heard a Drapsk produce. I kept my feet carefully together, not wanting to provide him with any clues as to the culprit. "Welcome back, Skeptic," I said warmly. Rael, watching from the safety of her chair, put her hand over her mouth. She never was good at keeping a straight face under any circumstances. "I have a challenge for you."

Maka hurried to the now-speechless Skeptic with a container of some drink—a peace offering Copelup accepted at once and clamped to his face. "One is always dehydrated after eopari," Maka explained to me, sotto voce.

"We are," I said politely but firmly, "running out of time." Copelup's antennae twitched. They were still partially coiled around one another, I supposed in the Drapsk-equivalent of a humanoid struggling to wake up from a too-sound sleep. "My sister and I thank you for your assistance, my dear Skeptic. Now we need you again." The antennae unwound with an alacrity suggesting alarm. I knew how to change that. "You see, Copelup, we'd like you to run some tests on Rael—find out more about how the Clan operates in the M'hir."

His yellow plumes, so striking among the purple-pink Makii, shot upward in absolute delight.

I hadn't been completely truthful with Rael, telling her only that I wanted to learn if Copelup's devices really did hide us from the Watchers. In that, we were not successful. The devices at close range gave the M'hir an odd, not unpleasant, metallic feel, hardly detectable unless one was aware to look for it; certainly nothing that appeared to disguise any other sensations. This was Rael's description, shared with me mind-to-mind.

Copelup's other test, the one we kept from Rael, confirmed what I'd both hoped and feared: that my sister's presence in the M'hir drew no unwanted attention from the M'hir life-forms. If it was my unbalanced power that attracted them, and worse, if my Power-of-Choice was rebuilding itself around me, I didn't want her to know. Not yet. Morgan came first.

Once we were certain of the results, I broached the subject to the Drapsk. "Captain Makairi," I began, keeping my voice calm and patient—no amount of belligerence or begging would sway a determined Drapsk, "the Skeptic feels Rael's presence in the M'hir will not endanger either of us. I ask your permission to have her attempt to contact the Watchers."

"You would not be at risk, Mystic One?" The Drapsk predictably focused on the member of his Tribe over a virtual outsider. "You would promise not to enter the Scented Way again yourself in this dangerous place?"

I thought of what waited for me there—waited with appetite—and had no problem saying with the utmost sincerity: "I promise. As I am of the Makii," I added on impulse, feeling this should carry some weight with him. Rael was glancing back and forth between the Drapsk and I. I shook my head slightly when it was my turn again, hoping she'd appreciate that the Drapsk would detect any nonverbal communication and rightly mistrust my promise if it occurred.

The Captain inhaled all his tentacles—the new ones had grown to match the others, I was relieved to notice, giving me one less item to try to explain to Rael. Two tentacles popped back out with the words: "We will remove the field, Mystic One. The Makii are relieved you are being sensible."

"Ah, about that," I said, drawing a deep breath. This was the trickier part and I wasn't prepared to take "no" for an answer. "Once Rael has sent her message, she can be traced here. We'd like to leave immediately and go into Jershi, to find Baltir."

"Leave the ship!" I could tell Rael was amazed by the unison with which the Drapsk could inhale tentacles and rock in place.

Before I could start arguing, a deep voice rumbled from the far corner of the bridge: "I will be with her." Huido, presently acting as a couch for three Drapsk crew, walked toward me, shaking off his passengers who bounced up from the floor and trotted away without complaint. "We must resume the search for my brother. This Baltir of the toads is the best lead we've had."

The Drapsk weren't pleased; the continuing sound of subdued tentacle sucking filled the bridge. I saw Rael preparing to add her comment and quelled her with a look. "Captain, we have come here with a purpose. You must accept that I know what I'm doing," *hopefully,* I added to myself. "Holding us on this ship can protect us today. What about the future? We have a chance to confuse my enemies, to recover the—" I searched my knowledge of them for an equivalent to describe my attachment to Morgan, settling for: "To recover the missing member of my own Tribe."

Tentacles popped out, forming the flowerlike ring that I thought signified if not agreement, then sudden comprehension. I just hoped they were comprehending what I intended.

INTERLUDE

With a frustrated growl, Morgan threw aside his bag of equipment, trading it for a bit of extra mobility and a second free hand. He'd chased the Clansman into the next room, only to find it was the antechamber to another, much larger space. A nightmare.

A nightmare built from a maze of tubes, most wider around than his arms could span, writhing upward to a ceiling lofted through at least two more floors, like some bizarre forest canopy of medical gadgets and industrial pipes. Any open space was filled with tables and counters, most of these connected by thick cabling that made it impossible to find clear footing for more than a couple of steps at a time. The Retian alarm system was fully active—silent, but with orange-red strobe lights careening from every corner, bewildering the eye.

Faitlen either knew his way through the place blindfolded, or had an inner guide. He had almost immediately disappeared from sight, running frantically not as though he feared Morgan, but as though he had to prevent something from happening at any cost. *What?* Intuitively, Morgan stopped and closed his eyes. He ignored the pounding of his heart, the sound of his own breathing. He shut out any concern about the Retians on their way down or how he was going to escape the Baltir. He became still, only then opening his thoughts to the M'hir.

An opening he immediately slammed closed, overwhelmed by what seemed to be blazing arcs of power, as if some deadly collision filled that void. But it was enough to give him directions in this madhouse. Morgan's eyes snapped open, and he began to run.

A twist, turn to the left, a sprint straight ahead. Morgan

glimpsed fabric, stained orange by the strobe lights. *Faitlen!* Careless of obstacles, Morgan accelerated, flinging himself over a table, rewarded by a second, closer glimpse.

This was it. Morgan grabbed a convenient pipe, hauling himself to a stop. Shields tight, Morgan crept closer, taking advantage of the abundant machinery to hide him, setting his feet with care. Ahead, Faitlen was motionless, as if staring. Realizing the Clansman was totally preoccupied, Morgan dared step out where he could see what was happening.

A figure lay crumpled on the floor a short distance away, a deathly-still figure the Clansman appeared to ignore, his attention on two of the vertical tubes. The tubes were opaque, as all the others, their surface marked with patterns of gauges and dials impossible to read in the flashing light. Morgan looked down at the figure. "Barac!" he cried involuntarily, hurrying forward.

Faitlen ignored him, too, seeming intent on the machines. Careful to keep the Clansman in sight, Morgan stepped over Barac's body and crouched beside him. Still breathing, the Human noticed with relief, and no outward signs of injury. Then Barac's breathing caught in his throat, his body arching as it fought for air. Morgan grabbed his shoulders, the contact enough to draw him into that other place . . .

. . . sharing utter anguish . . . utter loss . . . the bitter taste of failure . . . fading . . . fading . . .

Without knowing how he did it, Morgan *reached* for Barac, collecting the Clansman's fragmenting personality in a net of his power, striving to bring them both back from that brink. . . .

Success! Morgan shook his head, clearing his vision in time to see Faitlen launch himself at Barac's throat. The Human angled his shoulder to take the brunt of that assault, his own hands grasping the Clansman's wrists. He surged to his feet, hauling Faitlen with him—shoving the Clansman against the nearer tube before glancing at Barac.

Breathing, or rather groaning, Barac had already rolled to his hands and knees, head hanging down.

"You're supposed to be dead!" Faitlen shouted at Barac, struggling against Morgan's steel grip. When he realized he couldn't break free, the Clansman looked up into Morgan's eyes, and said in a strangely reasonable voice: "They wanted a body to examine. One of us. They told me he was already dead and I could release the restraint—but they lied. The ignorant fools brought an unChosen within reach," a note of rising hysteria. "They weren't supposed to die—understand me—he was!"

"Who has died?" Morgan said, remembering the anguish in Barac's thoughts. Then he looked past Faitlen at the tube. "Who is in there?"

"No one, now. You. You're Sira's Human! You'll both pay—" Morgan felt Faitlen gathering his power. Instead of gathering his own, Morgan released one hand, stood back a bit, and sent his fist into the Clansman's jaw.

With distinct satisfaction.

Chapter 46

THE Drapsk had been right.

I hated that. I truly hated the thought of staring into their kind, smug facelessness and apologizing for my folly. Of course, I'd have to survive a while longer to make that happen. From where I lay, stomach-down in a pile of very ripe and soggy refuse, it wasn't guaranteed I would.

My well-thought out plan had gone awry for one simple reason. I'd assumed I knew who my enemies were, putting them into neat piles of this group of Clan and that group of Clan.

Had it been a symptom of leftover Clan egotism that I'd forgotten the hundreds of other intelligent species in the galaxy?

At least three different ones pursued me now: Retian, Human, and Scat. I didn't know if they were working together or apart. To some extent, it was a meaningless distinction, since they all seemed to want me in their hands or claws, preferably alive, I hoped, although their willingness to use significantly nasty weaponry to achieve this outcome left me wondering if I was being overly optimistic.

I had only to look down the alleyway to see the glow from the fires lit by that last burst of blasterfire.

The poor Drapsk on the *Nokraud* were probably frantic. I hoped nothing worse, but given the reptilian snout I'd spotted in the group giving chase, there was little doubt in my mind that the pirates were involved.

I settled myself more comfortably into my pile, thinking back and trying to puzzle out what had gone wrong first.

Rael, Huido, and I had left the *Nokraud* under cover of darkness and a downpour unusually violent even for this season. Since we could hardly see one another, I'd been confident we could make our way to the groundcar without being observed by anyone else. That may have been the case. Our troubles had started once inside Jershi's mud walls, not before.

No one had bothered to tell us—and, to be fair, the not-infallible Drapsk probably didn't know; equally likely, the pirates did—that a torrential downpour coupled with a moonless night and the warmth of the season meant just one thing in the wee hours of the morning on Ret 7. We climbed out of our groundcar, Rael and I with ease, and Huido unloading himself from the back like a disembarking tug, only to find ourselves in a street full of sex-crazed Retians.

There can be a distinct titillation in observing the reproductive practices of other species. I've been told the aerial mating dance of the Skenkran makes their world a lodestone for Humans seeking to rekindle romance. The Retians, on the other hand, could disenchant the most loving couples.

We had to trace a careful path through the wallowing clumps; the ones with long chains of amorous males were the worst, since they rolled and thrashed like some fantastic snake completely regardless of whether they were about to knock our feet out from under us or bash themselves into a nearby wall with enough force to leave a pile of unconscious suitors in the mud. From what I could see through the rain and darkness, there was a steady supply of new ones eager to jump, grab, and otherwise dive into the fray.

It wasn't a particularly romantic-sounding exercise either. Between the thumps and bangs of entangled groups impacting on their surroundings, one could pick out rather violent and somewhat strangled croaking. I couldn't see which individuals made the noise, but found out later it was coming from the females within the clumps of males as they advertised their availability—implying they had as much trouble distinguishing their sexes as any humanoid visitor.

To totally finish any resemblance to the joyous coupling of other species, the handlights we brought out in self-defense revealed that the mud and puddles were coated with what looked like knotted strings of slimy beads, coated in a fine spray of some oily purple substance I didn't want identified and I hoped would wash off my boots. The strings, when not collecting on the wheels of parked groundcars or squishing underfoot, were floating away with the rainwater, presumably to end up in the marshes surrounding Jershi. I wished the next generation of Retians luck—they appeared to rely heavily on it.

Wouldn't it have been easier to do all this out on the mud-flats? I thought, but just to myself. The Retians were too busy to answer questions.

None of us believed all in the city would be so occupied; for one thing, less mature Retian adults were presumably keeping things running while their seniors caroused through the streets and alleyways. But there were enough here to make it difficult for us to reach our destination. Huido's bulk was a definite liability, since this time the Retians took no notice of him, making it necessary for Rael and me to lead in order to find the safest route.

Even worse, his low-slung frame acted like a rake. Within minutes, the Carasian was festooned in tiny glistening beads. I refused to look at him again once I caught Huido cleaning off his lower handling claws by simply consuming what he accumulated.

So when the Carasian was no longer behind Rael and me, we didn't notice for a few moments. The latest writhing Retian grouping had cut between us and I used my handlight to search the shadows. It shouldn't have been hard to spot him; his body armor might have been black, but those eyes reflected light like tiny circular mirrors.

There was no sign of him. "When did you last see him?" I shouted at Rael, holding onto her arm as we were almost pushed apart by another cold mass of writhing bodies. I gestured urgently at the protection of a doorway and we struggled our way to it.

"I don't know," she shouted back. She was gasping and beads of sweat covered her forehead after she drew back her hood to see me better.

"Did any of them scratch you?" I demanded, Huido's disappearance thrust aside by a new fear. Among their many virtues, adult Retians were poisonous. I'd seen the result once and would never forget it. I grabbed Rael, pulling her about so I could shine my light over her clothing, looking for any sign of a cut or gash.

"No," she said faintly, then jerked free of my hold to turn away and bend over, retching miserably.

Poor Rael, I reminded myself. Her experience with aliens—especially the messier sorts—had been confined to civilized Humans. A few days with Huido or the Drapsk hardly broadened her education, since both were very careful to act according to humanoid norms when in our company. *Most of the time,* I corrected myself, thinking queasily of Huido's latest snack food.

Had the Retians noticed and attacked him? I didn't think so. The number Huido had eaten, or even could, were insignificant compared to the millions being crushed under the press of passion in the street.

"Come on, Rael," I urged her, seeing she was either recovering or running out of stomach contents to share with the mud. "It can't be far now. Huido will meet us there if he can." And there wasn't much the two of us would be able to do, if the Carasian couldn't handle himself, I thought grimly. He was the one toting enough natural and technological weaponry to take out a small army. Rael and I had only our wits, our Talent being firmly off limits until the Drapsk were certain it was safe—a restriction Rael found ridiculous and would likely start to ignore any moment; a plea for common sense on my part I planned to take very seriously indeed.

We had only two blocks to walk to our goal, a reasonable-sounding distance in most humanoid cities. Unfortunately, the map the Drapsk had obtained for us had neglected to include the astounding number of stairs—currently waterfalls—in our path. This explained why most roads were marked as foot traffic only. From the occasional purr of an engine overhead, aircars were the vehicles of choice in this part of town. I spent a moment wishing I'd listened to the Drapsk and allowed them to follow us by air, but they were stretched thin as it was to keep the *Nokraud* secure, keep shifting through information, and hold the *Makmora* ready to lift if necessary. I'd been adamant, not wanting to have some Drapsk anxieties stop me so close to Morgan. They'd been convinced, not by me, but by Huido's cutting comments on the inability of the white and plumed beings to travel inconspicuously anywhere at night.

The lower Rael and I went—moving very carefully for, despite the lack of mating traffic here, the amount of water pouring over the stairs made the footing treacherous—the clearer it became that the Retians valued their real estate by its depth below the waterline. The buildings on either side of us, though still predominantly plas-coated mud, began to boast such expensive amenities as gilded doors and saddle-shaped ort-perches by the round windows.

It was a particularly silly place to put any research building, especially one housing damp-sensitive equipment. I began to sweat myself.

"Rael," I said, pulling her to the side of the stair just shy of the bottom, both of us reaching one hand to the wall beside us as if afraid of being swept down with the latest clump of Retian offspring. "This can't be right. This isn't the place."

"Why would your Drapsk give us the wrong address?" she argued reasonably.

"Where did they get it?" I replied with my own question. "I'm sure this can't be it. We've been led into a trap."

She turned to look back up the stairs and I followed her gaze. The rain had slowed enough to allow the feeble streetlights to make some progress in illuminating the city. There were figures, still impossible to distinguish, at the very top. Individuals who moved as though they planned to stay that way. *These were not,* I realized with a sinking feeling, *more sex-driven locals.*

"I think it's time to get out of here," Rael said, her fear pushing against my thoughts like a strong, cold wind. I felt her form a locate, *concentrate*—I knew she planned to take me with her and I *pulled* free at the last possible moment, using a burst of my own power to stay where I was. She vanished . . .

And that's when I had started to run.

And they'd begun to chase me.

So here I lay, catching my breath and probably a multitude of tiny pests and fungal spores, trembling in an alleyway while my sister tried explaining herself to the Makii. I kept listening for the comforting rattle of Huido's plates.

But all was quiet, including, the realization sank in slowly, the footsteps and shouting from the nearby roadway. Either they'd passed by me, or they were much better at walking silently over broken glass than I could believe. It had been, I congratulated myself, a stroke of genius to scatter the bits I'd found in the refuse within the first part of this tunnellike space between buildings.

Standing, I did the best I could to scrap off the larger clumps of mud and filth from my clothing. Spacer coveralls were made from tough, stain-resistant fabric, but I'd managed this night to tear holes in both knees and permanently discolor their blue into something closer to black. *At least,* I decided, *I was less conspicuous.* My hair, for a wonder, had remained cooperatively within its hood and so was dry, if inclined to act morose and tangle itself.

My appearance improved to the best of my ability, something I could hardly check in this city of windowless walls, I cautiously stepped out into the street. There was no sign of either mating Retians or any traffic at all, something easily explained, I decided, pressing the display on my chrono, by the fact only an hour remained until Ret 7's excuse for a dawn.

If I stopped to think about it—as if it mattered at all—I was exhausted, cold, wet, and tended to stagger when I wasn't giving strict orders to my feet to pay attention. But as I looked more carefully up and down the street, I saw something which took my mind off my state completely: a public vidphone. There were a few things less important to the Clan and few things more likely to help me now. I could make a list, and did as I walked casually toward it, looking over my shoulder every few steps: I could call the *Makmora,* I could call the Enforcers, I might be able to contact Baltir himself.

All of these things and more would have been possible, had procreating Retians not smashed the thing beyond any hope of usefulness. Garlands of dying eggs hung over the remains of the front plas panels. The inside was in worse shape.

The spurt of energy hope had provided was gone, leaving me feeling worse than before. I found a sheltered doorway as the rain started up again, shooing away the cluster of fungi busy slobbering over something in the opposite corner. I didn't see what it was: they must have somehow engulfed it at my approach or dragged it away.

What now? I asked myself, looking out at the deserted street, its puddles stirred by the now-heavy drops, the buildings to every side dark and full of incomprehensible things. I had no idea where I was. I could be leaning against the door of the building housing Baltir and his experiments right now, or be half the city away. As I recalled, there had been a great deal of blind running tonight, and very little careful observation. Morgan would not be impressed.

Morgan. There was temptation. He might be near enough to hear my voice if I called out in the night, a thought which quickened my heart rate until I was almost deafened by it. Of course, any shouting was more likely to bring back my pursuers.

Any other call might bring Morgan the instant attention of our enemies.

I sighed, dropping my head to my knees. My inaction wasn't helping anyone, either. I opened my awareness to the M'hir, just enough to reach for Rael's thoughts.

It was as though a sun—a decent yellow sun—had burst through the darkness and warmed me inside and out. There it was, within the darkness of the M'hir, that golden richness my power knew as its own and my mind knew as Morgan. Not his mind, not contact, but the scent, the flavor of his specific energy remained here.

Here? To be so strong, so immediate a presence, Morgan would have to have been physically near me. He could still be here. No longer caring about eavesdroppers, I was on my feet before I knew it, reaching out without being able to stop myself. Together we could defeat anyone. Together I could be whole again.

I touched . . . *madness, rage.*

It's Sira, I sent to him, beating with all my power against the wall between us, sensing—as though here I could see all around me at once—the simultaneous arousal of the M'hir's life, its hunger. *Jason!*

It was as if he turned an inner eye to look right at me. Through me. Time stopped. . . .

Then I fled the M'hir, not from the beasts and their deadly appetite, but from the terrible knowledge that behind his rage, Morgan could no longer see who I was.

INTERLUDE

When he found himself with a body again, the first thing Barac noticed was the one crumpled at his feet. Hard on that gruesome discovery was the observation that the world was being illuminated by disorienting and powerful flashes of reddish light: an alarm? Last, but not least, he realized he was standing upright solely because of the grip of two strong hands.

"Morgan?" he gasped, grabbing the Human's arms. "What—" He remembered and asked bleakly: "Where are the Choosers? Are they—"

Morgan's eyes were icy blue in a face showing considerable strain. "This is not a good time or place for explanations, Clansman." He glanced around. "Can you get us out of here?" Barac winced as the Human let go with one hand and pressed it firmly on his forehead, sending him a locate for the bridge of the *Fox*, Morgan's ship. With it came the assurance that Barac need not have the strength—Morgan would supply that as necessary.

"Yes, all right," Barac gasped, pulling back and free of Morgan's touch. The Human could also use a few more lessons in moderating his power. Then Barac looked around. Definitely not his cell. "What is this place?" he whispered, horrified.

Morgan had bent down and lifted the body, drawing it over both of his shoulders so he could hold it in place with one arm and hand, careful to keep one hand free—the kind of forethought, Barac realized distractedly, best developed on a battlefield. "I'll tell you later," the Human grunted as he settled the weight.

"You've killed Faitlen di Parth!" Barac exclaimed as the head rolled sideways with Morgan's movement and he could recognize the slack features.

Morgan frowned at him. "If I'd killed him, why would I be bothering to take him with us?" Then his frown grew. "Why would you think I'd kill him in the first place?"

"You killed the others," Barac blurted, "Larimar on Plexis; Malacan Ser here on Ret 7."

The strobe lights stopped flashing, returning the illumination to normal. The change was ominous.

Morgan's expression changed from impatient disapproval to merely thoughtful. He shook his head. "Much as I'd like to know what you're talking about, Clansman, I suggest we get out of here before the owners reach this level."

Barac nodded, accepting Morgan's strength as he accepted the hand on his shoulder. He *pushed* . . .

There was resistance. Just as he hesitated, startled by feeling a rebounding, almost yielding surface, he felt Morgan's power grow exponentially, as if the Human could tap into something more here. It was enough to force their own opening.

As he sent them toward it, a new force struggled against them. *Faitlen!* The Clansman had regained consciousness and fought to stay in place. His will, so much more than a sud's, became an anchor drawing them all back. Regretfully, and knowing Morgan would not be pleased, Barac set the other Clansman adrift.

. . . And found himself on the bridge of the *Silver Fox* for the first time in over a year.

Chapter 47

I'D found Baltir without any effort at all.

All it had required was a guide with local experience, such as that amply provided by the helpful being stalking beside me down the clean, white hallway. The Scats, it seemed, were very well connected indeed.

"Yes–ss, Fem Morgan, the *Nokraud* has–ss done cons–ssider-able bus–siness–s over the years–ss with the es–steemed res–ssearcher–ss of the Baltir," Grackik was telling me, waving her nub of an arm in emphasis, her other hand being occupied with maintaining a too-tight grip on me. "As—ss you can s–ssee, it is–ss a place as–ss well as–ss a name. The head of this–ss fac–ss–ility calls–ss hims–sself Baltir. A conc–ss–eit, I'm told. The toads–ss permit it."

I'd walked right into my pursuers, of course. I could have ported away—and into the formless jaws within the M'hir. It seemed the better part of discretion to allow them to take me where I'd been trying to go in the first place.

"Many of their findings–ss have proven us–sseful—" I heard the preening, hissing voice as though it were a vidplay in the background, preoccupied with something far more important to me than the Scats' weapons' testing: Morgan.

I understood—on some level, I could rationalize his failure to recognize me or to respond with clinical precision. To see me, to feel me in his thoughts, Morgan would have had to think past the layers of emotion, to push aside the clouding effect of the rage I'd both instilled and released in him. I understood this.

If he'd died in my arms, I thought, fighting back tears, *it would feel like this, as hurtful as this absence of me in his mind, this uncaring.*

And there was worse to face. When—not if, when—I removed my rage from his mind and restored his own inner balance again, I knew I had no guarantee Morgan would ever feel the same way about me, that all would be as it was.

All for my revenge. All for this place.

Suddenly cold and calm again, I started paying attention to my surroundings, plain and uninformative as they were, as well as Grackik's boasting. This dreadful night might have some value if there was a chance I could do something about what lay inside these walls.

"Sira di Sarc," the name was spoken with deep respect; the hand gestures and underlay of power were impeccably courteous, as befitted a Clansman whose power was less than my own.

Somehow, the presence of the well-armed and suspicious Scat at my shoulder took most of the shine from Faitlen di Parth's polite greeting.

"You have something of mine," I said smoothly, adding displeasure to my own power signature so that Faitlen's eyes winced ever-so-slightly in response. "I'd like it back." There was a bruise darkening under the skin of his jaw which, now that I paid attention, appeared to be oddly asymmetrical as if one side was swelling.

Someone, and I'd take any bet on who, had recently punched the Clansman in the face. It might even have dropped the slightly-built being to the floor. I found myself entranced by the image.

There had never been any love lost between myself and Faitlen, scion of a House always less powerful, yet always ambitious to be more than heredity granted them. We stood, outwardly polite and obeying the forms of courtesy, brought together by beings who were much more honest in their hates and treacheries.

Faitlen had chosen to meet me in a room remarkable for its lack of any features, a box with irregular walls as if here the Retian architect had tried desperately for some species' expression. There were three of us, then a second door opened and we were joined by someone I'd hoped never to see again.

"We are ready for the subject," the Retian I knew as Baltir announced to Faitlen without a glance at me. His wide, thin mouth was almost pink—a sign of agitation or excitement. That this being literally identified himself as his work was a characteristic I found intensely frightening, given he belonged to a species whose social structure relied on the details of relatedness recorded over thousands of years—a feat I found frankly unbelievable given what I'd seen of their reproduction, but they claimed to know.

I found myself pressing my hands against the scars on my abdomen, as if I could protect myself that way. "I thought you'd already stolen what you wanted, Faitlen. You were after the Sarc bloodline, weren't you? Are you acting for the Council or for your House alone?"

His fury leaked past his shields—a deliberate release, since Faitlen was too adept to willingly give me an opening into his mind. *Mine was the greater power,* I reminded him with a touch of threat he couldn't ignore. But any more overt attack against the Clansman was likely to be met by a more physical resistance, knowing the nature of his accomplices.

Grackik, for one, had concerns along those lines. As Faitlen winced again, glaring at me with very little of the urbane host left in his face, she drove her claws into my arm in warning, her heavy head swinging over and dipping down so her slit-pupiled eyes could regard me at close range. "No mindcrawler tricks–sss, Fem."

"I have no intention of touching his thoughts, Captain Grackik," I said grimly. "There's nothing in there I'd want to know."

"Really, First Chosen?" The title, given with a sneer, still had an impact on me. It belonged to the most powerful Joined female of a House. If I were the First Chosen for the House of di Sarc, it gave me considerable prestige and political power among the Clan—present company excepted, I knew full well. Of course, if my Power-of-Choice continued to accumulate, my status would eventually return to that of a lowly Chooser.

Instead of debating this or any other issue, I merely nodded regally, as though Faitlen only accorded me my due.

"Must you waste my time with this meaningless conversation?" Baltir interjected. "Everything is ready."

"For what?" I asked, keeping my eyes on Faitlen.

Baltir answered, Faitlen having turned an interesting dull red shade: "To see if the implant has taken hold, Clanswoman."

The blood drained from my head and shoulders, making me grateful for the uncomfortable support of the Scat's grip. The flesh beneath my hands suddenly felt foreign. "What implant?"

The Retian's lips turned a pleased yellow. "The one I put into your body on Pocular, of course. The chances were slim you would survive, naturally, but I never waste an opportunity to enhance the Baltir's knowledge of humanoid physiology."

"What implant?" I repeated, my voice threatening enough so the Scat gave me a shake. Without conscious intention, my power began to surge outward, as if already seeking a target in the room. Faitlen turned a ghastly color.

"Now!" he shouted, catching my attention so I missed the instrument in the Retian's webbed hand until it was too late to dodge the fine spray.

One breath, and it was also too late to do anything more than send out one desperate message.

Morgan!

INTERLUDE

Sira!

The name burst into Barac's nightmare with the force of an explosion, rescuing him from a damp cell filled with sharp-toothed fungi. He sat up before knowing he was awake, grabbing the sides of the hammock as it responded to his movements by obligingly offering to dump him onto the floor of the cubbyhole Morgan had euphemistically called his passenger cabin.

He swung his legs out and down, ordering on the portlight as he staggered to the door. The sending had come from Morgan, and its undertone of horror promised nothing good.

Morgan held his head between his hands, rocking back and forth in a futile effort to try and ease the pain there. Her sending had been so faint, so desperate. He'd almost not recognized it. When he had, and fought to reply, there had been only the emptiness of loss.

The wisp of Sira, the contact with a mind he knew as well as his own, was gone.

He heard pounding footsteps as Barac ran into the *Fox*'s control room, unsurprised the Clansman had overheard. His own head rang with the power he'd driven outward. It was as if all his longing for Sira, the need for her buried all these days, had been released in one second's plea.

A plea that he knew would go unanswered unless he could find her. It had been a call for help such as she'd never sent to him before—perhaps as she'd never sent. Whatever was happening, he had to stop it.

This time, Morgan welcomed the uproaring of his rage.

Chapter 48

SIRA! A call remembered from darkness, yet more than a dream.

Morgan lived.

I suspected I did as well.

Reason enough to open my eyes, no matter what they had done to me while I lay unconscious and at their mercy.

There was a ceiling overhead, white and sterile, broken by lighting panels set to produce a dim illumination.

I moved only my eyes at first, accumulating information at a rate that wouldn't upset the fragile control I had over my imagination. There were tablelike beds to either side of me, both empty, with their sheeting rumpled as though whomever had lain there had simply disappeared.

Beyond the beds—at some distance, making me realize I was at the center of a long room or even a hallway—were banks of busy machines. They hummed and chattered to themselves, some with what appeared to be windows to their insides as though what might occur within them mattered as much as what occurred without. I stared at them in fear, knowing too much to believe them harmless and too little to understand.

I raised my head so my chin pressed against my chest, the move sending a flash of agony through my head I ignored. My body was covered by a sheet. I ignored it for the moment also, more concerned with finding out if I was alone or observed.

Alone. Though there were probably vids set up to monitor me, I felt an instant relief knowing I didn't have to immediately deal face-to-face with any of my enemies.

My arms were free, if impossibly heavy to lift. I worked my hands into fists repeatedly until the prickly pain of returning circulation ran from wrist to shoulder. Then, I carefully brought my hands up, running my fingers lightly and cautiously where I'd been opened before. The new, wider medplas strips were easy to feel through the sheet.

At this rate, I told myself bitterly, *they should just install a zip.*

The bleak humor helped. There was nothing I could do now to undo or even discover what they'd done this time. What I must do was prevent anything further.

I looked around the room. *To me or mine,* I vowed.

Perhaps they hadn't expected me to awaken so soon. More likely, I decided, grimly reeling from step to step, they'd underestimated my willingness to climb off the table and walk. Since both movements were accompanied by the total conviction my insides would imminently spill out around my feet, I thought it just as reasonable they'd overestimated my intelligence.

But move I did, albeit unsteadily and, at times, almost unconsciously. So far, no alarms or investigations, despite it taking me what seemed a week to lurch from my table to the next, and then to the nearest wall. Firm objects were such comforting things.

What was less comforting was any thought of what moved with me, under those tidy strips of medplas. Or had Baltir merely removed something temporary, some experiment he'd housed in me and was pleased to be able to retrieve intact?

The door opened into an even dimmer hallway. I eased my way into it, the door closing behind me and, when I checked, locking as well. So much for the temptation of climbing back into bed, I told myself, feet already moving forward as if they knew the urgency even if my thoughts were prone to be sluggish.

Another door. This one would have been locked, except for the assault on its paneling, currently covered with a temporary patch. I pushed my way in, certain any room worth breaking into was worth my time.

It was. I caught my breath in short little gasps, counting the little incubators, guessing what they had to contain. This close to me; this close to Faitlen? It had to be what was stolen from me.

There was a way to confirm it. I leaned on the nearest, peering in at the tiny glob of tissue growing inside, opening my awareness of the M'hir.

Power flowed between us, almost imperceptible, but real. So did the link between mother and offspring begin and grow within the womb, the link the child, once-born, instinctively maintained up to several years after birth, allowing the separation of mother and child to build a pathway of power in the M'hir others could use at will.

It was, I recalled as I closed my eyes and fought to remain conscious, one of the potentials the M'hir life-forms used for food.

It occurred to me, as I hovered in that emotionally drained state, that if my existence as a too-powerful Chooser was a threat to the Clan, how much more a threat was this room full of Siras-to-be?

The answer spun around my thoughts until I grasped it, holding tightly. To save the Clan, I acknowledged with a pain rivaling the one in my body, there must be no more Choosers who could harm the unChosen. The *di's* must end. Only the *suds* held any promise for our future.

It was a heretical thought.

But it sustained me as I did what had to be done, forcing myself from box to box, turning out the little lights within each, then hunting every cabinet and shelf for signs of more.

INTERLUDE

Rael hadn't expected the Drapsk to take her arrival without Sira very well.

Still, she thought, gazing around the bland pink interior of the *Makmora*'s temporary brig—temporary because she'd had to wait in the corridor while the Makii unapologetically re-arranged a bulb in the wall into something resembling a room with a locked door—they could have listened.

She'd seen a sippik nest torn down once, a servant at her summer house hooking the round papery structure from its lodging under the eaves. While Rael wasn't fond of the out-doors, some of her guests enjoyed lounging on her balcony, an activity highly disapproved of by the fierce little insects. The nest had to go, and Rael, watching through the window, had seen the result: hordes of the small things climbing over the rail-ings, furnishings, and glass—far more than she'd have guessed from the size of their home—most taking turns to dash into the nest to snatch a wingless juvenile and carry it to some imagined safety, while the rest attacked the hapless servant. Chaos had reigned until the last of the sippik were gone, their nest an aban-doned ruin, and the servant sent home for treatment of his wounds.

The reaction of the Drapsk to Sira's disappearance had a lot in common with her remembrance of that day: a panic-driven yet well-coordinated hostility. They'd brought her from the *Nokraud* to the *Makmora*, ignoring her objections and holding her despite her efforts to port. More of their despicable technology.

Rael tried to be angry, but couldn't. The Drapsk were only acting how she herself felt. She'd use any method to find Sira and bring her to safety. In their opinion, this included keeping her, their one representative of the Clan, hostage.

Rael surprised herself by feeling sufficiently tired and calm to rest on the oddly shaped Drapsk bed, even if sleep eluded her. She kept her awareness of the M'hir open, hoping to sense something from Sira even if the Drapsk's devices kept her own thoughts trapped inside her head.

It was an awareness she paid for, when a mental shout ripped through her shields until she cried out in an echo of pain. *Sira!*

Wincing, Rael focused all of her power into a reply, knowing Morgan's mental voice beyond any doubt. Her efforts were in vain.

But when she lay back down, she felt unexpectedly comforted. If Sira chose to count on this Human, so would she.

Chapter 49

THE boxes had possessed alarms of their own, I suspected, listening to the rush of footsteps past my hiding place, concentrating on making my mental presence into a ghost, less substantial than the minds of those near me.

They'd have trouble repairing what I'd done, I firmly hoped, starting with the plasterlike substance filling the damaged access panel and ending with the empty tissue dishes. If they thought like Retians and looked down the drain for the missing bits of me, they might find some. *If.*

On the other hand, I had indeed thought like a Retian, it being the only possible way of eluding Faitlen and the Scats in this place. I squirmed, easing the cramp starting in my right hip, hissing involuntarily at the spurt of pain. There had been more benefit from having pushed myself into this closet of dormant Retians than merely hiding in plain sight. Too worn to feel any xenophobia—or care if I did—I found the dozens of soothingly cool bodies provided a gentle pressure that helped keep me on my feet when I'd otherwise have oozed to the floor like something boneless. The support was so firm I could doze a bit. I didn't, all too aware these sleeping juniors could be aroused to serve their elders at any moment. It was unlikely they'd be summoned during any search for me, however. Morgan had told me the juniors were none too bright and couldn't be given any creative tasks.

I didn't know how long I should wait here. *But,* I told myself, wrinkling my nose at the musty smell and feeling lumps of rubbery skin against mine, *I'd been in worse places.*

* * *

My world quivered, as though I were embedded in a bowl of gelatin tapped by a giant. I forced my mind to something closer to being alert, fearing at first the juniors were waking, the quiver being the outermost layer popping free into the corridor.

No further movement; perhaps the momentary shiver that had passed from one to another was a shared dream, remembering a childhood of mindless searching for food in the swamps before pulled by instinct to march onto land and capture by waiting adults.

Regardless, it was a warning giving me the energy to slide my way free, a task made much easier by the light coating of slime over each Retian. When I half-fell into the corridor, the space I'd left was immediately filled as my former closet comrades pushed themselves back together. I wouldn't miss them either.

I was, I thought, growing remarkably light-headed—a consequence of internal bleeding or possibly simply my body attempting to shut me down so it could survive. Walking down this corridor, under the now-bright lights, didn't seem a sensible course.

Something brushed past me; I raised a hand as if to sweep it away before recognizing the touch was inside my head. It didn't feel like a threat. I risked widening my perceptions.

This way, sighed the inner voice, a voice I didn't know, so weary it could have been my own. *This way.*

It was as good a guide as any. One hand on the wall for support, I began following the faint tug of that call, wondering what I'd find.

I didn't know the name, but I knew the House behind that face with its lean, haughty features: Parth. Whichever daughter she was, I felt the power flowing to and from her within the M'hir, the link to her Chosen unquenched by the imposed sleep holding her motionless within the box.

There were two others in this room I'd entered, a passage achieved by the simple expediency of slipping through as the Retian leaving it struggled to maneuver an overloaded cart. One of the disadvantages to having independently mobile eyes was their tendency to converge on problems and so lose any peripheral range.

All three Clanswomen were in some type of coma; all three were adult and Commenced. All three carried the tiniest of offspring, provided, I had no doubt, through the services of the Baltir, not their Chosen.

I wondered what they'd think upon awakening to find those offspring linked to my power, not theirs.

The other two were known to me; I'd met them briefly when they were Choosers, during the time when I conducted my research into our population. Neither had much power of their own. Demer sud Parth. I hadn't known she'd Commenced and so had no knowledge of her Chosen. The other, Est sud Parth, had Chosen Shedlat di Mendolar, taking the name of the more powerful partner as her right in the Joining to become Est sud Mendolar. Est had given birth to one child, a disappointing sud.

Three Clanswomen, I summed to myself, two of them suds and probably the third as well, all originally from Faitlen's House. Each bore what could potentially be my genetic double—an enterprising and original theft for di Parth, had the Retian technology been capable of overcoming one simple problem.

What was being attempted here was obvious to me. They—I didn't credit Faitlen with the resources or nerve to do this alone, although he was perfectly capable of substituting his own kin into positions of gain—were trying to increase the number of di's, specifically those duplicating my deadly power. At the same time, they were trying to increase the potency of the mother-offspring link in these Chosen using my flesh. It probably was irrelevant whether the Clanswomen had been willing or not. It wasn't going to work.

I could feel the power of the link fading, like three candles guttering in a wind. It was an invisible umbilical cord, forged through the intimate contact of pregnancy; without its steady strengthening until close to birth, the offspring would die. It had happened recently enough in our past to be one of the few medical details the Clan did know. Here was proof that it wasn't the physical location of the tiny unborn within the body of any of our species that mattered, but something deeper and more unique. These stolen bits of me had been doomed the moment Baltir took them and encouraged them to grow within another's power and out of range of mine.

I probably hadn't needed to destroy those in the incubators, but given the Retians' interest, I was grateful to have left nothing of mine for their experimentation.

My abdomen cramped in twin lines of fire just then, as though to remind me of one last subject to check. I felt no link to whatever might be inside me; I'd known the moment I awoke. *What else could the Retian have done?*

The other question, what was I going to do about it, required a certain amount of luck, energy, and bluff. I leaned on the case holding Demer sud Parth, knowing she wouldn't mind, and wondered if I could convince my feet to move another step.

INTERLUDE

Don't reach for her. Bitter advice, with the taste of Sira's despair layered within his own, but Morgan knew Barac was right. He couldn't yet conceal the use of his Talent in the M'hir— a Talent Barac referred to as blatantly obvious and undoubtedly Human. *Trust Sira's power,* the Clansman had urged him. *She'll reach you if she must. Don't lead trouble to her.*

Shaking his head at what wasn't an option, Morgan turned his attention back to what was. "Let's go through this again," he sighed, sweeping up the wrappers that constituted the remains of their practical, if decidedly tasteless, meal of c-rations. He glanced at the com system with its tally of messages—over seven hundred. Who'd have guessed his query for local artifacts would trigger so many prospects? Shame he was in no mood for business. He went on: "You don't know who grabbed you away from Huido. Let's assume Faitlen, shall we? You don't know why. He said something about having donated you for some research or other to the Retians."

"A role I'm quite grateful to have avoided."

Morgan gazed at Barac. He noticed again the Clansman's resemblance to Sira, a similarity that showed best when Barac's elegance was rumpled and he was too tired to put on the excess of charm he apparently donned like a mask for Humans. "And you don't know who might have killed the Clansman on Plexis or Bowman's contact here if I didn't. Did you meet any other Clan in the Baltir? Or on Ret 7, for that matter?"

"No—" Barac hesitated only a second. "There were no others."

Morgan decided to let that one alone. He could guess what had happened; Sira had given him ample warnings of the risks

Choosers posed to the unChosen. "So," he passed Barac a cup of sombay. "We have a lot of questions without answers, my friend."

The answers to several of these arrived before Morgan could take his first sip from his own cup, announced by a ferocious pounding on the small air lock, a pounding forceful enough to set off alarms, if not to echo through the bulkheads.

A second later, Morgan leaned back from the vid screen showing the *Fox*'s ramp and laughed softly. He waved Barac to the screen, quite delighted to share the first positive news since he'd arrived on Ret 7.

There, looking thoroughly wet, muddy, and miserable in the current deluge, raising his free handling claw to hammer against the *Fox*'s innocent hide while the other held a limp humanoid form barely out of the mud, was a very agitated Carasian.

Huido was home.

"I didn't desert you! Morgan, tell him!"

Morgan looked up, amused to see Huido still holding the Clansman overhead by the waist. "Put him down, Brother," he said calmly, returning to his efforts to bring Huido's companion back to consciousness. "I'm sure Barac would have preferred your company to what he's been keeping lately."

A grunt and thud from behind signified that Huido had listened, but remained in too foul a mood to be gracious about it. Leaving a trail of mud and water, he'd trudged through the *Fox* to drop his prize in a chair. He hadn't spoken yet—though overjoyed to see Morgan, a response Morgan's own bruises would attest to—the Carasian apparently was too anxious to deal with what he obviously considered the Clansman's disappointing sense of teamwork.

Before Barac could take further offense—to which he was probably entitled, considering what he'd been through—Morgan added: "I'll apologize for him, Barac. Being out in the rain like that? It's not a healthy thing for a Carasian. Tends to make them irritable, as well as swelling up the vocal membrane."

Released from Huido's grip, and quite likely sore about the ribs, Barac came to look over Morgan's shoulder. "I know him," he proclaimed in surprise. "What's he doing here?"

Morgan studied the wiry and very wet Human propped in the

galley seat. He'd searched him already, the result being a nasty trio of force blades now safely sealed in a cupboard. The eyes remained closed, the head with its thinning gray hair lolling back. It wasn't his sparse grizzled beard or unwashed state so much as the deep lines etched by suffering around the mouth and eyes that gave Morgan pause. Despite the good quality clothing, somewhat torn by Huido's quaint method of encouraging the Human to accompany him, this was not a person who'd had an easy life. "Who is he?"

Barac came closer, staring as though to make absolutely sure of his identification. "Well, it's hard to believe, but this is one of the Humans who tried to kidnap me on Plexis. A telepath." He turned his head to Morgan. "I can show you," he offered.

Morgan jerked a thumb back at Huido, the Carasian now more peacefully occupied tampering with the galley's servo-kitchen. "Let's not leave him out of any revelations, Barac. He's not in the best mood to deal with the, shall we say, less tangible aspects?"

Barac nodded a heartfelt agreement. Meanwhile, Morgan watched Huido. He wanted to be sure he could reset whatever the master chef was altering on the *Fox*'s perfectly functioning servo. More than that, despite what he'd said to Barac, Morgan worried why the Carasian hadn't spoken yet. A satisfied slurping as Huido sampled the beer he'd requested reassured Morgan that his friend's vocal apparatus was working. A slurp and a sly roll of a dozen eyes at their guest.

Of course. The telepath. An eavesdropper in their midst. "Barac, watch him, will you?" Morgan said, grabbing a willing Huido by an upper claw and tugging the giant to the wide galley door. "We'll be right back."

"My pleasure," Barac said grimly, taking up a perch on the table. Morgan raised one eyebrow. This story about the telepaths and the Clan promised to be interesting.

He just hoped Huido's secrecy meant the Carasian knew something about Sira.

Chapter 50

IF there was one thing I knew about myself by now, it was that anger gave me strength. It was an unreliable ally, with a tendency to disappear suddenly and leave me worse than before. But for now, I nursed the small flame inside me as all I had.

I'd found a closet of the white coatlike garments I'd seen the Retians use when they worked in their laboratories, helping myself to the smallest. It fit, after a fashion. They had no perceptible breadth of shoulder, their bodies starting where humanoids bore their ears. There were stacks of protective headgear, such as one might need to work in areas of potential infection. One of those disguised my definitely non-Retian neck, if it limited my range of vision. Fortunately, the species as a whole were shorter than most Humans, so my coat draped over my feet.

My smooth, slender hands were a different story. I spent precious minutes hunting for any type of glove, finally locating a pair near a sink. The extra fingers would just have to hang empty. Despite the difficulty of any added burden, I arranged some sharp-looking implements on a plas tray. It made sense to me that a busy worker wouldn't be accosted for another task.

I couldn't straighten without pain, and walked with a shuffle at my most energetic, a posture and pace which should pass a casual inspection. *Of course,* I sighed to myself as I made my slow way up the ramp, *there was no telling if the Retians relied on signals I couldn't duplicate, like my dear and clever Drapsk.* The Makii, I knew, would not accept the treatment given one of their Tribe. It was another thought keeping me in motion.

My imposture passed muster as three separate groups of Retians hurried by me on errands of their own, none of whom gave me so much as a glance. I shuffled slowly up the ramp to the next level, pausing to collect my breath and remember who was responsible for my condition before shuffling up the next. I thought wistfully of finding a lift and being whisked up the remaining floors to ground level, knowing perfectly well any such convenience would be a primary focus of their search for me.

At some point, having turned myself into an automaton as numb to my surroundings as the dormant juniors, I noticed there wasn't another ramp across the hall from the top of the one where I paused. Instead, there was—from what I could see past all of the Retians, Humans, and others gathered here—a set of doors through which passage was firmly linked to physical searches and the close inspection of Captain Rek.

I leaned forward so my feet had to move in order to save me from falling on my face. No time to hesitate and no point in retracing my steps. It was out this door or not at all.

I wasn't the only Retian in laboratory garb and there were others carrying trays and various packages. I was, of course, the only one on this level wearing a head covering. So I shuffled out as boldly as I could manage, mimicking the posture and demeanor of most Retians, aiming my steps directly at the Scat.

As I expected, that heavy snout swung until her predator's gaze fixed on me, slit-pupiled eyes blinking with menacing interest. I gave her a slow nod, using my tray to gesture toward a nearby door, ajar so that I could see it opened into some sort of maintenance room and was empty.

Rek stalked in behind me, the clicking of her claws louder than my soft steps. "What do you want, Toad?" she hissed. "Or—is–ss it?" The hood lifted abruptly from my head, pinching my ears as it went.

I turned to face her with what I hoped was an air of complete confidence, forcing my unhappy body to stand as tall as possible. "We meet again, Captain Rek," I said. "To our mutual profit."

The frills behind each eye pulsed with color, reds and purples supplanting the quieter yellow and blue. The tip of the long black tongue collected a stray bit of froth from between her teeth. She tossed the hood to one side, but made no other movement.

I had her interest; now to use it.

* * *

As an ally, the pirate had a great deal to offer—starting with a refreshingly no-nonsense approach to leaving the Retians' building.

She took me by one arm and hauled me through the crowd of those guarding the door and those wishing to pass the guards, snapping her jaws in threat when one of the guards looked about to speak.

It wasn't a plan that would have occurred to me, but I enjoyed it in spite of the agony it caused my abused middle.

Outside, the sky was bright by Ret 7's standards, with the clouds thinned to a pale, sun-edged gray. The temperature was soaring, sucking up moisture until the air was as thick as the drying mud underfoot. Rek's frills expanded, and her long jaw hung slightly open. I wasn't sure if this was to relish the heat or cope with it.

Her momentum carried us all the way to the side of a parked aircar on the other side of the street, three Humans who must have been *Nokraud* crew snapping to alertness as we arrived. "Get in," she ordered me. "With has–sste."

I did my best, helped by a strong shove from behind as I tried to ease myself into the farthest seat.

"Stop!" The word, and an upwelling of power against my shielding came simultaneously. I peered out of the aircar, just able to see past the pirates to where Faitlen had appeared from thin air. The Retians with him looked quite unhappy to have been transported, but after a moment's paralysis, began to rush at us.

From behind, I could see Rek's scaled sides heave and expand before she gave a strange cough, spraying a dark, smoking spittle over the nearest Retians. They screamed, wiping frantically at their faces. One fell writhing on the ground near enough for me to see the flesh dissolving.

I backed farther into the aircar.

A tingle warned me. Faitlen, standing out of range of the Scat's personal artillery, was trying to port me away. I relocated frantically, feeling the effort arousing the M'hir life as it drained my meager strength.

Fortunately, the Scat was not finished yet. A wave of a clawed hand and weapons' fire broke out as her crew took up positions to the front and back of the aircar. Faitlen vanished, leaving his horrified companions to run for cover.

As I slumped back, released from the strain of fighting Faitlen for the moment, Rek dove into the driver's seat of the aircar, sending it aloft with a terrifying rush that clipped the roof rail of a neighboring building and, incidentally, I was sure, left her crew behind.

Yes, Scats made interesting allies, I decided, daring to close my eyes and start to relax.

INTERLUDE

Morgan's experience of the M'hir was limited, granted only recently by use of the power Sira had given him, but even he recognized the burning pathways of power around this world. *The Clan,* he thought grimly, *had been busy.*

So, it seemed, had an entirely different group. Morgan steepled his fingers, gazing past their tips at the Human named Lacknee Sorl, burying—again—his image of Sira under that so easily summoned and useful rage. "Did you come to Ret 7 looking for him?" he asked, indicating Barac with a nod to where the Clansman sat at ease on the other side of the galley's long table. Morgan could barely detect the restraint the Clansman maintained around their guest's ability, preventing any of this conversation leaving the *Fox.* An interesting and useful technique. "I'd have thought the one attempt would have provided sufficient excitement."

Sorl looked confused, not the confusion of misunderstanding but as if he'd misplaced his sense of the world around him. "Find him, I did," he said in a rapid, muttering voice. "Showed them. Find him. Did right, I did."

Morgan looked over at Huido, raising one eyebrow. "I didn't do anything to him," the Carasian grumbled. "This is how he sounds. Started babbling at me the moment I caught him sneaking around the *Fox.* The only reason I brought him was because he'd say your name once in a while."

"Morgan, Morgan, Morgan," the wiry Human said agreeably.

Barac leaned forward, his dark eyes intent. "Back on Plexis. What were you and the others planning to do with me?"

The sunken, watery eyes became crafty. "Suck you dry, Man of the Clan. Take your power. Power. Power." Then he pointed

a gnarled finger at Morgan so suddenly Huido rattled to alertness. "Like he did. Morgan the Great. Morgan the Powerful."

Barac looked shocked and wanted to say more, but Morgan
stopped him with a look. "Lacknee Sorl," he said softly, willing
the other Human to meet his eyes. "What makes you think I'm
so powerful and that the Clan has anything to do with it?"

A sequence of blinks, then a protest, almost childlike in tone:
"You can. You can. He told us all. He promised us. Keep away
the bad place. Keep out the bad thoughts. Morgan has the power
now. We want it. We can have it." Another stab of his finger, this
at Barac. "They have it. They can give it. Like she did to you. Or
we can take it. Take it. Take it."

Morgan realized he was holding the palms of his hands down
on the tabletop with force enough to make his arms shudder.
The accompanying image, of Sorl's head beneath those hands,
sifted through his shields, making the smaller Human cry out in
panic, only staying in his seat because Huido was providing a
counterpressure on his shoulders.

There wasn't time for this—in their hurried conference moments before, Huido had told him where he'd been separated
from Sira and Rael, driven apart by scores of Retians in their
midsummer spawn. The Carasian had managed to carve a path
to the address where they'd been told the Baltir was housed,
only to find an empty house and no sign of either Clanswoman.
He'd decided the wisest course was to check the *Fox* once again
on his way back to the Drapsk. Where he'd found someone else
already snooping around her fins. Lacknee Sorl.

Morgan made himself relax, drawing on every scrap of disci-
plined patience he owned. Huido's catch might prove more
worthwhile than anything they could achieve running blindly
out into the rain. There was definitely something new going on.
The Human telepaths had never had organization or leadership
before. They'd never, that he knew, worked in groups even
when they knew one another. If the Clan was behind the kidnap-
pings Barac described, then they'd managed to achieve a una-
nimity of purpose among Human telepaths never seen before. A
rather pleasing irony.

Morgan was not, however, pleased by what he was hearing
right now. How did this scruffy, half-sane Human from the
subbasements of Plexis know anything about him or Sira?

One thing was certain: the knowledge hadn't come from the Clan.

"Who is this 'he' you speak of?" he asked. Huido stirred at the question, making a sandpaper hiss as he drew one claw edge past another. A simple fidget that startled Sorl, not surprising given that the Carasian loomed over his back. Morgan studied his friend, seeing nothing unusual in the whirling of his expressive eyes; Huido hadn't perceptibly relaxed since he arrived. "Who is he, Sorl?" Morgan repeated, keeping his voice as gentle as possible. "Who told you I had this new power?"

There was nothing simple or idle in the snap of Huido's massive handling claw. As Sorl almost fainted from fright, and even Barac looked startled, Morgan frowned at the Carasian. "You don't want me to ask the question? Why?"

"Because he knows. He knows. He knows," Sorl supplied, cowering under the Carasian's claws. "Bet he does. Bet he does. I do."

"Huido?" Morgan asked numbly.

"Psaat," the Carasian said rudely, heaving his bulk up to loom in front of Morgan, who stood to meet him. "The Enforcers are within a day of posting a reward for your hide, if they haven't already. Ask this one about the dead Clansman polluting my freezer. Ask him about the death of Malacan Ser. Ask him why he was hiding under the *Fox*. This other business can wait."

Morgan hardly listened, staring at his friend, feeling as though something solid in his life was turning to sand. "You know who has been watching Sira and me—maybe even who is responsible for all this—and you haven't told me?"

Huido's eyes suddenly deserted their focus, dodging away to look in every direction but into Morgan's face.

"Morgan," Barac said slowly. "Huido has only your interests in mind. Believe me. I know. Perhaps you should trust him in this—"

"Trust? Who can I trust? You?" With one smooth movement, Morgan tore the nearest stool from its latching to the deck, throwing it over Huido's head to smash into the door of the cubbyhole beyond. "Answer me! Who knew about Sira and me? Who told him?" Sorl had scurried under the table, but there was no doubt of Morgan's meaning.

Huido sank down until he crouched before Morgan, resting his great claws on the floor as if the gesture could counter the Human's towering rage. "There are some things best left under the rocks that hide them. Things that bite," the Carasian warned him, his voice not in the least conciliatory. Instead, he might have been some ancient oracle, about to pronounce a deserved doom.

Morgan clenched his fists, fighting to keep his voice level. "No more secrets, Huido. Tell me."

"You are close to a line, Brother, a line I fear you may cross. This could be the push, understand me? Do you still want to know?"

Morgan nodded, mute. Then, with a shudder of dread that started somewhere deep inside and roared through him like wildfire, he said one word to admit his past into his present: "Symon."

"Symon. Symon. Symon. Symon says. Symon says. Symon told us everything," came a frantic singsong from under the table. "Morgan has the power now. I feel it. Symon wants it." Then, words that made Morgan's blood run cold and brought Barac lunging to his feet: "Symon found her. Found her. Symon saw her. Symon. Tasted her power. Symon wants it. Wants it for us. Symon says."

It never ended, Morgan thought, reaching an unsteady hand to support himself against Huido's cool bulk. No matter what you did or how far you ran, the unresolved nightmares of the past would strike again as they chose.

But never at Sira, he vowed, fighting for control, feeling the room sway as his rage and what he owned of hers fed on one another until Barac cried out and Sorl began to sob. Symon would never threaten Sira; never take her from him as he had taken everything else.

Not while Morgan lived. He drew a deep steadying breath. Another. He waved an apology to Barac, who stood glowering.

"Huido," he began, his voice failing, then offered one hand to the dark gap where the Carasian's eyes nestled to converge on him, with the exception of the two twisted to one side to keep an immovable fix on the whimpering Lacknee Sorl—Huido didn't allow anything to distract him from an enemy. The remaining eyes parted and Huido's daggerlike mouthparts emerged, needle tips pressing into the skin of Morgan's hand with exquisite gentleness. Apology and forgiveness went both ways.

Morgan found his voice, though it sounded strained to his own ears. "I always knew your heart was bigger than your head," he said, rapping one knuckle against the Carasian's carapace. "I don't need you to protect me from the past, Brother. Not anymore." The Human stared straight ahead, not seeing the galley of the *Fox*, instead gauging the depths of his emotions, coolly assessing his self-control and its cost. "I see the line, Huido," Morgan said at last, understanding completely what the Carasian feared, and knowing he had good reason for it. "I won't deny it's difficult holding back from it, or that I've—changed—but trust me to keep my head, okay?

"Now. Tell me all you know about Symon—" Morgan drew in a steadying breath "and when he met Sira."

Chapter 51

IT took me some time to realize Captain Rek's aircar was not taking us to the relative security of either the *Nokraud* or the *Makmora*. Since this had been our arrangement, an arrangement which would cost my Tribe an astronomical sum I could probably never repay in three lifetimes, I was less than happy with the discovery. But there was no doubt. That vast stretch of open water I could see through my viewport, broken by mats of floating reeds—Retian agriculture—and the occasional low-lying island, lay to the north of Jershi. We were flying in exactly the opposite direction.

"Wher—" the word lost itself in my dry mouth. I looked around in the back seat and spotted a flask of some liquid or other. It contained, I decided, rolling the liquid around my thick tongue gratefully, the remains of a fruit juice, now on its way to an afterlife as a fermented beverage. Spoiled or not, I relished every drop I retrieved.

I tried again, more successfully: "Where are we going, Captain Rek?"

The driver's seat was an arm's length in front of me. Rek swiveled her long head around to regard me out of those chilling yellow eyes. "Do not be alarmed, Fem Morgan. This–ss maneuver keeps–ss us–ss from the vids–ss of the ss–city and the Enforc–ssers–ss. I will turn us–ss s–ssoon. My adherents–ss on the *Nokraud* us–sse this–ss time to cons–ssolidate my new pos–ssition."

I didn't like the sound of that, especially with some of the Drapsk and Rael possibly still on board. "This new position, Captain. Has it anything to do with our agreement?"

She laughed, her jaws clattering in so rapid a movement that tiny froths of spittle appeared and trailed down the sides of her throat. Her tongue darted out to accurately recapture each speck. "You have a delic-ccious-ss s-ssensse of humor, Fem Morgan."

What I had, I thought with more than a little self-pity, gritting my teeth to endure another wave of sick pain, *was a probably serious medical problem, and the only being near enough to help was accustomed to ripping apart those weaker than herself.* Or otherwise disadvantaged. "You're taking over the *Nokraud* from Grackik," I speculated. "Her arrangement with Faitlen di Parth and the Baltir didn't include you."

"To be more precss–is–sse, Fem Morgan, Grackik s–ssupported thos–sse with whom s–sshe had s–ssuccessess–s in the pas–sst." A jaw snapped in punctuation. "I look to the pres–ssent. There I s–sse you in asss–cendancsse over your enemies–ss and Grackik's–ss bones–ss in your jaws–ss."

I sorted all this out, surprised to find I'd been paid a compliment. So while Rek had gladly taken my promise of payment, she'd actually thrown in with the faction she believed would ascend to topple the other—mine over Faitlen's. While I approved of her faith, I had yet to see much proof of it. But who was I to argue with this obviously cheerful Scat?

Maybe, I said to myself, *she knew something I didn't about the situation.*

Rek didn't bother telling me the details of her plan to "consolidate" the *Nokraud*, which was just as well. Holding up my end of any conversation was becoming more difficult by the hour. I hunted surreptitiously for more to drink or something to eat, but the flask had been the only litter left behind.

At least I could snatch bits and pieces of sleep, having wedged myself along both back seats—taking the precaution of pulling over a seat harness in case Rek had to do any more serious piloting than running a straight course over nothing. I assumed the aircar had sufficient fuel for all this—not a question to ask, since it implied a possible lack of foresight the Scat would doubtless find offensive. I could only hope.

Unfortunately, as I'd found, hope wasn't enough.

When the first bolt of energy shot past the aircar, illuminating the interior with a brilliant white glare, I remembered a

410 Julie E. Czerneda

saying Morgan had taught me: the only thing a Scat chases faster than profit is revenge.

As the second took out most of the side of the aircar, covering me with ash and debris the howling wind tore away, I spared a moment to regret my choice of ally.

As it turned out, I was too quick to dismiss Rek's value. Her piloting skills, whether natural or inspired by necessity, brought the crippled aircar down on an island—if the glimpse I had of a flat strip of grass-covered mud qualified it as such—without so much as a thud. The heart-stopping slide and sudden stop wrapped inside most of a very tough and spiny shrub was hardly worth mentioning. I was frankly amazed to have lived this long.

Another streak of brilliance, this one overhead and followed by a dull explosion. I was hardly an expert, but it appeared to me as though there were now two aircars fighting above us. I wished them both luck, having no idea which one shot us down—or which one might be potential rescue.

"Out!" came a hiss, the Scat bending over me and tearing me free of the harness, green blood oozing sluggishly from several small indentations in her concave chest, as well as a few on her throat and snout. The wounds didn't appear to slow her down, her movements lightning-swift and urgent.

I didn't hesitate to obey. It was unlikely whomever had downed us planned to leave us walking around. Well, I tried to obey, but doubled over the moment I stood in the wreckage. The world kept spinning as though we were still in an aircar plunging to the ground.

"Asssssht."

Rek lifted me with one easy movement, despite keeping a blaster rifle firmly in one clawed hand, cradling me against her wounded chest quite gently, although this meant I was being soaked with her blood. I had no intention of complaining, instead looking for some uninjured part of her upper body I could cling to with my hands and so support some of my own weight.

"Hold s—sstill."

So much for that. I made myself as still as possible, if that was the only help she wanted, looking up at the outsweep of her long fanged jaw a hand's breath from my throat. Beneath the odor of singed cloth and plas, I could detect a dry, dusty scent—not unpleasant, merely different.

Rek moved cautiously through the wreckage, once grabbing some other piece of equipment—most likely another weapon, but I couldn't quite see it without squirming—after slinging the rifle to her more intact shoulder. The heavy weapon banged against my knees with every step. Before leaving the wreck completely, she switched me and her bag to the grip of one incredibly strong arm, using her now-free hand to manipulate some controls on what remained of the control panel. "Gss–sst." This a more satisfied sound.

Then it was back up against her chest, a clamber and jump over the side of the aircar and we were on the island. Rek didn't slow down, in fact breaking into a loping run through the scorch-tipped reed grass, her body leaning forward so that I had to cover my face with my arms to keep the sharp-edged vegetation from cutting into my skin.

Whomp! Clumps of mud and pieces of equipment rained down all around us. Since Rek didn't miss a stride, I assumed the explosion from behind us had been planned and wasn't a renewal of the assault.

It must have been a relatively large island. The ground was level and smooth, if occasionally spongy underfoot so that one or the other of Rek's long clawed feet would sink deeper unexpectedly, drawing a hiss of anger from her and one of pain from me. When she noticed I was trying to protect myself from the grass, she tossed me around so I faced her chest. I was fascinated to see her wounds closing as I watched. They had been relatively shallow cuts, probably from the shrapnel formed by the shattering of the front end of the aircar, but regardless, it was amazing to see Rek healing even as she continued to run with the burden of my body and the weapons. Such an ability must have proved a definite asset to a species so prone to physical conflict throughout its evolution.

Despite the ground she covered, it could only have been minutes since the crash and explosion before Rek came to an unannounced stop, startling me out of a state of semiconsciousness. "This–ss will have to do," she said, putting me on the ground.

"This" was a hollow in the mud formed by the toppling of a

group of the wizened, moss-hung trees. I looked around, seeing this wasn't the start of a forest, but must be a part of the island raised sufficiently above the water table to allow clumps of these drier land plants to take root and survive—not that any of them appeared particularly healthy. There was a general odor of advancing rot corrupting the fresh scent of the water lapping at the shore a few steps away, as well as signs erosion would soon weaken the hold of the next clumps, already bending to touch the water with their branches. Some of their leaves lifted up and down with each tiny incoming wave, drowning slowly.

I peered up through the tangle of dying roots over my head. The sky was darkening—not night, but the usual afternoon downpour gathering itself. No sign of our attacker or the other aircar. *Yet.*

Rek didn't waste time looking around. She reached into what I could now see was the aircar's emergency pack, pulling out a packet she shook into a large piece of fabric. This she laid right over the puddle of stagnant water at the very bottom of the hollow, before nudging me with a foot. "Down there."

Rather than stand up, which I doubted I could manage anyway, I rolled myself down the little bit of slope onto the blanket. It was waterproof, I noticed with relief, though my landing had splashed some of the foul liquid over its edges. Rek followed me down, examining my position with a tilt of her heavy head, then she took the sides of the blanket and began wrapping me up like a body for burial—an image I thought unpleasantly apt.

"What are you doing?" I protested weakly, prepared to trust her judgment if only because I couldn't possibly resist it at the moment.

"This–ss cover has–ss reflective properties–ss," she answered calmly. "It will dis–ssrupt their s–sscans–ss for you." She twisted free a piece of root, using it to disturb the sides of the hollow so they dropped on my legs and body.

Oddly enough, I found I was more comfortable with every passing moment. The water beneath me acted like a soft mattress, while the blanket held in my body's heat. The extra layer Rek was busy applying added to the effect.

"What about you?" I mumbled, already half asleep from exhaustion and the druglike effects of being warm and motionless at last.

"I mus–sst res–sspond to this—ss challenge from my brood-kin," Rek explained, twisting her snout to check the sky. "I will eat her heart." She returned to her self-appointed task of en-shrining me, a process I was relieved stopped below my neck, then showed me how to pull the last excess of blanket over my head while leaving a gap to breathe.

The light covering wasn't a trap. Even though only one of my arms was easy to move, I tested it with my legs and knew I could wriggle myself free despite my weakness.

Rek rummaged in the pack, returning with a cylinder she pressed into the fingers of my free hand—I recognized it as a tube of emergency rations and felt my mouth water. "There is–ss only one, Fem Morgan," she warned. "Us–se it s–ssparingly."

"What do you want me to do, Captain?" I asked quietly.

"S–ssurvive until I return from victory, Fem Morgan. I will wis–ssh to collect my profit from our arrangement." Her jaws clattered together in a laugh—Scat humor. Spittle landed in a hot streak on my forehead; she considerately removed it with a quick flash of her tongue.

"I wish you success," I said, smiling myself at the irony. Of course, there really wasn't anything amusing about it. I would die here, appropriately already half-buried, if Rek failed in her bid for power—a bid that appeared to me in my ignorance to be a hopeless example of biological hardwiring overcoming com-mon sense.

Then there was always the outside chance of being found by the Retians—who, after all, knew their world—and returned to the Baltir. I didn't count that as surviving.

A click and sullen hum brought my attention back to Rek, checking over her rifle; she used the tip of a claw to tease a length of reed grass from its entanglement in the mechanism, her frills pulsing with the colors of excitement. I envied her that attitude.

"There," she said, swinging the weapon up in both hands. Her head tilted so those cold yellow eyes stared down at me. "If you have died before my return, Fem Morgan, I vow to eat the hearts–ss of your enemies–ss."

"Thank you," I said quite sincerely.

Before I could so much as blink, she was gone—moving with the intimidating speed of an unencumbered and motivated Scat.

I opened the ration tube, allowing myself one blissful mouthful before closing it and tucking it inside the Retian coat. Then I pulled the blanket over my head, beyond worrying if Rek's idea of camouflage would work and I wouldn't be used for target practice as I slept.

As I drifted into the darkness of utter exhaustion, I couldn't even bring myself to care if the island's wildlife might consider my rolled-up body as delightful a source of nourishment as I viewed my ration tube.

INTERLUDE

Ru?

Rael's eyes were open, but she couldn't see in the darkness. The lighting in the brig was under Drapsk control, not hers, and they'd called this night. But she didn't need light to sense the tentative touch on her shields, identifying its source with surprise.

And its existence. Had the Drapsk released her power? She attempted to port, stopped immediately by the feel of the unseen wall around her.

Where are you? There's a strange feel to your thoughts. So Ru could detect it as well. Rael didn't bother to explain, aware the Drapsk might detect and sever this link at any moment.

I found Sira, Rael sent back, knowing Ru would feel the worry and uncertainty under the thought. There was no hiding them had she wished to try. *She's in trouble. You must help us.*

Ica's been summoned to Council, Ru's response was stronger, almost a shout to Rael's inner sense, colored by outright fear. *They could come for me next. She has supporters. I have none.*

Pella?

Ran home at the first sign of trouble. What did you expect from her? They'll find her if they wish. You know their strength. How did this happen? We have been betrayed!

One of the disadvantages of communicating mind-to-mind was the difficulty of controlling what was sent. Rael knew what she'd revealed even before Ru's furious *You?* burned through her thoughts.

What you're doing is wrong, she sent, forcing her conviction past the anger beating at her. *You had to be stopped. Sira—*

You told her, too?

416 *Julie E. Czerneda*

She plans to help us, Ru. There has to be a better way. Sira can guide us.

A pause, but their link remained; Rael felt it carving deeper through the M'hir as they both supplied power to hold the opening between minds.

You made your decision. The words in her mind were ice-edged. *Now the rest of us have to live with it—or die by it.*

Die? What do you mean? Rael strengthened her shielding, though Ru was no threat to her.

We will listen to Sira. You haven't left us any other options. But we can't leave evidence for the Council. We can't allow them to condemn us, to stop our work, Ru sent, her thought distant, as though her mind busied itself with other things. *We can't leave the Human telepaths alive.*

Ru!

Rael knew her mental scream flung itself into the M'hir without a target; the link was already gone.

As were, she realized with a shudder, the lives of beings who had as much right to survival as the Clan. Ru would not hesitate to make good her threat.

Sira had finally taught her to care about Humans, Rael acknowledged to herself. She had even come to see something worth puzzling to understand in the far more alien Drapsk. She was no longer the xenophobic Clan she had been.

It was, she decided with a certain sense of self-pity, *a lousy moment to become broad-minded.*

Chapter 52

THE harsh voice sounded desperate, as if afraid I no longer listened: "You must Join."

The darkness was the womb from which I refused to be born, knowing all without plotted against me. I would fool them. I would stay here until I died and was safe.

"Fool!" hissed a voice, a cough and spit breaking the sound with pain. "Death is–ss no bargain."

The round globe of a Drapsk face floated past me, sprouting multiple eyes of shiny black that milled in disapproval. "See how you bleed? How you bleed? You bleed?"

A new voice, with the crackle and snap of a campfire behind it. "Will you abandon him? Do you think he will survive? Can either of you live alone?"

The darkness was a moist haven, a cradle gentled by music and touch. "Why do you care?" I shouted, fighting the growing urgency threatening its safety. "Why won't you leave me in peace?"

"Peace is a lie," they shouted back, the words echoing through me until I couldn't breathe, I was choking, I was . . .

I really was choking, I realized as I awoke to feel pressure against my face. I pushed at it frantically, fighting to free my mouth and nose. Something gave and I sucked in air with grateful heaves that sent reminders of pain through my body. Even as I took the saving breath, I was struggling to get out, thoroughly panicked by the thought of truly being buried here.

Somehow the blanket came away, freeing my head. I lifted my face to the pouring rain, opening my mouth to collect the drops, feeling the nightmare's fear fade into something more tangible.

It was night. I was half-buried in the hollow. The music in my dream had been the rain pounding on the blanket; there'd been sufficient to start filling the hollow. As I moved, it felt as though I was semi-floating.

As for my lack of air, the culprit humped itself hopefully back toward me. An ort-fungus, smaller than its town brethren, probably attracted by the ration tube in my coat to crawl over my face looking for a way inside the blanket. I was very grateful I'd awakened first. The formless, fuzzy masses had their charm, I supposed—the Retians gave them free rein in their households, perhaps as living vacuums—but I wasn't comfortable with the thought of close contact.

Larger organisms ate them, so in a way the presence of the pest was a sign that nothing more formidable had considered me as an appetizer while I slept.

Other imperatives of nature made me pull myself free of Rek's nest-building, those and a sudden trapped feeling I couldn't rationalize away. The night's sleep—a full night, I saw from the brightening of the horizon—had been the best thing I could have done. While my wounds were quick to remind me which muscles I wasn't allowed to use, the rest of me seemed ready to try.

Once I'd stood and limped around for a few minutes, I felt even better. At least I wasn't going to topple to the ground immediately. I freed the blanket from the muddy hollow, knowing its value. There wasn't any dry ground—prime real estate here—but I spread the lower half of the blanket over a platform formed by the fallen tree trunks and their branches. When I sat on it, carefully, and drew the remainder of the blanket over my head, I had a shelter from the worst of the rain.

My feet were bare, I noticed idly, stretching my legs out so the warm rain could work at the dirt, soot, and mud coating my skin, rolling my ankles so it struck between my toes as well.

Using one hand to hold the blanket under my chin, I pulled out the ration tube and allowed myself to savor two slow mouthfuls before placing it in one of the fastenable pockets of my blood-stained and filthy coat. *At least it wasn't my blood,* I consoled myself, deliberately not looking too closely, afraid of what I might find.

By virtue of this being the highest point on the island, and most of the trees along the shoreline having fallen or about to drop, I had a reasonably good view in three directions. It was, I discovered, quite beautiful here.

The clouds were breaking apart, the rain falling in isolated showers. Over the expanse of freshwater sea in front of me, I could make out five separate patches of churning water—a sixth shower sat stubbornly over my head.

At the far horizon, the sun's beams drove lances of pink and yellow up through the clouds, catching the outlines of upper layers as they sped by on a wind I couldn't feel down here. Most of the water was so calm it took the clouds and replayed them in its depths, confusing the eye as to where sky ended and its surface began. Tendrils of mist wove patterns binding the island's shoreline to those of more distant, smaller protrusions. I thought, gazing into the distance through my personal curtain of rain, I could make out the curve of the planet etched in water and the beginnings of light.

Closer at hand, the shoreline was a busier place. Fat raindrops cut their holes in the pondlike spaces left by the undermined trees. Insects of some type jigged and danced on the calm surface wherever an overhanging branch acted as an umbrella. As I watched, entranced by this view of Ret 7 that didn't consist of mud or threat, a larger something, about the size of my thumb, drifted among the insects, snapping up a tasty jiggler with one gulp. It rose to the surface, allowing me to see its legs and arms hanging limply as it rested.

There was something very familiar about that pop-eyed stare and wide, rippled mouth. I bowed my head to it politely, positive I was looking at a very young Retian—a survivor of the first, most harrowing, stage of its life. It took sensible alarm at the motion, ducking back under the surface and propelling itself deep into the muddy bottom with kicks of its legs. I wished it luck.

Then I looked out at the vast inland lake with sudden comprehension. No wonder the Retians protected their land—or rather its watery coating—so fiercely against ownership by outworlders. It was as valid a form of parental care as the blatant offspring worship of Human parents.

My hand flattened over my abdomen, supplying a light soothing pressure. There was, I granted grudgingly, reason for the Clan to be so desperate, to act with such disregard for individuals. It was at the root of every being's existence: to have a living future. That, as Morgan would say, did not make it right. There had to be other choices, better methods. Some costs were simply too high for an intelligent race to bear.

He had taught me that—while I had been teaching him warfare and defense. Morgan saw every being as an individual and, despite the differences which made him spend much of his life alone, he valued others. It no longer surprised me he'd risked his own life to save mine before we'd even known one another. Now, it would surprise me more, knowing the measure of the Human, to expect anything less.

He would, I thought, *approve of my helping the Drapsk.* He would approve of my decision to try and help the Clan.

I allowed myself another mouthful from the tube, refusing to think about how long Rek had been gone or the number of mouthfuls left before I was reduced to hunting with the locals for nourishment.

Morgan would approve, I told myself, then allowed myself to be honest.

I might never know.

INTERLUDE

The *Makmora*'s trader's lounge was huge for a starship, suited to any gathering the Drapsk engineers could imagine. It had to be, to fit all those interested in this meeting.

Morgan sat at the head of the long bench-like table four Drapsk had magically produced from the deck. At any other time he would have lingered, fascinated by everything about the small, relatively unknown beings and their beautiful ship.

Today, he kept his hands in plain view, his weapon holstered, and his knives loose in their concealed sheaths.

To his immediate left sat Rael, her lovely face set and drawn into an expression of despair so deep he had been afraid to ask her what had happened. There'd been no chance for private conversation; the Drapsk had marched her into the meeting without a word, and two stood in apparent guard behind her, antennae rigidly upright. He was tempted to reach into her thoughts, but Huido had warned both him and Barac of the devices of the Drapsk.

Another amazing revelation Morgan would normally have found totally absorbing, had so much else not been at stake.

Barac was to his left, fully back in his charming, urbane role as former Clan Scout and spy, somehow able to make even a borrowed pair of spacer coveralls look tailored. His dark eyes roamed ceaselessly, but his expression was one of a partygoer ready to enjoy the revels. Morgan knew nothing was farther from the truth. Barac took the ambitions of Lacknee Sorl very personally indeed.

Huido amply filled out the list of those Morgan considered part of his contingent. The Carasian had finally worked out an arrangement with the Drapsk, who'd reacted to his arrival with distinctly counterproductive joy. Once convinced to stop climb-ing on his arms and back, they'd created a special seat for him from the cooperative flooring of the room, supplying a low stool for Lacknee Sorl next to it—Huido having assumed responsi-bility for guarding their reluctant guest, and neither Morgan nor Barac inclined to argue. It had apparently required twenty Drapsk to escort Huido and his responsibility to their seats, though by now Morgan suspected this was so more of the un-usual beings could touch the Carasian before they left.

Even now, there were three of them draped over Huido's back, having sneaked into the room as things settled, chubby little hands holding on to the ridges of his carapace for security. More information to file away until the business at hand was done.

The Drapsk response to Morgan had been odd as well. They'd rushed forward, exclaiming in delight when he'd first arrived, only to halt so suddenly several collided with one another. They had stood, just out of reach, antennae rigidly pointing at him and tentacles disappearing into their mouths. After a difficult mo-ment of silence, during which Huido grumbled something about "ridiculous featherheads," the Captain had reluctantly offered his hand in a politely Human greeting. Morgan's initial reaction had been to wonder darkly if the Drapsk had truly wanted him found, or if they preferred to keep their Mystic One to themselves.

When he whispered this suspicion into Huido's elbow on their way to the lift, the Carasian had said very seriously, if cryptically: "They are glad you are safe, Brother. It's only that your grist has the smell of—well, something I wouldn't serve in the restaurant. It will pass once you are yourself again." Morgan had to settle for this somewhat insulting reassurance.

The rest of the seats to Morgan's right were filled with Drapsk, starting with Captain Makairi and a very differently colored Drapsk referred to as the Skeptic Copelup. In some manner, this Drapsk belonged to Sira, or Sira was in his care. Comspeak, while a marvelous compromise language allowing commerce and communication among hundreds of species, entailed a certain creative flexibility of meaning when it came to details of relationships.

Which was why their frequent reference to Sira as the Mys-tic One, and to her as one of their Tribe—though not the Skep-tic's Tribe—made matters murkier instead of clearer.

What he could rely on, Morgan thought to himself, was that these beings cared about Sira and were more than ready to act on her behalf in famed Drapsk fashion—if they were given a target.

The two groups on the other side of the table, however, had different priorities altogether. First after Rael and her guards sat Sector Chief Lydis Bowman, representing the not-inconsiderable force of the Trade Pact Enforcers. Her interests were never totally revealed, Morgan knew, not even to the trusted constables at her side, Russell Terk and P'tr wit 'Whix. What brought her to this table was, on the surface, a regrettable suspicion about himself as a murderer—not normally part of an Enforcer's role, but she was more than willing to bend rules when one of her own contacts was the victim. Morgan nodded a greeting and received a challenging raised eyebrow in return. *Murder,* he decided uneasily, *was likely the least of her interests here.*

Which left Retian Port Authority, the arm of the local law responsible for dealing with violations of Ret 7's regulations by outworlders, represented here by three pink-lipped and non-committal Retians: Lord Lispetc and two others, introduced as his aides, Keerick and Mesnbatc. The aides were dressed in the drab hooded robes used by Collectors, the Retian officials enti-tled to reclaim property or person in the event of crime or tax evasion; their faces were customarily kept in shadow so only their expressive lips showed. It was understood by those pre-sent that these individuals were not the servants they seemed to be but rather interested parties to whatever negotiations were planned—understood with the exception of the Retians them-selves, who persisted in believing they fooled aliens with this strategy.

No doubt of the interest there, Morgan knew. Lispetc doubt-less remembered Morgan's *Fox* and her crew from the fiasco with sabotaged com parts a year ago. That Lispetc hadn't been charged for payment may not have compensated for the loss of face among his peers.

Meeting the Retians and the others here, on the *Makmora,* had been a calculated risk. Barac had been dead set against it, thanks to Huido's less-than-discreet and quite smug announce-ment that the Drapsk would be able to lock any Clan out of the

M'hir, preventing convenient vanishing. But Morgan convinced the Clansman by his own willingness to go where there was no possibility of retreat. It was a desperate toss of the dice, with his own freedom on the line. He thought, with luck, the gamble would be worth it.

Morgan needed to learn all that these others knew, he needed to clear away the obstacles keeping him from dealing with Sira's enemies, and, most of all, he needed all the help he could get to search for Sira without drawing the attention of her enemies to them both. This ship and Sira's plumed allies were the glue bringing all of these disparate groups together.

First things first.

"Greetings," Morgan said in a penetrating voice, shutting down the murmur of conversation in the room—mostly Drapsk complimenting Huido anyway. "I am Captain Jason Morgan of the *Silver Fox*, Karolus Registry. I am not a murderer." He raised one hand in a gesture to Huido. The Carasian nudged a thoroughly disheveled Lacknee Sorl to his feet.

"Sliced them, I did," Sorl blurted in a voice loud enough to carry throughout the room. "Had to slice them. Morgan talks to us, no one else. Symon told me so. Had to stay with Morgan. Had to follow. Sliced them all."

Morgan's eyes had been on those hearing this confession. He saw the flicker of recognition in Terk's face the moment Sorl rose to his feet, the Enforcer leaning his bulk right over the lap of his partner 'Whix in order to whisper urgently in Bowman's ear. She waved him back dismissively, 'Whix supplying a ruffle of irritated feathers. Morgan half-smiled.

"Who is 'all'?" Bowman asked, directing her question at Morgan. "Have we been remiss in our body count?"

"There was a Clansman on Plexis: Larimar di Sawnda'at by name." This from Barac. He and Morgan had agreed to give her the information; it was better than being accused later of withholding it. Morgan never underestimated Bowman's ability to turn over the heaviest rocks in search of her answers. She didn't bother writing down the name. Morgan suspected she'd had a recorder implanted—he remembered the days when she carried a worn noteplas with her everywhere, before becoming one of the brass. Maybe even a transmitter—his audience, Morgan suddenly realized, might be considerably larger than those in this room, unless the *Makmora* had some sophisticated jamming tech.

"Where's the corpse?" This inconvenient question came from Terk, of course.

Barac looked over at Huido, whose eyes milled around as if the Carasian were busy memorizing the layout of the lounge from ceiling to floor. "Let's say, it's not available for autopsy. But he was killed by a force blade used with—" the Clansman paused as if considering present company, "—some creativity."

Bowman tapped her finger on the tabletop. "A Clansman. Killed by this Human. With a force blade."

"Did it," Lacknee Sorl offered, nodding his head until his sparse hair flew back and forth. "Symon knows."

The Enforcer's eyebrow rose. "And who is this Symon?"

The question, Morgan noted without surprise, having seen the reaction for himself, sent Sorl into a state of almost convulsive muttering, hands on the top of his head as though in sudden agony. "Secret. Secret. Secret. Secret. . . ." Huido gave him a none-too-gentle rap on the shoulder, startling Sorl into silence.

"I may be able to answer this query, Sector Chief," 'Whix suggested, then waited for Bowman's brusque nod of permission before continuing: "He may be referring to a Renford T. Symon. This is a Human I have been tracking, the rumored leader of a growing faction of malcontents and, frankly, less reputable Human telepaths."

Morgan had already braced himself. This was no time to show any reaction to Symon's name—no matter how the mere thought of his betrayer made his blood burn inside and his rage batter at his control.

'Whix had gone on to say: "There have been reports of his spreading influence among other telepaths as well. My contacts believe Symon's group is paying for any information about ways to increase their telepathic abilities. They obtain funding for this payment—" here the Tolian's dry voice took on a decidedly disapproving tone, "—through illicit use of these abilities."

"Indeed."

"Chief Bowman," Lord Lispetc spoke up, his Comspeak deliberately thick and accented, as befitted one of the aristocracy. "I see no point wasting my time on this diversion into your Human politics. If you are satisfied this Morgan entity is innocent of the shedding of blood on our world, I will—reluctantly—accept your judgment. It was, after all, not a Retian involved. But there remains the more serious charge of espionage." He reached imperiously to one of his aides, Keerick, that worthy leaning forward to pass a plas sheet to his Lordship. A portion of Keerick's face showed in the light.

"Espionage?" Bowman looked at Morgan. "Are you aware of this charge, Captain Morgan?"

"No," Morgan started to say, then he hesitated as Barac's sending blasted into his mind. *That Retian is Baltir!* Simultaneously, every Drapsk in the room became alert, plumes tilting toward the Clansman.

"That is to say," Morgan continued smoothly, drawing on every bit of self-control he possessed to maintain that illusion of calm—to fight the burning desire to throw a force blade down a certain wide throat, "I wasn't sure if you were taking Port Authority into your full confidence, Sector Chief. About the investigation into the allegations of illegal research into humanoid biology—" Once he started, Morgan found it easier. The terrified pallor of the Retian's lips helped immensely. "—being carried out at the Baltir facility in Jershi."

There was a singular beauty in the way Bowman could take a lead and run with it. "We hadn't decided to release the details yet, Captain, as you so rightly caution," she said without blinking an eye. 'Whix was breathing very slowly, countering his tendency to pant when events took unexpected turns. Terk merely looked at Morgan with an expression promising a few broken bones if this gambit caused his boss any trouble.

Morgan opened his mouth, then hesitated again. The Drapsk had all stood, antennae erect, and were fluttering—there was no other word for it—their plumes toward the Retians. Even the ones crooning over Huido had slid down to copy this stance.

Captain Makairi spoke, his voice measured and low: "One of you comes from this place. You. The one called Keerick. We smell Makii—our Mystic One—on your skin." As one, the Drapsk turned to focus their attention on the Retian Barac had identified as Baltir. Morgan was impressed.

Baltir wasn't. He stood, backing away from them all, his protruding eyes wide with alarm, his hands raised and flexed so the poison spurs showed white in threat. "Lord Lispetc. I insist we leave. These aliens, these others—they conspire against me, against my great work. You can see that."

Lord Lispetc, who knew very well which side of this debate to take in a room containing the highest official of the Trade Pact within five days' translight, kept his lips shut tight and his wrinkled body firmly on its stool. His eyes blinked, one at a time, then closed completely in a Retian statement of disinvolvement. The other Retian immediately followed suit.

Baltir, perhaps knowing who was the true threat to his continued existence, launched himself not at Bowman or any of the Drapsk, but onto the table, in a lunge at Morgan.

The Drapsk acted immediately, hurrying toward Baltir with enthusiasm if little regard for personal safety. Terk was faster. As 'Whix knocked aside a protesting Bowman, the massive Human swept his longs arms around the Retian's legs, bringing him down just short of where Morgan sat, statue-still.

Morgan's perception of time became peculiarly stretched. He saw Baltir sliding toward him, mouth agape in surprised fury, clawed hands outstretched with their poison ready, before being dragged to a stop by Terk. He felt the vibration of the *Makmora*'s flooring as Huido thundered toward him. He saw Bowman shrug herself out of 'Whix's protective hold, her weapon already in her hand.

Yet there was time to think, to snap his wrist and drop down the force blade, to plan. *Which eye to carve out first?* he wondered. Had the left one seen more of Sira's pain or the right? *Which hand had held the knife?* Where in the mind should he cut out the memory of her agony?

Morgan blinked. The Retian's broad, wrinkled face had become something else, someone else. The soft throat between his fingers lost its wattle, becoming firmer, bristled with a day's growth of beard.

Ren Symon!

The force blade whined as if in hunger. Morgan bared his teeth, feeling an incredible rush of pleasure as he bent to take his own revenge in blood. He knew without doubt that none here would stop him. They couldn't—all this was happening in the space of a breath.

He was only defending himself.

Then, like some cataclysm had whirled within his mind, peeling away layers of emotion, the darkness and rage were gone. In their place rested the memory of a face, inexpressibly dear to him, perfectly clear as though Sira stood between him and the cowering being at his mercy.

No, Morgan realized, dropping his hold on the Retian, staggering back until he felt a wall. It wasn't a memory.

It was *her* voice in his thoughts.

Good-bye, my love . . . a whisper.

Forgive me . . . silence.

Chapter 53

THEY had drained me of almost all I had. I accepted it, too full of the joy of touching Morgan's mind at last to care about the cost.

It had been the only choice, the right choice. I rolled my head over to gaze at the ort-fungus waiting nearby. Others hung in the branches or floated at the shoreline like the foam produced from rotting leaves. They were polite scavengers. I was dying; they were patient.

Rek hadn't come back. I'd spent the long day resting, drinking only from water I knew had fallen as rain that morning and so was less likely to be full of the abundant life that existed everywhere else. I checked it for eyes out of habit. The ration tube lasted until the noon hour. I saw nothing at all appetizing near me and was too weak to travel farther.

I'd hidden myself once, pulling the by-now well soiled blanket over me as a Retian mudcrawler—a large one, perhaps a farming machine by the sound—sent its broad wake surging against the fragile shore, washing another layer of the island from the roots of its few embattled trees. There was no sign they were interested in my refuge, though the marks of the aircar crashing farther along the island must have been plain. Possibly they guessed them the result of a grass fire set by lightning, an unimportant event to a species focused on the water and its bounty.

My middle burned like fire. I didn't remember this particular pain from the earlier attack—if indeed Baltir had performed the same or a similar operation on my flesh, and I wasn't simply suffering the lack of care given to me by Withren and her villagers. The thought of my own flesh beginning to rot under the

medplas haunted me. At times, I imagined the stench rising
from any disturbance of the black soggy ground arose from me.

It was at sunset, well past the most pessimistic estimate I'd
made about Rek's return, when I recognized the final choice I
faced. The ort-fungus who had stayed near me, I thought in
hopes of my dropping the ration tube, had been joined over the
hours by a host of others. They busied themselves with fallen
leaves and litter along the shore, never approaching me, but I
knew why they had come. Scavengers survive by being able to
spot the weak and the dying. My choice? To save my strength
in order to thwart them for another night at best, or spend it.

I had not forgotten Morgan. There wasn't a moment of the
time I was alone when my awareness of him dimmed or faded.
Our minds might not be Joined, but I knew a closeness to him
that had to be more.

As I'd promised Huido, I owed Morgan his freedom from
my rage, from the vow I'd made him take: to seek my enemies,
to retrieve what was stolen. I no longer cared about the first,
and I had taken care of the second myself.

So I thanked the ort-fungi for their patience, wrapped myself
in my blanket where I could see tomorrow's sunrise if I lived,
and opened my heart and soul to the M'hir without hesitation
or fear.

Morgan!

I poured power into my search regardless of the frenzied
gathering of the M'hir life-forms, continuing as they instantly
fastened their cavernous mouths on the stream of energy and
sucked it to a pale shadow. What remained, as long as I could
feed it, sought the mind, the golden place that was both part of
me and someone else.

There! His presence blinded me, a brilliance drawing me near
even as I recognized with grief and regret the heaving walls of
emotion binding his power and thoughts. I tossed away my last
shields, massing all I was into a *reaching,* pulling back to me
all the rage, absorbing it, shunting it aside, furiously clearing
away anything standing between us.

Until I stared at the perfection of my Morgan in the M'hir,
feeling once more his caring, his need for me. Nothing of what
lay between us had been lost or destroyed. If I'd had eyes here,
I would have wept with the joy of it.

Until I felt the rising of the Power-of-Choice within me, heard its dark, wet demand for the Test, and knew I couldn't stay.

Good-bye, my love, I sent to him. *Forgive me.*

Somehow, I twisted free of those feeding on my power; somehow, I found my way back.

Morgan would be all right; I knew that now.

I closed my eyes.

It had been, in the end, all I'd ever needed to know.

INTERLUDE

It wouldn't happen! It couldn't!

The litany repeated itself over and over in Morgan's mind, as if his protest had the power to force away his fear, thrust away the feel of Sira's touch, so warm and real, fading away to nothingness, her vast strength exhausted.

She wasn't dead. He didn't dare accept the possibility.

If sheer will could have hurried the Enforcers' aircar, they would have broken the sound barrier before lifting from the ship-city. As it was, Morgan stood behind Terk's pilot seat, clenching the back of it with his hands until the knuckles were white.

'Whix, in the nav chair, kept rolling one eye toward him as though expecting Terk to protest this proximity. But the big Human merely found a little more speed, ripping through lanes of opposing traffic with a recklessness that suggested he'd only been waiting for an excuse. The aircar, mostly engine and weaponry, much of it likely Trade Pact secrets, was the best available in the quadrant. Bowman made sure of her equipment as well as her people.

She'd been sure of Morgan, coming to him as he sobbed, half-broken by the strain of finding then losing the other part of himself. She'd held him, he remembered dimly, as though he'd taken some blow in a fight and needed comfort while awaiting the meds. Her voice came back clearly enough: ordering the Drapsk in no uncertain terms to allow Rael and Barac full use of their abilities to help, assuming control of both prisoners—if Huido would move his crusty hide—and would Lord Lispetc prepare himself to immediately accompany a battalion of her troops to see firsthand what was going on in the Baltir? A visit, she added, to which the angry Drapsk were not invited.

Morgan should have been grateful, but stood numbly as others took control of the situation. The aircar arrived within seconds, depositing a pilot and two guards for Bowman, scooping up himself, the two Enforcers, and Rael.

Minutes only, but minutes might be too long. Barac and Rael had agreed vehemently with the Drapsk, that to use the Talent to go to Sira would only lure Faitlen to her just as quickly. So now they hurried at Human speed.

Morgan kept his own power tightly inside, hoarding his strength for what might lie ahead. Rael was their key. She'd picked up the scent of her sister's power in the M'hir and now guided 'Whix and so Terk with graceful gestures of her long white hand.

"There!" she called out, pointing ahead. Terk grunted, slowed their rush through the air, then pushed a control to release the aircar's portlights, sending them soaring outward, their broad white beams slicing through the night. Water. Water. Then a shoreline, reed grass burned in a long streak, wreckage—Morgan heard 'Whix muttering into a com—then the edge of a tiny forest, dwarf trees toppled this way and that, as though tossed by a giant before taking root.

"We'll land back at the wreckage," Terk began, slowing the aircar even more and beginning a banking turn.

Morgan didn't listen. His every sense insisted Sira was below them—and there was no time left. His hand was already on the latch to the emergency door. He heaved it open with one quick jerk.

Then threw himself out into the darkness.

Chapter 54

A LOUD splash brought me closer to consciousness again. I cracked open one eye, seeing light, and congratulated myself on lasting until dawn.

The splash had an echo; several echoes. Weight shifted off my legs as the orts abandoned their perch; I'd felt no discomfort with them there, but now my skin itched fiercely, as though inflamed.

What was coming? I fought waves of dizziness, quite sure I didn't want to die in the jaws of something slimy and large. If I wanted that kind of ending and still had the strength, I could *push* myself into the M'hir. There was, naturally, nothing I could do about either.

"Sira!"

Much better, I thought, relaxing and letting the darkness creep over me again. To fade away dreaming of Morgan's voice? My mind was kinder to me than I'd imagined.

"Sira!? Answer me!"

I smiled, sinking deeper. What a convincing dream.

Sira, wait for me. I'm here! His sending flooded my thoughts, pulling me away from that brink like a spray of cold water wakes a sleeper.

This, I told my subconscious, was going too far. How could I die peacefully with—

With someone dripping all over me? With urgent hands lifting me up?

I opened both eyes. The light was too harsh to be part of the afterlife I'd planned on and the face of my love, so close to mine, was too haggard, dirty, and scared to be anything but real.

"They'll be here in a few minutes with the med gear," Morgan was saying, the words coming out hard and fast, as though he needed the reassurance more than I. I probably, I thought, looked alarmingly like a corpse—and a freshly buried one.

"I'm sor—" My voice was another part of me in advanced shutdown, I discovered.

My dear Human wasn't really listening. I endured the discomfort of having the feeling restored to my arms and legs as he straightened them. I heard him curse under his breath as he eased open the blood- and mud-encrusted coat—suspecting the worst, I was sure, and finding it.

With each second, I moved closer to wanting to live and farther from being sure I could. I managed to twitch the fingers of my right hand. He saw, taking it immediately in his own. The warmth of his hand, even wet, was almost more than I could bear. *Jason,* I sent through that touch, giving him again all that I was, all that I felt.

He returned it, multiplied a thousand times by his own. Loving and loved, I drifted deeper into the darkness—knowing what was happening, I tried to push him back. This was not a journey he could follow.

No! he sent, the denial seeming to come from his very core.

Power . . . raw, unrestrained, forced into my mind as though I were drowning and Morgan tried to breathe his own life into my lungs. I grabbed at it, feeling the unbelievable as my body absorbed the energy and began to fight its way back.

With it came the eager tide of blackness; I was helpless as the Power-of-Choice surged through the link to smash against Morgan's outpouring of strength. We whirled into the M'hir together . . .

I was the center of all things, the glow around which all else revolved. I would fight to keep out the Other. This was my domain.

The Power-of-Choice, my deadly gift from the M'hir, lashed out. There was no memory here of who tried to save me—no cause except the Test.

The blow was met by one with the will and power to match it.

A struggle, endless, yet over in an instant. I resounded with desire, sensing completion at last . . .

Too late. I was lost, dying. Power bled from me in countless streams, to feed countless mouths.

I was empty, a husk, a need . . .

A flicker of brightness. I *reached,* feeling power flowing toward me, replenishing with a shock tasting of joy.

Another. I *reached* again. And again. It was as though there could never be enough of the flickers to satisfy me, yet there were always more to hold.

In the distance, if there was distance in this place, the streams of my bleeding power began to merge, seeking a new destination. One by one, then by their thousands, the feeders lost interest and faded away. The last, largest and with a mouth seeming to hold all of the darkness of the M'hir, passed through me as it left, leaving behind the taste of fate.

The M'hir was abruptly empty of all but pathways of power, crisscrossing its black eddies and depths in the closest this place could ever come to peace. Brightest of all were the ties of power newly forged between us, more real to my other sense than all the other pathways combined.

I was whole. And I was more. As I reeled with the delirious wonder of it all, I knew what Morgan and I had achieved.

I *pushed* . . .

Beyond all of my fear and on the edge of death, we had Joined.

. . . I opened my eyes to the solid, smelly world of Ret 7, and met the wondering eyes of my love, feeling the warm link between us in that other place as the way it should be and would be as long as we lived.

"Is everyone all right?" a deep voice shouted, causing the ort-fungi hanging overhead to drop to the ground and hump away in disappointment. "Morgan, if you ever pull a stunt like that again when I'm flying—" The voice trailed away.

"S'okay," I croaked cheerfully, my right hand squeezing Morgan's as tightly as I could. "Not dead yet."

"And that better be a promise," my love whispered, chill wet lips brushing mine, before standing to take part in greeting an astonishing assortment of beings and equipment.

I decided it was high time to faint and let Morgan take care of everything.

So I did.

INTERLUDE

"Yes, yes. They're both all right. Will you stop asking me?" Barac took longer strides to keep ahead of the anxious Carasian.

The Drapsk were just as bad. Everyone here seemed to think he was some sort of animated com system. The aircar had a perfectly good one of its own, he was tempted to retort to the next anxious query.

Except that the news from Rael was so much better than he'd hoped, it was worth retelling—at least a few more times.

"Are you ready, Clansman?"

"At your service, Chief," he said, amazed, as always, by Bowman's ability to move faster than anyone else when she chose, without seeming to hurry at all.

They joined a growing bustle of activity around the *Makmora*'s fins, Bowman's chosen staging ground. Three Port Authority aircars were already loading their share of battle-suited Enforcers, having sent armed Retians to provide a local presence in the massive troop transport. Lord Lispetc stood in the center of it all, snapping orders as though this virtual assault by offworlders on a facility within his capital city had his full support—surely an unusual attitude for a Retian of any caste.

When Barac mentioned as much to Bowman, she smiled cryptically, her keen eyes darting over the organized confusion. "Lispetc's only chance to come out of this whole is to seem to be in charge." Her smile turned into something closer to real humor. "Besides. You move fast enough, the action sweeps up even those who'd protest otherwise. Speed and decision, Clansman. That's the key."

Barac took one last look around before entering the lead aircar behind Bowman, her personal guards, and Lord Lispetc. Would all this be fast enough to catch Faitlen di Parth, Second Level Adept, member of the Clan Council?

That remained to be seen.

Chapter 55

THE universe had shifted itself obligingly in my absence. I could tell by the way I woke up—dizzied by a familiar duality of sensation. There were two pulses in my wrists, two heart-beats almost in synch—a comforting perception of another I dimmed with the ease of long practice before opening my eyes to what my body had already told me.

"How do you feel?" Morgan asked, his blue eyes dark with emotion. He wasn't smiling. I understood, knowing my Human would take longer to recover his inner balance. I smiled contentedly for us both.

"Clean," I said, surprised when my voice came out reed-thin. "Where are we?" A ship's med station, I'd known from my only glance away from his dear face.

"Bowman's cruiser: *Conciliator*."

I suspected a joke, but his expression remained serious. *There were ways to deal with that,* I said to myself, sending a touch of warmth through the link between us, rewarded by the softening of his eyes. His hand cupped my cheek, and I turned my face to plant a kiss in its palm, blinking to keep from showing any tears.

"Ah, the Mystic One wakes!" This was all the warning I had before I was buried in a blizzard of purple plumes; the Drapsk were delightedly fluttering over Morgan as well—I saw him look pleasantly surprised before he sneezed.

I spotted a pair of yellow plumes and said, "Copelup?"

They all pulled back immediately, letting me see the Skeptic. His bright red tentacles were in a happy ring around his mouth. Typically, he didn't waste any time berating me: "You should have listened to the Makii. And to me. We warned you not to leave the safety of the Tribe. If it weren't for Captain Morgan—"

"I know," I interrupted, rubbing my cheek into the hand still against my face.

"Ignore him," said a Makii wearing the ribbon denoting my old friend, Makoori. Though pleased to see any of them, I wondered what a tailor was doing as part of a delegation to Bowman's ship. "We rejoice with you in your reconnection to the Scented Way and to one another, Mystic One," Makoori continued. "The moment was one of great joy for all Makii."

I looked suspiciously at the group of ten or so Makii, checking the ribbons of the others. I didn't see Makairi. Maka was there, but he had a shoulder bag bulging with instruments. "Where's the Captain?" I asked, guessing the answer.

"But I am the Captain, Mystic One," Makoori said with chagrin. "Do you not know me?"

Copelup hooted, and I glared at him. "Gripstsa," I concluded. "When did the—happy event—take place?"

Maka spoke up: "We were all suffering from the shame of your capture and imprisonment, O Mystic One. Then there was the overwhelming joy of your rescue! There was no other way to recover our efficiency." Copelup hooted again, implying that at least one of the Drapsk had been able to keep his sense of proportion through it all. Or had he merely been without a partner?

Gripstsa? the word echoed in my thoughts and the Drapsk reacted by flipping their antennae toward Morgan.

So much for private conversation. "So you're the new med, Maka?" I asked politely, now remembering where I'd seen that bag of equipment before. Under the words, I delighted the Drapsk by sending Morgan my knowledge of the ceremony and its purpose in a quick burst.

For the first time, his expression lightened. "And you know everything about your new roles on the ship?" Morgan asked, eyes bright with curiosity. "Have there ever been cases of unsuccessful transfer? How do—"

"Captain Morgan. What is going on here? My patient needs rest, not a party!" The voice was stern, but the broad and friendly smile on the face of the Human female entering with two assistants belied its tone. All three wore the tech version of the Enforcer uniform, more like Morgan's spacer garb than the official-looking outfit Bowman and her constables showed off-ship. "How are you, Fem Morgan?"

"We wish you to tell us, Med Ginazhi," Captain Makoori insisted.

"That's what I'm here to determine. If you don't mind waiting outside?"

Morgan leaned his hip against my bed, definitely planning to stay, I realized with a sigh of relief. "I'll be here," he told the Drapsk, correctly assuming this would raise the drooping antennae.

I drew in a slow, deep breath, stopping when the flash of pain across my middle announced there was no doubt I was in the right place, with the right beings.

Which was why I wished Morgan and I could be anywhere else.

"Do you think I like it?" Morgan's voice approached a shout, startling us both. "Sira," he went on, quieter, but no less determined, "we have the expertise here, willing to help."

"He's done enough helping," I snarled, unable to restrain the anger I felt before it ripped through the M'hir between us. Morgan bore it with a tightening of his lips that said he felt the same.

Med Ginazhi had retired to wait in the next room, with the subject of this debate and the three grim-faced guards assigned to him. We didn't, she had told us bluntly, have much time to waste.

My feelings had been plain on the matter, given I'd screamed inside and out upon waking from a light dozing state to see Baltir looming over me.

They'd taken him away immediately; a process made swifter by Morgan literally throwing the Retian out the door, but Ginazhi had been right back in to explain to me.

The feeding burns of the ort-fungi, dehydration, and shock had been easily corrected. But the med was beyond her depth in repairing or even understanding what the Retian scientist had done to my insides. She wanted him to assist her.

Keerick. I now knew the name Baltir scorned to use, as if it made any difference. He was more than willing to participate. I knew why, if the Enforcer didn't; Baltir wanted to see the results of whatever experiment he'd conducted.

I would, I'd told her, trust her best efforts. I would not tolerate the Retian's touch on me again.

Morgan wasn't satisfied with that decision, which was why he'd asked the med to leave us for a moment. "Listen to me, Sira," he said, pulling up a wheeled stool so he could sit beside me, his hand warm on mine. "Regardless of his motives and methods, this being possesses the knowledge to repair what he's done to you."

"Jason," I pleaded, "Don't ask me this."

His face took on the implacable cast I knew so well. "The med can't guarantee you'll survive without his intervention. Are you willing to see us both die?"

The thought made me hold tighter to our Joining, reassure myself it remained whole and his presence was with me. "You never fight fair, Captain Morgan," I said, giving in, as he knew I would.

He didn't smile. "Consider it an order, chit."

Morgan called the rest of them back in immediately, perhaps fearing I'd change my mind if he delayed. The med had been sure enough of his ability to sway my decision that she and her assistants, as well as Baltir, were in their surgical gear, sterile fields glistening over their hands, arms, and faces. Two guards took up stations at the door, while the third hovered behind the Retian. Baltir ignored him, his wavy lips purple with anticipation.

"That's my spot," Morgan said in a flat, dangerous voice. The guard backed away, letting Morgan take her place. There was a faint whine as a force blade energized. I saw Baltir's lips pale to pink, his eyes protruding further, if that were possible. I could almost feel sorry for him.

Rest, Sira, Morgan sent to me, the absolute assurance of my safety in his thoughts enough to let me close my eyes on my personal nightmare.

INTERLUDE

Morgan wasn't sure which was worse, after a while: listening to the Retian's paper-dry voice discussing what he'd done to Sira and the results, as though he were lecturing to some group of admiring students, or hearing the sounds of the surgery into Sira's flesh. Both promised to become nightmares.

It did help to focus on the fold of gray skin marking the part of the Retian's knobby spine he planned to sever first if anything went remotely awry.

Med Ginazhi, her face pale and set, asked the questions Morgan knew needed answers—both for Sira's sake and that of the recording the Retian had been amply warned was being made. Baltir answered freely, as if the collecting of evidence against him and his work were some sort of validation of its worth.

"During the first—operation—you removed the egg-producing organs themselves," she confirmed again, seeming to have difficulty accepting what she was hearing.

"Yes, yes. But not completely. These humanoids, they call themselves the M'hiray, are a theta-class species, but have unusual internal adaptations related to the delayed reproductive state of their immature females. As you can see here, and here—" Morgan's hand shook and the Retian flinched. "Careful!"

"You were saying," Ginazhi urged him, her glance to Morgan full of complete understanding.

"There are three masses in which fertile eggs are produced and stored in a dormant state. We found this state ideal for transport, if difficult at first to overcome in the lab. But," he added with a note of satisfaction, "we were able to induce growth and chromosome doubling in ten percent of the tissue obtained."

"Stolen," Morgan gritted out between his teeth. "Then what did you do to her?"

"Really, Med—"

"Answer the question, Baltir," Ginazhi said in no kinder voice.

"Well," the Retian said, "my—patron—had no interest in seeing the subject survive, but I predicted she would live long enough to make it worthwhile trying another experiment. And I was right, you see. It was very worthwhile."

"What was?" Ginazhi gave Morgan a cautionary look. "We can get into the technical details later," she added. "An overview, if you would."

"The M'hiray aren't the only patrons of the Baltir," the Retian told them cheerfully, continuing his surgery at the same time. "And there are several with an interest in similar areas. This mental power business. It isn't something my species values, but there are those who seek it quite desperately. Compatible genetic material which could enhance these abilities is a much sought-after commodity. Really, they'd pay any price."

"So you conducted compatibility tests on Fem Morgan."

The Retian sounded huffy, as though he'd expected her to grasp the essentials the first time. "It was an unprecedented opportunity. All I had available to me on Pocular—such terrible working conditions and everyone in such a hurry—was some Human tissue."

"Whose?" Morgan demanded.

"I certainly can't reveal that—aghk—" Baltir reconsidered his answer as the force blade passed under a thick fold of skin. "Another patron. He donated a sample for just such an eventuality."

"A name." As encouragement, Morgan thumbed off the blade, watching the beads of yellow-brown blood that followed with interest.

"We don't ask for personal identification," Baltir said hastily. "Our patrons rarely use real names, you understand. I have a case number, that's all. There's tissue back at the lab—perhaps the Enforcers have a match on file." The Retian paused, lifting his hands to allow one of the assistants to check his work. "This is your mate, is it not? A poor choice, really, given the value you humanoids place on parenting—interspecies pairings so rarely work without extensive intervention. I'd have thought you'd want to know the result of my experiment, Captain Morgan."

"That's enough, Baltir," Med Ginazhi warned him. "Let me tell you plainly—and on the record—if you continue to bait Captain Morgan and there is some irrevocable result, he cannot be held responsible. Do I make myself clear?"

"Humans," the Retian muttered like a curse, lips rippling with agitated pink. "Yes, Enforcer. I understand your threats."

"What did you do to Fem Morgan at your facility on Ret 7?"

"We removed the tissue implant from her body to check its viability. It was—" Baltir said with distinct relish, "quite dead."

"That's not all," the med insisted. "There're alterations in local blood chemistry, nanoplants, a host of vessel reroutings. We didn't dare meddle with it, despite the deterioration in her surrounding tissue. What was all that for?"

"As I said. I have several patrons interested in the M'hiray's genetic material. I wasn't sure how long I would have this subject available, so I implanted their donated material all at once—with the requisite changes to improve the chances of a workable fit for each. However long the subject survived, there would still be useful data. She had already proved to be quite durable."

"Morgan?"

He understood why Ginazhi said his name, and nodded very slightly in reassurance.

"Viri. Make sure you get duplicate cultures from every one of those implants as Baltir removes them," the med ordered. "I'm sure the Sector Chief will want to know which species our friend here is referring to—just in case there's some difficulty obtaining the case files."

Her voice dripped scorn. "Now, Toad, this is what I expect from you. I want every foreign cell and every scrap of nanotech removed as if it had never touched her. I want complete restoration of every vessel and membrane you altered. I want Fem Morgan's system back in perfect working order. Or we shall see if my version of spinal surgery works as well as Captain Morgan's on your neck. Am I understood?"

Morgan found himself smiling for the first time since boarding the *Conciliator*.

Chapter 56

"TRY another. Deeper this time."

I regarded Med Ginazhi with some doubt, but obediently drew even more air into my lungs, cautiously at first and then with growing confidence when there was no answering lance of pain. "That's much better," I told her.

She grimaced as she refastened the front of my coveralls. I'd graduated from flat on my back to carefully mobile since the *Conciliator* left Ret 7, an improvement which included proper clothing. "Don't thank me. I hate to be the one to say this, Sira, but that scum of a Toad is the finest surgeon I've ever seen. I wonder if we could run a selective brainwipe—no, wouldn't be worth it."

"I will thank you, Med," I replied perhaps too forcefully. I made the gesture of appeasement. "Pardon me. It's a bit too soon for me to appreciate Baltir's skill for what it is."

Fortunately for my peace of mind, and Morgan's, Bowman had left Baltir in the hands of Retian Port Authority. There shouldn't be any question of his remaining where he was sent. Not only had Bowman left a small garrison of her troops to continue the investigation, but my dear Drapsk had let it be known there was a healthy price for the Retian's hide, preferably tanned. Not legal or civilized behavior, but even Bowman had twitched her lips upon hearing that bit of gossip.

The raid on the Baltir itself had been both more and less satisfying. They'd arrived in time to stop the wholesale destruction of records and evidence already underway, finding so much that the Trade Pact had ordered the building sealed and a special team to go though every item. It was plain within moments that an appalling number of experiments had been conducted, all banned by the Trade Pact of which Ret 7 was a full signatory, and many involving subjects who had been coerced or outright kidnapped from their homeworlds.

The *Nokraud* had also been a target of Bowman's ire, since the Retians freely admitted to using the pirates as a ready source of "new material." But the *Nokraud* had bribed her way to a docking tug and lift offworld within hours of Rek's leaving me to challenge her sister. I believed, if Morgan didn't, that Rek would have returned for me if she'd won. I found I was actually sorry.

Unfortunately, as Barac later told me, they'd missed the key to it all. Faitlen di Parth, whether warned by his own foreboding or simply cutting his losses, had disappeared. The boxes where Morgan and I had found the sleeping Clanswomen were empty. There was no evidence of the existence of the Choosers who had drawn Barac into their Testing. The Clan, I reminded him, weren't so many that we couldn't find out who they had been.

The Clan. That was the next target.

After saying my farewells to Med Ginazhi, I walked from the med area, using my link to Morgan as a guide through the maze of corridors cutting through the core of Bowman's immense cruiser. The *Conciliator* had been ready to lift in very short order after Bowman's return. In part this was due to Bowman waiving the use of a docking tug—the cruiser was fully equipped for independent liftoff from any port—but even more so because Sector Chief Bowman had also had enough of the Clan.

Especially—I thought to myself as I walked into the gathering already in progress and met Morgan's blue eyes with a sense of safety and homecoming—when Barac had told her the Council had ignored its promise to leave the rich Human world of Camos.

They should never have underestimated this particular Human. As the med cheerfully informed me, we were now within a day, translight, of the Camos system.

The occupants of the room, an antechamber through which Bowman could reach either the ship's bridge, her private galley, or quarters, fell silent as I arrived. I thought I'd startled them by walking so confidently after doing such a good impression of death a day and a half ago, and I started to smile. Then a trickle of emotion—Morgan's—shivered through the M'hir between us. It was fury.

Rael and Barac were there, too, as were Copelup and 'Whix, flanking Bowman's seat at the head of the rectangular table. Morgan had told me Huido and Terk were bringing the *Silver Fox*—he hadn't bothered to explain why he'd elected to stay on the *Conciliator* for this journey, as if I needed to be told.

"What was the verdict, Fem Morgan?" Bowman asked, breaking the ominous quiet I'd caused. "Fit for duty?"

"Systems norm, Chief, if a trifle slow," I answered in kind, making the gesture of respect and gratitude for my kins' benefit. "My thanks to you and your staff." I took the seat next to Morgan, brushing the back of his hand with my fingers in greeting. "Now, what's wrong?"

"Not so slow," Bowman said, her look sharpening in appraisal. "Very well. We're hearing something very disturbing from your sister. You were about to continue, Fem Sarc?"

Rael looked like someone who had struggled with a difficult choice and realized there were no easy ones. I'd faced such moments myself lately and recognized the symptoms. She glanced over at me, her eyes wide in distress. "Wait," I heard myself say with a ring of authority. "Do you know who I am, Rael?"

A slight frown. I sent a throb of my power through the M'hir between us all, testing their shields in reacquaintance. Neither Barac nor Rael had felt my full strength since the Joining. Now they should know.

"First Chosen," Rael acknowledged, starting to smile. She made the gesture of respect, echoed by Barac. Morgan's fury had vanished, replaced by a ridiculous amount of pride in me. I glanced his way to show I'd noticed, then turned my attention to a curious, if less than patient, Bowman.

"As First Chosen, Chief," I explained, "I am granted the respect due the head of the di Sarc House. There are certain responsibilities as well. For one," I nodded at Rael, "I choose to intercede in your questioning of this member of my House. Ask me your questions please."

"But—" Bowman closed her mouth over what she was going to say as Rael shut her eyes and sent me everything left for me to learn of the plans of our grandmother, the situation on Camos, and the probable fate of the Human telepaths. It took an instant, yet tears poured down her cheeks before she was done.

Then, I *pushed* . . .

Feeling a surge of pure joy—not only had my strength returned, but the M'hir was once more what it should be, its residents properly disinterested and out of sight, I hoped for good.

. . . Air sighed into the space where Rael had been.

I sighed as well, working my mind around this new burden but satisfied to free Rael of this part of her discomfort: the sharing with those who couldn't touch mind-to-mind. She'd never been good at that, not to mention this was hardly a safe place or topic for practice. As First Chosen, it was my duty to protect her.

So hers was now my story to tell; moreover, it was now my problem to deal with, if Bowman reacted as I expected.

Seeing Bowman's not-so-pleased look, I didn't waste any more time. "Chief Bowman," I began. "Rael belonged to a group of the Clan who sought another solution to our crisis than those proposed—or tried—by the Council. She believed they were planning to contact me, to ask for my help in finding a way to protect our unChosen." I turned to look directly at Morgan. "While that may have been true, they were also responsible for the kidnapping of the Human telepaths you are investigating. They hoped to locate suitable—subjects—from the list I generated, the list you were on as well, Jason." He lifted one brow. We were well past recrimination over what, in the end, had given us both so much. "Rael doesn't know what they planned to do with these beings. There was some talk of seeing if they could duplicate what Morgan and I achieved. They were fools." This last slipped out before I knew it, but it was true enough.

"Rael and I decided she should get a warning to the Council before anyone was harmed by this folly. She succeeded, but the Council blundered, failing to summon all of the conspirators at once. One remained free—may still be free. I have every reason to believe," I closed my eyes for a moment, regaining my composure. Bowman deserved facts, not my reaction to them. "Ru di Mendolar intended to kill the Human telepaths in order to eliminate evidence against herself and the others. Rael fears she has carried out this threat."

Bowman, I had noticed before, had a curious habit of tapping her eyebrow, quite firmly, at odd intervals. She did so now, even as she gazed down the gleaming surface of the table at me, her expression impossible to read.

Then, unexpectedly, she laughed. It was a short bark of a sound, but cheerful nonetheless. Affronted, I opened my mouth to object, seeing Barac about to do the same, when Bowman waved her hand apologetically. "Forgive me, Fem Morgan. You have just proved to me yet again that I'm an excellent judge of character, Human or otherwise. I had your sister pegged as owning a guilty conscience the moment I met her on Ret 7. And I knew you, First Chosen of the House of di Sarc, as one hell of a scrapper and," she bowed her head, "a person of honor."

She went on. "While we can't track your people through space or—it seems—through my own ship, we do keep our eyes open for what we can see. 'Whix?"

The Tolian consulted a set of notes, the emerald dome over each eye catching the lights as he read. "The pattern of disappearances suggested the Denebian to Camos corridor was significant."

I nodded. There was a generations-old pathway between the two systems, deeply ingrained and so safe to use we trained our young to 'port along it.

"The timing of the disappearances suggested only a few individuals were involved—perhaps, knowing some of the Clan's capabilities, as few as two."

"Larimar and Ru," I guessed.

'Whix fluttered his crest, as if shaking away the distraction of my interruptions to his list. A fascinated-seeming Copelup fluttered his plumes, then stopped, perhaps unsure he'd interpreted the movement correctly. I spared a moment to wonder if the Tolian envied the Drapsk its truly spectacular headgear.

"Based on the pattern observed, we were in a position to predict with 91.3% accuracy the likeliest next target and were prepared."

This time it was Morgan who jumped on 'Whix with a triumphant: "You bugged him, didn't you? You set up the bait and waited for the Clan to take it."

"We don't need to go into all the details of the operation," Bowman said. 'Whix clicked his beak in either resignation or annoyance—knowing Bowman, I thought the former. "Suffice it to say," she continued as though time were now of the essence, "once we were sure our subject had been taken to his final location—about the time we were searching for you, Fem Morgan—there was a reasonably successful intervention. There was no Clan interference or resistance. Two of the telepaths are still missing—possibly they were never involved. But we recovered the rest, alive."

"Why reasonably successful, then?" Morgan asked.

"We found them." Bowman examined the scar on the back of her hand. Barac leaned forward, as though what she was about to say had special meaning to him. "But the telepaths were not as fortunate as yourself, Morgan, to find a Clanswoman capable of, shall we say, restraint? Whatever they were put through left them brain-damaged. The experts can't make anything of it; there's no apparent damage. But they tell me the victims appear to have no reasoning minds left at all."

"They were given to Choosers," Barac said roughly, his face flushed. His emotions flooded the M'hir: anger, a desperate jealousy, pity for those lost. "Do you have any records of who was there? Who came to this place where they kept the Humans?"

Bowman's lips pressed into a firm line. "Let's say we have a lengthy set of questions for the Clan on Camos, Hom sud Sarc. You're welcome to come with us for the answers to your own."

Dangerous, Cousin, I sent, keeping it tight and private. Not tight enough. Copelup's antennae snapped toward me like the indicator on one of his own devices. Beside me Morgan shifted ever-so-slightly: not in protest but rather in curiosity.

"You could," I chided Bowman, "have told us all this from the beginning. It would have saved my sister considerable anguish."

Another short laugh. "But then I wouldn't have learned as much about you both as I have, Fem Morgan. And that was, to put it mildly, far more important to me than keeping anyone else informed of Enforcer business."

"Anything else to tell us while you're in so informative a mood, Chief?" Morgan's blue eyes had that icy tint they gained when he suspected something. I looked back at Bowman with a sinking feeling. Morgan was right. She'd gathered us here and told us what she wished, for her own reasons—not ours.

454 *Julie E. Czerneda*

"Oh, I have lots of news, Captain Morgan," Bowman announced. She steepled her hands and leaned her chin on the fingers. "What would you like first? Did I tell you about the extensive sabotage we found within the Baltir—damage the Retians swear was caused by unknown agencies before our little visit? Or maybe you can tell me about it."

A shock ran along my link to his thoughts, as though Morgan jumped to some conclusion he immediately resisted. I ran one finger over the back of his hand, tracing its shape. "There is no need to grill Jason," I said calmly. "If you are talking about Baltir's incubators, it was my right to deal with what they had taken from me."

She had the grace to look uncomfortable, sitting up straighter and meeting my eyes. "Actually, Fem Morgan, I was referring to some pretty sophisticated work on the entry, lighting, and surveillance systems. If you were the one responsible for the—termination—of Baltir's experiments, I'm the last one to object. I'd have been pretty angry, too."

"Angry?" I shook my head, rejecting her conclusion. "You misunderstand me. I destroyed those bits of me—those potential copies—to protect my kind. As a Chooser, I was capable of destroying those Human telepaths, or Barac, or any unChosen. Where is the logic in producing more of me? How long will the M'hiray last then?"

A sudden flood of emotion poured through my link with Morgan, as though a dam had burst. I knew then what he had gone through since leaving the Baltir: an endless round of second-guessing his actions and mine. Had he done the right thing in leaving the tissue alone? Had I done what I'd confessed to him because of the horror of the attack or for some better reason? Did I regret the loss of that future? These were questions he'd only asked himself.

None of this showed on the Human's well-controlled face, unless it was the upward curve of one lip I found quite fascinating.

I pulled my attention to the rest of those gathered here, trying to ignore the differing intentions of my hair as it persisted in sliding up Morgan's shoulder. "As to the sabotage, Chief Bowman," I continued, "do you really think you will discover the culprit? It sounds to me as though the place had as many or more enemies as friends. I'd suggest you concentrate on the Baltir's activities, not those who might well be on your side."

"You might be right, Fem Morgan," Bowman said silkily. "It's just a habit of mine. I like tying up loose ends. For example, did you know we can't locate Ren Symon? He seems to have vanished as easily as one of your people. Even those in his group we caught and scanned don't know where he's gone."

"That's a specialty of his," Morgan said, his offhand tone possibly fooling the others, but I shared his frustrated and now targetless anger. Then, remarkably, the emotion fell away as if dismissed from his mind, replaced by a swell of acceptance. "Let him chase his own demons. I wouldn't waste your time. If he doesn't want to be found, he won't—"

"Chief Bowman!" an Enforcer called from the portal to the bridge, entering as though being chased. "We have the *Nokraud* on approach. Her weapons are live."

INTERLUDE

"I have been sent by the First Chosen."

Pella looked at her suspiciously. Rael found it difficult to keep a straight face and knew her shields were barely holding back her glee at what she was about to reveal to her doubting sister.

"The First Chosen. Ica? I thought the Council—"

"The First Chosen of our House, Pella."

"Nersal?" Pella looked as surprised as though Rael had sprouted Drapsk antennae. Their elderly aunt, though powerful, was hardly an active part of the Sarc household any longer.

"There is a new First Chosen. Sira!"

Pella's face shone. "This is wonderful news! Why haven't I heard until now? We must plan a celebration! Everyone will want to know . . ." Her voice trailed away as suspicion wiped the delighted anticipation from her face and turned it into something closer to nausea. "It's *him.*"

Rael knew her smile was cruel, but she enjoyed it regardless. Pella deserved everything she was going to learn. "Sira wants us to prepare Camos to welcome her Chosen home, Sister. And that's exactly what you and I are going to do. Isn't it?" She didn't wait for a reply. "Now, where's the case for your keffle-flute?" Rael looked around Pella's home appraisingly. "And where's that pre-Stratification relic Kurr gave you at your Commencement? It still works, doesn't it?"

Pella blinked slowly. "The pistol with the jeweled grip? Whatever do you want that for?"

Rael's smile broadened as she whirled her arms exuberantly. "Changes in the wind, dear Sister. Changes in the wind."

Chapter 57

"THAT'S the *Makmora.*" The scan-tech's features, showing deep concentration, were highlighted by the greenish glow from the image suspended before his face. "There's *Nokraud.* The Drapsk—sir, it looks like they're chasing the pirate. The *Fox* is ahead of us. Fast little thing." This last an envious mutter.

I had to take his word for it. The symbolism used in the multidimensional display—from my viewpoint a jumble of digits embedded in what appeared to be a ball of rotating gelatin—must take years to learn and a particular bent of mind to enjoy.

We'd been allowed on the *Conciliator*'s bridge. Morgan wandered away on a self-directed tour, not obviously paying attention to the focus of interest, but I knew he was fully aware. Barac looked as confused as I felt.

"Hom Copelup?" Bowman was saying. "Care to explain what your ship is doing here? I thought she was fin-down on Ret 7, waiting for the results of the investigation for Fem Morgan."

His tentacles disappeared inside his mouth; one chubby hand wormed its way into mine. Profound distress? No, I thought, this was embarrassment. "The Makii chose to defer that duty for another," Copelup mumbled. "The Mystic One—one of the Makii—was betrayed by the Captain of the *Nokraud.* The Makii seek resolution for the Tribe in this matter." Four tentacles popped out, producing a spray of saliva but a clearing of the voice: "There's no arguing with them in this state."

"Fine," Bowman said in a voice that implied it was anything but. "So what's the *Nokraud* doing on an intercept course with us if she's trying to shake off the *Makmora*? She'd better not be trying to involve me." She turned to address the *Conciliator*'s

Captain. "Captain Arvy, be ready to sent a blast across the *Nokraud*'s course if this gets too close to us. A message to the *Makmora* to back off until we are clear. I want to be through translight and fin-down on Camos by tomorrow morning. Without complications, if you please." She turned to leave the bridge, motioning us to join her.

"Wait, Chief Bowman," I heard myself saying, then stopped. Her keen eyes fastened on me. "Make it quick, Fem Morgan."

"I don't think the *Nokraud* is running from the Drapsk. I think she's trying to rescue me—from you." At her expression of polite disbelief, I hurried on to add: "Let me talk to her Captain. I'll know soon enough."

Bowman looked at the display again. "Status, Scan-tech?"

"The *Makmora*'s weapons are powered up. She could fire on the *Nokraud* at any moment."

"Go," she told me.

Morgan came to stand with me at the com station, saying for my ears alone, "Even if Rek defeated her sister, Sira, you may be still be wrong now. Why didn't she come back for you?"

"I'll ask her," I said stubbornly.

"This is a Scat, you realize," he added a bit louder, as though I hadn't been paying attention.

"I've learned to overlook your species' shortcomings," I said wickedly. "Why not theirs?"

He shook his head, smiling nonetheless. "I see we have a lot to discuss."

"*Nokraud* com on, sir."

Bowman nodded to me.

"This is Sira Morgan to the *Nokraud*," I said, feeling everyone's eyes and antennae on me. "I want to speak to your Captain."

"Fem Morgan. This–sss is–ss a pleassant s–ssurprissse."

I couldn't tell by that voice; it always sent shivers of dread down my spine. "Who is this?"

Scorn even through the com system: "Assst. Captain Rek. Tell your Drapsssssk to power down their weapons–ss. We are not here for battle."

"Power down yours," Bowman snapped, leaning past me. "A gesture of your good intentions."

"Not a good idea, Chief," Copelup broke in urgently. "The Makii will fire the moment there is an advantage."

I raised my eyebrows. I'd attracted formidable, if not quite fair, friends. "Captain Rek," I said, "My colleagues wonder why you didn't return for me—and why you're here now. I assume you succeeded in your challenge."

A clattering of jaws let me picture her triumphant laugh all too well. "Grackik's–ss heart pounded its–ss final beat within my throat. A most s–sssatis–sssfactory moment."

Not the most amenable of beings, I thought to myself, but somehow I didn't doubt this one. "What happened on Ret 7?"

"S–sshe tried to avoid my challenge by fleeing offworld. My ss–supporters–ss gave me the opportunity to enter the s–sship before lift, s–sstaying behind to retrieve you while I tore the remaining limbs–ss from her body." The mudcrawler in the night, I thought, somehow without surprise that I'd hidden from my own rescue. "They failed but watched for any s–ssigns, fearing my dis–sspleas–ssure. When they reported your return and the attack on the Baltir, I s–stayed inss–syssstem. There was–ss the chanc–sse the Enforcers–ss would mis–sstake me for Grackik." An irritated snap. "It s–sseems–ss not only Humans–ssss do this–sss."

"Then why are you here, Captain Rek?" this sharp question from Bowman.

"Fem Morgan owes–ss me payment," the answer came so matter-of-factly I covered my mouth to keep in a laugh of my own; I didn't think the Scat would appreciate it. On the other hand, I'd been proved right in my judgment of her and grinned at Morgan, who shook his head in rueful acknowledgment. It was a nice change to best the experienced trader at his own game.

"She's quite right, Chief," I confirmed. "Let me speak to the *Makmora*."

Hours left until we reached Camos. I'd taken the capsules provided by Med Ginazhi and put them away in a drawer. There was no more time to waste on sleep.

Again, I sent warning.

I could just see the glint of Morgan's eyes in the dim night lighting. He sat, long legs outstretched, in a chair he'd leaned back against one wall of the small cabin Bowman had given me. Although I lay in a comfortable curl on the bed, my skin was wet with sweat. The exercises we were doing were hard on both of us.

Ready when you are, my love, he sent back. There was no strain to his thoughts, no fear. Only a distracting contentment, as though he saw the lances of power I drove against his shields, the tricks I played to bypass his defenses, as expressions of my love.

He was right, which made me even more grimly determined in my testing. It was the Council itself we faced tomorrow: the strongest from each House—most, if not all, my declared or secret enemies.

They would try to defeat me through Morgan, sensing our Joining as obscenity and opportunity. Once I would have quailed at the thought, fearing any risk to him. Now, testing the rugged, trained power of my Chosen, sharing his inner strength and determination, I was beginning to look forward to their reaction.

Clansmen, I thought, *meet Jason Morgan, Human, Captain of the* Silver Fox, *First Level Adept of the House of di Sarc.*

It had a nice ring to it.

INTERLUDE

The Watcher stirred. Felt the stirrings of the others holding vigil. No need to pass along the alarm: all shared it.

Something was gathering. There was the scent of change in the M'hir, a sense of potentials rising, of movements toward a core.

Threads of energy left trails, all converging on Camos. The Council had assembled. Others were coming.

The daughter of di Sarc remained outside the M'hir, but her essence shone within it like some jewel of power, her Joining to a stranger's glow plain to all who touched this place.

The Watcher consulted with the others, felt the concept she proposed fly from mind-to-mind as quickly as her first thought.

With her second, the Great Summoning went forth.

Chapter 58

CAMOS. I drew the pine-scented mountain air into my nostrils, feeling an odd sense of homecoming.

"Your memories didn't do it justice," Morgan said into my hair. "It's spectacular. Nothing like the restricted view of this world I had before."

The playful breeze did nothing to stop the heavy locks from preferring the Human's shoulders to mine, an intimacy of contact I savored almost as much as sharing my home with him.

This visit to the Cloisters, the ancient stone retreat where I'd lived, hadn't been part of the plan; Bowman was unlikely to be at all pleased at our disappearance from her ship just as it landed at the Gornwich shipcity. But these minutes before the conflict were best spent here, together, rather than bothering with the details of docking and Human means of travel.

The balcony jutted out into the air over the valley, making it appear we rode among the clouds. Behind us, the walls of the building, more than half consisting of the mountain itself, rustled as the wind toyed with the winter remains of the climbing vines coating their surface. It was, I supposed, bitterly cold. Tucked with my back against Morgan's chest, his arms around me, I couldn't say I noticed any chill.

The tip of my nose, maybe. As I thought it, Morgan covered it with the warm palm of his hand, chuckling: "I hope it isn't always this nippy up here."

I kissed his hand, then reluctantly disengaged from his embrace, shivering as I left its protection from the wind. "We don't have much time left, Jason," I said.

"I know." His blue eyes—fascinating how so cold a color

could be so warm—regarded me steadily. "Can we be sure the Council will even show up? They aren't supposed to be here."

"They'll be at the meeting place," I answered without doubt. "They have other things on their minds than preserving an out-lived secrecy on this world. And who would want to miss the opportunity to meet my Chosen?"

His tanned cheeks reddened. I cocked my head, amused by his reaction. "It is my kind who should be embarrassed in front of you, Human. That part of it, at least, should be entertaining."

"I'm glad you think so," he said under his breath as we went back inside. The table which doubled as my computer interface continued to make its whir of protest, but the machine had no defense, Morgan assured me, against the tunneling data destroyer he'd provided. The information of value I'd already sent to the *Fox;* any which could harm others was rapidly disappearing. Given the duplication of my list, this was too little and too late, but I wouldn't leave the temptation here again.

Morgan's com whistled for attention. He brought it to his ear, gave a brief affirmative, before saying to me: "The *Makmora* has docked. Copelup says all is ready for transport to the meeting. O Mystic One." His lips curled up at one corner. "Which should I start using, chit: 'Mystic One' or 'First Chosen'?"

I pretended to scowl. "Anything but 'chit,' Captain Morgan, if you don't mind." Then I grew thoughtful. "You have a point, though. Drapskii is not wholly reconnected with the M'hir. Perhaps after we settle things here." I sighed, finding it hard to think so far ahead.

There was nothing content or happy in the look this gained me. "At the risk of attack by those creatures you described? Why?"

"As I told you, they only appeared because my power in the M'hir was unbalanced. Now that we are Joined—" it was my turn to feel my cheeks burning, "—they have lost interest. I haven't seen any sign of them since. And the Drapsk . . . they matter to me, Jason. They need me."

His eyes softened until I could have drowned in them. "Befriending a Scat. Adopting the Drapsk. And coming here to knock some sense into your own kind with the help of some Humans. You've come a long way from life in this fortress, Sira di Sarc."

I looked around. The room was comfortable, full of things I

used to value, the favorite furniture shabby enough to welcome. The bars were still on the windows, placed there as reminders of the less visible barriers used to keep others safe from the dangerous lure of my power. "It wasn't life, Jason," I said, dismissing my past as he had dismissed his.

I reached for his hand. "Let's go."

INTERLUDE

The Watcher winced.

It was becoming painful to look in the M'hir toward Camos—painful and, at the same time, impossible to avoid. With each arrival, the M'hir flared with traces of more power until all pathways converged into one massive artery, pulsing to Camos, carrying the Clan to their Council.

There hadn't been a gathering like this since the day the M'hiray left the Clan Homeworld, power banded into one to forge the great path to carry them all outward, leaving the rest of their species behind—the day the first Watchers had stirred to awareness among the new breed of Choosers and their Chosen. Then, they had been shepherds to guide that journey. Today, they were guardians of the M'hir itself.

This inflowing was greater and less. The M'hiray had grown in individual power, if not in numbers. But they no longer blended their power into one purpose, not even for the good of their own kind.

This was opinion, and the Watcher removed the thought before it trickled to the others. Her duty was to monitor, to see if any faltered in the journey between worlds; if this occurred, she would notify their House of the loss. She expected none. The pathway was now so prominent in the M'hir, so well-formed, a child could follow it.

In fact, the Watcher doubted any Clan had sufficient power to resist it.

Chapter 59

TOTALLY without meaning to be, Sector Chief Lydis Bowman of the Trade Pact was the host for the first complete gathering of Clan in living memory.

As one would expect, she took it in stride, only saying to me, when the scale of things became apparent: "Thank goodness the Council was as paranoid as I was about privacy. Otherwise, wherever would I have put them all?"

The paranoia she meant was an insistence by the Council to meet where there were no eavesdroppers or hidden troops—there having been some uncomfortable experiences with such things in the past. So Bowman had cleverly arranged for the use of the Morris & Flag Tug Co. assembly plant, presently vacant as the company prepared for renovations.

It was, besides the largest freestanding building on the surface of Camos, well-lit, drafty, and as welcoming as you might imagine a vacant warehouse large enough to permit the construction of the mammoth docking tugs so essential to spaceports would be.

I'd read about the devices, in the ceiling, several stories above us, to prevent the formation of clouds. They didn't always work; there were puddles on the floor. Since Camos had very civilized weather control, I found this lack indoors remarkably appealing.

It was a distraction I needed, given what I was facing.

A carpet had been found and placed in the exact center of the vast expanse. *Somewhat like a target on a range,* I thought and felt Morgan's amused agreement. At the moment, the carpet housed Bowman, Constables 'Whix and Terk, two quietly dressed Pact officials she introduced only as "interested," Morgan, and

me. Enough, I thought, for now. We'd been the first to arrive—
some minutes before the appointed time—and now stood waiting.

A Clanswoman materialized on the cracked pavement to
one side of Bowman. Terk twitched, but held himself steady—
perhaps realizing her confused expression didn't quite match
the profile of an assassin. Shortly afterward, he had three more
to watch, then fifteen, then two hundred.

Now, as Bowman said, it was just as well she'd provided the
space, because the Morris & Flag Tug Co. building soon
housed what I guessed to be every living member of my kind.

With the exception of the Council.

All were silent, inside and out, the only sounds the breathing
and occasional movements of close to a thousand individuals.
All stood motionless, children to adults, their eyes focused
on where we stood—not in challenge, but in curiosity. There
were Choosers here. I felt their uneasy power, but it was oddly
dimmed, as though muted by some need beyond Choice, or,
more likely, overwhelmed within the presence of so many
others. It was enough to warn the unChosen. I saw them, Barac
as well, clustered at the far side of the gathering. The M'hir
itself seemed subdued, perceptible only as the faintest of traces.

I didn't know what—or who—had summoned the Clan here,
but I was glad of it.

"Here they come," I said for those blind to the M'hir, feeling
the surge of power as the Council announced itself.

Eight robed and hooded figures winked into place, standing
before us on the carpeting, plus two more: Ica di Teerac, First
Chosen of her House, and Ru di Mendolar.

The hoods were tossed back on shoulders, revealing faces I
knew very well indeed, the most powerful Talents from their
families: the First Chosen of Lorimar and Su'dlaat; the rest
Clansmen, Sawnda'at, Mendolar, Friesnen, and Teerac; the last
two my enemies in truth: Faitlen di Parth and my father, Jarad
di Sarc.

They all stared around the factory floor, as if transfixed by
the reality of what their inner sense must have told them was
happening. Crisac di Friesnen gave a faint gasp.

"Greetings, Councillors," Bowman said cheerfully. She had

a way of projecting her voice, quite startling given her rather small, sturdy frame.

She caught their attention, all but one. Jarad, as foremost in power, spoke as his right—but to me.

"What is this?" he demanded. "What have you done?"

"Greetings, Father," I said, making the appropriate power gesture in recognition of my equal. "This gathering? Wasn't it ordered by the Council?" The gibe let me touch his thoughts on the deepest of levels. *This time, Jarad, I need not keep your secrets. Morgan and I are safe from you now.*

"Greetings, First Chosen of di Sarc," he answered, smoothing his voice into something almost pleasant, his craggy features carefully noncommittal. "And our welcome to your Chosen." This with a gracious gesture to Morgan.

It was a tactic. Acknowledging Morgan as my Chosen, here among all of our Human-phobic kind, was asking for a riot. I hadn't thought him willing to risk that loss of control, not with the Enforcers present. My eyes narrowed. *Take care, Jarad,* I warned.

But, surprisingly, the crowd remained quiescent, as if what drew them here had nothing to do with Morgan or my private war with the Council.

Jarad bowed to Bowman. "And greetings to you as well, Sector Chief Bowman. And your warriors. Who might these be?" A wave at Bowman's other guests.

"Board Member Cartnell," said one, a Human male, tall and thin for his kind, slightly stooped as though accustomed to talking to smaller beings. He indicated his companion, the light scaling on her cheeks indicating she was possibly Papiekian, though that race had so many subspecies it was difficult to tell with any certainty. "Board Member Sta'gli."

Board Members. These individuals spoke for their entire species on Trade Pact issues. I made the gesture of respect and saw most of the Councillors and other Clan follow suit without hesitation. *We'd always,* I thought to myself with some cynicism, *been quick to identify true power when we saw it.* Jarad delayed perhaps a second. Faitlen's hands remained still.

"What is your interest here?" he said rudely, going so far as to step forward. Out of the corner of my eye I saw Morgan casually flex a wrist—a move that loosened his throwing knife in its hidden sheath. "We are not members of your Pact! We are the M'hiray!"

"Two–o Board members may invite a–iy new species into–o the Pact," Member Sta'gli said in a soft, singsong voice. "We are here to–o convey that invitation to–o the M'hiray–oo." Though begun almost in a whisper, the voice was immediately amplified by some hidden means, carrying well over our heads to reach everyone present. There would be no hiding that offer from the Clan, I thought. From Bowman's satisfied look, her side had brought some interesting tech.

Faitlen having broken Council protocol, Degal di Sawnda'at didn't hesitate to follow suit. "We have no homeworld, Board Members," he said bluntly. "This—" he gestured around himself, "—is the sum of our population. Why would you offer us membership? Where would be your gain—or ours?"

"Your gain would be what we all find within the Pact," Member Cartnell said equally bluntly. "Protection from interference by others; trade; and the right to call on the resources of other members when you need assistance."

"Our gain, Councillor, is to–o increase the diversity of the Pact." Member Sta'gli's tone took on a definite ring of menace. "And as members, you would agree to–o cease your interference with other species and to–o protect the rights of your own. This is a–iy more desirable solution than other options which present themselves."

"What interference?" Degal demanded. "We have no interest in other species." Several other Councillors nodded agreement, Faitlen emphatically.

The crowd remained still. I found myself picking out familiar faces. They might have been statues—or, I thought with an uneasy memory, Retians waiting for a summons.

"That is not quite true." I hadn't expected this stern admission to come from Jarad.

What are you up to? I sent.

Patience, that powerful, familiar voice said in my thoughts. I clamped down my shields.

"We of the M'hiray have harbored a criminal among us," Jarad said loudly, as if taking on the role of evangelist to the already converted. "A fiend who has dared tamper with the core of what we are—to bypass the Power-of-Choice and the rights of Choosers—to sell our flesh to species who lack our gifts!"

Jarad had the stage, I had to admit, looking around at a thoroughly spellbound audience. Perhaps not wholly so. Ica di Teerac was frowning at her son-by-Choice. They'd always disagreed, she'd told me once, even when he was fostered away from her for the first years. And Morgan had that loose, balanced look which meant he was ready to dive in any direction should it be necessary.

And Faitlen di Parth looked positively ashen. "What are you talking about, Jarad?" he began.

"You should know, Faitlen di Parth," Jarad said calmly. He gestured to Bowman. "This Human does have the evidence to prove what you've done with the aid of the Retians, does she not?" His voice rose again, power cutting under every word until what he said rang through the mind as well as through the ears. "Do you deny it? Do you deny stealing reproductive tissue from Sira di Sarc, my daughter, in order to attempt to grow—to grow!—some type of copy of her? Do you deny tricking Clanswomen from your own House into taking part in your schemes, so you might be the one to benefit?" *Aha,* I thought to myself, Faitlen's fatal mistake plain before me. No one tricked Jarad and survived it. From the look on Faitlen's face, he knew it as well as I did.

"And dare you," Jarad had continued, "dare you deny taking Choosers from the safety of your own House only to have them die for one of your experiments?"

"Are you challenging me?" Faitlen asked in a shrill, desperate voice. "Are you? When it was—"

"I challenge!" Jarad roared, his voice like a dim echo of the deadly force he projected into the M'hir.

It was over in an instant. Faitlen crumpled to the carpet, a shocked look on his face as his mind exploded from within, abandoning the needs of his body. When Terk and 'Whix moved as though to help, Degal stopped them with a brusque: "He has already died." What remained of Faitlen disappeared, discarded into the M'hir, most likely by Degal himself.

There was a disturbance in the hitherto motionless audience of Clan, individuals moving away to expose Faitlen's Chosen as she writhed on the damp floor, her soaked clothes making patterns as she rolled in helpless agony. Then she, too, was gone, granted mercy by someone from her House, her body following her mind into the void.

I looked at Jarad di Sarc, knowing what he had done and why. There was only one way he could have made those so-accurate and damning accusations. He had known. He had been the one to send Faitlen after what Jarad considered his: my power and progeny. He met my eyes; in his I saw only implacable purpose.

Well, I thought to myself, *I have my own.*

Bowman coughed lightly. "There is also the matter of kidnapped Human telepaths, Councillors. Do any of you have—revelations to make about that?"

Ica stood straighter. If anything, Ru di Mendolar appeared as though she'd like to sink into the carpet. She'd looked at me once, then stared at Morgan almost hungrily. Now she kept her eyes down and her power dampened. "I do, Enforcer, Board Members," Ica said. "It was my intention to counter the destructive path our Council was taking; to find other ways to our survival. We thought, in the Choice of Sira di Sarc for this Human, we had found such a way.

"I wish you to understand—you especially, Captain Morgan—that though we did take these individuals from their homes against their will, they were offered the chance to participate, or to leave with their memory of us removed. Two chose to leave." I saw Bowman's satisfied nod; she preferred things tidy, I'd noticed. I also imagined she would very soon be looking for those two and didn't envy them. Then, a quick guarded thought from Morgan echoed my own: *Had these been the source of Ren Symon's knowledge?*

"The rest," Ica concluded, "wished to stay."

"What were you offering?" Morgan asked. I wished he'd kept silent—any attention from the Council now could force our hand—but I understood.

"Why, power, of course? What else would they want? What else did you want?"

Fortunately, Morgan didn't reply. I wasn't sure what he could have said that Ica would understand.

"What they got from you, Clanswoman, was mindlessness,"

Bowman accused. "If this was such a failure, why did you keep trying?"

Ru's eyes flashed up. "It wasn't a failure! We were able to transfer the Power-of-Choice to several of the Humans. It wasn't much, but enough to prove the Choosers could, with the Humans' help, gain some control. No one was damaged. They were healthy—sane! Someone interfered. Someone didn't want us to succeed."

I didn't bother looking at Jarad. *You gave them my list,* I sent almost without emotion. *And you made sure they'd fail.*

"We shall investigate the matter, Enforcer, Members," Jarad said smoothly, words overlaying the sending just to me: *There can be no contamination of the M'hir. You will learn, Daughter.*

"No," I said out loud, "I think you will." I summoned my strength—sparing an instant to be thoroughly grateful for the med's tender care—and concentrated, *pulling* what waited just outside into this place . . .

A peacefully humming machine, nearly the size of Huido, appeared at the empty end of the carpet, surrounded by Drapsk, including Copelup. Their antennae were erect with delight. It might have been from traveling through the M'hir, however short the distance, but I suspected it had more to do with being surrounded by Mystic Ones. This would definitely result in some gripstsa, hopefully much later.

"We are not alone," I said, stepping away from Morgan to stand near the Drapsk, relying on Bowman's devices to carry my voice to everyone here, pitching my power to do the same. "We are not alone here and now. Four billion Humans and other beings inhabit Camos. Countless more share this part of space with us.

"And we are not alone in the M'hir. These are Drapsk. Their species not only exists partially within that place we've assumed was ours, their scientists understand it well enough to explore it with machines like this one.

"Maka, Makoori," I said quietly. The two Drapsk assumed the gripstsa posture with its echo within that other space. Then louder, to the Clan: "Reach to them. What do you sense?" The audience might have been silent, but it was attentive. I saw an expression at last on those watching faces: awe.

"Copelup?"

The Skeptic turned on his machine. It was a cobbled-together version of his M'hir viewing tube, borrowing from some Human display technology and definitely untested. I crossed my fingers surreptitiously.

The projection formed over our heads. It was—I gasped with the rest—it *was* the M'hir, the way we saw it within our minds. There were the bands of power looping back and forth to this world.

And there was what I'd hoped and feared: along one of those bands moved a group of, for want of a better word, grazers. Other things moved through the view too quickly to decipher. It was as well. They were disturbing enough as glimpses.

"That will be all, thank you," I told the Drapsk rather breathlessly.

Then I looked out at my kind again, aware of the Councillors and others at my back but no longer concerned with them. "We are part of this place. We are a part—and only a part—of the M'hir. The way we have chosen to live, to be separate, to exclude others, is an illusion.

"You know who I am," I said. "Here is what I am."

With that, I dropped every shield I possessed, opening my thoughts to them all, revealing everything: what had happened, what I'd felt. I hid nothing, not my caring for Morgan, not my mistakes, and certainly not what I knew of Jarad di Sarc. I refused to allow any shields to stand in my way, driving my thoughts outward with all of my so-vaunted power. It was an outpouring such as none of them had ever experienced before.

Let them make of me what they would.

INTERLUDE

Barac reeled under the impact of events and emotion, his head spinning after the rapid onslaught of so much power and so much information. What was Sira, that she could affect them all at will? How had the M'hiray produced such an individual and not known it?

The answer was there, in the memories she'd shared. There were those who had known, the same who refused to see Sira as anything but the future of their kind, blind to all that insisted an unmatchable Chooser would be its ending.

The death of Kurr, the one as responsible for his murder as Yihtor—that answer was also in these new thoughts, given to him freely as to everyone here.

Barac felt his lips pull back from his teeth. *Jarad di Sarc.*

With the understanding and the righteous anger came the dose of common sense Sira meant him to have. Jarad di Sarc had never been his to deal with . . .

He was Sira's.

Chapter 60

I SLAMMED down my shields when I was done, rather surprised not to have been attacked while so utterly vulnerable. It had been a trap of sorts. Morgan had been ready to protect me—by mind or, as likely, by the simple expedient of his knives.

But then, my enemies—my enemy—knew as well as I that simply sharing what I knew would never be enough to harm him. We were too used to our independence, too accustomed to letting others handle the big problems.

"I call for a Council Vote," I shouted. "A Vote to accept the invitation to join the species of the Trade Pact—to ask them for help in solving the crisis facing the M'hiray."

The crowd, so mute until now, began to shout in echoes: "A Vote!" "Join the Pact!" "Down with the Council!" and other cries until the overlapping confusion made it impossible to make out anything more than a dull roar.

"Jarad di Sarc," I asked, "will you call the Vote?"

He lost none of his confidence, none of his hauteur as he looked down at me for a long moment. *I see and glory in your power, Daughter,* he sent. *A shame you have perverted it. Such waste.*

I didn't bother answering in kind. "Call the Vote."

Knowing the Clan as well as I, he waved a graceful hand. The voices ceased. "I call a Vote from the Council of the Clan," Jarad ordered. "It must be unanimous to carry weight," he explained to Bowman. "We are not a democracy."

"Wait!"

This cry came from the audience. I think we were so used to their presence by now it startled us to be reminded these were all individuals. A group of three came pushing toward us. It was

Rael and Pella, the former carrying an ancient weapon and the latter with an empty keffle-flute case slung over one shoulder. Between them, they urged a young Clanswoman toward the carpet.

"This is Tle di Parth," Rael announced with a triumphant look at me. "It took some doing to get her to come forward, but here she is."

"My daughters," Jarad greeted them sardonically. Pella looked afraid but determined; Rael looked like some avenging goddess of war, hair lifted like a banner. Righteous wrath suited her, I thought, although I doubted the heirloom in her hands would actually work. "And what has Tle to do with the Council? As you can all feel, she remains a Chooser." The unChosen certainly knew, having backed well away.

"Tle is the most powerful member of her House with the death of Faitlen di Parth and his Chosen."

Morgan's approval washed over me toward Rael. She glanced at him with surprise, then smiled ever-so-slightly before turning a much sterner face to Jarad. "You must have eight for a valid Vote, Father, or had you conveniently forgotten?"

Tle raised her head, her vivid green eyes intense in that child-like face. Her body, adult-sized but not yet mature, was rigid. She was, I recalled, one of the older Choosers, almost forty standard years of age, and potentially another who would have difficulty finding a Candidate for her Choice. "There is no law against having a Chooser on Council. Only," she said scornfully, "habit."

"Very well. Do you accept Tle di Parth on Council?" Jarad asked the others. I sensed their probes testing her power. There was no doubt in my mind and shortly none in any others'.

"We welcome Tle di Parth to Council," Degal said. "Let us proceed. I vote to accept."

I nodded. It was his son, Larimar, who through my memories he had lost twice over to Jarad's scheming.

The others were quick to follow suit, Tle casting her first vote as a Councillor without hesitation.

Seven in accord; seven voting for the Trade Pact. They would not attack Jarad directly, but with this Vote they had turned their backs on his politics and schemes. But seven was not enough; there was one vote, now the deciding vote, left. I could see resignation in the faces of the Humans and Sta'gli, in the drooping antennae of the Drapsk, and in the limp feathers of the Tolian.

Every Human but Morgan. He stood, legs apart and hands ready, as though preparing for battle. There was a look of grim anticipation on his face.

"Then," said Jarad di Sarc, "the answer is no, since I vote against acceptance. We don't need these aliens."

"Ah, but, Father," I breathed, stepping closer to him, feeling my power surging as it demanded an outlet. "You have no vote."

"What? Has your link to the mind of this—this Human cost you the last of your wits?"

I pulled myself to my full height, feeling my hair starting to lift of its own volition, as if there was too much power within me to contain any longer. I questioned neither its source nor any price I'd pay later. Now was all that mattered. "As First Chosen and most powerful of our House, I claim the Council seat of di Sarc. Step aside, Jarad di Sarc. Your time is over."

Time. It narrowed itself down to this moment, forgot all that was before or might be after, focused on the breath coming from his nostrils and mine. I had Challenged him. He could flee—and I would permit it.

But not before he lost. There were too many here, starting with those from Acranam, who believed in his pattern of thought, his lust for power over all. They would understand this contest, this moment, better than all the reasoned arguments and cold logic I could give them.

Jarad smiled, knowing this and more, and struck.

He might have thought this first blow would end it, for, as I expected, he sent his power raging, not against me, but against my Chosen.

There were no rules in these struggles for supremacy among us, so none would cry foul if Jarad ended my threat to him by eliminating Morgan. My mind would dissolve into the M'hir, pulled there by our Joining, my body a mindless hulk.

A good plan? What a pity Jarad had not assessed his enemy.

Morgan's shields, trained and tested, were holding; I could feel their strength as well as Jarad's sudden and horrified comprehension. *Yes, Father,* I sent. *We are truly Joined. His power—*

*his Human power—is a match for mine within the M'hir. All of
your lies have been found out.*

"No!" the Clansman said out loud, as though he had no
power to spare to return my sending. His fists raised, clenched
above his head. "It cannot be! A Human resists me? Why have
the Watchers allowed this? He pollutes the M'hir! No!"

"Yes and yes again!" I countered, standing close enough to
Jarad that my hair lashed at his face, staring up into the madness growing in his eyes. "You have denied it—well, here is
your proof, Father. Morgan is my Chosen because he deserves
that place by all the measures of the Clan. End this now!"

"Never!" Jarad's power left its assault on Morgan with a sud-
denness that sent the Human staggering. Terk supported him
before he could fall, I noted even as my own shields took the
new attack and I prepared to attack in return.

My strength wasn't what it should have been—there was a
price demanded by my body for all I'd been through over the
last weeks. Jarad was at his prime. My goal wasn't as clear—I
needed his defeat, but couldn't afford a killing blow, knowing
this would cost Mirim, my mother and Jarad's Chosen, her life,
too. Jarad wanted the death of Morgan even more than my own.

But my purpose was too important for such minor details. I
gained strength from it, sure to the core of my being that it was
the survival of the Clan that was at stake. And, thanks to Morgan and the Drapsk, I did know where my duty lay.

Jarad never stood a chance. I began ripping apart his protections, layer by layer, methodically making my way to the level
of thought where the control of his motor functions resided.
Once I held those in my grip, he would have to admit defeat.

Then it was my breath stopping, my body abruptly losing
control.

I had time to realize that Jarad had wrapped his hands around
my throat and was choking me to death, before that hold was
broken. Morgan tore him away from me, throwing the Clansman to the ground with an oath.

Jarad, his fine robes spread over the carpeting like a stain,
crouched like some cornered beast, nothing left in those features but rage.

Then he was gone.

Unashamed to need it, I leaned on Morgan's arm, then looked

at the stunned Councillors. "I vote," my voice was oddly husky and I coughed to clear it. "I vote to accept."

Degal made the gesture of appeasement, with the undertone of acknowledging superior power. "First Chosen. Yours is the greater power," he said, as if unsure I'd leave any of them standing. "You must speak the verdict."

Politics by fear; rule by power. I looked over at Tle's unformed face and thought—one thing at a time.

I gestured my agreement. "The Council is unanimous," I said, looking at all of them and finding it hard to focus on any one face. "The Clan will join the Trade Pact. Our isolation ends here and now."

It might have been coincidence that my hair chose that moment to slide up Morgan's shoulder and tickle his ear.

INTERLUDE

Is she crazy?

"That is hardly the way to talk about the First Chosen of my House and the Speaker for Council," Rael answered Barac aloud, trying to sound offended, but the touch of her power against his in the M'hir glowed with joy. "If she is," Rael went on, "I suspect it will become contagious." She stretched lazily on the couch. They were staying in Ica's resort, the Clanswoman having decided to visit more distant relations. The Clan was still unsure how to deal with the respected and powerful First Chosen of Teerac. If it weren't for the new obligations to the Human telepaths under the Trade Pact, Ica's and Ru's crimes would have been forgotten, their ideas just another in the frenzy appearing throughout the M'hiray daily now as everyone discussed their future. Sira had made sure even the children knew what might lie ahead.

As Rael had said, they were all a little crazy at the moment.

"What will you do now?" Barac asked her, shoving another shirt into his carrysack. "Return home to Deneb?"

Her touch in the M'hir warmed even more. "I was actually going to ask where you were planning to go, Cousin. Back to your bar, perhaps?"

Barac gave a refined shudder. "I've had more than sufficient exposure to that lifestyle." He paused, not meeting her eyes. "I don't know. Kurr's murder gave me a purpose, Rael. Without it, I'm not sure what I'll do next."

Rael admired the suppleness of her ankle. "You could apply to Council for another Testing. With Sira there, you can be sure of some serious effort toward a good match."

His mouth twitched with irony. "The second Council vote

was to suspend any Testing of Candidates until our new allies in the Trade Pact can help investigate the Power-of-Choice. It may be months before any Choosers are permitted to Join. They can wait, you know. Time only passes for the unChosen."

Rael smiled mysteriously. "We'll see. But in the meantime, if you don't have any plans, Barac, why don't you come with me?"

"To Deneb? No thanks. It's a bit rich for my taste—"

Her smile broadened, reaching her dark eyes and sending them sparkling with mirth. "Oh, I have a new spot in mind, Cousin.

"How would you like to become a Mystic One?"

Chapter 61

"I CAN'T wait, Brother! The orders are piling up. There's— Good morning, Sira," Huido broke off what amounted to a tirade at Morgan as I walked into the main hall. His eyestalks were whirling.

Morgan smiled a greeting, looking rested and content— something I attributed as much to his checking over the *Fox* after her flight with Terk at the helm as to a good night's rest. Through the M'hir, I felt a wash of caring that brought warmth to my cheeks. "Huido is being crushed by his own success," he informed me.

I raised an eyebrow at the Carasian. He was pacing, an activity which not only generated a significant level of clattering and rumbling, but also threatened the furniture. The Cloisters hadn't been designed or furnished with his massive restlessness in mind. *As well,* I thought to myself, *drive a groundcar in circles around the vases.*

"The truffles," I said, understanding at once. "Poculan truffles."

"What else!" Huido's claws threatened a chandelier I was fond of and I winced. He noticed and calmed himself, but only slightly. "There have been orders from throughout the quadrant. Who knows how, but the word of my new recipe spread translight. The com system at the *Claws & Jaws* has been overloaded for two days!"

How Morgan kept his face straight I didn't know. Then, when he spoke, I found out: "Which means, my lovely witch, the *Fox* and I have to make a run to Pocular and do some digging, or my brother here could be out of business." There was an undercurrent of regret to the M'hir, a fervent promise to return along with a not-completely controlled and quite flattering frustration.

I settled into a chair, straightening the formal robe Enora had helped me put on this morning. There would be another Council meeting today. "We are Joined, Jason," I reassured him. "There is no real distance between us, no matter where you have to go."

A flicker of something, quickly suppressed. We might be forever linked in our thoughts, but Morgan had kept much of his inscrutability. *As it should be,* I thought, making sure I kept some of my own.

He sketched a bow. "Then we'll be off. Huido—" this with a definite glare of irritation, "has already scheduled a docking tug. And Huido is planning to go ahead to pay the fees—?" this hint bringing the Carasian to attention. He waved a claw at me.

"I'll make sure we send the first batch to your table, Sira."

With a satisfied snap, Huido left.

We were alone.

I looked at Morgan. "You'd better hurry. He might leave without you."

The Human hesitated, off-balance as if he'd been about to reach for me, then thought better of it. I kept myself perfectly still. "Of course," he said instead. "I'll be back as soon as possible."

I nodded. "I await your return."

"Huido! Huido! Where is he?" The muttering was coming close and I clamped down my barriers as tightly as possible. "Damn his shell, anyway. Huido! I need that spanner—"

Morgan stormed into the cargo bay, his cheeks spotted with red and his blue eyes stormy. There were lines between his brows and from the edges of his mouth to his chin.

"This spanner?" I said, coming out from behind the plas crate I'd been securing against one wall. No point taking the *Fox* out empty.

The way his face changed made me tremble, but I held my voice and thoughts light. "There's a lot to do, Captain, to make that schedule. Do you need the spanner or not?"

He took a step toward me. "The Clan needs its First Chosen," Morgan reminded me, blue eyes starting to glow.

"They know how to find me."

Another step. "The Drapsk need their Mystic One."

"I've arranged a suitable replacement."

A final step, bringing Morgan so close I could feel the beating of his heart, twin to my own. His eyes were deep pools I would drown in forever.

"The Trade Pact—"

"Has functioned quite well without me so far and will continue to do so." I watched my hair slide up to brush his now-pale cheeks and whisper across his smiling lips.

"You know full well, Captain—" I said softly, my arms and power wrapping around to hold him tightly: the farthest I ever hoped to be from my Chosen. . . .

"The *Fox* needs her crew."